TITUS

TITUS

ELON SALMON

ANDRE DEUTSCH

For Richard Simon

First published in 1996 by
André Deutsch Limited
106 Great Russell Street
London WC1B 3LJ

ISBN 0 233 99008 9

Phototypeset by Intype London Ltd
Printed in Great Britain by
WBC, Bridgend

ACKNOWLEDGMENTS

My thanks to my friends Maggie Body, Anne Stevenson, Peter Lucas, Moris Farhi, Richard Simon, and J. D. F. Jones, who have read drafts of *Titus* and gave me much needed moral support. I am grateful to Henning Langenheim and his wife Veronika and their two daughters Jori and Lili for their wonderful hospitality in Berlin which enabled me to research the story. I am indebted to Tom Sharpe, without whom *Titus* may never have seen the light of day. I should like to thank Cambridge University Press for permission to use the quotation from *Hanns Eisler – Political Musician* by Albrecht Betz, published in 1982.

1

Tsarytsin, Good Friday 1918

A horseman came riding out from among the birch trees. He reined in his mount in the open space where scattered items of soldiers' gear told of a recent defeat. The wood massed darkly behind him. The pale tree trunks stood out against a density of green like a palisade. The horseman moved on, skirting the clearing in a collected canter. He was lean, and young. But there was premature hardness in his tawny eyes. His cheeks were hollow and untidy with a few days' or maybe weeks' growth of stubble. He was hatless and wore a knee-length dark coat that hitched up over the long low-slung sabre at his side. In addition to the sabre, he was armed with a carbine, the butt of which protruded from a leather sheath at his right knee.

The mount was a large silvery grey stallion with dark flowing mane and tail. Whereas the rider looked haggard, the horse was spirited, in superb condition; its accoutrement was of the highest quality. For all the discrepancy in appearance, horse and rider moved in perfect harmony, as though time, practice and innate mutual empathy had forged them into one body – the supremely natural cavalry warrior.

Without moving his hands or upper body, the horseman turned his charger, bringing it to a tense halt in the sunlit grass of the clearing. There they stood stock still, looking watchfully ahead: a relentless caprice of violence captured in their gaze.

You could not tell whether the horseman had taken part in the battle that had been here a while before and, if so, if he was a survivor of the defeated or a victor. He looked totally disconnected from the events that had taken place here, as if

1

by some supernatural mandate he could set his own terms in any situation.

After a moment the horse backed a few steps and wheeled around. In an instant horse and rider disappeared, swallowed by the forest.

Primrose Hill, London, 1987

Alone in the house she had shared with Titus, Phoebe Whelan saw it in her mind's eye, and it speared her soul. Of all his diverse apparitions that visited her imagination in her bereavement, this one was the most vivid, the most persistent, also the most alien: man and horse possessed by implacable self-absorption which scrutinised without mercy.

She had seen that look in Titus's eyes on rare occasions; it had made her realise – then as now – how little she really knew him. And for all that he had filled her life in the time they had been together, what small a part she herself had played in his.

Titus's cremation had taken place the week before, a day ahead of Good Friday when she used to pray for him in church as the self-proclaimed infidel that he was.

The quaint irony of his death somehow, but only briefly, numbed the ache of her loss.

There had been an assassination threat from a clearly deranged Russian expatriate who claimed Titus had driven his father to suicide some half a century before. The would-be assassin's message read that he knew Titus's every move, and would strike him down in full public view, so that the world would see at last what Titus really was.

Titus ignored the threat; a load of nonsense, he called it. He refused to alert the police; didn't even inform John Lefebre. In defiance he announced to Phoebe that they would go out to a performance of *Rigoletto* at the Royal Opera, Covent Garden, followed by a dinner.

'You don't like going out,' she protested, because for all Titus's reassurances she was anxious.

'Tonight I do,' he replied. 'Wear that dark dress with the low neck, won't you?'

'But Titus, you hate opera!' she reminded him.

'So? *You* love opera. I'll sleep right through, ha ha ha . . .'

He did, almost. And at the intervals people were looking at them not always furtively. Some smiled, greeting them with a nod. She had experienced it all before. She could all but hear their whispers: *Isn't that Titus Alston, the notorious billionaire, and his youthful paramour? . . . Goodness me, I thought he died years ago! . . . No prize for guessing what keeps the old man going for eternity, eh?*

No assassin in sight for the whole evening. But it rained hard enough to kill. Coming back home, Titus lost his footing on the wet steps before the front door, and fell heavily. She managed to get him inside, then reflexively rang Lefebre, who arrived ahead of the ambulance. Titus had smashed his right hip. A week later he died at home of double pneumonia, having stubbornly and imperiously, against medical advice, discharged himself from hospital and refused any treatment other than painkillers.

She hadn't repeated to anyone his last words, uttered with a sardonic smile: 'Like bloody Tamburlaine! Serves me right, I suppose . . .'

She wasn't sure she had understood what he meant.

The obituaries in the press were extensive but sketchy, and mostly based on rumour. For someone who had been at the centre of world events for a considerable time, little was known about him, good or bad. The first was cautiously acknowledged; the second was darkly hinted at. As one tabloid caption had it: 'Titus Alston – an enigma from start to finish.'

Going through those obituary notices, Phoebe remembered what he had told her some time ago: a good secret was like a famous courtesan whom people loved to know but no one wanted to be seen with. She recalled his cynicism once again at the cremation, which turned out to be not quite the funerary event of the year: too many conspicuous abstentions of former friends, enemies, colleagues and victims from among the great and the good.

But Titus's four oldest friends were there, their aggregate age totalling over three centuries. Like porters of his life's monumental accounts come to bear witness, they stood together, excluding her. Except Chad, whom she knew and liked better than the others. Detaching himself from his friends, Chad had come over to give her a hug.

After the cremation, John Lefebre drove her home. She sat next to him with the urn in her lap. They didn't speak. And she was grateful when he declined to come in for a drink, saying with his peremptory smile that, as Titus would have wanted, The Alston Group never paused to mark losses; he had an important meeting in an hour. She asked if he wanted her in the office tomorrow. He replied, ominously but charmingly, 'No, honey, you take time off. I'll be in touch soon, I promise.'

He kept his promise sooner than she had expected. At the end of a breakfast meeting at the Stafford Hotel – Titus's old haunt – he sacked her, just as Titus had predicted. He did it gently and generously – waiting until after she had her first cup of coffee before letting her have it. Titus used to say he could count on Lefebre even to murder with finesse; that was one of the reasons he had hired him in the first place.

It was nothing personal, John assured her; she had been a tremendous asset to the Group. Only now it was better – for her in particular – that she should go. Thus, remunerated and flattered, Phoebe returned home feeling nevertheless empty and hurt.

The urn stood now on her mantelpiece. On the low table by the settee where she sat lay the pages of Titus's notes. Remembering a favour, the Group's computer whiz-kid had given her this, saying that surprisingly, even improbably, he had managed to hack it out of Charon before the file self-destructed. He thought the material rightly belonged to her. Her intuitive faith in him wavered when he swore it was the only existing copy.

All day she had been reading. Already at the halfway point she had understood how much of himself Titus had kept from her. Now she was on her own in a bleak stretch of no-man's-land, somewhere between his world and the one she had inhabited before their coming together; he had even warned her about that. But he had trained her in the discipline of fearlessness. Oh yes, he had tutored her into more than a

4

company boardroom guerrilla. She was prepared for the bomb he had primed and timed to explode as his requiem. And, as a dress rehearsal, she was ready to face his friends at the funeral lunch in Grantchester Titus had decreed.

Just how much or in what way she would miss Titus, she couldn't tell, except that, as with some chronic ache, the awareness of loss would surely hit her from time to time when least expected. Her father, in his perceptive innocence, had warned her. Unable to understand the nature of her love, he had tried to deal with it as though it were a rare uncurable affliction; or the outcome of a quirky accident. He could see the price to pay, but not the equally enormous benefit.

A part of that was that she no longer felt she needed to explain – even to herself – why she loved him. It had been she who had taken the first, tentative, step in their relationship, while Titus had been slow to respond. He had never flaunted his power, as some men in his position would have done, particularly with women – younger women – they wanted to win. In fact, at times she had wondered what it was that he had found in her. She saw him as being neither good nor bad but as someone to whom, being altogether beyond convention, such measures did not apply.

She remembered a trip they once went on, to Kenya. They had stayed for a few days on a farm belonging to a man Titus knew. It was on the eastern reaches of the Masai Mara. There was a huge bull elephant which had made the place its home. It hung about, coming close to the house. The gardener had befriended the animal. He would squat in front of it, talking to it. The elephant stood there, still, attentive, flapping its enormous ears. Then the gardener would get close to it and stroke its trunk.

The elephant was very old, and virtually blind. One of its tusks was half broken. Probably it didn't have long to live. Now solitary, in its prime it had been a magnificent, dominant and dangerous male, their host had explained.

Phoebe remembered the elephant when she thought of Titus. The essential inwardness of them both. And the inherent arbitrariness which, at least in Titus, could welcome affection and destroy with equal facility.

5

Implicit in loving Titus was a whole world of epic adventure and terrifying contradictions that always superimposed itself on reality. Such was the strange potency of her love that, without her realising, it seemed to transform her from a mere audience to a full partner in Titus's life and past. This, at last, she understood, albeit with some disbelief, especially when she searched her reflection in the mirror for any signs of a change.

Was that all? she could almost hear him protest and smiled inwardly. For there was another side to Titus's unpredictability that was sunnier.

'Aren't you ever going to grow up?' she would chide him at times, following one of his more than usually undisciplined bursts of enthusiasm.

'After I'm dead, maybe,' he would reply.

Now that he was, she could retrospectively love his amoral humour which at times had made her tremble. She could be angry with herself for her reticence, which made her hold back from his infinitely inventive and sometime reckless playfulness. If only she had entered with complete abandon into that rocking, rollicking sea of pleasure Titus so readily conjured up!

'One day I'll write a dissertation on the art and joy of loving a very special older man – a guide for the cautious and immature', she thought as she reflected wistfully on whether she would ever experience again the fun she had had with Titus.

The wolves were howling in Regent's Park Zoo. Phoebe poured herself another glass of wine, then shut her eyes and listened.

*　　*　　*

Halfway through the banana split Wanda Rutland began to cry. Her aged face which a moment before had concentrated with gusto on the dessert, turned still. Two tears, welling out of her dark eyes, edged over her cheekbones, raced each other down her cheeks, then dropped on her trembling hands one of which was resolutely grasping the spoon.

Theo Jablonsky, whose anticipation of Wanda was intuitive by now, leaned towards her and lightly touched her arm. After all that time – over half a century, goodness, how the years had flown past! – she could still move him, could still make his insides twist with a sweet ache.

'My dearest . . . Poor old Titus . . .' he murmured.

Wanda inclined her head to one side and smiled at him through an iridescence of tears.

'Why, Theo darling, you don't think I'm crying, do you? Good heavens! I don't think I've done that for at least thirty years. Just that my poor old eyes get tired.' But her lower lip gave a little tremor as she patted his hand. She dabbed her eyes with her napkin, then stared heron-like at the remains of the banana split.

'Delicious!' she pronounced. 'Curious how death makes you long for sweet rich things, don't you think, Theo?'

Her voice was strong, precise. She spoke with an exotic Hungarian lilt that gave her speech a musical undulation.

Theo blinked as he attempted to smile. 'Death . . . Ah, who would have imagined Titus would die while we are still alive?' he said pensively.

Phoebe Whelan, two generations younger, lowered her head as though an indefensible accusation had been thrown at her. At the other end of the table Sergei Aleksandrevich Pugachev, former General, Hero of the Soviet Union, succumbed to sleep. Like memories, commemorations were becoming too much for him.

'I wonder what's happened to Chad,' said Wanda, looking at her watch, then at Phoebe. 'He did say he would come, didn't he?'

'Yes, of course,' replied Phoebe.

Today she didn't mind Wanda treating her as though she were no more than Titus's secretary; after this, she would never see any of them again. To mark her farewell, she wore her best executive uniform with a vengeance, and put up her dark blond hair a little tighter than she normally did. But the boardroom attire did not subdue her youthful loveliness, nor regiment entirely her tall figure, somewhat fuller than a model's.

Wanda's assessing scrutiny was concealed in the sweetest of smiles. 'Ach! Chad is always late,' she said with a wave of a hand. 'Why doesn't someone order the coffee?'

Even though arthritic, Wanda Rutland could affect a

marvellous fluidity of motion in her dancer's physique. Imposing in her old age, she had undoubtedly been stunning in her youth. Her dark robe-like outfit accentuated the whiteness of her skin, which was miraculously smooth.

Theo Jablonsky was short, his centre of gravity conspicuously below the waist. He wore a grey suit, probably from Marks & Spencer or Burton, which looked as if it had become organically a part of him with continuous wear. Nobody in Cambridge had ever seen him wear anything else. Pugachev, slumped in his chair, wore a tweed sports jacket tightly buttoned up and festooned with Soviet medals.

A group of students breezed into the Green Man, bringing in with them a draft of fresh air and laughter. Chad Johnson entered in their wake.

'Chad! Darling,' Wanda cried, stretching out her arms.

Sergei Pugachev surfaced from his slumber, muttering Russian expletives.

'Hi, everybody,' said Chad.

Tall, tanned, athletically lean – years of daily tennis and careful dieting had seen to that – Chad Johnson, American *éminence grise* among international star journalists of his generation, stood at the doorway as if waiting to be photographed. A pale raincoat was slung over his shoulder atop a sky-blue cashmere polo-neck top. He had a shock of lusty grey hair, laughing grey eyes beneath dark heavy eyebrows and strong dazzling teeth.

'Do you think they'll ever get trains to run on time in this country?' he said in a resonant baritone reminiscent of Movietone newsreels from the fifties.

'Darling, who cares?' said Wanda, for whom time was an abstract irrelevance. 'Come and sit down. The food was so-so. You hungry?'

'No, thanks. But I'd love some coffee.'

First he went to Phoebe, put an arm round her shoulders and kissed her. Theo began to rise but Chad stayed him with a hand on his shoulder. Pugachev clambered to his feet. Well over six foot tall, he could look down on Chad, but only just. Having duly received the embrace, he mumbled lugubriously in his heavy accent, 'Now zere yiz wonly four of us left. Vot vorld yiz zis, I ask you?'

Wanda inclined her head as Chad, sitting beside her, drew close to kiss her cheek.

'Can someone tell me why here?' he asked.

'Because, darling, Titus willed it so. He still pulls the strings, like we were his puppets,' said Wanda.

'Blame me, if you like,' said Theo with a sigh. 'It was I who brought him here. He fell in love with the place.'

'Really, Theo? You never told me.'

'Well, Titus came to see me in Cambridge, you know. It must have been around 1953, soon after he arrived in England. I think Cambridge enchanted and, strange as it may seem, intimidated him. He said it made him feel like a barbarian at the gates of civilisation. We had dinners here at the Green Man. We went for walks in Grantchester Meadows. Titus said, "You know, Theo, this landscape is like a painted mediaeval allegory. There is a hidden meaning in all this pastoral tranquillity, with Cambridge in the background." '

'And what did you say?'

'I told him what you once said about me, that he was a great romantic.'

'As I remember, what I said was that you were an old romantic, not great,' she laughed.

'Maybe. But with Titus everything was "great". He had an absurd reverence for learning. I never noticed until he came here. Certainly not in Paris, nor in Copenhagen. It was as though all of a sudden he had become vulnerable, ironically when he was at the height of his powers. "Theo, I want you to recommend books for me to read," he said. "Whatever for?" I asked. "To improve my mind, of course," he said. "Titus," I said, "your mind needs no improving. You have a great mind. It's your soul you should worry about." '

'Did he?'

'I don't think so.'

'Did you?'

'Did I what?'

'Give him a list of books to read.'

'Of course. He never read any of them, I'm sure. Maybe he got them and placed them under his head at night, as Charlemagne reputedly did, hoping the learning would filter into his mind while he slept. God knows what really went on in Titus's mind.'

Suddenly Wanda began to laugh. Soon tears were streaming down her face. 'I oughtn't to be telling this now,' she said, linking her arms to Chad and Theo, 'but I simply must. Years after Titus arrived in England, I wrote to him. We might even have become lovers again. Except that he avoided situations that might lead to this.

'I got impatient with him. I said, "Look, Titus, if you no longer find me attractive, that's all right with me. Only don't be a *shmuck*. Tell me what's wrong."

'So he came clean. You know what he had done? The week before he had had an operation in a Harley Street clinic to put a foreskin back on his *Schwanz*. I said, "I don't believe you. Show me!" So he did. I said, "Titus, this is awful. It doesn't suit you at all; it makes you look years older. I don't think I want to make love to you ever again." '

She started laughing again, while Theo looked a little confused, a little sad.

'Oh Theo, my dear Theo, I'm sorry, I should have kept this to myself. Only it's so funny, so crazy, so Titus. Don't you think?

'And then he went on about the Jews fooling themselves and the world with meaningless convenants made with a non-existent, boring god. Maybe he had read your books after all, Theo. He said he wanted to reclaim something that was unfairly and unlawfully taken from him without his consent. He told me he had chosen a Jewish doctor for the operation and refused to pay him. "Let the bugger sue me, if he dares," Titus said.'

'Okay, let me tell you something even weirder,' Chad began . . .

Phoebe smiled inwardly as she only half listened. It was their day; like a kind of exorcism, their stories had to be told, now, perhaps for the last time. She was here only to perform a function, she had no illusions about that. And when these three old people whom Titus had in turn loved, manipulated and deceived, returned to their homes with their respective recollections hallowed but obsolete, she, not they, would be left to cope with the seismic shock of Titus's legacy.

2

W A N D A

When we were children in Vienna, my brother Stefan and I had a private game. We called it, 'What happened if . . .' You take a simple story, you interrupt it at an important turning-point; you introduce a new situation and carry on from there. Little Red Riding Hood, for example, is a good one. The slender fable offers interesting and timeless moral dilemmas. Is the wolf wicked or merely an opportunist? Is Little Red Riding Hood as innocent as she appears to be? And what about Grandmother? A victim, or exploiter (we drank Socialism with our mother's milk)? As for the actual story, it will support countless permutations. Which is why it was the top card in our childish pursuits.

Here, then, is Little Red Riding Hood, alias Wanda Hephziba Popper, happily strolling in Berlin's Tiergarten on a beautiful spring morning with no particular aim in mind. She is not so little any more. She's not wearing a red cape, either. The wood, however, is as magical as it is real, with enormous trees in lush green foliage, with birds, and squirrels – all inviting any number of metaphors.

Along comes the Wolf. The recognition is mutually instantaneous. Little Red Riding Hoods – modern ones in particular – can tell a wolf when they see one just as wolves instinctively know who is a Little Red Riding Hood and who isn't.

This wolf is not sinister or in any way threatening. Far from it. Nor is he a morosely shy *Steppenwolf*. He is young, good-looking, sexy. He gives Little Red Riding Hood the once-over with his laughing lupine eyes before sitting down beside her on the park bench. If he is hungry, it is obvious that Little Red Riding Hoods, not to mention wizened crones, aren't on his preferred menu. For all that, our Little Red Riding Hood might

11

easily have pointed him to the imaginary address of a non-existent grandma in Moabit and watched him trot away, never to be seen or heard of again. End of story.

At this point I stop to ask: what would have happened if I had not walked through Tiergarten that morning? Or had sent Titus packing? Probably I would never have met my future gentle English husband, Tristan Rutland . . . Instead of finding a haven in England, I would have been bussed out of a gathering-point in Oranienburgerstrasse, ten years later, to Dachau, along with Berlin's Jews. To die, like my father Istvan, my mother Magda, my sister Eva and brother Stefan.

Or what would have happened if the wolf had become tame, turned to me and said, 'Wanda, my love, I'm really rather tired of being a wolf. I want to be a nice plump dog. Let's marry and have children'?

What of the sorrow? The ecstasy, the yearning? The intoxicating ordeal of unbearable awareness? The ache for lost opportunities you can never regain?

What of Theo?

Death and Fate. When it came to playing one against the other, Titus was the consummate juggler to the last.

A horse had dropped dead, smack in the middle of Kurfürstendamm. Its rider, a policeman with a Hindenburg moustache, stood over it, perplexed, the riding crop silly and redundant in his hand. A heart attack, Titus had diagnosed – he knew about horses.

'To think the poor old bugger was just a week away from green pastures or the knacker's yard, by the look of him.'

'Aren't you afraid?' I asked, thinking suddenly of my father. He looked at me, those amber wolf's eyes laughing. Swallows whistled in the dusky light, among the darkened chestnut trees on the pavement. At the corner of Fasanenstrasse two pretty whores gazed impassively at the dead horse.

'Afraid of what?' Titus asked.

'Death,' I said.

He pulled the brim of his black felt hat lower over his face. 'Why?'

'Just so.'

12

He smiled. 'Not any more. Sometimes I'm afraid of life, though. Only sometimes.'

That was one thing I learnt from Titus, in retrospect. I mean, now, at my age, who's afraid of death anyway? He is a polite companion walking beside you in the park, on your shopping rounds, ready to pick you up when you fall. Funny how we think of Death as male, and the earth which receives you when he has done his work as female . . . I digress, but not altogether pointlessly. Death, you see, always lurked about Titus, that was what I felt. Perhaps because Death – if he is, if he possesses intelligent awareness – simply couldn't believe a man could live so intensely, raise the stakes all the time, and not crash rather sooner than later.

Berlin, spring 1929, when I first encounter Titus in Tiergarten, is a city resting between upheavals, a city shaped by turmoil and drawing her strange vitality from it. Berlin . . . I think of it as a vibrating mass of disparate agitating forces, fighting each other yet bound together, generating energy which is indivisible. Berlin is a profound caricature of humanity – greatness and flaws exaggerated to absurdity.

These are the fat years: the cafés are full; shops are trading briskly; culture blooms in a riotous variety; art leaps and loops about itself; depravity defies imagination in its inventiveness; foreigners flock here as if to a mythical city of delights. A drugged contentedness smothers the savagery of internecine conflict. You know this cannot last. You don't care. If there is such a thing as the last fling before the end of the world, it must be now, here in Berlin.

I want to be a writer but I can't write. I want to be a painter but I cannot paint. I would like to perform in cabaret, like Claire Walldorf, only I don't have a voice. I open myself to love, I turn my life into an artistic experience. In this way, you might say I am an artist.

How different it all is to ten years before, when we arrived from Vienna with a bundle of scuffed luggage right into the epicentre of chaos.

If my mother Magda had had her way, if there had been enough money, it might have been New York instead. Ever heard of a middle-European Jewish family that didn't have some relatives in Brooklyn? My father Istvan, however, the self-taught philosopher – *Luftmensch* par excellence – the committed Marxist revolutionary who could never strike roots anywhere, not even in our native Budapest, became obsessed with the notion that Europe, if not immediately the entire world itself, stood trembling at the dawn of a new age in which injustice would be banished and mankind would be liberated from the brutalising stupidity of capitalism.

Where would the redeeming luminosity manifest itself? Where else but in Berlin! Here it didn't matter if you were poor, if you had nothing but the clothes you stood up in. Here you witnessed History (a term my father uttered with religious reverence) at work. The revolutionary disorder which presaged a new harmony levelled everybody to his and her fundamental humanity (I quote him, more or less). That, I understand with hindsight, was a failure's most comforting refuge from the torment of failure. My beloved Papa, you see, was a *shlemiel* if ever there was one.

We stood at Görlitzer Bahnhof and waited in vain for the *Spartakusbund* comrade Rosa Luxemburg had written would come to meet us. More than two hours passed. Porters were staring at us. Stefan sulked. Eva fretted. At last, Mama too, began to cry. My father's defeats didn't stop at national borders but shadowed him everywhere he went, like secret agents.

We found lodgings in 17 Wildenbruch, Neukölln, a working-class area cluttered with ugly tenement blocks in the east part of the city. A week later the news came that Karl Liebknecht, co-leader of the revolutionary Spartacus Movement, had been murdered and Rosa Luxemburg was missing, presumably dead. Papa wept inconsolably. The next day, however, he was his usual self again. Did perennial failure immunise him to sustained grief?

A qualified operating theatre nurse, Mama got a job somewhat beneath her qualifications in Charité Hospital. In a typical Berlin spirit, fate soon played a cruel joke on her: she found herself one day towards the end of her shift looking down on Papa's death-pale and bloodied face in the emergency ward – an arbitrary casualty of the day's street riots.

The incident and the demise of the Spartakists notwithstanding, Papa's faith in Berlin's historical destiny remained undimmed. No sooner was he on his feet again than an undemanding job was secured for him as assistant salesman in a second-hand bookshop in Leipzigerstrasse, owned by a sympathetic *Landesman* – a Budapest Jew. At last Istvan Popper had found his milieu: he wrote occasional pieces for the Communist *Die Rote Fahne*, he frequented Romanisches Café where intellectuals and literati of the left met; he played chess with an Odessa-born genius whose landlady, it was said, let him stay rent-free because, being a sensitive woman, she feared posterity's judgment if she turned out the new Einstein into the street; he attended political meetings in Alter Jacobstrasse; and, of course, he had walked innocently into a rough spot of street violence.

As for me, I grew up. To my adolescent imagination Berlin was a teeming, painted Babel suspended in nothingness. Full of allure, full of hazards, endless contradictions bumping against each other nose to nose. At dusk prostitutes came out like beautiful night flowers along Kurfürstendamm, around Kaiser Wilhelm Gedächtnis Church, in Oranienburgerstrasse. Some of them were young men dressed as girls; you couldn't tell the difference. During the days of the hunger, in 1923, you might have seen your school friends – boys and girls – all made-up, soliciting in Tauentzienstrasse. And you thought, there but for the grace of God, it might have been me! Children starved in Neukölln. At the Hotel Adlon in Unter den Linden the chandeliers were bright, champagne flowed. Theatres played to full-capacity audience . . . Could somebody say, please, where the Revolution was revolving? . . Demobbed soldiers sold their weapons for next to nothing by the Brandenburg Gate, which were discharged in mob warfare the next day in Alexanderplatz.

A morning in March, 1920. Wolfgang Kapp's putsch – a comic operetta from start to finish – is over. The workers of Berlin, not the timid government, had put an end to it. Ehrhardt's Marine Brigade march out through the Brandenburg Gate, singing. Then suddenly, without provocation, they turn, aim their rifles at the crowd of onlookers and fire.

15

Goodbye Red Berlin! Jews! Cosmopolitan degenerates! Traitors! Twelve dead, many more are wounded. The newspapers have their headlines. It was business as usual for the eating and dancing places that evening.

What do the lions, the tigers, the leopards and the hyenas in the Zoo get for supper at the end of those murderous days, when the streets are cleared of corpses?

'Endure!' says Papa. 'Only when suffering becomes intolerable will mankind learn.' Regeneration after destruction? What happened after the Flood? After Sodom and Gomorrah? Our household is under a cloud of dispute: it had taken me another quarter of a century before I could discipline my argumentative nature.

At the height of Berlin's hyper-inflation (how politicians and historians find sanitised words for plain misery!) Mama succumbed to nervous exhaustion and lost her job in Charité. The bookshop where Papa worked went bust. His own endurance, like the Reichsmark, devalued to nothing. Papa was right on one thing: the intolerable induces change.

It resolutely followed tearful scenes in our bleak two-room apartment. My parents, with Eva and Stefan, were to return to Vienna, to the bosom of Mama's family, where a modest job in Uncle Georg's men's retail shop awaited Papa.

'Wanda is a survivor. She's strong, she's clever, she's beautiful. She's made for greater things. She's all I always wanted to be. Let her stay. You know, Magda, you can't argue with your daughter once she's made her mind up on something. It's fate,' Papa pronounced. Poor Mama still had faith in Papa's apprehension of life's inscrutable forces. She wasn't one to argue with Fate, either.

I see them off at the station. The wrench is unbearably painful, though we all show a brave face.

'Write frequently, Panni, promise you will,' says Mama fighting back her tears.

'I'll send you money regularly. Ring to Uncle Georg's if you need anything, and don't forget to reverse the charge,' Papa says.

I hug and kiss them both, I hold Stefan and Eva for a long

moment. I return to the empty apartment. I sit on the bed and cry my eyes out, stopping only to smoke cigarettes.

But oh, how I wanted to stay . . .

I was nineteen at the time. I suppose Papa was more or less right: other people also said I was clever, and good-looking but not sexy. Beautiful in an ethereal way. I had the kind of body painters like to paint, and did. Otto Dix, for one. I can't say I was flattered by the result. Mine was a dancer's body, lean but not thin or angular, and I had a Modigliani face and neck to go with it. My skin was pale in a radiant sort of way. I must confess that, when I stood naked in front of the mirror, I was pleased at what I saw. Why not? If there were visible intelligence and integrity in a face, couldn't they be seen in a body too? My modelling brought in the bacon when bacon was in very short supply. Literally so; some of my employers, patrons, call them what you like, paid me with food.

My parents didn't like this but these were hard times. We were hungry, tired of the daily intake of turnips and other things that passed for vegetables. Modelling for artists isn't prostitution, either, if you don't want it to be.

The year before, I had lost my virginity to a painter I modelled for. Detlev Gestner lived in Grunewald but kept a studio in Pfalzburger Strasse, Wilmersdorf. The son of wealthy parents, he had taken to painting as therapy for severe depression after witnessing the murder of Walther Rathenau in a street near his parents' villa. He was gifted, too. He lived to enjoy modest success before blowing his brains out the day the Nazis came to power.

We were friends. Detlev was shy, delicate, a committed artist. On that day, near to lunchtime, we heard shots from the street, very close. Detlev began to tremble. He dropped his brush and palette, sank to his knees, holding his hands to his face. I went over to him. I knelt beside him, put my arms around him and held him as I held my brother Stefan many times when he was upset. We made love on the exotically-covered couch, overlooked by his unfinished picture of me as a naked 'Madonna of Sorrows'. Afterwards Detlev wept. And for all the tenderness I felt for him, I asked myself, 'Is that what it is all about?'

At home that night we had a royal meal: half a dozen

sausages and a pound of smoked beef. You could have feasted on the smell alone. Suddenly there was a frantic knocking on the door. It was Frau Schmuckler, our neighbour from upstairs. Two days before her tortoiseshell cat Mitzi, her sole companion, had disappeared. The whole block had heard her laments.

'*Guten Abend,* Frau Schmuckler,' said Mama. 'Is anything the matter?' Because the poor old widow was staring wild-eyed.

The woman sniffed. 'You are eating my Mitzi!' She screamed. 'I knew it! Savages! Cannibals!'

'Calm yourself, Frau Schmuckler,' Papa said in a quiet, reasoning voice. 'How can you say such a thing? We are Jews, would *you* eat a cat? You know cats aren't Kosher.'

This surprising though perfectly logical argument did not calm our Jewish neighbour. But she retreated. Her cries of 'Cannibals!' echoed in the stairwell, sending a chill down our spines – Berlin was all agog at the time over the serial killer Karl Denke, who stored barrels of his victims' smoked flesh in his house.

After my family left, I joined the KPD – Germany's Communist Party. I moved to a pleasant room in Kreuzberg. I earned my living waiting in cafés, modelling, doing the odd secretarial work at the Party head office, for Ruth Fischer, whom I detested, and her common-law husband, the political commissar sent from Moscow, Arkadi Maslow. I went on street demonstrations. I made friends, dearest and most revered among them the gentle artist Käthe Kollwitz . . . I had lovers . . . I lived from day to day, sustained by endless cups of coffee, and cigarettes. There were serious conversations that stretched into the small hours of the night. You were dazzled and repelled by Bert Brecht. You held forth on subjects you barely understood – how Art should serve the aspirations of the Proletariat, not be merely a meaningless bourgeoisie aesthetic self-indulgence. You secretly prayed: 'Dear God, please keep the future at bay, please let things stay as they are, for a while at least . , ,'

Communism? Put it this way. In my heart of hearts I didn't take it lock, stock and barrel. The doctrine left me cold. Fashion never held sway over me. Even before I met Titus I had an instinctive suspicion of all 'isms'. I wasn't moved by the cynical pessimism of intellectuals like the poet Kurt Tucholsky who thought everything in Germany, from the Republic to democracy, was a sham. Nor did I share Brecht's and John Heartfield's fascination with America. My idea of revolution was gentler, bourgeois, I dare say, closer to the sentiment of Beethoven's Ninth Symphony than to the Party's ideology. My anger at social injustices was perhaps best echoed by Hanns Eisler's eloquent irony in his song *Frühlingsrede an einem Baum im Hintershaushof* – Springtime advice to a tree in a courtyard:

> I earnestly request you to blossom, Mr Tree. Do not forget: it is spring! Are you on strike because of the terrible courtyard? Are you on strike because of the frightful rented barracks? You are surely not being so impossible as to dream of green forests. Adapt to your surroundings, if you don't mind! Perhaps you think that it is superfluous to blossom in our day and age? What are tender young leaves to do on barricades? You would not be at all wrong, Mr Tree! Forget it is spring!

You may well ask why Wanda Hephziba Popper was sitting on a bench in Tiergarten on a brilliant spring morning, in the middle of the week, in March 1929, allowing herself to be accosted by a foreign stranger?

Since the beginning of the week I had been walking with my head in the clouds, an exhausting exercise which calls for frequent rests. I had been appointed personal assistant to Herr Willi Münzenberg, the impresario and publishing maverick genius of the Left, who in a few master strokes created the *Rote Konzern*, a growing conglomerate of opinion magazines, book publishers, and political theatre featuring agitprop groups. The office was in Nollendorfplatz, close to Erwin Piscator's Proletarian Theatre, which now came under Willi's supervision. The pay was good. More importantly, I should be working at close quarters with interesting, important people. I would become *involved*! There were projects under way. How soon could I start? I am asked. Right away! No, come on Monday.

I took the rest of the week off to write to my parents. To see

19

art exhibitions. Go to the cinema, go on leisurely walks while digesting this stupendous piece of good fortune which would transform an outwardly committed Marxist crypto-bourgeois bohemian into a fully-paid Communist apparatchik on a bourgeois salary.

'Excuse me, Fräulein,' says the stranger, 'may I sit here beside you for a while?'

He speaks with a Russian accent. He is about five foot ten, and sinewy. He moves like an athlete. His hands are large, strong. There is a pale scar, like a plastered-over crack in a wall, running down his forehead from the line of his dark blond hair to the corner of the left eyebrow. He is wearing a knee-length leather overcoat that has seen too much wear – probably been slept in for God knows how long – and calf-high boots. An anarchist, I think. Berlin is full of them. Maybe a criminal to boot.

I look around. Not more than twenty metres further on there is another bench. Why would this fellow want to sit here unless he was up to something? But the stranger doesn't look aggressive. In fact, he has a pleasant manner: after all, he didn't have to ask my permission. There is gentle laughter in his tawny eyes. People are strolling by in either direction. Anyway, in a moment or two, I'll get up and walk on. I look at him with confident indifference. I think, well, maybe this wolf had already gobbled up a grandmother and a Red Riding Hood. Maybe all he wants is to digest his dinner in peace. But I remember that only a month ago a prostitute was found dead not far from here, stripped of all she possessed, including her clothes, and nailed to a tree with six inch construction nails. I have seventeen Marks in my purse. At worst, I'd give it all to him.

'This is a public bench, please yourself.'

'Thank you,' he says. He dumps his carry-all bag on the ground. He sits down – not too close – and stretches out his legs. Sunlight shafts through the tree branches and hits his face. It is a tired face for a young man. Crow's feet run crookedly from the corners of his eyes.

A few sparrows come down from the trees. They skip about

not far from the man's feet, glancing impudently with cocked heads. Even the sparrows have more *chutzpah* in Berlin.

The man takes out of his coat pocket a lump of bread, breaks it up and tosses bits at the birds. We watch the brief scramble.

'I'll bet you anything you like the little one on the right takes three out of five crumbs,' says the man.

'I don't bet.'

'No? Well, that's too bad,' he says, shrugging his shoulders and smiling. He has a most attractive smile, there's no denying.

'I'll bet on your behalf, then.'

Five crumbs, the little one takes them all. I have to laugh.

'You cheated. You threw the crumbs its way.'

'Cheated? No no. Well, maybe I helped the little bugger just a little bit. Ha ha ha.'

'Okay. So what did you lose on my behalf?'

He half-turns towards me. 'Ah, that's my secret. You place no bet, you make no win or loss.'

'That's fine by me. I told you, I don't bet. Are you a gambler?'

He shakes his head. 'No, I'm a player. I'd play at anything I know. I size up the odds sensibly. That's hardly gambling.'

'And you know about sparrows, do you?'

The man tilts his face upwards and laughs silently. 'I know damn all about sparrows. What I do know about is survival . . . Moving in to grab a chance, that sort of thing. You see, I recognised that little sparrow. I saw at a glance he had more pluck than the others. He will live through winters. He's the one that will fool the cat.'

'You've come to the right city, pal,' I tell him. 'For survival experts, Berlin is the ultimate playground.'

'You think so?' He looks me full in the eyes, smiling, as though knowing nothing about him, I had made a foolish presumption. But it is too late to retreat. I feel a latent reckless-ness about him which excites me, emboldens my curiosity. Temperamentally as well as ideologically, I am also sympathetic to Russians. I am on the verge of flirting with this man.

'What are you? A Russian agent, or an anarchist?' I ask.

He laughs. 'What do you think?'

'Without doubt, I think you are both.'

'I am a Russian sparrow. But not out for crumbs, I get by

with these. Actually, I'm looking for a little nest. You see, I just lost mine this morning.' And he touches his bag with the toe of his boot.

'And I thought you were a wolf. A Russian steppes wolf.'

'Not today. Sorry if I disappoint you.'

There is something Titus and I always had in common: an impulse to act suddenly, intuitively. Oh, what dreadful situations that can get you into. What wonderful experiences pass you by when you don't have it.

'What's your name?' I ask.

'Titus. Titus Altermann.'

'Well, Comrade Titus Altermann, it so happens a room has just become vacant where I live. If you can afford fifty-five Marks a month payable in advance.'

'I can,' he says.

'If you don't mind living in a room a whore lived and worked in.'

'I don't mind.'

'She was a first-class whore, mind you. Kind, cultured. Very clean. She paid her rent on the first of the month without fail, and had the best room in the house.'

'That suits me fine.'

I can see Frau Dumke's face when I bring this fellow in, her mouth gathering to a point until she sees the money. If she sees the money. That is not my problem. I can hear her think, 'What, another foreigner from the East? What is *der Vaterland* coming to?' And I can see her looking him over, saying as an afterthought, 'Ah well, why not?' Frau Dumke has a soft spot for ruggedly handsome young men. What woman doesn't?

'Is it far from here?' Titus asks, getting up.

'Kreuzberg.'

He wants to take me out to lunch first, a thank-you gesture. Anywhere I want. *He* take *me* out to lunch anywhere I want? Goodness, what would my friends think? . . . I haven't started working and already I'm thinking like a bourgeois.

'We'd better settle the business of the room first. It might be taken already, for all I know,' I tell him.

It's nearly an hour back home in the tram, the walk from Gneisenaustrasse to No. 5 Kloedenstrasse, the climb up four flights of stairs to Frau Dumke's apartment, and Titus doesn't think to ask my name!

He counts the money into Frau Dumke's palm, and pays for a bath. He goes into his room and shuts the door. The invitation to lunch is forgotten.

3

Frau Elsa Dumke's apartment on the top floor of No 5 Kloedenstrasse in Kreuzberg is spacious: four good size bedrooms, three of which she lets. She inherited the place from her parents – her father had been a civilian quartermaster with the nearby army base. This is one of the first things Frau Dumke proudly tells all new lodgers. In her living space, as on her person, traces of past middle-class prosperity linger amidst the ravages of prolonged hard times. The plumbing is erratic; the pipes rumble as though afflicted by chronic indigestion. Black dampness spots canker the walls in the bathroom. Elsewhere, too, the paint flakes off in patches, and the wallpaper bulges from the walls even in Frau Dumke's own quarters. But not in the large room where we have our breakfast, or evening tea, or where, with Frau Dumke's approval – a mere formality – we receive guests. Here, under the stern gaze of the absent Herr Doktor Otto Dumke, whose framed photograph stands on the mantelpiece, respectability is affirmed in the unchanging tradition of a bourgeois German home: a marriage of staidness and kitsch from the wallpaper to the curlicued silver-plated teaspoons on the table.

Frau Dumke embraces modernity, which she professes to detest: there is a telephone in the passage, and a cathedral-like wireless in the breakfast room.

Don't misunderstand: I like Elsa Dumke. Beneath that irritating coyness lies genuine integrity; behind all that boring stereotype respectability there beats an honest heart. Her nosiness, as her greed, is without malice. All she expects of 'our guests' is that they pay the rent on time, refrain from making noise, uphold good manners, keep the bathroom clean, stay out of her kitchen and address her as Frau Doktor Dumke.

24

Subject to these rules, all are welcome. Except Nazis and pimps; there Frau Doktor Dumke draws the line.

My room isn't large. I've decorated it myself, by special permission. I've stripped off the dreadful floral wallpaper. I've painted the walls a pleasant shade of cream, and the ceiling, which has plaster carving along the edges and a boss at the centre, white. I've polished years of grime off the heating stove so that its brown tiles shine. I've bought a colourful rug with two matching cushions at the market in Marheinekeplatz to place over the bed. I've hung a print of Egon Schiele's *Sitting Girl* above the bed so that I can see it in the mirror of my dressing-table when I sit down.

'*Ach, wie hübsch!* I could tell at one glance that you were young lady of good taste,' Frau Dumke had said, clasping her hands to her ballooning bosom.

A French window facing east opens onto a tiny balcony with a wrought-iron balustrade. Here I've created a miniature tropical garden in pots – a tangle of exotic greenery, with two bountiful tomato plants – that twines about the railing and spills over in a cascade of colour.

Every morning I stand for a few moments on my tiny balcony, putting my thoughts in order. This has become a daily ritual, when the weather permits. I watch the sun rays slant on the long grey roof of the block across the street, where the curtains are being drawn open. A peachy-faced boy in the middle flat is struggling into his Hitler Youth shirt. The mother bends over him, adjusting the swastika arm band. He is a sweet little boy. I have met him on several occasions in the streets, and he has always greeted me with a smile. Above, a man stands staring blankly straight at me. He is wearing a grey dressing-gown, holding a coffee cup in his hand. Behind him is a piano. He is a composer, a widower. Sometimes I hear him at work late at night.

These are our moments of contemplative privacy, when greetings, even glances of recognition are forbidden. And should the other lodger, the morose accountant, Herr Rausching, come out on to his own little balcony, which is separated from mine by that of the room where Titus now lives, he too would look out but not at me, and utter not a word.

25

Down below, the glistening cobblestones form a band of refracted light all the way down to Fidicinstrasse. I am alone, at the reticent beginning of a spring day, waiting for the routine sequence of ordinary motion in the street to commence. The French window of Titus's room is firmly shut, as it has been for three consecutive mornings ever since he moved in. There is not a sign of him. Is he habitually a late starter? Maybe he is ill . . . I haven't seen him at all from the moment he shut the door of his room behind him the day he arrived. I know the room well. It is the best in the house, the only one with a double bed – one which has a brass head and foot ends, like you see in movies. And two armchairs. And a gas fire. Even a desk, on which Hildegard had a standing exhibition of postcards from all over the world, sent to her by devoted clients – all regulars. Hildegard never picked men off the streets. She worked from the bar of the Eden Hotel in Kurfürstendamm. Despite what I've told Titus, Hildegard never brought her clients here, either. For that she had another rented room in town.

The emptiness of the balcony where Hildegard used to share my morning ritual inexplicably disturbs me: I miss her silent companionship all the more because I keep thinking about Titus, wondering if I shouldn't knock on his door later to see if he is all right, or at least tell Frau Dumke – what must she be thinking of him?!

Suddenly the French window opens. Titus comes out naked but for a towel wrapped round his waist. Instinctively I turn my face away, but from the corner of my eye I an see what a wonderfully athletic body he has. He raises his arms and yawns loudly. I feel as though a tremor from the street has bucked up the height of the building to amplify in my stomach.

'Hello there,' he calls out.

I half turn and give him a terse smile.

'Anything wrong?' says Titus, a big grin on his face.

There is nothing wrong. Not with him, anyway. He is being natural, isn't he? Isn't this the way people normally behave? I am annoyed at myself for stiffening up just because he had burst in on my little ritual, which I had originally devised – quite needlessly – to discourage Herr Rausching.

'You'll catch a cold, standing half-naked like that.'

'On such a lovely morning? I don't think so. But thank you for thinking about me.'

'Well, it's only natural, isn't it? I mean, when you don't see a neighbour for three days, you begin to wonder . . .' I say this with exaggerated nonchalance, which does not escape Titus. He smiles mischievously.

'Has it been that long?'

'More or less.'

'Ah well. I slept very soundly. Every three years I do this. Recharging my batteries.'

'A rather long recharging, isn't it?'

'Big batteries,' he says, winking at me.

'I'm pleased to see that you are recharged and well. You must get hungry after such a hibernation.'

'Ravenous! Which reminds me, I invited you to lunch. How about today?'

'I'm a hard-working girl. Lunches are out, I'm afraid.'

He gives me a look as if to say, 'Hard-working? Well, well . . .'

'You seem surprised. Don't you go to work?'

'Not if I can help it. How about dinner then?'

'We can talk about that over breakfast. You are coming to breakfast, I take it?'

'Sure. Let's see now. I've missed three, right? I wonder if I could have them all retroactively. What do you think?'

I ought to tell him what breakfast amounts to in this establishment, but I don't.

'Try it on Frau Doktor Dumke,' I say, laughing.

'You bet I will.'

Herr Rausching comes out. Seeing us, he stops abruptly. Disconcerted, he retreats like a snail into its shell, closing the French window. I feel sorry for the poor man, deprived as he is of his scheduled daily moment of silence in the fresh air.

'What's the matter with him?' says Titus.

'That was Herr Rausching. I think you've shocked him. He's not used to seeing naked Russians first thing in the morning. Who talk, moreover.'

'It seems I have a lot to learn. See you in the breakfast room.'

I look at my watch. 'In half an hour. Breakfast is a punctual business here, you'd better get used to it.'

'Is that so?'

'Exactly so.'

Titus shrugs his shoulders, goes inside without a further word. In all the years that I've known him, if there was one thing I could say about him with certainty it was that he hated routine, schedules, instructions – all of which, at the height of his power, he would ruthlessly, implacably, set for others.

I am not as calm as I wish to be, when at last I get down to preparing myself for meeting Titus at the breakfast table. I want to look my best and I'm angry at myself for wanting to. The two parts of me, Woman Wanda and Rebel Wanda, have a slanging match with each other as I gaze at the mirror. Rebel Wanda wins. I wipe my face clean of make-up. I pin my hair up in a bun. I slip into a plain but neat outfit which I have recently bought at a second-hand clothes shop in Nollendorfplatz . . . I wish I had a picture of myself from that morning: quietly intense, intelligent, but not dull; a Rosa Luxemburg look-alike?

Breakfast at Dumkehof is a simple regimented affair. Two tables are laid the night before. Herr Rausching has one to himself. Hildegard and I shared the other. Since Titus now occupies her room, he has naturally inherited her place at my table. The repast itself is strictly symbolic. Even though there is now food in plenty to be had in Berlin, Frau Dumke commemorates an austere past by providing only milk, one roll per person, and a cup of coffee or tea. Anything else we are expected to buy ourselves, and keep in the cupboard designated for our provisions. Except Herr Rausching. Along with the statuary *brötchen* he gets an egg and a slice of *schinken*, which Frau Dumke brings on a tray from the kitchen. She feels protective about him. He is a lonely man who needs looking after, she says. Herr Rausching must have a solid breakfast because this is the most important meal of the day, he insists: 'If you don't feed your brain well first thing in the morning, your brain won't serve you well for the rest of the day.'

Herr Rausching is Chief Accountant in the Town Hall. What

calamities might overtake the city if Herr Rausching's brain were starved even for one morning, is too horrible to contemplate. Frau Dumke is a responsible citizen.

On the stroke of eight from the nearby clock tower, she enters bearing Herr Rausching's sustenance, Egbert her tabby cat at her heels. '*Guten Morgen, Herr Rausching, guten Morgen, Fräulein Popper, guten Morgen Fräulein Pfilz,*' she would say. She would turn on the radio, stand there listening for a moment, sigh a doleful '*Ach . . . doch . . .* ', shake her head, then leave. We have grown accustomed to breakfasting with the radio recounting yesterday's disasters. And Frau Dumke has just become reconciled to breakfast's flawed symmetry created by Titus's absence.

A chimpanzee had escaped from the ape house in the Zoo, the announcer says. It bit two storm-troopers before climbing to the top of a tree. The police shot it dead. But the volley of gunfire hit a balloon piloted by an ex-cavalry officer called Hans Grimm, who had been throwing down leaflets from the sky, calling on the citizens of Berlin to unite in loving kindness as the Day of Judgment was at hand. Oberleutnant Grimm fell to his death right in front of the Kaiser Wilhelm Gedächtnis Church . . .

In Weimar, seven right-wing chemistry students who had burnt down the house of a professor with a Jewish name, known for his Republican sympathies, have been fined by the judge to pay a mere 300 Marks each! . . . In Wannsee, a young pianist and his lover committed suicide by jumping in the lake, leaving a note saying the world was too ugly for them to want to live. The sex psychologist Dr Magnus Hirschfeld opined it was all Goethe's fault.

Herr Rausching is visibly disturbed. Not, I suspect, because of the lovers' tragic death, or the miscarriage of justice, nor because one ape and a former soldier turned preacher lost their lives in the cause of freedom and human understanding respectively. No, he is upset because it is already five past eight and there is no sign of Frau Dumke. How will his diligent brain perform in the service of fellow Berliners without breakfast?

29

He glares crossly at his copy of the *Berliner Tageblatt*, avoiding my eyes.

There is no sign of Titus either.

'Herr Rausching,' I say rising from my chair, 'it seems something is delaying Frau Dumke. May I, in the meanwhile, make you a cup of coffee?'

He peers at me over the top of his glasses. Such a worried look, like a plump little schnauzer forgotten in a railway station by his owners.

'Well . . . er . . . That would be most kind, Fräulein Popper. If it is not too much trouble.'

'Not at all, Herr Rausching.'

Yesterday I bought a fruit cake on the way back home. I cut a slice for Herr Rausching – it is nutritious; should keep his brain ticking over nicely until help arrives. I am set to pour out the coffee when I hear shuffling behind the door, which opens. In shoots Egbert, high-tailed, followed first by Titus carrying Herr Rausching's breakfast tray and then Frau Dumke, limping pitifully. An attack of lumbago, worse than usual, she explains. Only duty dragged her out of bed. And if it weren't for kind Herr Altermann's help, *Gott in Himmel* knows how she would have managed.

'I think you've made a friend for life. Frau Dumke doesn't forget kind gestures,' I tell Titus when he joins me at the table.

'More to the point, I am getting a free breakfast. Not bad, eh?'

'You were counting on three,' I remind him.

'I'm always amenable to compromise.'

'Good for you. But if you don't catch Frau Dumke in the kitchen before she disappears into her room with her lumbago, my guess is you can forget about your breakfast.'

Titus makes a dash for the door. A few minutes later he returns triumphant with a laden tray. It's more than one Rausching breakfast but not quite two. He wolfs down the food; I've never met anyone who ate so fast as Titus did.

'Now, what about that lunch or dinner we're having together?' he says, wiping his mouth with the back of his hand.

'How can you think of food when you've just gobbled up a large breakfast in record time?'

He laughs. He thinks it's a joke I've made. 'I can always think of food. Always. But I was thinking of the occasion.'

'The occasion is timely. As it happens, it's my birthday on Friday.'

'Wonderful! We'll go out again on Friday!'

Paris, Autumn 1937: before we once again vanished from each other's life, we dined late in Montparnasse one night. Titus had polished off a dozen oysters and a large sole in white wine sauce, while Theo, Chad, and I had barely touched our own main courses (and there's never been as much as a pinch of fat round his waist!). Then he withdrew into a kind of impenetrable autism as he often did when he had things on his mind. We talked but he wasn't listening; he was miles away. I touched his arm. He surfaced. I said, 'Titus, you're like the Wolf in Little Red Riding Hood, do you know? That's how I thought about you when we first met.'

'Little Red Riding Hood? What's that?'

'It's a nursery story. For little children.'

'I've never heard it. Never been to a nursery. Tell me . . . But not now.'

'You are free tonight, aren't you?' says Titus.

I want to go out with him. I want to feel his hand on my arm as we cross a street. I want friends to see us and think, Who is this mysteriously handsome fellow Wanda is with? I want a little more than a vague guess at what he might be like as a lover.

World-wise Hildegard once said to me, 'A man who eats hurriedly fucks hurriedly. Good thing when you're working. Hopeless if he happens to be your boyfriend.'

I want him also to understand that I'm no pushover.

'Yes, I am. Where would you like us to go? The Hotel Adlon? The Eden, perhaps? Restaurant Horcher?' I rattle off a whole list of posh exclusive eating places. 'Or maybe one of those special cafés? For intellectuals, journalists, actors, film people. Take your pick. Of course, we could go somewhere cheaper. There is a nice Italian restaurant just round the corner in Belle Alliance Strasse. It's all the same to me, truly.'

31

He is smiling ironically, as if to say, 'Not bad, for a champion of the working classes who works for a Communist organisation.'

'Why not let it be a surprise, a last moment decision. Is eight all right with you?'

'Eight is fine.'

At work, we are preparing the schedule for the song and dance troupe from Moscow – the Blue Blouses. My boss, Willi Münzenberg, is enthusiastic as always.

'Wanda,' he tells me, 'we're going all out to promote this event. There's a cultural war going on here. We've got to win.'

Of course we've got to win. And we're in with a chance on this occasion: the troupe is first class; Russian songs are melodious, as everybody knows. No choir sounds better than a Russian choir. Cossack dances can stir the dead. Etcetera . . . Etcetera . . . Etcetera . . .

Will the German working masses accept this meticulously choreographed Moscow-packaged Socialism? Will children of German workers in Neukölln, Moabit, Oranien – you name it – sit through it patiently, let alone remember? Even to doubt is heresy.

As I plot the course of the forthcoming tour, I think of Titus. Where will he take me tonight? Will the promised surprise end in disappointment? Or would this be the beginning of something I could only dream about? What would he say about my endeavours on our cultural battlefield? He is, after all, a Russian!

'Who goes to your political theatre? The working masses?' I ask myself on his behalf. 'No. Our political theatre of the Left is poorly attended. A small group of intellectuals who continuously quarrel with each other in the columns of little-read journals like *Rote Fahne, Weltbuhne, Kurvlinie*,' I answer. 'There you are,' he says sardonically in my imagining, 'better if you organised puppet shows in the parks.' But . . . No, wait! Better still, rent the Sportpalast. Bring in from Russia Communism's champion fighter, a killer wrestler. Match this frightening beast of a man against the Aryan hero of the German

Right. Nothing attracts the masses better than a good scrap, believe me.

'Imagine: In the red corner, weighing mountains of Marxist revolutionary doctrine, champion of the oppressed proletariat, bone-crunching savage of the steppes, the one and only Tartar Terror.

'In the blue corner, weighing tons of pure Aryan racial garbage, the knight of the Third Reich, scourge of the *Untermenschen*, The Teutonic Tiger!

'*Meine Damen und Herren*, I give you the battle of the Titans, to the death. No holds barred.

'Why, Wanda, isn't this a brilliant idea? Tell your bosses Titus Altermann will promote and stage the whole show for a mere five per cent of the takings! Ha, ha, ha!'

This he actually said. And laughed. And mocked my foolish idealistic innocence. Much later, of course, after we had become lovers. Did he deliberately set out to discredit my beliefs for his own amusement? Titus loved contests. And, like a primitive god, he was as merciless to the victor as to the vanquished.

I am grateful for the busy day at the office because it keeps me from thinking too much about the evening. I accept Willi's lunch invitation. 'Come and meet Tucholsky and Eisler,' he says. 'Tucholsky will depress you. Eisler will make you laugh, he is so witty.' It's like taking simultaneously a purgative and a bowel stabiliser.

I stay in late to do some extra work which could easily wait until tomorrow. I arrive home at a quarter past eight. Let Titus cool his heels waiting for me.

But when at last I am ready, dressed to kill, in my fashion, nearly an hour past our appointed time, it is I who am waiting for him! I go and knock on his door. Silence. Then a much delayed, '*Herein!*'

The room is in a mess and stinks of French tobacco. A twist of clothes spills out of Titus's open bag onto the floor. Titus himself is lying on the bed, bare-footed, dishevelled, his crumpled shirt open over his naked chest. He is reading the *Vossiche Zeitung*, no less – Berlin's top Liberal daily newspaper. He puts

33

the paper aside when he sees me, but does not get up. He lights up a Gauloise, offering me one. I decline.

'Is this your idea of a surprise? Or have you forgotten you've invited me out to dinner?' I say.

'Forgotten? Of course not.'

'It's nearly nine! We were supposed to go out at eight!' Even as I utter the rebuke I marvel at my own hypocrisy.

'So? What's the hurry? You're not starving, are you?' He laughs and gets up.

When Titus became a powerful man, he once fired a top executive because the poor man was five minutes late for a meeting. But here in Berlin and later in Paris, where the cafés turned him into a night bird, time means nothing to him. In fact, he does not even own a watch.

'All right. Give me five minutes and we'll be on our way. No, don't leave. Hang around while I get dressed.'

'One day, Titus, maybe I'll take you round to buy you some decent clothes.'

'One day,' he replies with a laugh, 'I'll be paying people to go out and buy for me whatever I need. And have the best tailors come round to measure me for suits.'

'People like me don't run errands for anybody, Titus. Especially not for a lout who is too lazy to go out and buy his own clothes.'

He stops what he is doing to look at me.

'No, I didn't mean you. You are special. I'd never take advantage of you, Wanda. But in general people will do anything you ask of them, for the right reward. It's just a question of judging how much will buy them.'

He grins impishly while buttoning up the fly of an unexpectedly superior pair of trousers.

'The whole business of living is getting enough money to buy what you want, including people, without paying too much yourself.'

'Is money everything?'

'Absolutely! I'm not talking about pennies, either. I'm talking about big money. Life is worthless without it.'

I might have walked out on him there and then, but I remembered the hovering air of vagrancy about him the day

34

we first met in the wood. And the seriousness with which he held the wad of bank notes out of which he peeled off the rent money into Frau Dumke's palm. What did I know about this man, the things he had been through, the awful deprivation he had probably experienced?

'On the understanding that I'm not for sale in any way, and that you don't try to prove your theory on me, I'll go out with you to wherever you've decided to take me tonight.'

He is relieved, I can tell. 'Understood and agreed. Let's be comrades. Let's say tonight we celebrate our comradeship, right?'

Should I be surprised if Titus takes me to an exclusive restaurant in Berlin's West End? I make up my mind not to be. The man is unpredictable, an unknown quantity. The only surprising thing about him would be his failure to astonish. With him, *Alors, étonne-moi* isn't a sarcastic dismissal nor an appeal. It is simply a sequence you can count on.

And were he to take me to one of those sleazy so-called clubs in Potsdamerstrasse where criminals and fighters hang out, and semi-naked girls dance, what should I do? Leave and go home? I decide I'd stick it out. I am no missionary; I do not believe in forcing my values and tastes on other people. I might even enjoy seeing the criminal side of life. Besides, I know in my bones I'd be safe with Titus anywhere.

Let me also say that when Titus decides on a celebration, it invariably turns out to be a full-blooded one.

'We'll take a taxi,' he announces.

'Where to?'

'The Russian Tea Rooms in Kleiststrasse.'

I had never ridden in a taxi before that night. Nor have I ever been able to overcome completely the feeling that taking a cab was irredeemably decadent. Except in London, when old age provided an excuse for just about everything.

This Russian place is without doubt respectable and far from cheap. The light, shining from a superfluity of crystal, is dim. The atmosphere recalls a Russia that no longer existed except in the stubborn memories of expatriates. A dreamy-looking singer dressed as a Cossack is playing a Russian ballad with his

35

balalaika. It is the kind of Russian haven you read about, where clients settle outstanding accounts with family heirlooms, jewels, gold – mementos from past lives that had been destroyed by the Revolution. Could Titus possibly be one of them?

The tables are almost all occupied. I am not quite dressed for such a place. Titus certainly isn't. He is not in the least bothered by this. Nor is the proprietor, who greets him with friendly familiarity and personally conducts us to our reserved table.

Titus wants real vodka, which he says he hadn't had for longer than he can remember. He asks for a whole bottle. And for me a red Caucasian wine of which I had never heard.

'Quail's eggs, Wanda. They are simply delicious. You must try. And then we'll have venison, shall we?'

From across the room a burly man with a Rasputin beard nods at Titus, who nods back. A White Russian agent? A Communist renegade, at least? Who is Titus, for that matter? Who will pay for this sumptuous feast?

'Wanda, you're not eating. Don't you like the venison? Would you prefer something else?'

'I'm really not hungry.'

'Why, that's perfect. Hunger would spoil such food. Savour it, let your senses caress it.'

I recognise Hans Moltke sitting with a very beautiful young man a few tables away. He is a Liberal among liberals, publisher and art collector of impeccable refinement, a man who is as generous with his time as with his considerable wealth to all the dying causes that still serve decency in Berlin. That was how the painter George Grosz described him when he introduced me to him only two days ago. Graf Moltke had kissed my hand. 'Sweet Wanda, we must meet again,' he had said.

The Count is looking vacantly at me. I lower my eyes.

Titus has eaten all that was on his plate, and has drunk three-quarters of the vodka. Now he picks desultorily at what I have left.

'Now, Comrade Popper, you must drink a little vodka with me. Then I'll know we are friends,' he says, simulating drunkenness. But he is not drunk. For the moment we step outside into the cool night springiness returns to his step, and he is clear-eyed. It is I who am befuddled and I have hardly drunk more than one glass of wine!

By the time we get back to Kloedenstrasse it is past two in the morning. His arm round my waist, Titus almost carries me up the four flights of stairs.

'Good night,' I say at the door of my room. He looks at me for a moment, then pulls me gently by the hand into his own room.

Poor Hildegard; she didn't know all that much about lovers after all, if Titus was anything to go by. He wolfed his food but made love patiently, sensuously, interminably.

The pale light that filters into the room illuminates the line of the scar on his forehead. I run my finger along it.

'How did you get that?'

'A moment of carelessness . . . Which, but for luck, would have cost me my life.'

'But how? Where?'

He takes hold of my hand and kisses my fingers. 'In a faraway country, another world that I want to forget.'

That was when I said 'I love you' and immediately regretted it. He didn't answer. He turned his face from me and went silent.

'I didn't mean it . . . I mean, I make no claim on you when I say I love you.'

'I know.'

I begin to feel embarrassed. I stop stroking his chest. I move a little away from him.

'I don't understand what people mean when they talk about love,' Titus mutters, more to himself than to me.

'Different people mean different things, I suppose. I can only tell you what I mean.'

'What do you mean?'

'That right now and here, you are everything to me. I want to know all about you. I want to know how to make you happy.'

'You make me happy.'

'I want to know what makes you afraid.'

'Emptiness.'

'What you value most.'

'I've already told you. Money.'

'I can't believe that. It's too awful.'

'No. Money is like a weapon. What you do with it can be awful, not the thing itself.'

'Why do you want a weapon?'

'Because violence is always around, like bacteria.'

'What are you really, Titus? Tell me.'

He turns on his side and takes me in his arms. I can't see whether his eyes, enlarged by the darkness, are serious or mocking.

'I am the supreme specialist in chaos. A master at winning and losing with utmost economy. That's what I am.'

I feel his groin stir against my belly. I take his penis in my hand and guide it into me. As I hold the hair at the back of his neck, I think, One day my love, I'll know where you're weak. Not to hurt, but to heal.

4

If you're lucky it happens to you once in a lifetime, no more. You fall in love completely. You love with total commitment, ignoring whatever warning lights your intuition flashes at you. You tell yourself: 'Here is the man Destiny has chosen for me. Welcome the consuming intensity of life without which existence is a drudge! Nothing else is remotely as important.'

If you are luckier still, you get over this illusion before too many bills come in. For Destiny, if there is such a thing, is neither a dispenser of fortune nor a stage director but a bailiff – quick and unrelenting with the accounts.

How should I describe my love for Titus? The imagination inflamed by the enigma of impossibilities, then made feverish by an uncertainty of a future and the obliteration of a past? I am grateful for the experience. I am even more grateful that my passion for him had matured into a lasting care; a loving recognition of his greatness of spirit; of the enormity of his flaws. For he himself foresaw and accepted the desolation of his end.

Often when we lie deliciously exhausted side by side, I trace my finger along that pale scar on his forehead which is like the frozen imprint of lightning.

'Tell me what other scars you have, inside?' I ask.

He takes my finger in his mouth, bites lightly on it. 'None. I have no scars at all other than this one. Disappointed?'

'If you were to be turned into an animal, what would it be?' I feel like Delilah, probing the secrets of his strength.

He considers my question for a long moment. 'I don't think it would be an animal at all . . .'

'What then?'

'A rock, maybe. A plain slab of stone on the seashore or in the desert. An eternal passivity of witnessing would be the ultimate reward . . .'

'Or punishment?'

'That, too. They're often indistinguishable from each other . . .'

We make love so much it worries me. Have I developed an insatiable appetite for sex? Will my brain go soft? That's what they say excessive sex does to you. I look up *nymphomania* in the dictionary: morbid and uncontrollable sexual desire in women. Grouped with it is *nympholepsy*: a yearning for the unattainable. I decide there is nothing morbid or uncontrollable about my desire.

As for nympholepsy, here is a cause for concern. It is a collective condition in Germany nowadays, particularly in Berlin: everybody is frantically thrashing about to suppress yearning for unattainables, like a secure future, a semblance of permanence, ordinary stable continuity. We are citizens of an apocalyptic Babylon, revelling in the last almighty orgy before the end of the world. Nympholepsy is a symptom we must dull with the drug of pleasure. I don't think any but the most stupid of my Marxist colleagues truly believes the awaited Revolution will come to redeem us in our days. They only pretend they do.

But Titus, he yearns for nothing that is unattainable. That's not in his nature. For he does not recognise what he cannot grasp. Yet he too lives from day to day. Making no plans, aspiring to nothing, he hones his reflexes to meet the flux of turbulence that agitates at the periphery of our lives. Theo said of Titus that he was the most beautiful and perfect barbarian he had ever met. Only barbarians were truly free, the real survivors, Theo had said. Because the process of becoming civilised diminished both your freedom and your ability to survive. If Berlin imploded in fire, Titus would rise unscathed from the ruins, holding on, I hoped, to what was left of me.

One day, without warning, Titus disappeared for a week. I didn't know where he had gone or whether he would ever return. He reappeared, looking drawn, went straight to his room and slept. I let him be.

Eventually, I confront him for the first and last time.

'Where have you been?' I ask crossly.

He looks through me. 'Here and there. Why, is anything the matter?'

'I was worried. I nearly went to the police . . .'

'The police!' he sneers. 'I'm surprised at you, Wanda. You ought to know by now that you don't even ask the police for the time of day.'

'I don't know, actually.'

'Take it from me then. Stay clear of the police. Anyway, you needn't worry on my account.'

'I shan't in future. But you might have told me . . .'

Again that unfocused look.

'All right. I'm sorry. We are both free people. We come and go as we please. No questions, right?'

'I'll try to remember to let you know next time,' he says noncommittally.

'Oh, so you're going to make a habit of it, disappearing like that, are you?'

Irritation flickers about him like a tiger's tail. I'm not his wife; I'm no less independent than he is, either! Foolishly, I won't let the matter drop. I stare at him.

'Maybe yes and maybe no. What's the fuss for, anyway?'

I am angry. Not at Titus, at myself, for engaging in such a petty argument, for being on the verge of tears over something I should simply accept. He is unmoved. His eyes are unnervingly dispassionate as he says:

'Wanda, I do what I have to do, when I have to do it. I have vowed many years ago that I shall never be accountable to anybody.'

I think to myself, what a desolate vow to make! How can I make him realise the impoverishment he is unwittingly inflicting upon himself. And I know in the depth of my heart, that I can't.

'All right, Titus. No more questions. Ever.'

After that exchange Titus is demonstratively loving. The next

41

day he turns up in my room with a brand new gramophone and a batch of records, all bought at the posh Wertheim department store in Leipziger Platz, no less. He places the contraption on the table, cranks it up, pulls out a record from the batch. My little nest of culture resonates to the sound of Berlin's queen of operetta, Fritzi Massary's, latest hits.

'Isn't this wonderful?' He strokes the ornate megaphone, clearly impressed more by the outpouring volume than by the music itself.

'You don't like it? There's Beethoven, Schubert, Chopin, Tchaikovsky, jazz, shmaz, anything you want.'

It is all there, the full range. The shop assistant at Wertheim had selected a catholic assortment of records. Titus never does anything in half-measures. I look at him standing, one hand on the new toy, and burst out laughing.

'What's funny?'

'You. I love you. Whatever gave you this idea?'

'A belated birthday present. You always tell me how much you love music. Perhaps now you won't drag me to concerts.'

I hear a dreadful noise down in the street one evening, like an aeroplane about to crash. A few minutes later Titus is at my door. He is wearing a scuffed leather jacket, high boots, and a ridiculous pilot's leather helmet, with a pair of goggles perched above the floppy visor. A yard of white scarf trails down his front. He sports a fresh black eye, too. He is grinning all over his face.

'Don't tell me. You've got an aeroplane. You force-landed in the street. The furious neighbours beat you up,' I say.

'Not a bad guess. Come down and have a look.'

I've just had a bath and washed my hair. I am in my dressing gown. But Titus won't allow me a minute to get dressed. He drags me down as I am to see the new acquisition, which came with the jacket, boots, helmet, goggles and scarf, not to mention the black eye.

It is an elderly BMW motorcycle. The exhaust manifold had fallen off. That's why the machine makes such an infernal noise, Titus explains. Otherwise it is in perfect working order. He did not buy the motorbike; he fought for it. Six rounds of boxing against Schönberg's middleweight champion, Gypsy Joe, in a fairground on the edge of Tiergarten not far from Potsdamerplatz. Gypsy Joe retired with a broken rib halfway through the sixth round.

'At least I hope he's a Nazi,' I say, not being able to think of anything else.

'Naah . . . He's just a poor mug trying to get a few more easy fights before his lights go out. Maybe he'd want to be a Nazi now, since I told him I was a communist and a Jew. After the fight, of course. Ha ha ha.'

'Why did you say that?'

'He was a bad loser, so I thought I'd make it even worse for him. Wanda, why don't we ride to Wannsee tomorrow? Have a picnic at the lakeside?'

It is Friday. The weather looks set to be beautiful. Barely half an hour from Berlin, Wannsee is lovely. There's nothing I would like better than a picnic at the lakeside with Titus. I look nervously at the machine. I have never been on a motorcycle before. The very thought of it terrifies me.

'Shouldn't you first get some practice on this thing? We could take the train . . .'

'Nonsense! There's nothing to it. Easier than riding a horse. Wanda, don't tell me you're scared!'

'Me? Scared? What on earth gave you such an idea? If only you'd said right away it was easier than riding a horse . . .' We have a good laugh. He knows I've never been near a horse in my life. As we climb up the stairs, his arm around me, I rack my brains for a ploy to make him change his mind in favour of the train.

Avus is a stretch of road flanking Grunewald on the way from Berlin to Wannsee and then Potsdam. Straight and wide, it invites speed. Automobile races are held here regularly, and are popular sporting events with Berliners.

No sooner are we on Avus than Titus shouts over his shoulder, 'Hold on tight!' He leans forward, opening the throttle full. If all the Luftwaffe took to the sky in a body, they would not make half the noise Titus's BMW makes as it roars at top speed, vibrating violently.

'Poor Wanda,' says Titus when at last we arrive. 'You deserve a medal for courage.'

Wannsee lake, surrounded by woods, is sparkling blue. Sailboats move languidly across the calm water. On the shore, families set out their picnics. Children wade in and out of the shallows. It is a hot day for the time of the year, yet too cold for swimming, except for the few dedicated older swimmers. A heavy barrier of cloud lies on the horizon; dark but unthreatening in its immobility.

We spread a rug under a tree a few paces from the water line. I unpack the picnic basket. Titus had brought a bottle of good Riesling. The wine is pleasantly cool because the first thing he did after we dismounted was secure the bottle between two rocks in the water.

Not far from us, under a wide-canopied beech tree, sits a young family. The woman, her hair bobbed fashionably, is pretty. Probably she is a secretary in some business. The man is slightly overweight. There is an air of contentment about him. Their two little blond children are pretty too. They run about chasing each other. When they come too close to us, the mother cries, 'Thomas, Hildchen, come here,' and smiles at us apologetically.

They had eaten their lunch. The husband is fiddling with a camera: he wants to take a snapshot of his pretty family with the lake as a backdrop. Titus lies, his head in my lap, overcome with lethargy. And suddenly that nympholeptic yearning for the unattainable overwhelms me.

'Ah . . . sometimes I envy the bourgeoisie. Don't you think it would be nice to have a nice little house in the country, with a garden, and a dog . . . Just think what lovely children we could have . . .'

I have said it; mentioned the unmentionable. Titus lies squinting at the sun, pretending he hadn't heard me.

'Titus?'

'You'd hate it. You'd be bored out of your mind in no time at all.'

'What about you?'

He pulls a face, half a smile, half a grimace. 'Probably the same. I don't much care for the countryside.'

'Why not?'

'Emptiness. Nothing happening there. Just open spaces you have to cross on the way to cities. Armies like the countryside because that is where war is easier. Where you can kill, and move on and kill again. Cities are life. Cities are civilisation.

'People romanticise about the countryside without even thinking what it means. They believe peasants are wise and happy. Have you ever talked to peasants? They are ignorant! Stupid! They live and think like pigs! No, you can keep your countryside. It's not for me.'

'So why are we here?'

He laughs scornfully, 'This? Countryside? This is the city people's playground. Besides, I know you like getting out of town. I like giving you what you like. Also, didn't we want to test the bike?'

'You mean *you* wanted to.'

'Okay, but don't tell me you're not happy to be here.'

I wonder if Titus ever counted lost opportunities. And if he did, whether he ever regretted the loss. I suspect that, as with grudges or favours given or taken, he never kept count of either losses or gains.

He loved the races. He was knowledgeable about horses. How many times he dragged me to Hoppegarten, or to the Grunewald-Rennbahn I cannot remember. When he won a large sum of money, as he often did, he would say: 'Celebration! Where would you like to dine tonight?'

Once I suggested the outrageously extravagant Hotel Adlon in Unter den Linden.

'No,' Titus said, 'I never go there.'

Instead, we went to Horcher in Lutherstrasse, which was probably as expensive. We both shared a reckless disdain for saving money.

He had an obsessive fascination with boxing. Here I put my foot down: I refused to go to fights with him. Concerts, theatre, left him cold, but he enjoyed cabaret. The only theatre he actually wanted to go to was Brecht's *Mahagonny*, because he had heard it was staged in a boxing ring. In the event, he liked it.

One Saturday afternoon, at a race meeting in Grunewald, Titus lost heavily. We were on the point of leaving when Chad Johnson suddenly emerged from the crowd. 'Hi,' he said, putting a hand on Titus's shoulder, 'I've been looking everywhere for you. Where've you been lately?' Chad was handsome, with a friendly open face. I liked him at once.

'Hello, Chad! It's good to see you. We were just leaving. I've been losing on every single race. It's obviously not my day.'

'Really? Then maybe it's my day. Normally you always win and I always lose,' said Chad cheerfully.

'Wanda, this is Chad Johnson. Chad writes for the *Boston Globe*, and is the smartest foreign correspondent in Berlin! Why were you looking for me, Chad?'

Chad started to say something then stopped. 'Gosh, I forgot,' he grinned.

Chad was not alone. With him was an English friend called Tristan Rutland. He was older than any of us, very tall, angular, soft-spoken. He explained that he was First Secretary at the British Embassy. He said this with appealing diffidence, as though it were a mild disorder he was suffering from. Then, possibly for my sake, because he identified me intuitively, he added that he was no longer enjoying Germany, and would be relieved to return home. His family lived in an old country house in County Durham, in the north of England.

'Look after Wanda while I go to answer nature's call,' said Titus. 'And don't talk her into placing a bet, ha, ha, ha.'

Chad was full of praise for Titus. He had never met such a brilliant unpredictable man, he said. Titus would either perish before his prime, or reach greatness, because he always played for the highest stakes with courageous virtuosity.

I asked him where they had met. 'Why, at the Adlon, of course. His habitual haunt. How come he's never brought you there?' Poor Chad, he looked so uncomfortable when he realised the faux pas he had made.

I have two daughters and seven grandchildren. From that tentative encounter in Grunewald there grew a steady friendship between Tristan and me. Never emotionally demonstrative, he eventually offered marriage out of the noblest of generosity. We never made demands on each other. The bond between us deepened out of mutual respect, affection . . . Yes, with time love too: a slow, comfortable, knowing kind of love.

In adjusting my own hectic illusion of freedom to Tristan's ordered world, I attained the only kind of real freedom life can afford: recognition of its limitations; acceptance of its responsibilities. Tristan taught me how to give of myself without self-congratulation, without regret, without even expecting acknowledgment. How sad for poor Theo, who needed me most, that my apprenticeship in giving was not nearly completed at the height of his need.

And Titus? Out of a hostile void he created the mighty empire which in the end imprisoned him, emasculated his gifts, relegated him to the loneliness of old age. Strange how irony, like wisdom, is often perceived only in retrospection.

I wanted to point this out to him once, many years later, but didn't. He more or less pre-empted me.

He had invited me to lunch at the Stafford Hotel, St James's Place, across the way from his office. He had with him a volume of Christopher Marlowe's plays he had just taken out of the London Library.

'Why, Titus, fancy you interested in Marlowe of all things!' I said.

'I don't much care for *Faustus*,' he blurted out.

'Why not?'

'I find him boring and stupid. He's supposed to be the wisest man on earth. Does he utter anything remotely wise? Nothing at all. The ugly old goat wants the most beautiful tart in the world in return for his worthless soul! When he gets her, he's scared, he whines, he wants redemption. What's redemption, anyway?'

'I never saw it quite like that. Maybe I should read it again.'

'Don't bother. Read *Tamburlaine*. That's the one to think about.'

'A rather imperfect play, I believe.'

'No, Wanda. On the contrary, it's the most perfect play there could be. Tamburlaine comes from nowhere into the heavyweight division of life, and beats everybody in sight. Wins everything. Then, when he has it all, he's licked by the most ordinary things of all, a common bloody virus or something.

47

Nothing's left of his achievements, only pain and emptiness and loneliness. Isn't that wonderfully tragic?'

For the first time ever I saw a kind of helpless fear in his eyes. I wept inwardly for him.

Titus has fallen asleep. He lies on his back, arms crossed over his chest, the empty wine bottle discarded at his side. A dark inflation of cloud at the horizon turns the water grey. A breeze whispers coldly in the leaves; people are packing up their picnic paraphernalia. I ought to wake Titus, we too should move before the storm breaks, but he sleeps so peacefully that I haven't the heart to disturb him. I cover him with the rug. I suddenly have a vision of him as a corpse laid on some foreign battlefield, waiting to be collected by the gravediggers of war.

The rain comes rushing across the lake, pounding on the water. Titus rises, astonished, annoyed. Hurriedly we assemble our stuff.

'There's no need for us both to get soaked to the bones. You'd better go back on the train,' he says.

'No. I came with you and I'll go back with you.'

He protests. It's foolishness, he says. What's the point? I'm adamant. I want to be with him, I insist.

We thunder back to Berlin through a spray, my face pressed against his back.

I am numb with cold when at last we stand dripping water at the bottom of the stairs.

Titus takes my face in his hands. 'You look like a drenched kitten. How do you feel?'

'Like a drenched kitten, I suppose. I don't ever want to ride a motorbike again.'

'All right, I'll get a car.' He laughs. 'What we need now is a hot bath and something to drink strong enough to kick-start your system.'

'Titus, if you make another reference to motorbikes I swear I'll pass out!'

Frau Dumke stares in horror at the pools we are making on the floor of her hall, but she is not unsympathetic. Yes, there is hot water, *Gott sei dank*. But not too much.

'Fräulein Popper, you go in first, poor lamb. *Und Sie*, Herr Altermann, you'll have to make do with what is left.'

'Okay, "poor lamb". You go in first,' Titus says the moment Frau Dumke is out of sight. 'Don't lock the bathroom door.'

I don't quite latch on to what he means. I decide to be selfish. I run the bath to the full. I sink into the bathtub up to my chin in the hot water. Dreamily I watch the heavy condensation forming on the windowpane. A moment later Titus steps in. He lets his dressing gown fall to the floor and stands over me stark naked with a bottle of plum schnapps – my lovely *zwechken schnapps* – in his hand.

'Move forward, darling,' he says.

'Have you gone mad! Frau Dumke will throw us both out. We'll be out on the street this afternoon!'

'No, she won't. She won't know. And if she did, she'd pretend she didn't. Trust me.'

'Titus, you're not going to get drunk here in the bathtub, are you? We'll drown, both of us. I couldn't bear the disgrace.'

'This, my love, is to rub your back with. It works like magic. You'll feel reborn.'

His hands are strong and gentle and practised. The spirit seeps through my skin, deliciously warm. I lean back against him. He removes the towel from my head. My hair tumbles down, intertwines about his arms. He licks schnapps off my shoulders and neck . . .

'How does that feel?'

'You know damn well how it feels. How many women have you done that to?'

'You're the first.'

'Liar.'

'Once I brought a horse back to life, rubbing it down with vodka strong enough to burn a hole in you. Not in a bath, though.'

I twist around to face him, put my arms round his neck and kiss him on the mouth.

'I'll never know when to believe you. I don't mind any more,' I say.

I am sure Frau Dumke registered what had gone on in the bath but she said nothing. Titus was right, again. If she had

49

protested, we would have left, Titus and I, just like that. We walked back to his room openly. We made love once again in bed, then fell asleep.

I am the first to awake. The room is untidy; Titus doesn't care about tidiness. I think, if I'm going to spend more time here, I'd better do something: messy rooms depress me. I get out of bed and slip into my dressing gown. Treading softly, I let my mind idle on where I should start when I see something dark jutting out from beneath a jumble of clothes in a half-open drawer. I pull at it and draw a very large pistol from a wooden holster. Next to it are two cardboard packets full of bullets, a couple of clips, and short thick barrel – a silencer?

The weapon is heavy in my hands, and frightening. I am dumbfounded; I don't know what to think.

'What are you doing, Wanda?'

Titus has half risen to rest on his elbow. He is looking at me as though I were a harmless but irritating intruder whom he has woken up to discover in his room.

'Titus, what is this?'

'You can see, can't you? It's a pistol. A German-made Mauser pistol, to be precise. Put it back where you found it.'

'Titus, why do you keep a gun with bullets and a silencer? I want to know.'

'I just happen to have it. There's nothing sinister.'

'Why don't you get rid of it? What do you need a gun for?'

Panic is rising in me, pushing to the surface all the recurring doubts about him – the money he will not tell how he earns, his disappearances.

'I don't *need* a gun, Wanda. Like I said, I happen to have it.'

'Why don't you get rid of it? Surrender it to the police or something.'

'Come here,' he says, stretching an arm to me.

He takes the gun; it is clean, thinly oiled. The metal gleams. He strokes my shoulder with the barrel.

'See? It's just a piece of machinery, Wanda, nothing terrible or awful. No different from a pen, or a spade, or any other implement, really. What makes the difference is who uses it and for what. Actually, this is a very good pistol. I've had it for some time and I have no intention of getting rid of it, and certainly not surrendering it to the police.

'The Nazis have guns. The *Stahlhelms* have guns. Your Communist *Rotefront* have them. So do crooks. This is a time when people keep weapons. So if you have one, you hold on to it because you never know when you might need it.'

My need of faith makes his reassurance unassailable. Titus can always talk his way out of anything.

'Now, put it back where it was, and don't worry your head about things that needn't worry you. One day I might teach you how to shoot.'

Berlin's police chief, Herr Karl Zörgiebel, has personally issued a warning against street demonstrations on the First of May. We discuss the matter in the office. A rumour is circulating in town that the militants will ignore the police warning. Besides, these days, who are the police to give such orders anyway, corrupt and ineffective as they are?

Our own organisation is predominantly cultural; we neither organise nor participate in street events, even if these are traditionally a part of the Berlin way of life. But the First of May is special: anybody with even a faint flush of pink in his political complexion marches with the red flag on this day. All the more because Nazi fascism is on the rise; we must therefore show our red banner defiantly. Berlin is ours. The Nazis should be made to understand that here their barbaric progress will be halted.

I am assigned to march with our Neukölln branch comrades.

'Where are you gathering?' Titus asks.

Does he want to join in? Would he come, just for my sake if for no other reason?

'Hermannplatz.'

'Hmm. Can't you go some other place?'

'Of course I can't. That's where I've been assigned to go. Why?'

He shrugged his shoulders. 'It's an ugly place. If you must go demonstrating, I thought you might at least choose a more attractive location.'

'Really? Since when have you become so fastidious?'

51

'I was thinking of you, not of myself.'

'Then why won't you come with me, Titus?'

'I hate crowds. And I've seen enough First of May parades to last me a lifetime. I think I'll stay in bed today.'

'How can you say such a thing!'

'Easily. Tell you what, why don't we meet outside Karstadt department store when your parade is over? We could have something to eat.'

'Don't expect me to go round looking for you; I'll be with my friends. If we run into each other, then maybe.'

'Oh well, in that case I'll certainly stay in bed. First of May days are always a write-off for me.'

They wrote in the *Berliner Tageblatt* the next morning that it had been a planned Communist provocation, directed from Moscow. Ten were shot dead by the police in Hermannplatz alone. In the whole of Berlin, thirty had been killed and many others wounded. The hospitals were stretched to capacity on that black Tuesday, May 1st 1929.

But I was there. There had been no provocation. We were disciplined. The procession was orderly, with no Nazis in sight, either, only police: row upon row of grey grim men in their helmets. Rifles held diagonally across their chests. The *Schupo* secret policemen circled about like jackals at the site of a kill.

We formed. We marched singing the *Internationale*, red flags held high. 'Well, what did you hope to achieve? You couldn't even give Berlin a dose of German measles with all those red flags,' Titus would later say.

All of a sudden the shots rang out. Then they charged at us with batons. There were screams and shouts. Comrades began to fall. A stampede got under way. Someone gave me a shove and I lost my balance. As I struggled to my feet, one thought pounded in my brain: 'Run, Wanda, or you'll die!' But my legs would not obey me. I felt a sharp pain in my left knee, probably from the fall.

Then I saw Titus. He was standing at the far end of Karstadt, in the shadow of an alley between the store and another building. Whatever or whomever he was looking for, he seemed to have found. He drew the Mauser pistol from inside his coat.

Calmly, as though he had all the time in the world, he inserted a clip into the magazine sleeve, slapping it home with the flat of his hand just as he had demonstrated to me in his room. Then, cocking the gun, he knelt down on one knee and took aim, holding the pistol with both hands at arm's length. The gun gave two little kicks upwards.

'Titus!' I screamed. Perhaps he didn't hear me. He turned away. The next moment he was gone.

I was arrested along with tens of others, then released a few hours later. My knee was the size of a football, and throbbing. A friend took me to hospital where it was X-rayed. Nothing had been broken. When I got back home, Titus was still in bed.

'You look terrible,' he said, jumping up. 'What happened?' I told him. He made me sit down so that he could take a look at my knee. I said, 'Who did you kill today?'

He stared at me in surprise. 'What are you talking about?'

'I saw you. You were by Karstadt. You had your pistol. You shot someone. Twice!'

'You are imagining things. I was here all day, in bed, like I said I would be. Had I known it would turn out as it did, of course I'd have come. You might have been killed.'

I started to cry. 'Why are you lying to me, Titus? I love you. Even if you did something terrible . . .'

He put his arms round me and rocked me slowly back and forth. 'You're upset, Wanda. I'll make you a cup of tea with lots of brandy. Then you'll go to sleep. Tomorrow you'll feel much better. You'll forget all this nonsense.'

'I'm not crazy or hysterical, Titus. I saw you . . .' Remembering a gangster movie we had seen together, I blurted, 'Show me your pistol. I want to smell if it's been fired.' As if I could tell.

'Why, Wanda. I got rid of it. Like you wanted me. I sold it for fifty Marks a few days ago to a Pole. I thought I'd buy you a present with the money. Tomorrow you can tell me what you'd like to have.'

We were having a good summer. Thanks to our enterprising mayor Herr Gustav Böss, Berlin was celebrating a prestigious

Festwoche. The conductor Arturo Toscanini gave concerts with the Berlin Philharmonic. Wilhelm Furtwängler conducted Beethoven's *Fidelio.* The Catalan cellist Pablo Casals enchanted or bemused Berlin's musical cognoscenti with his idiosyncratic brilliance. Paul Hindemith, whom I knew personally, conducted the gala performance of his latest opus.

I took Titus to see *Fidelio* at the Opernhaus. He slept through the first act, then again after the intermission but woke up towards the end of the second and last. 'Let me guess what happened,' he said cheerfully. 'Another flopped revolution, right?'

At the end of the year comes the great crash, recalling the dreadful days of six years before. Only this time it is worse. Or better. Depending on the vision you hold: they say that worldwide capitalism is collapsing for good. Once again the money is worthless. Unemployment spreads like the plague, sparing no class. As winter sets in, people burn furniture for fuel to keep warm, and paintings – those that cannot be traded for something useful. Any commodity is currency for barter. Criminals rob innocent people in broad daylight. Formerly blameless citizens turn into criminals. The police are nowhere to be seen. Everybody knows they take bribes. That's Berlin all over again: forever at the extreme ups and downs of fortune.

Will I lose my job? Will I become destitute like so many others? Do I really believe the long-awaited revolution is at last on its way? Do I really want it? So much of what I have grown accustomed to is at stake; can ideals overcome moral cowardice? I ponder uneasily over these challenges.

'We are moving forward, Wanda. History's on our side,' my boss Willi announces. 'This is no time for gloom but for resolution and extra effort.'

Since you can't count on History to give a helping hand, we trim down our activities to the minimum; our paymasters in Moscow are quick with advice but slow with funds. Ever since Professor Einstein formulated his theory, Relativity with all its variations has been the buzz word in Berlin. Thus we are only relatively badly off; relatively starving, scrounging around for anything we can get. But relatively speaking, business is as

usual. Even Frau Dumke, who is not encumbered with ideological baggage, understands this. I draw courage from her
tough Berlin resilience.

'Think positively, Wanda,' says Titus, 'At least you can walk
in Potsdamerplatz without being killed by millionaires falling
down from the top floors of office buildings like in Wall Street,
New York! Ha ha ha . . .

'Know the difference between a *shlemiel* and a *shlemozel*? The
first is a guy who tries to kill himself jumping from a first floor
window. The second is the sucker he lands on.'

In adversity Titus always turns Jewish. His response to bad
news is to produce the joke equivalent of chicken soup.

I tell him what they say in my office.

'Rubbish. Your communists couldn't destroy capitalism in a
hundred years of revolution. The only thing they destroy is
humour, like the Nazis. In time humour will destroy them.
Remember I said that.'

Always my communists! As if I owned them!

'Your communists think the world is changing in their favour.
They couldn't be more wrong. This depression is nothing but
a blip, soon to pass. Your commies aren't even the winners of
the moment. The Nazis are. For every day of hardship
hundreds flock to swell their ranks.'

Everybody I know, except Titus, says the Nazis are a 'passing
blip'. Chad Johnson and Tristan Rutland, whom we see frequently, also dismiss the Nazis as a transient phenomenon, a
flash in the pan: you get such movements in many countries
whenever things get tough; Germans tend to overdo things,
that's all. Look at Berlin! Here the Nazis are in nowhere near
a winning position and Berlin is the heart and soul of
Germany . . .

Who am I to believe?

If Titus had been helpless I would have shared everything I
had with him, to the last crumb of food. In sharing, I might
have been healed from the haunting memory of what happened in Hermannplatz. However, he is far from helpless.
The apocalypse of capitalism's demise, so welcomed by my
communists, does not affect him in the least. My doubts return
with a vengeance; our differences seem wider than ever. We

55

quarrel over trivia. I drink coffee, addictively. I suffer when I don't have it. Titus prefers strong black tea, which he slurps noisily through a lump of sugar in his mouth. I want to kill him when he does that. I tell myself, 'If he were to up and go this minute never to return, how relieved I'd feel!'

'Wanda,' he says one evening, smacking his lips after a particularly long and noisy gulp of tea, 'I've got good news.'

I look at him, wondering what fantastic enterprise or purchase he has brought about this time.

'Clearly what we need is more space. So I've found us a new home. A flat. Three large rooms, with high ceilings, wonderful views and good solid furniture. Old-fashioned but very presentable. You'll love it.'

I am speechless! Just like that, without even asking me if I wanted to move!

'It's in Schillerstrasse,' he goes on. 'Number 27. The top floor, like here, only there is a lift. Just think, Wanda . . .'

I listen in disbelief as Titus rhapsodises about the flat. Charlottenburg is an expensive middle-class area, not like Kreuzberg. Where will the rent money come from?

'We move in tomorrow. I've already informed Frau Dumke, and paid her for the week we should have given notice.'

'*We*, Titus?'

'Who else? Do you think I need three rooms all to myself? There's one for you, one for me, and one for us to fight in when you feel like it. Ha ha ha.'

He affects hurt surprise at my hesitation but a wicked, knowing, devil smiles from behind his eyes.

I understood even then that he knew how I felt, knew I wouldn't move in with him. Then, as ever, Titus liked to create situations for people he was involved with, then sit back and amuse himself at how they reacted. As though he were Wotan, bound by a universal contract to non-interference in the mess he himself had set up for his minions.

Titus moved out the next day I went to work. When I returned, he was gone. '*Come for a house-warming dinner, Friday 7.30, 27 Schillerstrasse top floor. See what you're missing. All my love, Titus*,' he wrote in a note he left for me.

I took the few belongings I had kept in his room back into mine. I drank what was left of my *zwechken schnapps*. I put a record on the gramophone he had given me – Richard Tauber singing Lehár arias – and felt comfortably foolish when it made me cry. I got into bed with the thought that I was doomed to sleep alone for the rest of my life. In that mood, I picked up Robert Musil's new novel *The Man Without Qualities*. What a desolate title! Who are such men? What qualities do they lack? Who suffers most thereof, they themselves or those who love them?

I visited Titus frequently, often sleeping with him overnight. On the face of it, nothing had changed between us; except that we no longer quarrelled. He never again asked me to move in with him. The handsome flat soon succumbed to untidiness, like his room in Kloedenstrasse. Only here the untidiness conveyed a tension of impending departure, like a nomad impatient to begin his migration. I noted this with uncomprehending sadness. I did not understand that his indifference to his domestic environment camouflaged a savage tenacity of purpose, until I witnessed its working when we met again in Paris in around 1935, when money – the complexity of power it offered – began to obsess his imagination.

Theo understood. Right from the beginning.

Here we are, having a good dinner with quality burgundy at the Café Josty. Chad is here, with his new girlfriend, an American student calling herself Jay. Tristan is also present.

Titus is in an expansive mood. He repeats his assessment that the depression in the west is nothing serious: bankers' loss of nerve, that's all. And serves them right if they get so stupid as to kill themselves. In fact, Titus emphasises, this is the time for anybody with a bit of money and lots of balls to make a killing in the financial markets. He cracks jokes, then laughs at them himself. Chad, too, laughs. He says that Titus's robust realism is a sure antidote to gloom. But Jay is quiet. Her erstwhile rich daddy had recently become depressingly less rich. Besides, she loathes Titus. You can see her hatred in the cold smiles she gives him.

Tristan and I exchange glances. There is a growing conspiracy between us; a pretence to mutual understanding unshared by the others.

One day, quite unexpectedly, Tristan rang. He came to the point in a roundabout way. Would I mind ... would it be impertinent and altogether awful if he asked a personal question? No, I said, go ahead. Was I ... well ... romantically involved with Titus? Please, I must understand, he was not prying into something that clearly was none of his business. Only I seemed to him a little unhappy, which made him sad. He was wondering ...

I told him, somewhat disingenuously, that Titus and I were friends. Very good friends, as I hoped we too would become. He asked if he might take me out to dinner. I said yes, gladly.

We had been going out a number of times before I told Titus. He said he was delighted. Tristan Rutland badly needed a friend like me. I would do him a world of good. What about me? I asked. He stopped to think.

'It's very good for you too, Wanda.' A small pause. 'Better start learning something about botany.'

'Why?'

'Because the English have slow sap in their veins, like trees, not real blood. Your Mr Rutland is very English.'

It is past midnight. Josty is still full of people with money having a good time. Animated with wine, Titus is in full flow: we are treated to an idiosyncratic analysis of what is happening in Germany and in the Soviet Union where Stalin, he says, is doing to the Russians what Hitler wouldn't even begin to dream of doing to the Germans were he given half the chance. I stare at him in silent outrage. Tristan glances at his watch. It's late, he has a busy day tomorrow, he says.

'But we're going to the Adlon,' Titus announces.

'At this hour? What the hell for?' Chad may protest but he is really game for anything

'Have you forgotten? In a couple of hours Max Schmeling is fighting Jack Sharkey in Madison Square Garden for the heavyweight championship of the world. We can listen to the fight on the wireless at the Adlon. It's almost as good as being there.'

'Sorry, not me,' says Tristan. 'I can't stand boxing.'

'Sharkey will knock the shit out of Schmeling,' says Chad.

'I bet you a hundred dollars Schmeling wins,' says Titus.

'What makes you so sure?' asks Jay, snake-eyed.

'Call it intuition. It's Germany's call, her first in a series of victories. Until she gets her come-uppance.'

'I've never heard such nonsense in my entire life!' says Jay. 'Take him on, Chad. Or I will.'

It is early morning, Friday 13 June Berlin time, when Max Schmeling – Germany's current national hero – becomes the world heavyweight champion. Not quite a victory, for Sharkey is disqualified after flooring Schmeling with a low punch. The crowd which had gathered at the Adlon to listen to the fight is ecstatic. I suddenly get the notion that it isn't the fight alone which has so interested Titus. He has come here to see the people's faces. He watches them in fascination. To feed his intuition about the things to come?

He holds the bank notes he has won from Jay like a hand of cards.

'Want this, Wanda? Clean American money.'

'No, thank you.'

'No? I'll keep it as a long-term investment for you. In a few years from now you'll be blessing me.'

'Just as a matter of curiosity, how will you invest it?' asks Jay.

'In me, of course. Ha ha ha.'

Chad told me what Jay had said when they left the Adlon: 'I don't know what you find in that Titus guy. I know his type. He's like a dog. What he can't eat or screw he pisses on.' Unkind. Totally untrue as well. Chad thought it was funny.

In the September elections the Nazis win 107 deputies in the Reichstag, thus becoming the second largest party after the Social Democrats. Nobody is making jokes about Hitler anymore. Titus claims that unless our KPD makes common cause with the Social Democrats, the Nazis will surely come to power at the next elections. Which is probably what Stalin wants. That is the drift of Chad's report published in the *Boston Globe*

59

following the elections. Although I still see a lot of Titus, I see even more of Tristan. We are comfortable with each other. There is no sex between us, only calm intuitive understanding and quiet humour. Like a brother and sister.

Years later, in London, I befriended an American poet. She wrote a wise, sensitive poem about a departed friend: a '*bright look of tireless inquiry . . . the attentive courtesy of that look.*' I remember it because this is how Tristan's early and enduring companionship could best be described.

I cannot remember a darker, colder winter than that of 1933. The day after the Reichstag fire I rang Titus at his home. The line was dead. None of his friends seemed to know where he had disappeared to. Six months later I got a postcard from him. It showed the mermaid in Copenhagen harbour. The message was brief and esoteric: '*Retreated to re-group. Love to you both – Titus.*'

Tristan and I went for tea to Max Liebermann. The grand old painter lived in a flat in Pariserplatz from where you can see Unter den Linden and the Brandenburg Gate. The day Hitler became Reichskanzler, Liebermann told us he lowered the shutters of his windows so as not to see the Nazis' torchlight victory parades down below.

He laid his hand on Tristan's arm and uttered what was to become one of the most quoted sayings of the time: 'My dears, nowadays one cannot eat as much as one wants to vomit.'

Tristan never spoke to me about what he thought might be the future for Jews in Germany. But one evening, shortly after our tea with Liebermann, he broke a long silence saying, 'Wanda, I know this might sound a little odd. I'm not going to speak about love, that kind of thing . . . I can only say very sincerely that I'd be very, very happy if you'd marry me. And I'd do everything I can to make you happy. On this you have my solemn promise. And I will not hold you if at any time you wanted to leave me. If Titus . . .'

I held his head in my hands. I said, 'I believe you completely, Tristan. I will happily marry you and pray to God I can make you as happy as you deserve to be. As for Titus, you needn't worry about him, ever. He is and always will be a part of my life for as long as we both live. But never as a lover.'

I suppose because I was on the verge of tears that Tristan went down on one knee saying, 'Well, we might as well do this properly. Wanda, darling, will you marry me?'

Then he told me that he planned to apply for a transfer, ideally to Paris but, if that didn't come off, back home to England.

5

PUGACHEV

Back in Russia I had a wife. Her name was Varvara Kaganova. I was happy with her. She died. I don't remember when, only that it was very long ago. We had two daughters, Maria and Ekaterina. Both are now married and have children. Sometimes they write to me. I would like to see them all before I die.

Maria is a doctor. She is gentle, like her mother. Ekaterina is a scientist... I don't remember her too well. Varvara used to say Ekaterina was like me: stubborn. But I am also a simple man who believes in God, and that evil is evil and good is good and we are all somewhere in between. I don't think Katya has ever been like that.

Then I had another wife, Zhenya Richter, whom I married in England. She, too, died. Now I live alone in the house she owned in Richmond. Zhenya had money of her own. She gave piano lessons. The piano still stands in the living-room, open, with the music pages on top, just as she left it when they took her to hospital. And there's a large framed photograph of Tsar Nicholai and his family on the mantelpiece above the fireplace. Zhenya worshipped the Romanovs, used to say a prayer for their souls every night.

Mrs Short from the Council, who comes in to look after me, often stares at the picture with great interest. 'Is this your family, General?' she once asked.

I laughed. I find the ignorance of the English working class charming. I said, 'Yes.' Why not? Zhenya believed Tsar Nicholai was father of all Russians, and we have been orphaned since he was murdered. I fought for the Reds. Zhenya Vladimirovna bore this as a penitent bears sin.

'Nice,' said Mrs Short. 'So many medals! Obviously he was a military man, like yourself, General, wasn't he?'

She brought me a cat to keep me company. The cat was large, ginger and white. It wore a red collar with a little bell attached to it. She put it in my lap, where it sat purring, blinking at me. 'Isn't he beautiful, General? What will you call him?' she enquired, talking to me as though I were a child.

I summoned a voice from the past: 'I'll call him Vassily Igorevich Scratchinsky.'

'Oooh, that's a bit of a mouthful!'

'Vaska for short.'

'Aahh, isn't that nice.'

Vassily Igorevich was a serf on my father's estate east of Voronezh. He lived to be a hundred. He looked after our horses. He was the wisest man I have ever known. If you want the truth, seek it from a wise old *mujik*. *Mujiks*, when they are not stupid or lazy, or treacherous, are the salt of the earth. They know from the heart more than professors can learn from tons of books. The *mujik*'s knowledge is the pure poetry of life. All the more so if he's been working with horses. Horses teach you patience. And endurance. Horses and cats understand each other like no two other animals do. Therefore, my Vaska is now a sort of link with my past. My life had been full of horses . . .

'Memory,' Vassily used to say, 'taunts you like the devil when you're old. And when you lose it, it's as much a blessing as it is a curse.' Another thing Vassily used to say: 'If you want to know whether or not you can trust a man, don't listen to what he says. Look in his eyes. That will tell you what you need to know. Same as with a horse.' In the old days I used to instruct my mount requisition officer to avoid whenever possible getting mounts which showed too much white in the eye, because they tended to be unreliable.

How many times I've asked myself what Old Vassily would have made of Titus Altermann. How many times I've looked into his eyes and was none the wiser. They told me nothing, and everything. Like gazing into the uncanny eyes of a strange, part good, part wicked icon.

I turn on the gas in the fireplace where a real fire used to be. I sit in my armchair. It has two dark stains where my arms rest, like we've grown into each other, the armchair and me. Vaska jumps into my lap. He likes it when the fire is on. Another thing Vaska likes doing. Even now, when I stoop a little, I am a tall man, yet the cat can leap cleanly onto my shoulder, like a circus acrobat. Then he rubs against the back of my head as if to say, 'I'm with you, Seryozha. Together we'll walk paw in hand to the end of the road.'

As I stroke Vaska memories come back. Still pictures, faded, a little blurred . . . or reels of film, interrupted and jerky. More often just whispers of long-forgotten voices struggling against a background of mixed noises and dim light.

My father, Aleksander Sergeivich, was a melancholic man. His serfs cheated him, all except Vassily. The overseer robbed him dry. I can see the house in its slow decay. I can see the untilled fields overgrown with weeds.

But the horses were always bright-eyed, their flanks shiny. In the stillness of my mind I hear the muffled crunch of their hooves in the snow by the wood streams, frozen opaquely grey, like a blind man's eye . . . the dark green and black lichen on the pale birch trees . . . the tense silence of the woods, broken by the noisy flight of a woodcock. Oh, Vaska, we had some happy hunting!

My older brother Oleg was a drunken rogue. My mother, Tatiyana Ivanovna, her hands always clasped to her thin chest, couldn't wait to go to heaven. Her mouth never smiled but held a ready prayer like a lump of sugar: 'God forgive me, Sasha. I should have locked myself in a convent rather than marry you,' she would say tremulously, when my father shouted and cursed his fortune for having a wife who crossed herself whenever he touched her.

When I came back from the war, she was dead. Oleg had disappeared, gone to St Petersburg. I never saw him again. I heard that he had been shot dead in a duel. My father lay in bed, sick with debts, dirt and dust gathering about him . . . Then came the Revolution. I returned home one day after six months' absence to find Vassily sitting at my father's bedside. The serfs had taken away everything that could be moved, all but the bed and the chair on which Vassily was sitting.

My father died two days later. Vassily and I buried him where seven generations of Pugachevs slept eternally. Then Vassily came to me, leading a liver chestnut colt. 'I hid him so he wouldn't be taken away. The world is falling apart, Master Seryozha. Ride away from here and God be with you.'

So I stuffed a few belongings in a saddle-bag, shouldered my rifle, belted on my pistol and rode away on the colt. Five versts away from home, I stopped. Fires were flickering from the dusky forests. You could hear men singing in the distance. I took a coin out of my pocket. Heads, I ride south to join General Denikin. Tails, I ride north to join the Bolsheviks. The coin bounced against a stone, spun, then fell flat. I leaned from the saddle to look. I rode north, to Moscow. That must have been late autumn 1918; the leaves were dying on the trees. There was a taste of snow to the air.

What can I tell about wars that you couldn't read in books? . . . I can tell about people I knew. About Titus, the strangest of them all.

I was a good soldier, a General, Hero of the Soviet People. I have seen cities bombed to dust, old *babushki* sucking on the bones of dogs, children burnt to charred heaps of sticks. *Bozhemoy, Gospedyn,* dear Lord, and the horses, dying vacant-eyed in the icy snow . . . What is so damn important about one Jew, Titus Altermann, I'd like to know?

My Vaska digs his claws into my knee: awake, memory, speak!

The small plane stood at the far end of the airport, away from the lights. The dark green minibus with blacked-out windows drove right up to it. 'That's it, *Tovarish,*' said the Major who sat beside me. We stepped out into the chill, first the Major, then me, then the other man in civilian clothes who sat beside us all the way from Lefortovo without uttering a word.

Two men were standing by the airplane, smoking cigarettes. They were KGB, no mistake about it. Any Russian with an ounce of wit can smell KGB from yards away. Our silent civilian, who was also KGB, walked towards them. They talked. He took out a file from inside his coat and handed it to one of them.

The man who took the file read something with the aid of a pocket torch, signed a form, and handed it back with the file.

Delivered and received: one misguided enemy of the people, transferred to Lefortovo Prison psychiatric section from Perm, to be exported . . . where to? Why?

'What's the difference? Enjoy the flight. Happy Christmas, *Tovarish*!' the young Major said. 'Say goodbye to Moscow, to Mother Russia.' I looked back. The lights of the air control tower were blurred. So were the pyramids of dirty snow along the runway. It must have been the cold that made my eyes water. The Major was grinning heartlessly. He must have been told by someone that to Russians, unlike Jews, exile is a fate worse than death.

On the way here I had asked if he truly believed I was a mental case. 'Why, of course, Seryozha. What else can you be? Anybody who thinks he can beat the system must be a complete lunatic. A bit like your eighteenth-century forebear, the Cossack Emelian Pugachev, aren't you? And he was brought to Moscow in a cage, like a crazy animal. Maybe madness runs in your family, eh, Seryozha?'

'Seryozha'! I can take *Tovarish*, but not that impudent familiarity. I should have hit the mother-fucking son-of-a-bitch!

This madness I was supposed to suffer from, when did it begin? What was its nature? What brought it on? Not one of those who sentenced me had the goodness to explain. To appeal is like pissing against a storm: you get it all back in your face.

I fought under Budenni in the Revolution. I survived the purges of the 30s. At Stalingrad, I became a hero. Tovarish Malenkov personally appointed me to head petroleum development in Baku. I've lived in an official dacha in Morozovskaya. Who helped bring millions of US dollars to the Soviet economy? Sergei Aleksandrevich Pugachev did! Then all of a sudden, someone decided there had been 'corruption and incompetence' in my department. Naturally, I protested. No sooner done than I was whisked away, tried in secrecy by a panel of KGB masquerading as psychiatrists, and incarcerated as a certified psychopath!

The plane droned through the darkness. I thought, 'What

kind of a Christmas present is in store for me? This is 1964, not the 50s. . . . People don't just disappear like that any more, do they? . . .' Suddenly it flashed through my mind: Titus. He's behind this, with his quirky sense of occasion. I leaned back in my seat and dozed off.

We landed in Berlin. I was driven through empty streets to Checkpoint Charlie. Their watchtower and gate were visible at the end of a stretch of road from ours, through the rain which alternated with sleet. A section of infantry was manning the point.

'That's it, General Sergei Aleksandrevich. You're going over to the other side,' said the Major who accompanied me. I strained my eyes but could see no one over there. 'Don't be nervous, it's all right. The best of luck to you,' the Major said. After a lengthy talk on the telephone, the Major summoned a young lieutenant to take me across. We started walking, the lieutenant holding his sub-machine-gun across his chest.

'Too bad about the weather, Comrade General,' he said. 'Do you have a watch?' I had an old Swiss Omega with my name inscribed on the back. It gave the time as three in the morning. Already Christmas Day. The lieutenant slowed down so we were hardly moving. 'Won't you please give me your watch, General? You can get yourself a new one on the other side,' he said. I gave it to him; what the hell.

We walked on, side by side, the muzzle of his gun brushing my arm. I wanted to talk, to hear Russian. But the young lieutenant, having taken possession of my watch, fell silent.

Two figures came towards us. We met halfway in no-man's-land – the American marine and a civilian who looked as downcast and confused as I must have looked. Who was this poor devil being traded for me? I walked to the West with the American marine, the spy – for surely he was that – East, with the Soviet soldier.

Freedom? Beyond Checkpoint Charlie spread a pale diffusion of the city's light. I had nothing but the clothes I wore. Not a word of English. I knew nobody. But I was a General: *someone* over there must have wanted me; there would be a welcoming party headed by a soldier of my rank; and the press, maybe. I would make a short dignified statement which an interpreter would translate. I would be taken to comfortable accommodation. A prolonged de-briefing would follow in a congenial environment. Of course, I would be careful not to compromise friends back home, my family. I knew as well as anybody how to say all in saying nothing.

A sleepy American captain was waiting at the other side. He didn't even salute. Having confirmed my identity, he took me outside again to where a Mercedes car stood parked, its engine running, the driver at the wheel. A man in an expensive-looking overcoat and fur hat was standing by the car. I couldn't see his face.

'Seryozha?' he said. It was Titus. He put his hands on my shoulders. He hadn't changed a bit in all those years. How long had it been? Ten, maybe less? I couldn't remember.

'All considering, Seryozha, you don't look too bad at all.'

Was that all? I felt cheated. Humiliated. I was no common criminal. I had served my country well. I deserved more than that!

'I'm hungry. I haven't eaten a thing. Even a dog gets a good meal on Christmas.'

'I know. We'll take care of that right away.'

It must have been one of the best restaurants in Berlin. Obviously Titus had made special arrangements with the pro-prietor, as it was hours past closing time. A table was laid for us in a private room. With candles, and a three-piece band which played Russian music. I could have laughed. Or cried. I'll say that for Titus, he never skimped on anything he did. The food was delicious. Titus didn't eat. He just sat opposite me watching while I ate as much as I could, and drank a lot of vodka. Then he took me to a posh hotel, The Bristol, it was called.

'You have a good sleep, Seryozha. At about noon, I'll come round. We'll talk.'

'What about official de-briefing?'

'Don't worry about that now. First rest.'

Rest never comes on order. I slept poorly and woke up early to see a sunny day. The room was too warm. The bed was too comfortable. The sheets smelt fresh. Everything so easy, so luxurious . . . I kept wondering where was the catch, what price I would have to pay for all this?

I turned on the television; a large screen. A street scene. People going about their business. They looked well, prosperous, happy. I tried to understand what the commentator was saying; it was no use. But I couldn't help thinking how well-dressed he was, a smooth-faced, confident man, smiling as he talked. We beat the living shit out of these people in the war. Look at them now! Look at their cars, their clothes, the way they live!

I went for a walk along Kurfürstendamm, where the hotel was situated. A broad tree-lined street, crowded with people. I wanted to buy something – a bottle of Coca Cola; to taste that nectar of western capitalism. But I had no money in my pocket. I couldn't even tell the time. And the people passed me by, looking through me. If I had been truly mad would I not have shouted at them, 'Hey, you lot! Only nineteen years ago I rolled with my tanks into your city. You don't remember? Peer over the wall that separates you from another reality. Your brethren on the other side will tell you. They haven't forgotten.'

Titus arrived at the hotel late.

'Well, Seryozha, did you sleep well? Are you rested?'

'Yes, Titus, I'm rested.'

'Is everything here to your liking? Anything you'd like to have?'

He was sitting on the bed, elbows on knees. I sat opposite him, in the armchair. How many times I have held his life in my hands! Now he was playing cat and mouse with mine, knowing I fully understood that he had already decided my fate.

I suddenly remembered the grey stallion . . . Could it be that Titus bore me a grudge on account of the horse? After so many years? After we had fought side by side and had worked together? That look in his eyes, which I never understood . . .

Budenni once asked me what I thought of Titus. 'He's dangerous, Semien Mikhaelovich. But a brave soldier. A first-class cavalryman,' I replied. 'Dangerous? How do you mean?'

69

'I mean he's completely fearless. You can't buy him. You can never tell what he'll do next.'

'Well, Seryozha?'

'I want Coca Cola.'

He raised his eyebrows. 'That's simple. You pick up the 'phone. When you hear a voice, you say "Coca Cola". They bring it up to you, okay?'

'I can't tell the time. I want a watch.'

Titus pulled off his own watch and tossed it at me. 'Will this do?' It was a Rolex. In Moscow top apparatchiks would denounce their grandmothers for such a watch.

'Next?'

'I want a good dentist to fix my teeth. I want proper clothes.'

'No problem. As soon as the holiday is over, we'll do all that. But now, Seryozha, we must talk about your future.'

'Who was the spy they exchanged for me at Checkpoint Charlie?'

'How should I know? Probably some small-time English pederast who thought he was an idealist and sold secrets. What does it matter?'

'It matters a whole lot to me. I'm not a nobody.'

'You needn't tell me that, Seryozha. Unfortunately, there's no fixed rate of exchange for such transactions. It all comes down to supply and demand.'

'Damn it, Titus, I'm a General. I was your commanding officer in two wars! I've helped you. You might've done better than have me sneaked across Checkpoint Charlie at three in the morning, like I was a mail bag! My life has been ruined because of you!'

'No, Sergei Aleksandrevich. You ruined your own life by indiscretion. By not playing by the rules. You made a fuss when acquiescence was called for. Also, your luck had run out. Just be grateful you are here, not rotting away in Siberia. I can't influence the way things are done between the Americans and the Soviets. But now that you've got out, I can and will help you. All the way.'

'I want to talk to journalists. I want to sell my memoirs to a publisher. I have a lot to tell.'

'I can't help you with that. Publishers aren't interested any

70

more in defecting ex-soldiers from the Soviet bloc, Seryozha. There've been too many.'

'I thought Jews had powerful connections everywhere. Everybody knows all the big capitalist publishers are Jewish. What's so difficult about that, when you've fixed everything else?'

It was being helpless that made me burst out like that. Personally, I have nothing against Jews. I apologised immediately. Titus rose to his feet, walked round the room, then sat in the other armchair. There was no anger in his eyes or in his voice.

'As soon as possible you'll have the best dentist in Berlin. He'll fit you with a full set of 24 carat gold teeth, if that's what you wish. You'll get all the clothes you want. It wasn't I, by the way, who helped with your release. You must thank Chad Johnson for that. His Christmas present, in gratitude for the help you've been to him in Moscow. Now, can we talk about your future? Where would you like to go, America?'

'No. I don't like Americans.'

'Fair enough. How about England? I think England would be better. You'd like it there. The English are nice to foreigners. With a bit of luck you might even find a publisher for your memoirs. The English are romantic.'

At the door he stopped, looked at me for long moment. 'I should forget about talking to journalists, here or anywhere. I don't think that would do anybody any good, least of all yourself. Happy Christmas, Seryozha.'

The de-briefing with the British and American intelligence was short, polite and inconclusive. A man from the British Consulate gave me my new papers. I was told I must contact the Home Office and the police the moment I had a place of residence. I had six sessions with a dentist who had gentle hands and Mozart pouring out from somewhere in the ceiling. He virtually reconstructed my mouth. I bought a dozen shirts, six silk ties, four pairs of shoes, and four custom-tailored suits. We drove to Tempelhof airport in Titus's hired and chauffeured limousine. Before parting he gave me a sealed envelope.

'A colleague will meet you at Heathrow, Seryozha. He'll help you with everything. If ever you need something, he would be the man to contact.'

We hugged. 'Don't think I'm not grateful, Titus. In spite of the bad things I said earlier.'

'Forget it, Seryozha. We're even now. Take care.'

He walked away to the VIP lounge, to board a private plane. I opened the envelope he gave me. It contained £10,000 in cash. There was also a note: *There'll be more to come. Your unpaid commission for past contracts, which I've invested for you.*

6

Where the Volga and the Don bend towards each other before parting again, the one to the north-east, the other to the west, lies Tsaritsyn, later renamed Stalingrad. A sprawling, undistinguished town, it was twice chosen by Providence as the site where our country's destiny was decided in war.

Here, too, Titus's life and mine converged on each other. First during the Civil War, then in the battle of Stalingrad nearly a quarter of a century later. You might say that in the mud and dust and snows of Tsaritsyn, Fate manacled us together.

The rivers flow past acres of wheat, barley, alfalfa. Where the fields and villages end, the woods begin. In summer Cossack peasants stay out all day with the harvest. Carts laden with hay stand by the stacks. Underneath them babies in makeshift hammocks share the shade with dogs, as they did on my father's estate not far from Voronezh. At night you can see their fires, smell the smoke in the air, hear their singing and laughter.

When the rains come, the paths and roads turn into impassable streams of mud, for the soil here is heavy and dark. The horses slosh about fetlock-deep in the mire; wagons sink down to their axles; tanks get stuck. As winter sets in, the mud freezes into sharp combs beneath the snow.

Beyond the rivers and the fields and the forests, the land heaves upwards to the vast steppes. No trees grow there, only wild grass, whipped by the punishing winds and pounded by the hooves of Cossack herds.

The railway from Moscow to the Caucasus turns on Tsaritsyn. Whoever possesses the town commands a strategic position for an advance on the capital.

In 1918 we had infantry, we had armoured trains, we had artillery, tanks, some aeroplanes too, but no cavalry to speak of. The Moscow commissars didn't understand the vital importance of cavalry in the kind of war we were fighting. They thought cavalry was a thing of the past, something the noblemen in the days of the Tsar liked to play around with. I blame Comrade Trotsky for that fatal shortsightedness. Not Stalin, or Voroshilov, or Tukhatchevsky. They knew better.

Only after Tsaritsyn fell, when Denikin's army stood a mere 100 miles away from Tula's armament depots, 200 miles south of Moscow. When Mamontov's Don Cossack horsemen were wreaking havoc behind our lines, riding unopposed anywhere they liked. Only then did War Commissar Trotsky see the light . . .

Semien Mikhaelovich Budenni transformed a rag-tag body of ill-disciplined Cossacks into the *Konarmiia* – the First Red Cavalry Army; the finest fighting horse troops the world has ever seen.

If it hadn't been for him, Tsaritsyn would not have been regained. General Wrangel would not have been defeated. Denikin would have marched north to take Moscow as he boasted he would do in the spring of 1919. Whatever historians say, I know in my heart that is what would have happened: the end of the Soviet Revolution. Mine, too, along with many other comrades. I'm not sure about Titus, though.

Semien Mikhaelovich came from Cossack peasant stock. In the war he served as a cavalry sergeant in the Tsar's army, whereas I was a lieutenant. He only learnt to read and write when he was a man. But what a fighter he was! I'm proud to have served under Budenni. He led his troops from the front, like a squadron leader. Such became the style of all who fought under his command.

Like Semien Mikhaelovich, I too have Cossack blood in my veins. We were alike in other ways as well. Big strong men, we loved nothing better than a rough gallop on a spirited mount and a good scrap. We both wore moustaches. His was upturned, for he was a dashing jovial man. Mine was downturned. 'If we have a good day, bless Budenni,' he used to say, tweaking his moustache. 'If we eat shit, blame Comrade Pugachev.'

74

In the spring of 1918 Comrade Kliment Efremovich Voroshilov came down from Moscow to organise Tsaritsyn's defence. He was stocky, bullet-headed, a first-class administrator, courageous and single-minded. Stalin came too. The two liked and respected each other but loathed War Commissar Trotsky. Voroshilov took Budenni under his wing. Budenni gave me my first command: an under-strength battalion recruited from the remains of other units. Cossacks, most of them. Whose only taste of battle had been defeat.

Spring had been particularly icy, as I remember. Fodder was scarce. Our horses were run-down, the men restless, quick to quarrel. We were camped thirty miles west of Tsaritsyn, in what had been a village before General Wrangel's raiders had razed it to the ground. Not even its name remained, only a few walls, barely standing. Belongings that weren't worth taking lay scattered about the place along with half-eaten carcasses of livestock. We buried the mutilated bodies, cleaned up the place. I made the men rebuild some of the houses so that we would have shelter, storage places for the ammunition and provisions, stables for the horses, a headquarters above which to fly the flag. We had intelligence that Wrangel had promised Denikin he would give him Tsaritsyn and a lot more besides before the summer was out. He was a good fighter, Wrangel. A cavalryman in the blood.

On the level wilderness beyond our camp, I put my men through the rigours of the training Budenni had devised. They made a sorry spectacle. I thought: 'Any day now we'll be up against the real thing. If Wrangel's Whites are half as good as they are said to be, we'll surely die.'

The day before two young Cossacks who had deserted were caught and brought back to camp. They were put in irons in a room that had the bare earth for a floor. I sent a message to Budenni, telling him what had happened, asking for instructions. He sent back a hastily scribbled massage: *Comrade Pugachev, you know what to do. If you don't, your regiment's commissar will tell you. Semien Mikhaelovich Budenni.*

The two lads were brothers. One of them had a good voice. They had had enough of the war, they said. They wanted to go back home to their farm on the way to Rostov, deep in enemy territory. Their father was ill, too weak to work alone on the farm.

The commissar said, execute the bastards. I didn't want their blood on my hands. The commissar, a tough former metal-worker from Kiev, was adamant. An example had to be made of the two. He would assume full responsibility. So they were taken out to a far end of the camp where they were made to kneel in front of a wall, their hands ties behind their backs. They asked not to be blindfolded. I said no, they must. I didn't want the firing squad to look them in the eye when they shot. Two salvos were fired. One slumped dead on the ground. But the other, the one with the good voice, was still alive, struggling to get up. I pulled out my pistol and shot him clean through the head.

You remember for ever the first time you kill, like the first time you make love. Eventually, killing becomes easy; doing it no longer shocks you. That's the terrible thing about it. I had killed before, in battle. Never like this. And when I saw these two lads lying on the ground slumped against each other, their blood mingling, I thought, 'Dear God, what kind of war is this, when we have to kill our own people?'

There was this fellow – a kid – come from nowhere. I hadn't noticed him until I turned to go back to my office. He just stood there, looking, with a grave expression on his face. His head was bare. His overcoat had no buttons. A half-torn kit-bag lay at his feet. He looked as though it had been weeks since he last had a proper meal. A mere boy, aged by whatever experience he had gone through. He didn't look at me as I passed.

I called in my adjutant.

'Yefim Ivanovich, who's that kid I saw outside?'

'A newly arrived recruit, Comrade Pugachev.'

'Is that so? How the bloody hell did he get to see the execution!'

Yefim Ivanovich shrugged his shoulders. He was an absolute scoundrel; he had been a convicted thief. No one in the entire Red Army could get a battalion outfitted and on the move quicker than he could.

'I don't know, Comrade Pugachev. He must have wandered in by chance.'

I slammed my fist on the makeshift desk. 'What is this, damn it! An army camp or a collection point for delinquents?'

'It will not happen again, Comrade. That fellow, Comrade Semien Mikhaelovich Budenni sent him. Apparently he came down from Moscow with Voroshilov . . .'

'Let's see him then.'

As I sat waiting for this new recruit, I brooded over the execution and our situation: the battalion's low morale; the dire shortage of mounts, weapons; shortage of just about everything in fact, except bad luck. My own inexperience . . . What would be my fate when we lost the war? It seemed probable at that point that we would.

The last thing I wanted at that moment was to interview another raw recruit who had just witnessed a dreadful spectacle. There was a knock on the door. I reached for a batch of order papers, fanned them out on the desk, pretended to be preoccupied.

'Come,' I called out, determined to make a short business of this untimely meeting.

A blade of light thrust into the room as the door opened. The new kid advanced to a few paces from the desk. His boots were scuffed, caked with dried mud. He must have walked all the way from Tsaritsyn. He dropped his kit-bag insolently on the floor.

'Your name?'

'Titus Altermann.'

'No patronym?'

'None.'

I noted with irritation the relaxed irreverence of his stance. A rebel, not a soldier, I thought. I'll break him soon enough.

'Your papers.' I glared at him.

He pushed his recruiting order towards me. It was signed by Budenni all right. There was no patronym.

'Everybody has a patronym. How did you lose yours?' I demanded.

'I didn't lose it, Comrade, I just never had one. I grew up in an orphanage. If it's that important, I'll take any patronym you'd care to suggest.'

I thought to myself, if I were to have this fellow taken out and shot, he probably wouldn't even blink.

'How old are you, son?'

'Eighteen, Comrade.'

He was lying, I could tell. But he was a well-formed youth, a mature, tough-looking kid who could easily pass for eighteen. I was only twenty-three, damn it. And I, too, had lied about my age! His papers were in order, that was all that mattered as far as I was concerned. He could be from the Party, though, since he had come down from Moscow with Comrade Voroshilov. Undoubtedly Jewish, with a name like Altermann. I needed no commissar apprentice in my unit. I had no use for Jews, either. But Budenni had sent him to me.

'Are you from the Party?' I asked.

'No, Comrade. I'm an ordinary soldier, here to fight, like everybody else.'

'A soldier, eh? Can you ride?'

Titus nodded. 'I was with Count Bagritsky in Lvov during the war.'

'Really? What were you, a drummer boy or something?'

Titus ignored the sneer. I couldn't help admiring his coolness. 'I rode with him,' he replied.

'Were you frightened by what you saw out there?'

'No, Comrade. I've seen worse.'

'They were good men but they deserted. We shoot deserters.'

'I guessed that was what they were. A pity.'

'Can you shoot?'

He sort of nodded. So I repeated the question a little more sternly.

'I don't like to boast. I guess I'm a better shot than most you're likely to meet in the course of this war. And that's the plain truth of the matter, Comrade Pugachev,' he said quietly.

I smiled sceptically. 'Is that so?'

'Yes, that's about so.'

He was confident but not cocky. I knew the type; better to take them at their word. My reason said, 'Here is trouble.

78

Throw him out.' The devil in me whispered, 'Go on, Seryozha, have some fun, it's been a bad day.'

I slid my cavalry revolver across the desk at him. I had another weapon, a loaded Colt .44 automatic in the drawer. 'Go on, show me how good you are,' I said.

Titus picked up the revolver, examined it, balanced it in his hand, then swung in a half-turn and fired three times in rapid succession. The day's orders sheet was pinned on the wall to my right. He had grouped all three shots tightly around my signature at the bottom of the page. That was really good shooting!

Men burst in, guns at the ready, but Titus had already returned the pistol. I motioned them to leave.

'You don't exaggerate, young Comrade. However, without a horse and weapons you aren't much use to me here. We have none to spare.'

He shrugged his shoulders, looking at me blankly. 'I was ordered to report for duty here. That's what I'm doing. Whatever you tell me to do, I'll do.'

I have to say this about Titus Altermann. In time he proved to be more than an ordinary soldier. More than a good soldier, too. He was a one-man raiding party. An independent loner, inventive, unpredictable, but undoubtedly an asset.

When, soon after the Korean war, I chanced to meet an American General, we had a drink or two and exchanged stories. I told him about Titus. 'That doesn't surprise me at all,' the American had said. 'I had a Jew in my outfit. His platoon commander wanted him transferred out. I called this fellow in. I said to him, "Goldstein, here's a machine-gun with 800 rounds of ammunition. You're in business on your own. Get the hell out of here!" Damn it, he nearly won the Korean war single-handed!'

A joke, of course. Titus was no joke.

I dismissed him to go find himself a place to sleep. I called in Yefim Ivanovich. I told him to detail Titus Altermann to the battalion kitchen where the cook, an irascible character, would keep an eye on him.

The men were saying Titus had been with grain requisitioning

79

parties which shot peasants. That he had ridden in Trotsky's armoured trains. They even said he had been sent from Moscow to spy on us. I didn't believe that for a moment. It was the cook who spread those rumours; he was a bad man, a bad cook too. A year later I had him shot for stealing provisions and selling them on the black market. I tend not to listen to idle talk. If a man is trouble, you get rid of him. That's my view. Titus wasn't. Moreover, Budenni had sent him. Besides, I had more important things on my mind.

In the middle of May, General Pyoter Wrangel with his Kuban Cossacks defeated the Tenth Red Army in four days of fighting at Velikokniazheskaia, a main railway junction to the south. Then, at the end of June, he beat us again, capturing thousands of trucks, hundreds of machine-guns and artillery. Only two hundred miles stood between him and Tsaritsyn which he had vowed to capture.

He had new British tanks. Tsaritsyn's defence, so energetically organised by Voroshilov and Stalin, consisted of barbed wire fences and trenches manned by ill-trained, demoralised troops. My own cavalry battalion had not yet fired a shot in anger. I realised that our first combat engagement would be a retreat.

At the height of all this, the cook petitioned for an interview. He complained bitterly about Titus, said he was lazy, insolent, unwilling to learn. He swore Titus spat into the broth on at least two occasions. At the end of a long list of alleged misdeeds, the cook concluded that he would rather face the firing squad than work with that son-of-a-bitch Altermann for another day.

The real reason emerged later. Our quartermaster, an elderly one-eyed Cossack called Yegor Spiridonovich Chesnakov, had a daughter with him, a dark-eyed beauty called Dunia. She could ride and shoot and had a wicked temper. The men flirted with her, called her 'Little Sister', but none dared make advances to her. Dunia had apparently taken a fancy to Titus. The cook saw them together in the barn where the fodder was stored, so he said. With Dunia's legs up in the air. He told the quartermaster, who announced he would kill Titus. I wouldn't have minded losing the cook. The quartermaster was another matter.

80

I called Titus to my office.

'I'm told you're worse than useless in the kitchen,' I said.

'I told you I could shoot and ride. I never pretended I knew how to cook.'

'Nevertheless, we have to eat.'

He said nothing.

'If you can't do your job in the kitchen you're just another belly to fill,' I said.

'What would you have me do, then, Comrade Pugachev?'

'This. Go find yourself a horse. If in ten days you are not back with one, consider yourself a deserter.'

'Where will I find a horse?'

'That's your problem. Only don't come back without one.'

I gave him my .44 Colt with an extra loaded clip, and wished him good luck. He pocketed the pistol and left without thanking me.

Three weeks passed. I had all but forgotten Titus. Having decamped, we moved north of Tsaritsyn, closer to Budenni's headquarters for exercises in preparation for combat. The Cossacks were good hardy horsemen. They could shoot. Their use of sabre and lance was crude but generally effective. What they lacked was knowledge of methodical cavalry warfare. Budenni devised the training framework. Day in, day out, we exercised, often under his supervision. It all paid off: sooner than I had hoped, we were becoming a cohesive disciplined body of cavalry, growing confident in our ability and in our commander Semien Budenni.

It was a Friday. My battalion had been exercising from dawn. Catching the morning sun, the River Don glimmered. Tall lush grass swayed in the breeze against the huts and barns of a hamlet called Pavlovka. On the other side of the river where we were, the grass had been trodden flat by the repeated charges of our squadrons.

We had watered our mounts and let them graze. The men sat or lay in groups not far from the river, their rifles stacked in pyramids. Behind us, not more than quarter of a mile away, was the wood, dense and leafy. It was from there that we had issued at a full gallop, practising an ambush.

I gathered the four company commanders to discuss what

we had achieved, what needed improving, and the next stage of the training. A distance away the cook was brewing tea. We had hardly settled down when two of the officers rose to their feet. They were staring in the direction of the wood. Some of the men also got up, pointing in that direction. My first thought was, Enemy! And I had posted no sentries! The second thought was, Budenni, on a surprise inspection. Which was even worse! I jumped to my feet.

It was a solitary horseman skirting the edge of the wood. He came towards us in a slow collected canter. I was struck by the immaculate balanced coordination between horse and rider. But the horse! Heavens above, it was magnificent. A large dappled grey stallion – you could tell from its flexed neck and its proud bearing – with pale flowing mane and tail.

As the rider got closer you could hear the rhythmic snorting of the horse declaring its superb condition. I recognised Titus with surprise and a pang of envy; it was the first time I had seen him mounted.

How he had changed in so short a time! Or maybe it was the horse that made him look different. No longer a raw kid, he looked every inch a man, relaxed and confident. He had lost weight. There was a rugged fluff of beard on his chin. He still wore the same old coat he had when he first arrived. An English rifle was slung on his back, and across his chest a bandolier. He also had a long sabre hung low over his thigh.

Titus saw me and turned his horse in my direction. The men gathered round to admire the horse, which pranced on its toes, eyes flashing. We had no such horses. It was not a Russian breed but German with a lot of Arab blood, I reckoned.

You may well ask what went through my mind at the sight of that animal. In a word, jealousy. I didn't care where it came from, how Titus had got it. No. Every part of me said, 'I want it! I want it!'

Titus didn't dismount. He leant forward, a hand resting on his knee. He said loudly, for all to hear:

'Well, Comrade Pugachev, I'm back, with a horse. I hope you'll not have me shot as a deserter for being somewhat late.'

Officers and men were looking from him to me and back to him.

'No,' I replied. 'You've done well, Titus Altermann. I underestimated you. Tell me where and how you got this animal?'

'You might say I stole it, if taking from the enemy is stealing.'

I laughed in disbelief. 'For taking from the enemy you'd deserve a medal. But such a horse must belong to someone very important. I would go to the end of the world to retrieve this horse, if it were stolen from me.'

'General Wrangel owned it. And I can tell you, he is heading this way with a very large party, not altogether on account of the horse,' said Titus.

According to our intelligence Wrangel was still more than a hundred miles to the south. Titus said he was now less than fifty miles from us, having moved north with a fully mechanised army and cavalry. On hearing that, I left my second-in-command in charge, and galloped with Titus to Budenni's headquarters.

For three hours Budenni with three senior officers and myself interrogated Titus. He told us how he made his way south doing odd jobs in villages, but mostly living off the land, until he came upon the Whites' forward camp. He pointed on the map where it was. It was a hardly more than a large scouting detachment. But General Wrangel himself was there, wanting to see things for himself, as was his custom.

Titus had been arrested. Beaten. He showed us the fresh weals on his back and arms.

'What did you tell them?' Budenni asked.

'Everything I knew,' said Titus.

'Our strength in Tsaritsyn?'

'Whatever I knew. It was no news to Wrangel. He seemed to know he had nothing to oppose him.'

Twice he had been taken out to be shot, only to be taken back again.

'Why didn't they shoot you?'

'I said I would lead them to the weakest spot, where they could take the Reds by surprise.'

'Did Wrangel believe that?'

'Maybe not. He reckoned he could shoot me any time he wanted. There was no hurry. Perhaps he didn't mind too much

83

my escaping with his horse, so I could come here and put the fear of him in you.'

'Would you have betrayed us?'

'Everything I've told you is true,' Titus replied after a pause. 'Now it's up to you whether or not you consider that a betrayal.'

'So how did you get away?'

'They untied me. They put a stupid guard over me. I tricked him. I took his boots and weapons, then I sneaked out. The horse was there, apart from the others. I saddled it and galloped away. The guards didn't shoot for fear of hitting the horse, I think.'

Everything Titus described – General Pyoter Wrangel's appearance and manner, the men who were with him – corresponded to what was known to our High Command. At the end of the interrogation Budenni came out to look at the horse a second time. He stood by it, patted its neck, talked to it softly. At last he turned to me and said with a sigh, 'What do you think of all this, Seryozha?'

'I think he was telling the truth. Whatever else he might be, Titus Altermann is no liar, no traitor. That's my belief.'

He pointed a finger at my chest. 'I'll hold you to this, Sergei Aleksandrevich. Well, then, now that your scullery boy returned a hero, what do you want to do with him?'

'What I believe you'd do in my place, Semien Mikhaelovich. Make him a squad leader.'

'And the horse?'

This is a test. I could see from his eyes.

'Unless you want the horse, Semien Mikhaelovich, I say Altermann has earned it. Let him keep the horse and the devil take them both.'

Budenni laughed. 'That's a good decision, Comrade Pugachev. You do that.'

Vassily Igorevich used to say, 'Every child is brought into the world with one God-given secret talent. Happy is he who fulfils it.' True, without doubt. For how else than by divine gift could a Jewish foundling from Odessa, if Titus really was that, possess the finest attributes of a natural mounted warrior? I have seen many, but there was none better than Titus Altermann. The way he rode that stallion and fought . . . Let me tell you, it was perfection itself. It was magic. How could he do this without years of hard training, which he had never had?

He was quick and fearless, at times foolhardy, taking too many risks. But he knew what he was doing. Judgment. Concentration. The swiftness of the horse. That's what kept Titus alive when many others perished. The men, in their idle superstition began to believe he was invulnerable. Until he was felled, which was due to me, not to a fault of his own. One way or the other, Titus's luck ran out. And I rode away taking the grey stallion with me, leaving him for dead on the battlefield. And I told myself, 'I'm a commander. I have responsibility. I *must* have this horse which has special powers!'

Look at it this way. If you are an infantry rifleman dug in, or a soldier manning a field cannon, you see enemy cavalry charging at you, sabres drawn. In a few seconds they will be upon you, cutting you to pieces. Amongst the rushing fury of horsemen, you select your first target. Which? The one which stands out the most, of course: the rider on the large pale horse! Titus never hung back. Every charge, there he was out in the lead, with bullets flying about thicker than curses. Chestnuts, bays, blacks fell like skittles. Titus always returned unharmed.

Fedya Bogdanov, our battalion's story-teller, used to say: 'Every bullet has a name inscribed on it by the Angel of Death. When your name comes up nothing will save you.'

Where was the bullet carrying Titus's name?

I read in my mother's bible about King David who, coveting Bathsheba, sent her husband to a certain death in battle so that he himself might have her. I did the same to Titus, so that I might have the horse, not once but time and time again. And he came back to mock me.

In the autumn of 1918 Tsaritsyn fell to the enemy. We retreated northwards. That was the last year in which the Whites stood within grasp of victory. When he realised what horsemen could do, Commissar of War Comrade Trotsky personally decreed that the first priority should be given to establishing the First Red Cavalry Army – our *Konarmiia* – led by

Semien Mikhaelovich Budenni, who appointed me his second-in-command.

We destroyed Mamontov's force. We captured Voronezh, then regained Tsaritsyn, then rode down along the Volga to take Rostov. General Denikin was finished, along with Wrangel. Next, we campaigned in the Ukraine. We outfought and beat every force the Whites sent against us. General Mikhail Nikolae-vich Tukhatchevsky, overall commander of the southern front, was a brilliant soldier, no one will deny that. But the one who brought us victory in the south was Budenni, nobody else.

In the summer of 1920 we faced our greatest challenge: the vaunted Polish cavalry. One day, perhaps, someone will make a movie of that campaign. If I'm still alive, I would tell what happened there, free of charge. Money doesn't matter to me any more. What I did to Titus Altermann does. I would like to make a clean breast of it.

Picture to yourself a flat stretch of land not far from the Polish border, somewhere between Pinsk and Brest-Litovsk. It is a hot day, very bright, early in the morning. There are fields, copses, villages, most of them deserted. The bombardment had started at daybreak, theirs and ours. Ahead, a distance of not more than a mile, is a half-levelled village. A large one, almost a townlet strung along behind a shallow stream. Dug in among the ruins are Polish infantry and artillery. There is cavalry, too, only we don't know exactly where. The village is in the way of our drive towards Warsaw. It must be taken. We are about to charge again. On the first attempt we were driven back with many casualties; there are men lying in the open space, horses kicking the air in their dying throes.

However, that first unsuccessful charge has shown us where the enemy's strong positions lie, and where their cavalry is mustered for a counter-attack. One spot on the flank, not far from the church, is particularly troublesome. And it is in my section. We have to take it first if the attack is to succeed. You cannot see what lies in the background; there are too many buildings clumped together sheltering a concentration of artil-lery. I know that if I were the Polish commander, that is where I'd keep my best cavalry, ready to outflank us.

I calculate that a two-wave charge might do the trick. The

first would be cut down. But the second would reach the church and then our centre would be able to gallop right into the village.

I instruct my command group accordingly. The adjutant asks, 'Comrade Pugachev, who will go in first?'

I look around. I see Titus on his grey stallion amidst his battered squadron. I think, Let's see how your charmed life stands up to this one. I summon him. I tell him to take two squadrons and charge straight at the church.

'Wouldn't it be better if I circled round and came at it from the south?' he says.

'What are you, a fucking general? You do just what I tell you,' I bark at him. 'We haven't all day to spend being stuck out here!'

He gave me a look I'll never forget, then he trotted off to join his men.

Titus led two squadrons at full tilt across the open space towards the church. The enemy's fire was hellish. Above the noise of the gunfire and shouts of hurrah, you could hear the horses scream as they fell. Titus reached the village with less than half of his force. I followed close behind with the main assault, just as the enemy cavalry came out to him.

More than five hundred of our men died that day. We took the village. We shot the Poles who surrendered. We prepared to move on. I saw the grey stallion standing alone by the church. I rode up to it. There was no sign of Titus. I thought, Surely this time he must be dead. Certainly wounded. The medics will gather him along with the others. I handed my own horse to my adjutant and mounted Titus's stallion.

It was Drogichin. Yes, that was the name of the place, I think . . .

At the end of that summer we rode back to Voronezh. That was where Titus caught up with us again, with a train of supplies. He was nearly half his former size. A festering wound seeped blood and pus through the bandage on his head. He limped a little, most likely from sheer weakness. I couldn't believe how dull his eyes were; the fight had gone out of them. He showed no emotion as the men gathered round him, cheering, clapping him on the back. He smiled at me wearily.

'Well, Sergei Aleksandrevich, I am back. You didn't miss me too much, did you?' he said.

'I'm glad to see you. I thought you had died.'

'Did you, now? Well, I very nearly did.'

'Good to have you back. In case you're wondering about your horse, he's well and sound there in the stable. You can take him any time you like.'

He gave me a strange smile. 'Have you been riding him all that time, Sergei Aleksandrevich?'

'That I have.'

'Then keep him and enjoy him. He is yours.'

Saying that all he could think of was a bed to sleep on, Titus walked away. He never mentioned the horse again.

Before the war was quite over, Titus disappeared. They said he deserted. It wouldn't have surprised me if he did. He was never quite the same after he came back from the dead, so to speak. Perhaps a part of him had died out there by the village church. What is one to think of a man who wouldn't as much as take a look at the horse he loved? Who walked out on his comrades without saying goodbye?

Lenin died. Stalin became General Secretary of the Party. I was promoted to Colonel, serving under Budenni. Whenever I came near the horse I would feel guilty. In the end I passed him on to a cavalry stud farm. Some years later, it must have been around 1927, we had a small reunion – comrades from the Red Cavalry. Vodka flowed, stories were recalled. Then someone mentioned Titus. 'Does anybody know what has become of him?' the fellow asked. There was in the company a former quartermaster who had joined the GPU secret police. 'Titus Altermann?' he said, 'Why, I seem to remember someone by that name. He was sent to prison in Solovetskii Island, I can't remember on what charge. I don't think he has been executed yet.'

The next day I contacted Budenni. 'Semien Mikhaelovich,' I said, 'do you remember Titus Altermann, our Jew, who rode with us?'

'The one who stole Wrangel's horse?'

'The same.'

'How can I forget?' he laughed.

'I would like a personal favour, Semien Mikhaelovich, for which I'll be forever in your debt.'

I told him what I had heard. 'Whatever he has done that has landed him in prison I'd be grateful if you did all in your power to have him pardoned.'

Budenni promised he would talk to Voroshilov. Voroshilov in turn promised he would take the matter up with Stalin personally. A month later Budenni informed me that on Stalin's instruction Titus Altermann would be taken care of. 'You can forget about the fellow now, Seryozha,' he said.

I didn't stop to think what being taken care of might mean. I had done all I could for Titus. My guilt was expiated by this timely intervention in his fate. I felt free. I didn't believe I'd ever see him or hear from him again. Old Vassily would have told me otherwise.

Stalingrad, that unbeautiful town, with its endless factories, new housing compounds, forever under the pall of industrial smoke. There are strange compensations in heaven that such a place should become legend. For it was here, alone, left to our own devices by false allies, that we defeated the Nazis in the winter of 1943.

Nothing in Stalingrad resembled Tsaritsyn except the horrors of war, magnified a thousandfold. Except the inexorable killing winter, and the bravery of Soviet soldiers. And the horses, dying and eaten by man and dog. And the River Volga, flowing under an armour of ice.

I was there. So was Semien Mikhaelovich. Our commander was General Vassily Chuikov. From September 1942 to January 31st the following year, when General Friedrich von Paulus, Commander of the German 6th Army, surrendered, every street of Stalingrad had been fought over, left littered with burnt-out tanks and the dead . . .

I ran into Titus a little before our big offensive – Operation Uranus – that smashed the German 6th Army. Rather, he ran into me outside my headquarters.

'What are you doing here?' I asked. I was so surprised to see him. He gawped at me as if he didn't understand what I was saying. I repeated the question, and asked. 'Why have you come back?' He said nothing. I thought perhaps he was shell-shocked. He looked terrible. The wind rose. We could barely hear each other. So I invited him inside for some tea. Then I asked, 'Well then, where have you been all these years?' And he told me a long story I can't remember. But I couldn't forget what a good fighter he was. I needed men like him. I took him to my command.

Titus didn't disappoint me. He distinguished himself . . . I recommended him for a medal for bravery.

My mind is getting tired. Sometimes, you know, my memories fight each other like enemies and bits of the past become frayed, like a worn-out tapestry.

Titus was right, I should not write my memoirs. Everything I have seen has already been written about. I'm glad that he died in this country, blessed with years . . . more likely cursed with them. Men like him and me should die in our prime, in the full swing of something important, not decay like an old empty house that's falling apart.

Vaska is purring in my lap. I'll shut my eyes for a while.

7

THEO JABLONSKY

My home is in Newnham village, Cambridge. A modest house of manageable size, it overlooks Grantchester Meadows where, on several happy occasions, Titus and I had walked. I enjoyed living in the splendid Peterhouse rooms that looked down on a beautiful court, but here I am happier still. Bought with money I have earned teaching and writing in my adopted country, it is my own first real home. When I sit at my desk in my study on the second floor, I can see from the window my very English garden. I've become a modestly competent gardener, a soothing occupation loaded with comfortable metaphors. The old Riley car is parked by the gate. The creaking floorboards on the landing are like familiar bodily noises: we are growing old together, this house and I. And when my time is up, I'll be taken straight to the crematorium without fuss. Like the former owner – an unhappy Theology don from Emmanuel College – who defenestrated fatally, thus enabling me to purchase the house at a bargain price.

Soon after my eightieth birthday, a young lady from Radio 3 invited me to Broadcasting House for an interview. She was charming in an intense sort of way; a little like Wanda when I first met her, in Paris before the war.

'Professor Jablonsky,' she began by way of warming me up, 'a Festschrift collection of essays by leading scholars has just been published. How do you feel about that?'

'Good,' I said.

'Good?' Hilarious incredulity.

She was on the thin side, clever, likeable. She had a lovely throat, alive with sensuous energy. Her name was Jane. She wore large red-framed glasses. I remember that as vividly as I remember her throat.

'Good? C'mon, Professor Jablonsky.' She laughed.

'Very good,' I said. 'Very happy.'

'You've written prodigiously. Let me see, *Tyranny and Reason*, 1952; *Man the Measure – Plato and Political Socialism*, 1954; *The Philosophy of Nationalism in 19th Century Europe – Collected Essays*, 1961; *Childhood and Logic – Autobiographical Notes*, 1966; *Reflections on Jewish Universality*, 1968; *The Yearning for Asymmetry – a Study of Thought Currents in Weimar Germany*, 1970; *Why We Need Religion – Letters to an Imaginary Grandchild*, 1983 . . .'

She let the list fall from her hand. 'An impressive output, I'd say.'

'About two feet of bookshelf space, I reckon,' I said.

She looked at me in puzzled consternation. Did someone warn her Old Jablonsky could be awkward?

'My dear,' I said, 'I didn't mean to be frivolous. Ask me anything you like. I'll try to give straight answers.'

She had a pleasant laugh. 'Well, for a start, how would you prefer me to address you, Professor or Sir Theo?'

'Whichever you feel more comfortable with.'

'You were interned for about six months during the war as an enemy alien, weren't you, Professor Jablonsky? Would you rather we didn't talk about that?'

'I don't mind, if you think it's relevant to anything.'

'But then you were enlisted to the team that cracked the German secret code.'

'Enigma . . . Bletchley Park, Leighton Buzzard. Yes. I was there.'

'That must have been a welcome change. How did it come about?'

Tristan, in a word. He got me out of internment and into Bletchley Park. Even without Wanda's urging he found the irony of a German Jew interned in warring Britain as an enemy alien insupportable.

'They were looking for clever people. Someone in a high place must have got the notion that I fitted the bill. I was pleased and grateful to be of use.'

'Professor Jablonsky, four years ago you created a furore

when you wrote arguing that democracy wasn't the best political system. That it encouraged' – she looked down at her notes – 'greed, mediocrity and shallowness as the ruling forces in society. Are you still an unrepentant élitist?'

She hurled the charge with such a charming smile. I paused to think, then said, 'Politicians, and journalists, tend to invest words with properties which aren't necessary intrinsic to them but which turn them into being politically correct or otherwise, as the case may be.

'I was talking about ideals. I suggested that democracy mutated into something different from what the word meant, when the society in question was very large, diverse, motivated by material, and constantly manipulated by media propaganda.

'If you isolate what you have mentioned from the whole argument, it becomes perhaps sensational but not necessarily meaningful.

'As for being an élitist, I'm not sure I understand what you mean.'

My life. My work. My views on society. Education. History. What did I think the future held . . .

I could sense Titus materialising in the studio to stand at my shoulder: 'Who are you, for Christ's sake, bloody Nostradamus? Beware of humbug, Theo. It's worse than immortality. Two feet of bookshelf space? That's good. Stick to that sort of stuff.'

Cambridge, 1954. Titus paid a surprise visit. I didn't even know he was in England.

'Congratulations, Theo. I heard about your new book; it sounds very serious. Do you think I'm up to reading it? Let me take you out to dinner tonight. Can one get a decent meal in this place?'

We embraced. A delicate fragrance of aftershave lotion on his face: did it indicate a new vulnerability or a new disguise? I thought: Dissemble as you will, Titus, like all barbarians, you stand trembling and confused within the city's gates. You've never seen me in my natural habitat. You had lugged me along – 'your scholar' – in your booty caravan, like a conqueror on the march. Welcome to my city of ideas, which you venerate uncomprehendingly. Relax, enjoy yourself. You'll find me a considerate host.

'Why don't we have dinner in my rooms? Better than going out,' I suggested.

I arranged for dinner to be brought to my rooms, boeuf bourguignon and a bottle of good claret which Titus liked.

'Excellent, Theo. But you know, eating with so many books around tends to give me indigestion.'

He ate uncommittedly a few mouthfuls then sauntered over to the window. Some undergraduates were crossing the darkening court. We could hear snatches of their conversation, and their laughter. Titus looked down pensively. Impatience and thoughtfulness always alternated with each other in his quiet moods.

'How things have changed,' he said.

'They always do, Titus.'

He turned, smiling, his eyes shiny in the dim light. 'We had some terrific times, you and I. And Wanda . . .'

'Oh yes.'

I had thought he had come to see me for a special reason, to tell me something. Now I knew he came simply because he was lonely.

'I like the way you've changed, Theo. You even look different, a great improvement. I'm very glad.'

'You too look different.'

'You think so? Smooth contoured and dull-eyed. Like a big cat in a zoo. Ha ha ha. Well, I'd better be going.'

I walked with him to where his car was parked – a new Riley, dark green like a loden coat.

'Theo, what do you normally use for transport?'

'Here? I bicycle. Like everybody else.'

'Quaint but restricting. Like this car? Have it. A present from me.'

'You always give things away. Why?'

'Why not? I like giving.'

I protested. I couldn't drive, I told him. But Titus wouldn't hear. When he gave something it was irrevocable, like a decree.

'Drive with me to the railway station, Theo. How far is it, ten minutes? Don't say another word.'

94

We arrived at the station with five minutes to spare before the next London train. He parked the Riley and gave me the keys.

'Get someone to take the car away. I'll send you the papers tomorrow. Learn to drive, Theo. Take Wanda out for picnics, she'll love it. Have fun. I'll keep in touch.'

I am an early riser. Early to rise, early to bed. Winter in Copenhagen is a long wind-blown affair. The days are short, crepuscular, at times marrow-freezing cold. My rented flat at the cul-de-sac of Strandhøjsvej, Charlottenlund, overlooked the Travebane stables where at weekends trot races were held. At six in the morning the horses wake me up, neighing and kicking the doors of their boxes as the stable-lads clutter about the yard preparing their morning feed.

I would dress, go for a walk. Always, except when the wind was so fierce it drove needles of ice into your face. Morning ablution and breakfast would come later. Then I would be ready to face a day at Københavns Universitet, where I taught Philosophy.

Mostly, I would walk down Kystvejen, the coastal road that ran along the sea front all the way to Klampenborg. You wouldn't see many people about at this time of the morning. Not in winter, that is, when a grim Norse twilight challenges the man-made comfort of human habitation.

On such mornings the ice groans on Øresund; the grey sea clutches at a winter-blanched shore. Mist moves over the face of the water where, on a clear day, you can see the coast of Sweden. A boat, seemingly without orientation, trudges along a depthless horizon coughing smoke doughnuts into the air.

I arrived here a refugee. Half my mind is still impounded in the past. The other half is grudgingly cajoled into wakefulness with absurd mental callisthenics: Hegelian theses, antitheses, syntheses centred on domestic triviality, leading to imponderables such as, 'Is Modern Man still sufficiently resilient to adapt to permanent deprivation of commodities like toilet paper?'

Not me? *Quid sequitur?* I'm not Modern Man. *Ich bin Heimatlos!* An irregular condition. *Ergo*, why bother to adapt to anything at all?

I was standing in Rådhus pladsen. Clouds tumbled past Copenhagen's green steeples. Wind whiplashed the puddles on the sinking cobblestones. There was no use complaining; it was free air, after all. And there was that cock pigeon, copulating with a dead mate on the busy pavement at the foot of a sausage vendor's booth.

That was the first time I really felt homesick. Only the central premise no longer existed: you had to redefine for yourself concepts like 'home', 'sickness', 'humanity' against the heartbreaking failure of language.

Fruken Liselotte von Freisleben, a Danish aristocrat of German extraction, wiped tears from my face with her starched handkerchief.

'My dear Theo,' she said, 'it is a well-known fact that the wind in Copenhagan is merciless. Why, it can literally knock you off your bicycle at any corner, not to mention what it does to your eyes. Come, let's go have a beer. I know a nice little place just round the corner.'

Linking her arm through mine, she led me away to the grand Hafnia Hotel – bless her outrageous euphemisms – her tall sparse figure leaning over me like a bracket.

'Theo, what is happening in Germany could never happen here,' she said, downing a shot of schnapps. 'We Danes are too simple, too fun-loving, too easy-going. History has drained the violence out of us. Just look around, won't you?'

That coat with the thick fur collar which I wear on my morning walks, against the cold wrath of the north sea, is far too large for me. A gift from Liselotte, it belonged to her late father, Count Henning von Freisleben. He was six foot five. I am five foot six. Designed to be knee-length, the coat reaches down to my ankles. I would rise from bed, put on my winter boots and get into the coat in my pyjamas. And I would pull my hat down as low as it would go, until its brim touched the collar. The hat, like me, is an exile from Berlin. Cocooned thus in Count von Freisleben's outer shell, I would enjoy a twofold asylum: first in Denmark, second, in the warm encapsulation of the coat.

One morning I was standing on Kystvejen esplanade against

the concrete barrier. It was ten degrees below freezing – I always made a point of looking at the thermometer outside my study window before going out. The air stung your lungs. An anticipation of snow frowned in the dense nacreous sky. I was enjoying a moment of privacy in that inclement vastness when I saw a man and a dog lumbering along the beach among frozen flotsam of broken pieces of timber. He was wearing high boots, a knee-length military coat belted at the waist, and a Cossack fur hat. The dog – a black Labrador – discovered a pool in the ice-bound sea and jumped in.

'Smoky, come out of the water, you stupid animal!' the Cossack called out in Russian-accented German. But the dog, exercising atavistic instincts, ignored its master. So the Cossack stood there, hands on hips, watching, until Smoky clambered out and shook himself, covering him in spray.

'*Schweinhund!*' the man swore, jumping back. Smoky looked at him and wagged his tail.

'What the hell, you do what you like,' said the man and patted the dog's head.

As he straightened up, our eyes met.

'Maybe he thinks he's a polar bear,' he said in English.

'Maybe that is a good thing for a dog to think, in the circumstances.'

'You're right. Ha ha ha.'

He made for the nearest point of exit from the beach and soon joined me on the esplanade. The dog, exhausted from his aquatic exertions, waddled behind.

'Smoky,' he said, 'is an old dog. Tomorrow he'll be lying half-dead unable to move because of arthritis. You're German, aren't you?'

'I thought I was.'

'Ah. It's rare to know what you really are before it's too late. You live around here?'

'In a peripatetic sort of way,' I replied, mindful of the rumour that Copenhagen was crawling with foreign agents of all nationalities.

'Yes, I think I've seen you before. Here. At about the same time. The coat. I remember your coat. Unless, of course, it sometimes peripatets on its own . . . Ha ha ha.'

'That is a thought. But it was probably me and it, one inside the other that you've seen.'

'I live in Klampenborg. More accurately, Smoky does. You see, he's not my dog. I am his, so to speak. In his employ. I look after him while his owners tour Europe. Now they are in Prague. Next week, maybe London. They send Smoky post-cards which I read to him. It's part of my job.' He took his glove off.

'My name is Titus Altermann. My papers say I'm German. My heart tells me I'm Russian. My memory reminds me I'm neither. Ha ha ha.' His handshake was warm, honest. I felt instinctively that I had nothing to fear from this man.

'Theo Jablonsky.'

Mutually attracted as if by a common dislocation, we walked together towards Klampenborg, talking about Berlin, where we had both lived. Every now and again Titus would stop to wait for Smoky.

'You see? He's already dead tired. But also he is a perfect Danish gentleman, polite to a fault. He doesn't want to intrude on two foreigners having a chat.'

'Well, I must be turning back. It was nice talking to you, Herr Altermann.'

'Likewise,' says Titus. 'It would be nice if we could meet again.'

The dictionary defines *Heimat* as home, native place or country, homeland. The word's deeper meaning, however, is untranslatable. It sums up Herder's Germanic romanticism. *Heimat* is what you are, what you feel, the peculiar emotional and spiritual reverberations evoked intimately by your own language. Rooted in specified geography, *Heimat* is thus untransferable and immutable.

Like Germans, Russians too have a gut and blood understanding of the concept. That is why both peoples make such sorry immigrants. That is also the reason why Communism will fail in the end, in Russia as it has in Germany. For Communism is a cold creation of insulated reason at odds with the heart's intuitive knowledge of which *Heimat* is part.

Should I elaborate on this to my students?

'You have a free hand, Theo,' Liselotte, the Faculty's formidable secretary, has told me. 'Do what you like. We are pleased and honoured to have you. No one will tell you what to do.'

This was her kindly way of letting me know that as a Jewish escapee from Nazi Germany, the University placed my moral comfort above, though not contrary to, curricular considerations. I was grateful. My colleagues – she above all – had been splendid. Liselotte found me the quiet, affordable old-fashioned flat in Charlottenlund. I was invited to dinners. New friends visited me. With my status and pay clearly defined outside the common struggle for advancement, everything was done to make me happy.

Not content with giving me her father's coat, Liselotte presented me with a black second-hand bicycle. Coat and bike are mutually incompatible, each requiring its own distinct personality. Inside the coat, which is pedigree Danish, I am the reclusive German longing for the *Heimat* which no longer exists. On the bike, which is German-made, I am the jolly Danish academic wearing a cheerful bobble hat, trailing a yard of red scarf, happily pedalling to Frue Plads.

What should I teach? Germany has reverted to prehistoric barbarism. Elsewhere, disillusionment drugs the so-called civilised world . . . Prophesy the death of humanity? Affirm the promise of everlasting light?

When I was a child, I read a book that stuck in my memory. In it a strange catastrophe has happened. People had been turned into wild beasts. Yet individuals could still recapture their former humanity by pressing a paw, a wing, a hoof to their hearts. Only a few know of this, and they run around at great risk to themselves, trying to make a tiger or a wolf press a paw to its heart.

So, I made a decision: not a word from me about Fichte, Herder, Hamann, and the like. Let others unravel the brooding German spirit. In my classes let there be ancient Mediterranean clarity and the simple elegant symmetry from the bedrock of our civilisation.

'Wonderful, Theo!' said Liselotte.

I met Titus again at the Kystvejen waterfront. He returned

home with me to share a breakfast of coffee and wienerbrød. Smoky lay by the oven, a look of sad resignation on his benevolent face. He was sad, Titus explained, because yesterday he had received a postcard from New York. How could he tell if he would ever see his beloved owners again, since America was eternity away for his devoted canine mind? 'Ha ha ha.'

Why did I like Titus?

He had warm spontaneity. There was an air of raw, reckless courage about him, not merely physical, which was appealing. And he was funny, in an earthy devil-may-care way. And, of course, our shared uprootedness drew us to each other. But whereas mine was circumstantial, his was inherent – a strength and a weakness of his character. It took me a long time of knowing him to understand this.

In those early years I thought of him as an errant knight in a wild timeless landscape where allegory was immanent but vague; where symbols were vivid yet meaningless. Neither a seeker of redemption nor a rogue. Simply a warrior skilled in combat, wandering at random without mission and without a quest, looking for action. A man with no pattern to his existence and no forfeit for his mistakes.

'Theo, the way I see it, things aren't that bad for you at all. All you need is the crucial prompt to tell you when to move on. I'm good at that.' He winked at me.

A bright Sunday noon. Eight degrees below freezing. Tree branches sparkling with hoarfrost. Barely a fortnight from Christmas – will it be a white one? Titus offered me two to one against.

We had been to Dyrehaven. Titus insisted we hired a horse-drawn carriage rather than walk, for Smoky's sake; arthritis had got him at the hips. We ate venison in a forest inn called Raadvad. Titus knocked back three measures of Ålborg schnapps, I two. Back in Smoky's owners' red weather-boarded, garden-girdled Klampenborg villa, the fire was giving off a pleasant aroma of burning birch logs. Titus stretched out in an armchair, hands clasped behind his head, eyes half closed.

'So you were one of those privileged *wunderkinder*, eh? Shows you how life can level differences, doesn't it?' he said lethargically.

100

Well, yes. I grew up in a home not unlike this one. A house in the heart of Grunewald, Berlin. Large, full of books and paintings and music. I won prizes at school. I graduated from Tübingen University in Philosophy *ausgezeichnet*, and followed that in record short time with a *cum lauda* doctorate from Berlin University. They said mine was the most precocious Ph.D. thesis of the generation.

'Doctor what's-his-name,' said Titus.

'Faustus?'

'That's him.'

'I fought a sabre duel!'

Titus sat up. 'No kidding. Who sewed your head back on?'

'I won! My opponent was so hopelessly drunk he lurched forward onto the point of my sword.'

Titus laughed.

I was the youngest scholar ever appointed Lecturer in Philosophy at Berlin's Friedrich-Wilhelm Universität. And I was peremptorily sacked by the new Nazi sympathiser Head of Faculty. I thought life had become meaningless.

'You know what's your trouble, Theo? Duel apart, you think too much and live too little. Try the other way round for a change. It would do you the world of good,' Titus said.

My father Otto was a successful pianist and teacher. Herta, my mother, had a disciplined contralto; she sang German Lieder. Enticed into Zionism, they had fulfilled their commitment in translating themselves to Palestine six years ago. They had built a lasting home in Ahuza Mount Carmel, Haifa, where they taught music to bold-eyed young *sabra* children – the apotheosis of the New Jew.

But my younger sister Ingeborg . . . I used to tremble for her. She married a Berlin priest, outspokenly anti-Nazi.

'Is she pretty, Theo?'

'No. She looks like me.'

'God will look after her,' said Titus, yawning. 'And I'll look after you.'

'Really. How?'

'Life, Theo, is an ongoing game of poker. I'll deal you a good hand, teach you a trick or two. Ha ha ha.'

'*Und sonst?*'

'And then you play like the devil, for high stakes. With me standing behind you, prompting. Ha ha ha.'

'A Helen of Troy, perhaps?' I said laughing.

'Could be, Theo, could be. If that's what you want.'

Once, on one of our walks, Titus momentarily put his arm around my shoulders as he was explaining a point of argument. The firm weight of it, the latent potency of his body . . . the feel of it is lodged in my memory like a childhood recollection of smell. That night, touching my own soft virginal flesh, I thought of Titus's masculine body.

'Coffee, Theo?'

'Yes, please.'

'Tell me, Theo, how are you for money?' he said as he returned from the kitchen with the coffee.

'All right, I manage. I don't need much.'

'That's not what I meant. I need some. Can you lend me 2,000 kroner, for a couple of days?'

I was taken aback, and replied acidly: 'Don't tell me Smoky has withdrawn credit.'

'Don't be so damn silly. Well?'

'I haven't got that amount. Not nearly.'

'How much can you manage?'

'Maybe 500.'

He looked disappointed. 'That's not much. Still, do you have it in cash? Can you let me have it today?'

'I suppose so.'

'Good man. We'll have coffee then go over to your place. In a couple of days you'll have your money back, like I said.'

He volunteered no explanation. He stuffed the bank notes into his pocket without counting. Only a moment's strained hesitation suggested that he hoped I wouldn't ask.

When I got to know him better I realised this had been a test of friendship. For on the rare occasions when Titus borrowed money from individuals, he never gave reasons nor suffered them to ask for any.

Two days later, at around midnight, he rang.

'Did I wake you?'

'Yes.'

'Sorry. I forgot how early you went to bed.'

'What is it, Titus?'

'Get up, Theo. I want you to meet me in town. Now.'

'Titus, do you know what time it is?'

'What does that matter? You've had a couple of hours' sleep, haven't you? Don't you know what Napoleon said about sleep? Five hours for a man, six for a child. More than that for a fool.'

'I'm a fool, Titus. I need sleep. I have a hard day's work tomorrow.'

'Theo, don't you think I know what you need? Don't worry about tomorrow. Trust me.'

His voice was cajoling, but charged with authority. I could hear music in the background.

'Now listen, I've sent cab to fetch you. It should be with you in a few minutes. You'd better take down the address all the same. Got a pencil and a piece of paper handy?'

The Decameron nightclub was in an old building in Lille Colbjørnsengade, not far from Vesterbrogade in the centre of town. The entrance was painted blood red. Above it, in red lights, was the name. I have always been amused and bemused at how names, mutating through diverse contexts, form a thread of cultural continuity.

Past the door, I was faced with a steep red carpeted flight of stairs from the top of which came the sound of swinging music. The nightclub itself resembled the inside of a huge gaping mouth – dark red, glistening, and hungry.

At the centre, beneath a large dim chandelier, was an oval parquet dance area where a few couples danced mechanically to the music of a three-piece band. Beyond stretched a length of bar where women sat perched on high stools. They were mostly young, pretty, and mercenary. A tableau of masquerade ball personas featuring sultry vamps, anaemic-looking femmes fatales, sexy schoolgirl nymphettes, fallen nuns, and an assortment of straightforward no nonsense harlots.

A sombre major-domo in tails and white tie kept watch over a team of dinner-jacketed waiters who moved between the tables with immaculate discreet proficiency.

Seeing me, the major-domo approached.

'Herr Theo? This way please.'

But I had already spotted Titus at a table on the dimmed fringe of the room. He was grinning at me.

'Theo, I wouldn't have missed seeing the look on your face for the world! Why, you're as white as a sheet, and trembling! The philosopher in the den of vice. Ha ha ha.'

He wore a dark suit with a deep burgundy shirt and a matching handkerchief that bloomed like an exotic flower from his jacket pocket, and no tie. The absence of the latter somehow underscored the confidence with which he could take on decadence.

'Is this one of your haunts?' I asked foolishly.

'Hell, no. I chose it specially for you. Like it? Well, don't stand there like a lost soul. Sit down. What will you drink? Champagne, of course. A bottle of Veuve Cliquot is on the way.'

I obeyed, feeling like a captive.

'Hungry, Theo?'

'No.'

'Not even a little? They serve excellent gravad lax here.'

'Truly no, Titus.'

'All right. Well, here comes the champagne. Let's settle the loan first.' He took his wallet out, bulging with money.

'Five hundred kroner. Returned with thanks. And another five hundred, as bonus. Faith and trust rewarded.'

I protested weakly. My will-power was all but gone.

'Do you want to know how I got all this loot? Poker. I couldn't have got into the game without your 500 kroner, so, you're an accomplice. Does that make you feel depraved?'

'Not yet.'

'Good. Cheers. Drink up.'

The band began playing 'I've got you under my skin'. Titus hummed out of tune, his right foot flicking in rhythm.

'What do you think of the girls here, Theo?'

'Pretty, I suppose.'

'Pretty? What are you talking about? They're gorgeous, Theo! Each one a top-grade whore. They will turn any trick you like. Makes you think, doesn't it?'

'About what?'

'Life. Appearance and reality.'

'I don't think I follow, Titus.'

He refilled my glass, and looked at me askance. 'Look around, Theo. Fancy any of them?'

'Oh no, Titus. I most definitely don't.'

'Don't you? How about your Helen of Troy? She was a whore too, by the way. Inside, you're trembling with excitement. But you're also frightened, aren't you? Don't be afraid, Theo. Just look. Like they were books in the most exciting library you can imagine. No harm in that.'

I was frightened and confused and, against myself, excited as I obeyed him. And an absurd thought kept preying on my mind: what if someone from the university should be here and recognise me?

'Suppose, just for fun, I choose your Helen for you,' I heard him say. 'Let's see if I can tune into your secret fantasy.'

'Titus, please . . .'

'Don't worry, it's just a game. Drink, man.'

I empty my glass, and refill it with the last of the bottle.

'All right, just for fun let's see what's your idea of my dream woman.'

'That's the spirit, Theo. Give me five minutes. You stay right here. Don't move. First, let's get another bottle of champagne.'

What dread scenes Titus directs in the film studio of his inscrutable mind! How profound and shallow he can be all in a moment. How quickly his acquired good taste can fall apart to reveal inherent vulgarity. Or is he, underneath it all, subtle and cruel beyond imagining?

The demi-goddess he returned with was large. An opera diva voluptuously overflowing, she reminded me of Alma Mahler a little past her prime. She was beautiful. Her hair was Titian red, gathered into a lustrous coil on a splendid, imperious head. Her skin, from face to throat to shoulders and a heaving expanse of bosom, was smooth as silk. She had a kind, friendly smile, showing teeth that had undergone dedicated dentistry maybe a little too long ago.

'Inge, this is my friend Theo. Theo, meet Inge. Sit down and have some champagne with us, Inge, won't you?'

Strangely, Inge began to grow on me. I liked her quiet manner. She talked intelligently, English, in a deep slightly husky voice which was vaguely Germanic but certainly not Danish. I thought I sensed a private guarded integrity about her. And I was deliciously hypnotised by the little mole on the side of her cleavage.

'You like Copenhagen?'

'Oh yes.'

'The Danes are so friendly, no?'

'Oh yes.'

'All Europe has gone crazy, but not Denmark. Are you here on business?'

'Yes. Oh yes.'

'I meet many businessmen from abroad in my work.'

'Work opens up horizons, I always say.'

'Yes, I think so . . . But I don't think you are a businessman. Maybe a young professor?' She smiles understandingly.

'Please excuse me, I must go a moment . . .'

'Across and to the right,' said Titus.

When I returned he was gone.

'Your friend,' said Inge, as if to a child whose parents had left him in a doctor's surgery, 'said he had to leave.'

We looked at each other in silence.

'If you want to go, it's all right,' she said quietly.

I lowered my eyes.

'I don't mind, really,' she said.

'No, I'll stay.'

She laid her hand on mine. 'Your friend has paid me. I'll be with you for as long as you want. We can sit here and talk, and dance . . . Or you could come to my place. Would you like that?'

I nodded.

For work, Inge rented a one room flatlet in a run-down house a few minutes walk from the Decameron. It was warm and clean. A large, sagging shell-shaped bed all but filled the tiny bedroom. Above the wooden headboard, on which were carved figures of mermaids and tritons, there hung a large gilt-framed reproduction of a slumbering semi-naked Boucher shepherdess: sea and earth united in the business of love. The

106

only other furniture in the room was a rustic kitchen chair with a wicker seat, and a table on which stood a gramophone and a thin stack of records.

I took my coat off and helped Inge out of hers.

'We don't have to prove anything,' she said, touching my face.

'I know.'

She embraced me. Her breath was like a warm mint bon-bon.

'I'm going to the bathroom. Why don't you get into bed?'

Datum: Inge is German. That is clear enough. So she clearly recognises that I too am from Germany, even without our having spoken a word of German to each other, and Jewish. Titus knew she was German and said not a word about it to me.

Questions: Why is a German Wagnerian diva look-alike working as a prostitute in Copenhagen? A placed Gestapo agent, ready to be activated? What is Titus up to? A game in bad taste which is potentially dangerous? Or something more sinister? How could I be so stupid not to think of all that before getting naked into this woman's bed?

Ergo: Be on your guard, Theo. Don't be carried away, or your ethnic dignity and a lot more bedsides may be in danger.

The bathroom door opened. Her hair down, Inge stood against the light in a diaphanous dressing gown – *O forma divina!*

She came and sat on the edge of the bed.

'This is your first time, I mean, with a woman like me, no?'

I made no reply.

'I know. I can tell. Then I think you'll always remember me.' A sudden sadness came over her.

'Would you like some music?'

'Yes, that would be nice.'

As she put on the record I noticed another object beside the gramophone. It was a family snapshot: a smiling couple holding a smartly dressed boy and a girl.

Inge returned to the bed, slipped out of her dressing gown and got in. I pressed my face to the delicious amplitude of her

107

breasts and the music reached my ears muffled by the thumping beats of her heart. It was Max Bruch's *Kol Nidrei*.

She heaved a sigh. 'Yes, I think I too shall always remember you. Maybe this is the last time for both of us,' she said, hugging me.

8

I hadn't heard from Titus for some time. I thought, 'Well, if he had done the serpent on my innocence – the loss of which, as it happened, I thoroughly enjoyed – let him crawl in shame and guilt.' Then I rang. There was no answer. I tried again, repeatedly, without success. He seemed to have disappeared completely. I knew no one I could ask about him.

Once or twice I was tempted to revisit the Decameron. Perhaps the head waiter could tell me where Titus was. I also thought with some longing about Inge. Would she be as wonderful a second time? Could the magic of illusion be sustained after I had counted out into her palm the fee of her love?

I began to go out with Liselotte von Freisleben: to arty foreign films that aroused an undefined nostalgia; to quaint eating places she knew. The grave humour of her eyes, the intelligent austerity of her face, and her Adam's apple working up and down her throat like a piston as she talked, kept reminding me of the familiar constants of my life.

The ice was breaking on the canals, floating slowly under the bridges in great chunks. And then it was spring, migrating season for scholars. I met an English Philosophy don from Peterhouse, Cambridge. His name was Donald Quest. He was fascinated with Søren Kierkegaard, but not yet compellingly. He said to me: 'I very much admired your essay on Herder in *Mind*. But . . .'

I thanked him, 'but' notwithstanding. I said his name suggested to me an enigmatic contradiction of terms. He laughed. We talked lengthily over flagons of beer at the Tivoli Gardens.

He said, 'I've been told you're a great success. The Danes are so charming. I love Copenhagen. Don't you? Are you happy here?'

'Yes, and no,' I replied.

'Oh?' he questioned, peering over the top of his glasses.

'I'm very happy at the university and in Copenhagen,' I explained. 'But Germany is too close for comfort. I've heard ideas, like plagues, can be contagious.'

'I could never decide whether being separated from the Continent by the English Channel was good or bad,' he mused.

'Count your blessings,' I replied.

So he scribbled his address on the bill, saying, 'Do let's keep in touch. If you should ever want a spell in England, perhaps I could help.'

I phoned Titus again. This time a man answered. Herr Altermann was no longer there, he told me coldly. When did he leave? 'Oh, a month ago, maybe more. I'm not sure.' And there was no forwarding address. He had no idea where Titus had gone, and clearly didn't care.

A week later Titus rang.

'Titus!' I cried, at once happy to hear from him and annoyed at his inconsiderate disappearance, 'Are you all right?'

'I'm fine, Theo. How are you?'

'I was worried about you.'

'Ah, that's nice. There's no need to worry.'

'You might have let me know before you disappeared.'

'Yes, I'm sorry. I just didn't get round to it.' The line crepitated and echoed as if he were talking from the other side of the world.

'Where are you?'

'Paris, Theo. Mind, heart and genitals of Europe.'

'What are you doing in Paris?'

'What does one do in Paris? Having the time of my life, of course.'

'You haven't got into some sort of trouble, have you?'

'Trouble? You ought to know better than that, Theo. I don't get into trouble. I get other people into trouble. Ha ha ha.'

'So whom did you get into trouble? The man who answered the phone?'

'Nobody. It was just a joke. That fellow was Smoky's father. There are two of them, you know. Well, poor old Smoky got very ill, and I had him put down. Those two fellows, instead of being grateful that I had looked after Smoky while they were traipsing around the world and offered him a painless dignified death, said it was all my fault. Can you imagine civilised intelligent men being so childishly irrational over a sick old dog? Anyway, I'm settling down now. Everything's in order.'

'You mean you're living in Paris for good?'

'Nothing's for good, Theo. I'm here for the time being. That's what I want to talk to you about.'

'I'm listening.'

'I think you should come to Paris.'

'Just like that?'

'Just like that. Trust me, Theo. Remember I promised I'd prompt you when it was time to make a move? Well, it's time. And the move is good. You'll love Paris. Just think, Theo, of all the museums, the cafés, the beautiful women . . . Why, Theo, there are more intellectuals and artists here in Montparnasse alone then anywhere in the world! Even the sparrows are brilliantly original! Paris will do for you what . . . Theo?'

'Yes.'

'Can you imagine I'd ask you to do anything that wasn't for your good?'

Of course I could. Not deliberately; Titus wasn't wicked; it was just that he didn't think of other people when he wanted something.

'Titus, I have a job. I can't just up and go at a day's notice.'

'Of course you can. They are nice understanding people, in your university. You said so yourself.'

'For that very reason.'

'Theo, listen to me. Copenhagen University's Philosophy Department won't suffer much because you've left. It will be just another run of the mill administrative inconvenience. But you'll be the loser if you stay on. You're meant for bigger things, Theo. You never wanted to stay in Denmark longer than was necessary, did you? Well, it's not necessary any more. You don't owe anybody anything. Not me, either. Take what you can, when you can.'

'The flat: I've signed a lease to the end of the year.'

'*Narrengeschwätz*, Theo. Forget it. I'll take care of that.'

'Let me think about it, Titus,' I said.

He laughed. 'You, think about it, and think hard. Let me make it easier for you. It's the end of term or something now, right? Play it safe. Let's say you're just having a terrific holiday in Paris, all expenses paid. You like the arrangement, you stay on. You don't, you go back your university. How's that? I'll ring you again tomorrow at the same time. Good night.'

'I think you should listen to your friend,' Liselotte said, her gaze a little too luminous to discount a hint of tears. 'If I were in your place, I would think very hard about his offer.'

'Why, Liselotte?'

'Because . . .' She sighed and turned her face away. 'Maybe things are changing.' She looked at me again. 'Certainty is becoming less certain, Theo,' she said with sudden levity, as if to make light of something that was too weighty for an evening's outing. 'And Paris in spring! Isn't that too beautiful to miss? Wouldn't it be better to make important decisions strolling along the bank of the Seine, with the sound of Notre Dame's bells in the air? I can be romantic vicariously, no?'

'And wouldn't it be too late then?'

She reached across the table to hold my hand.

'No, Theo. You can always come back. I promise you that.'

'Dearest Liselotte,' I said, 'you give me courage to decide that for once in my life I'm not going to hedge my bets. If I go, I go; meet Titus on his own reckless terms and take the consequences, whatever they are.'

'My father used to say that every person must do something wildly reckless before he or she is forty.'

'He was probably right.'

'Promise me something.'

'Of course, whatever you want.'

'Promise that whatever you decide, you decide with your heart. Without fear or regret. And that you'll remember I'd do anything to help, if you needed help.'

'I promise.'

'And send me a postcard from Le Marais.'

'I will.'

112

Titus rang on the stroke of midnight, not the following day as he said he would, but the day after.

'Well, Theo?'

'I'll come.'

'Excellent. Now, take a piece of paper and write down what I tell you. First, this is my number in Paris. Don't telephone unless it's very urgent.'

I was to proceed to Esbjerg in a week, and there board a French freighter called *L'Aurore* bound for Le Havre. I was to book my passage, and pay for it, with an agency whose name and address in Stormgade Titus dictated. I was to carry as little luggage as possible – absolutely no more than was ostensibly needed for a normal vacation. When I reached the ship, her captain, Gomez, would take care of me.

'Titus, why all these strange manoeuvres? Can't I simply get on the train? I love trains, whereas the mere thought of a ship makes me seasick.'

'It's very important you follow my instructions,' he said impatiently. I thought he meant that travelling through the Ruhr on a German train full of Nazis would be unpleasant if not dangerous.

'You'll have the owner's cabin, which is very comfortable. You'll be served good food and good wine, I promise. Just think, Theo, quiet evenings on deck, watching glorious sunsets on a calm sea.'

'All right. Who is the owner of this mysterious vessel, by the way?'

'I am. A good ship. There's nothing mysterious about her at all. Now, there's one more thing. Listen carefully . . .'

L'Aurore would dock for one day in Amsterdam. I was to go to No. 37 Gabriel Metsustraat and ask for Herr Jan Albers. He was short, fat, about forty years old, balding, with thick-lens glasses and a red beard. Titus repeated these details twice.

Albers would give me a leather briefcase – very similar to the kind I used – which I was to take back to my cabin and hand over to Titus in Le Havre.

'It's a very simple operation, Theo. If for any reason you don't get the briefcase, ring me at once at the number I gave

113

you. Have a pleasant trip. Go see the Rembrandts or something in Amsterdam. I'll meet you in Le Havre.'

Liselotte saw me off at the Hovedbangaard. The ferry crossing to Nyborg should be pleasant, she assured me. Esbjerg was a boring fishing port. A good place to leave. But if I should have time for a meal, absolutely the best in Denmark for fresh fish. Practical information filled our last moment's together.

'Here's yesterday's copy of *Le Temps*, for you to catch up on what is going on in France,' she said. 'You will eat *croissant chocolat avec un grand crème* for me in Saint Germain, won't you?'

'I promise.'

'Don't say you'll write. Maybe your friend is right. Maybe life is like a hand of cards you get dealt. So make the best of it.'

The train pulled out. Liselotte von Freisleben stood on the platform, waving, until her tall figure was swallowed in the moving crowd. I sat down to read *Le Temps* but kept thinking about her, wondering if she too had been a card dealt to me, which I had too hastily returned to the dealer.

L'Aurore was a rusty hulk and the owner's cabin a far cry from the luxury Titus had described. And the sea was rough from beginning to end, except on the day we arrived in Le Havre. There *L'Aurore* was piloted to a less busy and more run-down part of the port. Tired and feeling slightly sick, I stood leaning against the deck railing to look for Titus amidst the bustle on shore.

I saw him standing by a black car talking to three men. Wearing a pale light suit, a fedora hat and dark sunglasses, he looked leaner, almost theatrical.

No sooner was the ship moored, and a gangway thrown across the littered brown water, than Titus came on board. Captain Gomez greeted him. They exchanged a few words then went in together. Shortly afterwards Titus re-emerged alone and seeing me, spread out his arms.

'Theo, welcome to France. Gomez told me you had a dreadful passage. How do you feel now?'

'Better. I can't wait to have my feet on solid ground again,' I said.

'Be patient for just a little longer. There are a few procedures before disembarkation and then we'll be on our way.' He had a healthy suntan. He had also grown a thin moustache.

'The briefcase, Theo. Do you have it?'

'Yes. It's in my cabin. Do you want it now?'

'No. Hang on to it. Give it to me later, when we're out of here. Now I must leave you for a while to attend to some business. The ship is departing tonight. There's some paperwork to do.'

'Where to?'

He pulled a face. 'Another port. See you later.'

Once outside the port, Titus examined the briefcase. Satisfied, he tossed it onto the back seat of the car.

'I really appreciate what you've done, Theo. I'm sorry if the ship was a far cry from a Cunard liner. But now it's all behind you, and ahead is Paris. A new life, Theo. Sit comfortably and enjoy the view.'

He was driving with great panache, speeding through the rolling Normandy countryside. While I was wondering just what it was I had done which had earned his appreciation.

'In Paris, Theo, you'll be right back in your own element,' Titus said.

'What about you, Titus? What's your element?'

'Oh, anything volatile. Ha ha ha.'

'Like owning ships and cars?'

'You disapprove? They mean nothing to me, just useful machines to serve a purpose. Easy come, easy go. I won the ship, by the way. But I bought the car and got swindled.'

I said, 'Pull over, Titus. We need to talk.'

To my surprise, he did. He ran the car over on the verge of the road, turned the engine off, and lit a cigarette.

'All right,' he said. 'Let's get this over and done with.'

'I want you to tell me what all the secrecy was about that briefcase. And I want to know what *L'Aurore*'s cargo was. I'm not interested in your business, Titus. What you do is your own affair. But you've brought me here in a manner that was not open and above board. And you've involved me in something

115

without my knowledge. If I'm to be an accomplice to something, Titus, I have the right to know what it is. To consent or not to consent . . . Titus, this isn't the way friends treat each other.'

He drew on his cigarette then stubbed it out in the ashtray.

'Okay, I have used you. And I apologise,' he said gravely. 'But you're jumping to conclusions. That, too, isn't fair. You seem to have decided on no evidence, that something sinister is under way. I've never lied to you. You do believe that, don't you?'

'Yes.'

'So let me tell you, the briefcase contains certain information. If you had been caught with it, which would have been extremely unlikely, you'd have suffered nothing worse than embarrassment and possible brief inconvenience. But a few good brave men and women in Germany may have lost their lives. I needed to get the briefcase safely here. It was a small calculated risk and it worked. If it had been a dangerous mission, I wouldn't have drawn you into it, I'd have done it myself. Do you accept that?'

'Yes, I think I do.'

'I'm glad. As for the ship, you don't want to know about her any more than what you already know. It's better that way. What I do does not and will never concern you. This I promise. And because I have used you, as you said without your consent, I shall make it up to you. Again and again. Without counting the cost. All right? That's all I want to say on the subject. Can we not put it behind us and concentrate on getting a decent lunch?'

In Louviers we found a pleasant inn. Titus ordered a platter of escargots and grilled sole for both of us, with a bottle of Meursault.

'To happy days and good times,' he said, raising his glass.

I raised mine too. Then, all of a sudden, the sea caught up with me: overcome by nausea, I vomited all over the table.

9

A student once asked me what was the meaning of life. I replied that there was no meaning whatsoever to life; it just happened. Its progress was unpredictable. And the only certainty about life was death.

So what is the purpose of life? she persisted. I glanced demonstratively at my watch. There was no purpose to life either, I said. But, since one was alive, it was best to endure, to explore, to try to be happy and try not to make other people unhappy. That, in a nutshell, was what continuity of civilisation was about.

Anticipating another question, I said that because there was neither meaning nor purpose to life, similarly there was neither meaning nor purpose in ending it prematurely.

The student went away disappointed. Soon afterwards, she dropped my classes to join Wittgenstein's.

I'm not proud of this kind of stoic reductionism. You fall into it either as a result of role-playing, or old age, or both. Also, it's a bald unromantic way of viewing life: I don't believe truth is either absolute or always necessary.

The last time I saw Titus, he said to me, 'Theo, I've always envied you a little, you know.'

'Why?' I asked.

'Because for one thing, you were never distracted by bodily appetites.'

'How do you know?'

'Just a good guess. I'm good at guessing. And I know you. Ha ha ha.' How weak his laughter had become.

'Think, Theo. We eat too much, we fuck too much. A few moments of pleasure followed by indigestion, or remorse. And emptiness. What is it all for?'

'Because,' I replied, 'implicit in those few moments is a whole universe of imaginary possibilities.'

'Ach, you're a romantic after all. Go now, Theo. I'm tired.'

I try in vain to recollect the imaginary possibilities that may have been implicit in two years of longing for Wanda. Paris, '35 to '37? A sustained marathon of indolence. A surfeit of emotion and of food. Ecstasy alternating with despondency. The wild arousal of the senses and the imagination that leaves you as limp as if drugged.

Titus was right. Paris, with the war only a few years away, had everything; was everything.

He rented a flat in rue Lacépède, not far from Panthéon. You walked past a sullen concierge, up four flights of dirty stairs, to face a heavy brown flaking wooden door. To open it, you pulled hard at the doorknob while turning the key, then kneed the door panel at a certain spot in conjunction with the turning of the key.

'See what I mean? The French are like that. You'll get the hang of it after a while,' Titus said.

It was a large flat, clean but untidy. Titus announced right away that he didn't mind things lying about all over the place so long as the flat was clean; dirt depressed him.

'Yours is the larger room facing east. It has more morning sunlight than the rest of the flat. That should cheer you. And I've got you a proper desk and a German typewriter.'

'Thanks, but I can't type.'

'Learn, Theo. Learn. If you should have any problems with the door, or anything else for that matter, when I'm not here, don't go to the concierge. She and her husband are total pigs. Don't let either of them in here. There's a painter one floor down. Wolman's his name. He'll help you. He can fix anything. You'll meet him soon enough. I've already told him about you.'

We stepped out onto the balcony. An unbroken row of haughty old houses looked down on the street. Immediately below stood Titus's black Citroën, one wheel on the pavement, like a cleric who had just crossed the street. Above the houses' pigeon shit-stained roofs the skyline of Paris rose and fell.

'Panthéon there. And there, the market. You'll find good second-hand bookshops over there. And some nice cafés. I'll

118

be away a good deal, so I think it's best I leave you always enough money to see you through a month in advance, okay? Just enjoy yourself, Theo. Read. See the sites. Write. Do anything you like, so long as it's fun.'

He didn't say anything about Wanda. He sprang her on me as a surprise later, like so many other things he did. Maybe it had all been by inadvertent design – Titus's way of doing things created complex oxymorons. One thing I feel certain about: were it not for Wanda I would not have been saved by coming to England and Cambridge. Spellbound like one of Circe's swine, I'd have remained in Paris to perish.

Chad Johnson believed Titus had had foreknowledge of Hitler's invasion of Czechoslovakia. He had tried to warn high-placed officials in the French government, and the British Embassy in Paris. No one had listened to him. Chad has claimed that after Guernica Titus had no doubt that Hitler was preparing for an all-out war. That Titus understood with uncanny accuracy what would follow.

Intuition? More than that, Chad had said. Titus had worked out the puzzle from pieces of information he possessed. No one wanted to believe him, except Chad. But at the time Chad was still a couple of decades away from the eminence he was later to attain.

When Titus was at home, he usually slept late. We had breakfast in the kitchen at around eleven, strong coffee and hot croissants. A mostly silent repast because Titus would be busy with his newspapers. A news addict, he read daily just about all the newspapers he could get: French, German, British, and American.

If you removed the newspapers Titus fanned across the table, and replaced them with, say, a baguette and a round of cheese, the kitchen would be transformed into a Bonnard interior: an iron stove, the rustic wooden table covered with a chequered table cloth, wicker-seated chairs, a near-empty bottle of wine from the night before; sunlight filtering in through tulle curtains on an open window. The tableau, infused with Bonnard's peculiar immanence of latent threat, is completed with us sitting across the table from each other.

'Look, Titus. There's a story about your ship in *Le Temps*.'

Stuck at the bottom of the page was this report about a French freighter called *L'Aurore*. At some unspecified time but not long ago, she had been fired upon off the coast of Valencia, then impounded for a while. Then mysteriously allowed to slip out of harbour.

Probably a filler taken from a news agency, the story wasn't clear about who fired on the ship, why she was impounded, nor who intervened to have her released.

Titus lowered his newspaper to look at me. 'My ship? What are you talking about?'

I paraphrased the story for him.

'You mean you didn't know about it?'

'*L'Aurore* for a ship is like Marie for a girl. There must be hundreds floating about on the high seas,' he said, and resumed reading. 'Besides, I sold the ship a while ago.'

'Oh? You didn't tell me.'

'I promised to keep you out of my affairs, didn't I? Isn't that what you wanted?' he said nonchalantly.

I knew in my heart the ship was Titus's *L'Aurore*, and suspected the event coincided with his recent absence from Paris. Thus, if Titus had been gun-running, as Chad had implied, then I was an unwitting accomplice. But who were the beneficiaries? Surely not the fascists. Surely the Republicans . . . Or both?

I tussled with a moral dilemma: was guilt by complicity compounded if the crime were ignored? Yes! Mitigating circumstances? Yes. First, I would never get a straight answer from Titus. Second, but more significantly, while I could easily be kept in the dark, concealing the truth from Chad was quite another matter. Chad firmly supported the Republicans. Chad was Titus's friend. *Ergo*, whatever Titus was up to, it must have been to the benefit of the Republicans. *Quod erat demonstrandum!*

The truth of the matter is that Wanda, not moral lethargy, was the chief reason why I didn't confront Titus with a 'level with me or I leave' ultimatum.

Tristan Rutland was First Secretary at the British Embassy. He and Wanda lived on the Right Bank, in a neighbourhood favoured by foreign diplomats. Chad buzzed around in Moscow, Berlin, London, Washington DC. In Paris he kept a pied-à-terre near the Place des Vosges.

My introduction to them followed a sudden announcement one afternoon: 'Theo,' Titus said, 'tonight we are dining out. Get your tie and best jacket ready.'

We often dined out. Titus had an insatiable appetite for restaurants and cafés. It was the way he emphasised 'tonight' that indicated it was to be a special occasion.

'You're going to meet some friends of mine. You'll love them, my oldest friend, Wanda, in particular. And she'll love you. The two of you are the perfect antidote to each other's foibles.'

'And what are they?'

He ignored my question, poured himself a glass of wine and sat down at the table, feet up. The afternoon light fell on the table, highlighting age-long stains along with breadcrumbs left over from our late lunch.

'So what have you been doing with your mornings?'

'Playing boules in the Jardin du Luxembourg.'

'There you are,' he said, grimacing. 'One foible to start with.'

'I like boules. I've become rather good at it.'

'You're too young for that silly game. Wanda will cure you of boules.'

'Really? What will I do for her?'

'Ah, that isn't quite as simple. You might discipline her seriousness.'

'How could I, when I've lost mine?'

'All the better. I need a snooze; wake me up at around seven, will you?'

We took a cab to Julien in rue Faubourg-St-Denis. Wanda and Chad were already there. If Chad wasn't quite so memorable that night, it was because Wanda was overwhelmingly so. She wore a black sleeveless dress which showed the natural elegance of her body, the linear loveliness of her dancer's arms. Now as then, when I think of beauty in the deepest meaning of the word, I think of Wanda that night at Julien's.

'Tristan isn't here?' asked Titus.

'Another late night at the Embassy. He sends his apologies.'

'What a pity. This is Theo. He brought my ship home, but he didn't like her. So I think I'll junk her. Ha ha ha.'

'You said you sold her,' I interjected.

'Did I? Well, maybe I did. Chad, what's the latest with our friend Stalin?'

'So you are Titus's philosopher,' Wanda said in a voice that matched the allure in her eyes.

'I must be Titus's something or other. The title feels uncomfortable. What about you?'

'Just an old friend. No other title,' she said, smiling. 'Titus talked a lot about you. He said I should like you.'

'He said the same to me about you.'

'Ah well, then we mustn't disappoint him, must we?'

'That would be easy, as far as I am concerned.'

She looked at me quizzically.

'What are you two whispering about? Wanda, what will you have?' Titus interrupted, pushing the menu at her.

She said to me. 'What do you do all day?'

I replied. 'There is this painter Wolman in the house where we live. He wears a drooping moustache and a sad basset hound expression. I imagine I'm him when I go out. I play boules in Jardin du Luxembourg. I wander like an old dog along the Seine – one way on the Right Bank, the other way on the Left Bank. I eat. I think, sometimes. I browse in the second-hand bookshops. But I have not started to read. And I've not started to think about writing anything.'

She said, 'That's too unbearably bleak.'

I said, 'It could be worse, believe me. I don't mind any more.'

She said, 'Why did Titus bring you over here?'

I said, 'Didn't you know he liked dogs?'

'No, seriously,' she said.

'Well, seriously, perhaps to save me when Europe catches fire,' I said.

'He cares about his friends,' she said.

'Oh yes. If there were a market for friends like Le Marché

aux Timbres in Champes Elysées, you can bet your life Titus would be there, trading vigorously,' I said.

'No,' she said, 'that's unjust. Titus collects friends but not to trade, he's like a conservationist of threatened species.'

'You think I'm a threatened species?' I asked.

'I think we both are,' she said.

'How do you think he spends his days, when he's not dining us out?' I asked.

'Oh precariously, I should think,' she replied with a laugh. 'Fencing off order from chaos is fast becoming a practice of diminishing returns.'

'Why bother?' I asked.

'Because,' she said, 'Titus needs both like God needed the Infinite Void and the Garden of Eden.'

'I think I'm in love with you. Does that shock you?'

'No,' she said.

'I want to make love to you. I've never said that to anybody,' I said.

'I know,' she replied.

'But it isn't possible, is it?' I asked.

'It doesn't matter. Believe me, Theo. Fucking isn't what it's cracked up to be. We'll have a good time . . . go to Musée Carnavelet and the Louvre. We'll sit in the Jardin des Tuileries like two friends taking a rest. We'll watch artists in Montmartre, and we'll eat in Café Cyrano and chat with the intellectuals. And when that gentle mental laxative begins to work, you'll start to write. You'll be a new man. No longer a Wolman-like basset hound.'

But we did make love. Once. Tentatively, clumsily, in a little hotel room on the corner of Boulevard Haussmann and rue Tronchet; not far from the Opéra. Not far from where years later I stayed in another more luxurious hotel, and remembered that day with Wanda.

It happened like it begins to rain, for no particular reason, without anything significant leading up to it. We saw the hotel. We checked in. We undressed and made love on the bed, Wanda on top, me under. And it was just like she said it was: not quite what it was cracked up to be.

Afterwards we ate onion soup in the bistro across the street. Wanda said: 'It doesn't matter, Theo. Truly.'

But it did. There had been a betrayal, for one thing. All that for next to nothing? A feasibility balance of risk and reward never accounted in Wanda's reckoning – another reason why I loved her. Maybe that was why she wasn't disappointed.

'Whom had we betrayed?' I asked myself as we lay in each other's arms in the creaking love-worn hotel bed. Not Tristan Rutland. Titus! That, I think, was implicit in our awkward silence.

'Where is he?' Wanda asked, as if meshing into my thoughts. And I might have replied, 'Can't you hear his steps walking in the garden in the cool of the day? His voice charged with irony calling, "Who told thee that thou wast naked?" '

'Chad thinks he's in Spain.'

'I've always wanted to visit Spain . . . I thought one day I'd journey along the Via Compostela.'

'Why not? When that war's over.'

'Who can tell what Spain will be like when it is?' she said.

Silence again.

'Chad told me something funny about Titus,' she said.

'What?'

'Titus had a fight, a boxing bout, with Hemingway. Hemingway had boasted he could lick Titus with one hand tied behind his back. Titus had him out cold in the first round. Poor Hemingway, nobody had told him what a mean crafty fighter Titus was.'

Of all the streets in Paris Wanda loved Boulevard St Germain best. And of all the cafés there, the one she favoured most was one with a generous stretch of *terrasse* not far from the intersection of Boulevard Saint Germain and Boulevard Saint Michel.

We met there one morning late in spring. I had walked from rue Lacépède. She arrived by a cab from shopping in Printemps. I ordered for her a glass of Noilly-Prat, and bock beer for myself. A loitering busker serenaded the beauty of Paris in spring, accompanying himself on a wheezy accordion. Relaxed and cheerful, Wanda was looking here and there when

124

suddenly her expression turned grave. She was staring over my shoulder, straining to see better.

'What is it?' I asked.

'A dreadful thing has happened. In Spain,' she said in a low voice. 'It's on the front page of *Le Figaro* the man at the next table is reading. Guernica's been bombed to rubble by the Luftwaffe.'

She had gone quite pale. I had no idea where Guernica was. I thought for an instant it was Titus she was worried about before I remembered that he was in Paris, not in Spain.

'Hundreds of people, mostly women and children, killed. Hitler's reached right across France to strike at Spain. When will everybody wake up to what is happening?' Wanda said.

I wanted to tell her – because I was feeling gloomily prophetic that day – that we were all over-sleeping, and when we woke up, it would be to a nightmare. I wanted to say that this lovely April day in Paris was probably at the boundary of a retreating reality, soon to vanish altogether.

'Oh Theo,' she said putting her hand on mine. 'I feel weary and frightened and unable to decide. Isn't it terrible to feel like that already at the age of thirty four?'

'It'll pass,' I said without conviction.

She shook her head. 'Do you know how I know it won't?'

'How?'

'Titus. For the first time since I've known him I feel he is hesitant. He casts about like a man who fears he is about to lose everything. And I ask myself. "If Titus is at a loss, what will happen to the rest of us? What will become of my mother and father, my brother, my sister?" '

Tears welled up in her eyes. The man at the next table had paid his bill. He folded his newspaper and for a moment looked at us thinking, no doubt, that we were lovers having a sad moment.

A year later almost to the day, Wanda informed me that she and Tristan were leaving Paris. He had put in for a transfer back home some time ago, and at last it had come through. She was relieved but nervous. Relieved that at last she was to settle down in a permanent home; nervous because she had never been to England before. She couldn't bear the thought of being separated from Europe by a body of water.

'You will write, Theo. We *must* keep in touch. Promise me.'

I promised. I mumbled something about the English Cambridge don I met in Copenhagen.

'Do please write to him, Theo, won't you?' Wanda said.

I told her I had liked the idea at first, but the appeal was all but gone. The notion of living on an island made me uneasy, like mild but permanent seasickness.

Wanda got annoyed: 'For God's sake, Theo! I'm worried to death about my family. I don't want to have to worry about you too!' she almost screamed at me.

That evening, Titus invited us all to dinner at Voisin's on the corner of rue Saint-Honoré and rue Cambon. Voisin was one of the most distinguished restaurants in Paris. Halfway through the first course, he stopped eating. A grin spreading over his face, he looked at each of us in turn.

'Well, Tristan and Wanda are leaving. Chad is always on the move all the time anyway. Poor Paris. Poor Theo.'

'Why poor Theo?' Wanda asked. 'Theo could come to England.'

'Indeed. Perhaps you'd better start thinking about it, Theo. Chad, would you kindly pay the tip at the end?'

We all stopped eating. Chad said: 'Sure. What's the problem?'

'No problem at all. On the contrary, everything is wonderfully simple for a change. I'm broke.'

He was smiling, as though he had said something funny. Only Wanda looked horrified.

'Broke?' Chad repeated incredulously.

'As the Ten Commandments. I'm good for this meal, but I'd like you to tip, please. Austerity from next week. Ha ha ha.'

'Jesus, Titus! Let me . . .'

'No,' said Titus raising a hand, 'there are rules to the game.'

'My dear fellow, being without money isn't a game. Look, if we can help '

'My dear Tristan, I thank you with all my heart. You're wrong, you know, being without money is part of a game. The rules had been changed without my noticing. Everything's part of a

126

game. I'm glad for Wanda's sake that you believe otherwise. Enough said about that. Let's drink and eat and remember the end of a wonderful period,' Titus said, raising his glass.

A scream was suddenly heard, followed by gasps of horror from the tables around us. A man at a table not far off had stabbed his sweetheart with a fork through the eye. Blood streamed down her face to cover the escargot on her plate. There were shouts of 'Get an ambulance . . . Call the police . . .' She was a healthy young thing, and she sat there mouth gaping and stunned like an animal in an abattoir.

I thought what anarchy was let loose on the world, when Titus is trumped by a sudden change of rules, and violence erupts at Voisin's!

Let me say for the record, in Cambridge I never competed with Ludwig Wittgenstein. Not for honour nor for disciples. He was a genius whom nobody understood but pretended they did. I was a methodical plodder whom all could understand but pretended it didn't matter.

10

CHAD

Okay, how should I play this? It has to be short. I'll stick to the main events for now. One day perhaps I'll write a book about those years with Titus. On second thoughts, probably not. There are things that are better left unwritten. Besides, I'm getting kind of tired of writing. Nowadays I only write when I must. Never much liked doing books, anyway. I prefer to talk, you see. Always have.

Titus was one of my oldest friends. We had kept in touch for over half a century. I should be able to say I knew him well, right? The truth is, I can't. I never *really* knew him. But then who did? I'd lay a bet no one. I don't even know if Titus was his original name. He died Titus Alston. When I first knew him he was Altermann. One is tempted to say Titus, whoever he was, invented himself. Full of riddles, but left no key to any of them. A total enigma. A damn good one at that.

He was the kind of guy who could enter a game, play for the highest stakes, win, then walk away leaving the prize behind because all of a sudden the challenge he had just overcome disappointed him and there was nothing more to play for. Well, maybe not quite. What I mean is Titus was unpredictable beyond imagining. A maverick of mavericks. Nothing he ever did that I know of was done in half-measure.

That day, when we all stood under the ash tree by the river Cam, I looked at Wanda who had loved him, at Theo who had worshipped him, at Pugachev whose feelings for him I could never understand, and at lovely Phoebe who had been with him to the last. And I thought, Which one of us, if any, really understood what he was about? And then I thought, He was the only man I've ever known who pursued wealth and power not out of vanity, not out of wanting to prove a point, not out of greed, either. Titus did all that out of pure curiosity. Like a scientist, you might say, often experimenting on himself. And when he attained it, I think he came face to face with the ultimate futility and emptiness of it all. Imagine a religious mystic dedicating his entire life and energy to building a mighty monument to God. A cathedral, say. And when it stands there complete, in full glory, he hears a voice he cannot deny, saying, 'Sorry, there is no God!' I guess that's how it must have been with Titus. But he had fun on the way. Fun was in everything he did. If you ask me, I'd say he died deliberately.

I think it's fair to say that in different ways we've all learnt a great deal from Titus. The first lesson was that nothing in life, absolutely nothing, comes for free. I dare say I was the luckiest in the sense that I paid the smallest price. Maybe I've also gotten the least. It's difficult to judge such things.

I've written three books. Articles. Lectures. Essays. I've twice been awarded the Pulitzer Prize. So I'm not being immodest when I say I've made it to the top league in my line of work. I have a lot to thank Titus for.

You raise your eyebrows? Let me put it another way. Ever read the American poet Wallace Stevens? He wrote a poem called 'The Blue Guitar'. It bowled me over when I first read it. One line in particular: *Things as they are are changed upon the Blue Guitar.* But I don't think I fully understood what it was all about until I came to assess for myself what rôle Titus had played in my life.

Some years back, a former girlfriend called Jay, who later headed Media Studies in Chicago University, invited me to give a talk to her sophomore students. I began by telling them that anyone who aspired to write should read that poem. Because it summed up what writing was about, the nature of truth and of reality. Neither is constant, let alone absolute. Played on the Blue Guitar, they sound different each time, depending also on who the player is.

Now, Titus was a virtuoso Blue Guitar player. Not only that, in his hands the Blue Guitar could change colour without anybody noticing.

That is not to say that he lied. He saw possibilities, perceived more permutations of truth and reality than most people

129

could. A fine line, you might say. Sure. The point is, however, that more often than not he was right. His uncanny intuitive imagination hardly ever let him down. He could foresee a whole sequence of events from the first incident. He could anticipate trends. That's how he was able to make fortunes on the world's stock exchanges, among other things.

Journalists don't always report the truth; I'm no exception. The bad ones would knowingly report falsely and not care. Good ones would sometimes do so inadvertently. I've always *wanted* to write the truth as I understood it, and mostly did my level best to do so.

Titus had a slightly different approach. He said anything *could* be the truth so long as it conformed with the surrounding reality. In other words, informed guesswork.

Once we argued about truth. Paris. 1936 or '37. We were having a late dinner in some smart restaurant in rue Fontaine where Titus habitually played cards. He brought with him a gorgeous French girl he was sleeping with at the time. She sang in a Pigalle nightclub. He said something like this: What was history if not chronicled events selected arbitrarily? Didn't omission affect the truth no less than the selection?

An historian studies a period or a war. He chooses evidence which suits his ideas. Another historian with other ideas, who studies the same thing, comes up with a different picture. But what about things both had omitted? And what about things that no one recorded at the time? So how do you know what *really* happened? Or what *really* caused this or that to happen?

Take the war in Spain. The Republicans are fractious and incompetent. The Nationalists are allied with fascist regimes the civilised world hates. They will win. Not because they're good, but because the Republicans are useless, all the more so for the help they are getting from a whole bunch of foreign idealists. Meanwhile journalists are buzzing about the battle-fields filing stories their chosen side wants to hear. The underlying truth is that this war is about the most stupid and brutal that's ever been fought at any time, anywhere in the world. Political anarchy taken to extreme. Whoever wins, when the dust settles it wouldn't make the slightest bit of difference to the lives of the poor bloody Spaniards.

130

'So why are you risking your neck getting involved?' I asked, without quite knowing in what way he was involved.

'That's different. I'm not in the business of reporting,' Titus replied with his mephistophelian laughter you couldn't forget.

'Titus eez 'elping ze Republicans in a very important way,' the girl interrupted in her husky voice.

'See what I mean? Minou hasn't a clue about what I do. But she's certain I help the Republicans because that's what she wants to believe.'

Okay, here's a main event only a few know about.

By 1962 Titus was a big shot in business and finance. Among other things, he had been trading vigorously with the Soviets for a number of years. Then came the Cuban missile crisis. I was then Foreign Editor on the *Washington Post*. There was a lot of sabre-rattling. The international tension was electric. I had a contact in the White House, a friend way back from Harvard whose name I shan't mention. And I was altogether on very friendly terms with the Kennedy team.

One late evening this guy rang to invite me for a breakfast meeting.

'Chad,' he said, 'I want to sound you out on something. Strictly off the record, you understand. Not for news. We have a problem. We've got to defuse this crisis before it gets real serious. We'd like to know what kind of deal we can do with the Soviets.'

I said I thought Khrushchev was bluffing. I didn't believe he'd risk a confrontation that could lead to war.

My friend said, 'We think so too. But it's a hell of a gamble. What we need is a safe dependable line of communication to the Kremlin, Chad. Unofficial and unknown.'

I had an idea. I asked him to give me a few hours.

He said, 'You got it. If what you come up with looks good, we'll put it to the President.'

I phoned Titus in London.

He said, 'I'll ring you back in a moment, on a better line.'

Security was a reflex with him. When he heard what I had to say he asked, 'How much time do I have, Chad?'

'Virtually none. Do what you can as soon as you can.'

131

'Two days. If I have something real I'll meet you in Washington.'

In mid-October the US naval blockade was deployed. The Soviet ships had not yet started steaming towards Cuba. But the entire world was shit scared. Titus arrived in Washington three days later. Maybe Khrushchev was bluffing but it would be too dangerous to count on it, he told me. Khrushchev thought Kennedy was too inexperienced and insecure, and public opinion would force him to back off. Khrushchev didn't want war any more than Kennedy did. The danger was that both could be drawn by events to a point of no back-off.

Through his own contacts, Titus confirmed what the White House already knew: a deal was possible. It entailed an American promise not to invade Cuba and the removal of American missiles from Turkey's Eastern borders. In return, the USSR would pull out its own missiles from Cuba. It was now a question of credibility. The Soviets wanted to be sure the deal would be all hush-hush, that we wouldn't turn it into a propaganda victory.

I passed on the message. My friend came back: 'Chad, we've checked out your man. Bring him over, won't you? The President wants to hear it straight from him.'

Titus had a brainwave: use Pugwash for a double check, as a kind of honest broker. He had some friends there.

Founded by the philosopher Bertrand Russell, the Pugwash Movement was a prestigious international organisation of scientists working for East–West nuclear disarmament. Its members were predominantly scientists from diverse disciplines and nationalities, including Soviet and American. Many were Nobel Prize laureates. The organisation was, above all, eminently discreet. It had authority; it was universally respected.

So, said Titus, why not get Pugwash to act as a behind-the-scenes go-between on each stage of the deal? Well, it wasn't quite as simple as that. But it was a brilliant idea, and it worked.

The rest was choreographed drama: the world held its breath as the Soviet ships, under full media coverage, sailed towards Cuba with orders to turn back before contact with the American naval force was made. A great universal sigh of relief. The US agreed not to invade Cuba, and to lift the blockade. There followed a muted denial about the missiles-in-Turkey part of the deal. But less than a year later, they were pulled out – 'redeployed'. As always, both sides claimed victory. Both protagonists were heroes in their own country. End of story. Titus thought the real winner was Khrushchev. He was wrong, for once. The missiles in Eastern Turkey were obsolete. They were scheduled to be scrapped anyway.

Boy, how I remember the gratified look on Titus's face as he shook hands with Jack Kennedy in the Oval Office on Monday October 29, 1962!

I met Titus in the bar of the Adlon Hotel, Berlin. It must have been 1930. The last French troops had gotten out of the Rhinelands that summer, I remember. Max Schmeling beat Jack Sharkey to become world heavyweight champion. We listened to the fight at the Adlon. Titus made a tidy sum betting on Schmeling who was very much the underdog. And that fall, the Nazis became the second largest party in the Reichstag. Titus was wrong on that one: he had predicted they would come first.

I had not been long in Berlin. I had graduated in History from Harvard two years before, then did one year at Christ Church, Oxford as a Rhodes Scholar. Then, back home, I did nothing for a while, undecided about what to do next.

We lived in Boston. My older brother Rex was gearing himself for a political career. My sister Meg was doing postgraduate biology. For Dad, a banker from an old Boston family, politics was like baseball is for some – a total addiction. He had made it a lifelong hobby to cultivate friends in high places. Mom was famous for her parties which always got a few lines in the *Boston Globe* social columns because so many important people came to them.

Dad said to me, 'Chad, you'd better start thinking about what you want to do in life. Now, Rex got drive and ambition. Meg got brains. You, Chad, got good looks and charm. The way I see it, there are two things you could do with that. You could become a film actor, which I wouldn't recommend. Or you could join the State Department and be a diplomat.'

I said, 'Dad, I want to write.'

He told me writing was a mug's game. Unless I was talking of journalism, which he also didn't rate too highly.

I settled for journalism. I got a job with the *Boston Globe* as a reporter. Soon, as luck would have it, the *Globe*'s Berlin man died in a car crash and it so happened I was almost fluent in German, having taken it at Harvard, and with a gentle nudge from Mother, who always invited the editor to her parties, I was posted to Berlin.

The received wisdom was that if the greatest story of the time was hovering about looking for a place to happen, it would be Berlin. Everybody who was anyone – writers, artists, scientists – passed through Berlin. You had there some of the top foreign journalists in the world. Men like William L. Shirer, who worked for the *Chicago Tribune* and later CBS, and H. R. 'Knick' Knickerbocker, to mention but two.

At first I felt a bit like some greenhorn cowhand coming into a saloon bar full of seasoned gun-slingers. Or like a lamb among wolves, if you prefer that simile. They were not unkind. On the contrary, I was shown the ropes. I was helped a good deal, particularly by Bill Shirer whom I consider simply the greatest journalist of his generation. I was taken, almost as a first port of call on my initiation tour, to the Adlon.

I can't really blame any of these guys if to begin with they didn't hold me in high regard. They were, after all, battle-tried reporters who had earned their spurs, whereas I was a rich boy with connections from Boston. But out of that isolating temporary disadvantage I gained one telling and lasting benefit which, in the long run, gave me an edge over many of them: Titus. I think that, more than any of my colleagues, I recognised his value as a source of information. And that recognition grew into the most important friendship of my life. I guess I've always been kind of lucky.

Hotel Adlon, at No. 1 Unter den Linden overlooking the Brandenburg Gate, was unlike any of Europe's great hotels that I've known. That it was splendid in every way, romantic, evocative, all that goes without saying. Perhaps the most remarkable thing about the Adlon was that throughout all the violent vicissitudes that visited Berlin, up to the day the Russians occupied their part of it in 1945, the Adlon remained a fortress of uncompromising excellence, maintaining the highest standards of European culture and tradition.

Whenever the lights went out in Berlin, in the Adlon, which had its own generators, the chandeliers went on shining. Hot water went on flowing in the luxurious bathrooms of its rooms and suites. The best food continued to be impeccably served in its dining-room. And wines from its legendary cellars never ran out. The Adlon catered for the world's élite which, in turn, remained loyal to it to the last.

It is said that when the Soviets entered Berlin, they arrested the proprietor, mistaking his title of Director-General for a military rank.

The bar had its own distinction, being the Number One watering-hole of the city's foreign press community. Informers, spies, boring raconteurs, anybody who thought he or she had a story to sell, even for the price of a drink, came here too.

I've gotten to be where I am in my profession through a lot of hard work. Okay, I might not have been quite the natural, like Shirer. But when it came to stamina, methodical preparation, intuition, I reckon I could hold my own with the best.

From the day I arrived in Berlin I wasted not a moment. I did the rounds to places like the Josty Café, Romanisches Café, and Adler near the Ullstein Building where the Berlin press met. I spent nights reading Alfred Döblin and the other novelists of the day. And Kurt Tucholsky – the fat Berliner who was trying to save Germany with a typewriter, as someone unkindly described him. I read Lukács, Korsch, Spengler, Heidegger, Müller van der Bruck, Jünger – intellectuals of the left, intellectuals of the centre, intellectuals of the right, as well as a whole assortment of down-market propagandists.

If one night I went to a new play by Brecht, or some satirical cabaret with George Grosz, the next night I'd see the Tiller sisters or the singer Anita Berber. What I mean to tell you is that I *did* Berlin comprehensively; day and night, high life and low life. I made friends with the editors of *Berliner Tageblatt* and *Vossiche Zeitung*, and with that most enchanging man about town, Graf Harry Kessler, who knew absolutely everybody worth knowing.

All this is by way of pointing out that by the time I met Titus,

I was no longer a total innocent abroad who could be sold a pup.

That spring evening a whole bunch of us were at the Adlon Bar. Ed Murrow from CBS, on a brief visit from the States, Henry Bridges of the London *Daily Telegraph*, Laurie Christie from *Time* magazine, Milton Strobe, *The New York Times* chief of the Berlin Bureau. Knickerbocker had come with a friend, Walter Duranty, *The New York Times* man in Moscow who was nominally under Strobe and whom Strobe detested. A short repellent Englishman with facile charm, Duranty was a big name. He was universally considered the best informed authority on the Soviet Union. Only later it transpired how much of what he had written was untrue – not even plausible speculation. He was the man who tried to explain Stalin's atrocities with the glib but memorable excuse: "You can't make an omelette without breaking eggs". He had lost a leg in a train accident but had put it about that it was a war injury. Duranty came often to Berlin, much to Strobe's chagrin, mostly to have his spare wooden leg readjusted.

Von Sternberg's *The Blue Angel*, starring Marlene Dietrich, had recently opened in town. Laurie, the only one who had already seen it, thought it was so-so. When Duranty wasn't sizing me up – he liked to put down anyone he could, inexperienced newcomers in particular – his eyes were darting about the bar. There were many pretty girls there and Duranty had the reputation for being a mighty womaniser.

Then Titus walked in.

At first glance I thought he looked out of place in the Adlon. With his casual, almost scruffy appearance, he might have fitted better in the Rheingold in Potsdamer, where gangsters hung about. But he had a calm, assertive presence and clearly he was more at home here, and certainly better known, than I was.

He nodded at us, then sat at a far table which had just been vacated. Bridges went over to join him. They talked for a while. Then Bridges got up, waved us goodbye and left.

'Who's that fellow? I seem to remember his face from somewhere,' Duranty inquired.

'He goes under the name of Titus Altermann. Russian. A cool customer. Comes here a lot. I can't make him out. NKVD, I guess,' said Strobe. I think he was trying to faze Duranty.

'Is that so?' said Duranty, unfazed, which put Strobe's nose out of joint. But after that, he went silent. Soon he excused himself and left with Knickerbocker.

When they were gone, Strobe remarked, 'I reckon Duranty knows damn well who that guy is. He just pretended he didn't.'

'Is he really NKVD?' I asked.

Strobe, a cunning old buzzard, laughed. 'Titus? Who knows? But I doubt it. I'll tell you what he is, though, a great drinker. He could drink ten Irishmen under the table, then walk a straight line. Also, he's a great story-teller. On any given topic this guy could spin you three likely yarns. Two would be utter nonsense. One could well be priceless information.'

'How could you tell which was which?'

'Experience, old buddy. Pure street-wise experience. Until you have it, use Titus's tales at your peril. And another thing. Nothing comes for free with him.'

'You mean he charges?'

'Sure. One way or another.'

Another time I found Titus in the bar when I came there alone. Our eyes met. He came over. He already knew who I was but waited for me to introduce myself. There had been a Nazi demonstration in Unter den Linden that morning. A fight had broken out between the Nazis and Socialists. The police had stood by and done nothing. Some fifteen people had been carried off on stretchers. We talked about it. Rather, for once, I did and he listened. We were about the same age, yet Titus seemed older, in demeanour not in appearance. I repeated what Strobe had said about him. Titus misunderstood.

'Duranty said that?' he asked with a laugh.

'You know him?'

'Only that he is a fraud, albeit a damn good one. You know the difference between a good fraud and a good journalist?'

'Tell me.'

'The reporter will tell what he saw. The fraud will tell the same story without having seen it.'

'Which are you?'

'Both. Duranty was right. He should know.'

'What do you mean?'

'Well, I know for sure that all his stories about Stalin's great achievements originate at the bar of the Metropole in Moscow, from which he hardly ever stirs. He's the most accomplished and widely-believed liar in a profession that's full of them. You should study him. No offence meant.'

'None taken.'

We spoke German, I with an American accent, he with a Russian. When we became friends we switched to English and never spoke German to each other again.

I figured Milton Strobe wouldn't thank me if I put Titus right. As for Duranty, I didn't much care for him, but there was one thing Duranty did say to me. He said, rather unkindly, that if I wanted to get to know Germany from the inside, I should get a German girlfriend. Preferably a Wagnerian-size Nazi. That I did repeat.

'Sounds to me like a good advice,' said Titus. 'You like large blonde women who want to breed?'

'Yeah, I guess I do. Not the breeding part.'

'You like riding?'

'Sure, I like riding.'

'And zoos?'

'Not so hot on zoos. Any connection between the three?'

'None that I can think of. If you like riding and zoos, we might see each other. Personally, I don't care for large blonde Nazi girls.'

That laughter of his! People would turn to stare.

The beer or two I bought Titus that day at the Adlon was one of the best investments I've ever made. Over the years he gave me many crucial tips, always in triplets. And remembering my introductory story, he would say, 'Disregard these two. This one is the real stuff.'

Sure he took money. Before he had plenty of it, he needed money. That is not to say that Titus was in any way mercenary. He valued friendship. He was to the end a loyal if unpredictable friend. Always dependable, in crises as in easy times.

There was a livery stable on the edge of Tiergarten. We sometimes hired horses and rode in the park. That was for minor stories and for fun. For the serious stuff we met in the Zoo.

Like I said, zoos leave me cold. I asked Titus what turned him on about the Zoo. He answered:

'You like libraries, don't you? You go into a library. You can't read all the books, so you pick one. You browse though a few more. For the rest, you watch other people, the expressions on their faces as they browse. You make guesses about the interesting ones. Well, in some ways, for me a zoo is like that. Only instead of books you have animals. I get more peace of mind for reflection in one hour at the Zoo than I would in a whole day at the Staatsbibliothek.'

That summer in Berlin political scores were being settled, a trend that was to reach a gruesome climax shortly after the Nazis came to power three years later. Titus rang me one Sunday morning. I was still asleep.

'Are you doing anything special today?' he asked.

I mumbled something.

'Why don't we meet at the Zoo at around noon?'

I was wide awake in an instant.

'Okay. Where?'

'Anywhere. Walk around. Enjoy yourself. Buy a packet of peanuts. Feed the monkeys.' Then he hung up.

If ever there was a line straight out of a spy movie. In retrospect, I realise Titus had played it up for his own amusement.

It was a beautiful day. The Zoo was full of people. Through Titus I've become a bit of a zoo connoisseur. Zurich, London, New York, I've been to them all. But Berlin is something special. It has a certain claustrophobic intimacy: Germanic sentimentality plus middle-class *Gemütlichkeit* plus Old World whimsy with a lot of *Entschuldigen Sie bitte, mein Herr, Bitte schön, meine liebe Frau.*

And there I am, trilby pulled forward, jacket flung over one shoulder, a copy of *Life* magazine under my arm, doing the secret agent routine in this arboreal neatness crowded with strolling families and Nazi brown-shirts who, for once, are politely doffing their caps at passers-by.

There's a commotion at the baboons' landscaped pit. I squeeze through the crowd to get a look. The baboons are in a state of excitement, females scurrying to and fro, males jumping about with erect penis, all of them screaming. The focus of all this agitation is one baboonette hotly pursued by a young amorous baboon. Whenever he gets near her, the older dominant ape sets upon him, fangs bared, shrieking murderously.

The spectators are divided: some hold forth about propriety – the young baboon should show respect for his elders, wait his turn, grow up, learn more about life, etc. But the majority is rooting for the young baboon – why should the old one have all the fun? they argue. Look at him. He's so ugly! Jewish, no doubt. Think of the poor pretty young baboonette!

A few protest: disgraceful! A zoo is a respectable place for family outings, a showcase of God's creation. Children shouldn't witness such obscene goings-on. Call the keeper to put an end to these unseemly shenanigans!

Cheers alternate with boos. A group of youths show initiative. They distract the old baboon with peanuts, cakes, fruit. And while he's stuffing his face with food, his young rival copulates vigorously to still louder cheers and cries of 'Shame!' Suddenly the old baboon turns to catch his erring wife *in flagrante*. A half-chewed banana is hastily discarded. With a blood-curdling scream, he charges. This time the young baboon doesn't flee; his morale is high. Or perhaps he's too tired. The two roll on the ground. There's fur and blood all over the place. The dreadful din brings two keepers running to the scene. Armed with long poles, they separate the combatants. The old baboon – defeated? – is driven away, exiled into an isolated cage. End of an era?

An elderly man shakes his head and says to his wife in a sad voice: '*Entsetzlich!* Violence and disorder even in the zoo! What is the world coming to, I ask you? Thank goodness we're both old, Helga.'

One man remains standing at the pit's railings when the crowd disperses. He is leaning forward as if immersed in thought, perfectly still. Short, rather fat, and not young, he is wearing a cheap dark suit. His hat is pitched forward to reveal a pink flashy back of the neck. One foot is twisted awkwardly. The heel of his shoe is worn down and tipped with metal.

'*Entschuldigung, mein Herr . . .* ' says one of the keepers.

The man doesn't move.

'*Mein Herr, bitte!*' When he touches his shoulder, the man slumps down to the ground like a sack.

'Otto! *Komm schnell!*' The keeper cries to his mate, who comes running. '*Es muss ein Infarkt sein. Was denkst du?*'

It is no heart attack. When they turn the man on his back a small bloody spot beneath his jacket's lapel is clearly visible.

What I can't remember clearly is at what point I ran into Titus. Was it before or after the police had arrived and sealed off the entire zoo? Was it by the baboon pit or elsewhere? Anyway, there he was, sitting, legs outstretched, arms spread out across the back of the bench, face turned to the sun, eyes closed.

'Hi,' I said.

He opened his eyes. 'Ah, there you are.'

'There's been a murder by the baboon pit. A man's been shot.'

'Is that what the commotion's about? How do you know he's been shot?'

'I saw the gun wound. I was close by. Looking for you, actually.'

Titus grinned. 'And here I was all the time, missing the excitement.'

'A man's been murdered, for Christ's sake. How can you be so blasé about it?'

'Berlin's like Chicago nowadays. Bang bang everywhere. But here in the zoo . . . That's real bad form. No consideration at all. Did you hear the shot?'

'No. The monkeys and the people were making too much noise. Or more likely the killer used a silencer.'

'A silencer. Hmmm . . . Very professional.'

'You wanted to tell me something?' I said, suddenly remembering why I was here at all.

Titus raised his eyebrows. 'Did I? I forgot. It couldn't have been terribly important. Why don't we go and have lunch somewhere? I'm starving.'

The police were at the gate, interrogating people as they came out. I showed my Foreign Press identification. Titus raised his arms in mock invitation to be frisked. The police waved us through.

The man who had been shot was a German communist, opposer of Stalin and a follower of Leon Trotsky. His name was Krauss. The Monday newspapers ran a short story about him. I went to interview Chief Inspector Karl Zörgiebel, Berlin Police. Apparently Krauss was shot at point-blank range with a small calibre pistol, a semi-automatic Beretta 7.65mm Brevet-tata. The weapon was found discarded in a litter bin at the other end of the Zoo, with no fingerprints on it. There was no silencer either, unless the killer had removed it before throwing the gun away. What were the police going to do about it? Following the usual procedures, Herr Johnson. There were no leads.

I filed a story about it. My editor wired back: 'CHAD WHO GIVES A SHIT ABOUT COMMUNIST KILLED IN ZOO STOP DO IN-DEPTH STORY ON HITLER'S CRONIES.'

I've heard many stories told about Titus. A lot of them pure fantasy, in my opinion. I don't believe he was ever involved in killing people. I won't believe he would be so treacherous as to use a friend for cover to slip away from the scene of a crime.

I got myself a girlfriend, but not quite what Duranty suggested – she was an American. Her name was Dido Jane Merryweather but her friends called her Jay. She was a Wagnerian beauty, all right: large, blonde, clear-skinned, and a nose like a miniature sculpted ski chute. Originally from a small mid-west town, Jay was both clever and uncompromisingly ambitious. She had graduated from Ann Arbor in European History, majoring in German. We met at the Staatsbibliothek, where I often researched and where she read Heidegger like he was the new Messiah. Jay was the closest I've ever come to being involved with a Nazi. She claimed to have loathed Titus. For all that, I think they slept together at least once. I don't grudge Titus that. Jay was a lousy fuck anyway.

I admired Wanda a lot, but she never turned me on. To be

frank, I can't for the life of me understand how she and Titus were lovers for such a long time. They seemed to me totally incompatible.

After the Nazis came to power and Titus decamped to Denmark, I did a stint in Moscow. We kept in touch. That is, *I* kept in touch. Titus never rang me. Unlike Duranty, I didn't hang around the Metropole. I went out to see things for myself. I saw the famine with my own eyes. And I wrote about it with all the passion and anger I had in those days. You know what? They didn't believe me. My editor told me to cool it. He had read what Duranty was saying, that it was all an exaggeration, and believed *him*, like everybody else. Titus had warned me about that. I quit the *Globe*.

We had a good time in Paris, Titus and I, and Wanda and her English husband, and poor old Theo who was so much in love with her. I had joined the *Washington Post*, where I was much happier. I did some reporting on the war in Spain. Don't ask me what Titus was doing there. I've learnt not to ask too many questions where my friends are concerned.

Then we lost touch during World War II. I went with the marines on D-Day. Titus? He disappeared altogether. I thought he had been killed. When we met again in London in the mid-fifties he told me he had been back to Russia and fought at Stalingrad. Only Titus could've done such a crazy thing.

Khrushchev didn't trust him too much. But when Brezhnev came to power, Titus prospered enormously. Oil, gold, furs, you name it.

Hey, want me to tell you something? Titus was a damn lucky guy. But luckiest for having had Phoebe, and that's God's honest truth. If it hadn't been for her I guess he would have died years ago out of sheer boredom.

11

That Christmas might have been Phoebe's last with Titus, as with the Group. She would always remember it as a watershed where she witnessed him at his most inadequate and vulnerable; when, for all that, she loved him more compassionately than ever.

Titus had been in what John Lefebre labelled his 'rooting-out-sedition frame of mind' and she, like John, got caught in it. Titus had summoned her to his office to give her a good dressing-down for allegedly siding with Lefebre against him over the take-over of an ailing leisure consortium. Phoebe protested at first calmly, rationally, then indignantly, losing her temper. It made no difference to Titus, who dismissed her from his presence with a chilling stare.

'You're like bloody Stalin!' she shouted at him.

'You wouldn't know Stalin from St George if he breathed in your face,' he snorted.

She started making tentative inquiries about openings elsewhere, and injudiciously confided in John.

'Hey, take it easy. You wouldn't think of running out on *me*, would you?' he said, holding her by the shoulders. 'C'mon, let me buy you lunch.'

He took her to the place he favoured, at the bottom of St James's Street and at the first glass of wine said, 'The dragon's wrath has abated. He's all sweetness now.'

'I don't give a damn.'

'Sweetheart,' purred Lefebre, putting his hand caressingly on her arm, and leaning over until she could smell the mint on his breath, 'don't be like that. You know you're happy here. You're doing a great job. Titus needs you, and loves you. So do I, by the way.'

She pulled back, twisting her mouth sceptically. John raised his glass, looking at her askance. 'Cheers! Here's to you,' he said. Then he pushed up his left sleeve to reveal an enormous white gold Rolex watch. 'Look what I got by way of an olive branch. See? He's sorry. Let me know what he gives you. You know, it's amazing, I still can't figure Titus out. I don't know what he likes, and more importantly, what he hates. That puts a keen edge on the concept of living dangerously.'

'Crab.'

'Sorry?'

'He hates crab. A friend had committed suicide by jumping overboard on a channel crossing. Titus was told the channel was littered with suicide corpses on which the crabs gorge before being fished up and themselves eaten in London restaurants. When Titus heard that, he went off crab meat permanently. That's his weakness. He has a crab phobia.'

'Is that a fact?'

'It is indeed,' said Phoebe. 'Better remember when you next dine with him.'

Titus never apologised. That evening, however, he cheerfully, as though nothing had passed between them, suggested they spent the holiday somewhere in the Swiss Alps. He suddenly longed for high snowy altitudes.

'I promised my parents I'd spend Christmas with them,' she said sullenly.

'We can take them with us,' he suggested after a pause.

'What a bizarre thought, Titus. They wouldn't come. They want me home. And they hate travelling anyway.'

'Home,' Titus echoed as though the very idea puzzled him. 'What if I came with you?'

She gave him a look. 'You can't be serious!'

'Sure I can. Sometimes. Once or twice a year maybe.' He laughed.

He didn't ask what, if anything, she had told her parents about him. He made no attempt to guess how her parents would feel at meeting their daughter's lover, who was just about old enough to be their own father.

As for Phoebe, having with some difficulty come to terms with Titus's unexpected suggestion, she said with a touch of

145

irony that being a retired vicar – and a liberal-minded one at that – her father was well equipped to deal with life's strangest aberrations. She wasn't certain whether Titus's silence indicated trust in her discretion or indifference. So she just passed on her parents' message, which was that he would be most welcome and that they both looked forward to meeting him.

They flew to Teeside Airport where a rented car was waiting for them. It was cold, with a premonition of snow in the air. Driving to Romaldkirk in Teesdale, where Phoebe's parents lived, she said it might be a white Christmas for once. Titus offered her ten to one against a single snowflake falling throughout the entire Christmas holiday. Phoebe produced a ten pound note and stuck it in Titus's pocket. 'You're on,' she said, adding after a pause, 'Titus, you will be careful, won't you?'

'Of what?'

'What you say . . . My parents, my mother in particular, are not the kind of people you're used to.' Her eyes on the road, she didn't see his smile.

When they reached the village Titus noticed the Rose and Crown inn, and remarked that it looked a good place, which Phoebe confirmed.

'Where is your parents' house?'

'There, on the other side of the green.'

'Pull over. I'll stay here at the Rose and Crown, if they have a decent room vacant.'

'Titus!' she began to protest, because her mother had taken the trouble to prepare the best room in the house for him.

He stroked her cheek with the back of his hand. 'It's better this way, truly. You know how I need to have my own bathroom. Why don't we extend borders this Christmas and declare home and inn one unit?'

She knew Christmas would be unbearable if she made an issue of it.

Titus came out of the Rose and Crown beaming. 'I have a splendid little suite. I can't see your folks' house from my window, but I'll blow you a goodnight kiss all the same.'

'Won't you come over to say hello and for a drink?' she asked.

146

'Later,' he said.

'I'll come to fetch you, shall I? In two hours or so?'

'I'll walk over. See you later.'

But he didn't show up until mid-morning the next day, leaving Phoebe with the burden of explaining his absence.

She managed this immaculately for, coming round from the back of Hallgarth Cottage just as Titus passed through the garden gate, Rupert Whelan greeted him without so much as a hint of strain.

He was a large man with enormous weather-beaten hands, a splendid equine head and a mass of white hair, like sea foam. His eyes gentle and alert, his whole manner evinced diffident, good-humoured intelligence. Above all else Phoebe admired that delicate balance of steady confidence and vulnerability in her father. She noted it was more precarious than ever when he came in and stood with Titus in the living-room against a backdrop of demure Christmas decorations.

A more explicit unease was reflected in her mother Mary's eyes as she came forward to shake Titus's hand. In her youth Mary Whelan would have looked like a softer version of her daughter, for Phoebe's focused directness seemed to come from her father.

They were all a bit too formal, too awkward with each other, Phoebe thought; as though there were an embarrassing illness in the air nobody wanted to mention. Left with the ordeal of providing a three-way bridge of familiarity, she was angrily blaming herself for imagining it could have been any different. Had not Titus taught her there were divisions which were irreconcilable, and problems that were insoluble, and that any attempt to do so was bound to end in disappointment and heartache? She should have reminded him of that when he had offered to come here.

Not a word was said about Titus's last-minute decision to stay at the Rose and Crown. For all Phoebe's apprehension, she and her parents survived Christmas Day lunch and a protracted afternoon without too many tense moments.

On Boxing Day Phoebe's parents were enough at ease with Titus to suggest that they all went for a walk, as it was a beautiful frosty morning.

'Why not?' said Titus.

They took a footpath that led from the edge of the village down to the River Tees, crossed the stone bridge to the other side, and walked along the bank.

'A little further on,' said Rupert to Titus, 'there's a footpath that leads through the wood up to the ridge. The climb is rather steep, but the view from the top is magnificent. We can go up or turn back, whichever you prefer.'

'Let's go up.'

'It's not that difficult when you take it very slowly,' said Rupert.

Titus pretended that he hadn't heard.

Phoebe and her mother trailed behind, so that on reaching the top the two men had a few moments' head start. Walking on, they soon reached a rocky promontory from where you could see the river bend flanked by trees, a plunge of more than two hundred feet. Beyond the river there were fields and farmsteads and winter-naked copses and still further on, the lofty wilderness of the fell, above which a barrier of dark cloud was massing.

'This spot,' said Rupert, 'is known as Percy Myre Rock. It is believed that the last of the medieval Fitzhughs, Lord of Cotherstone Castle, fell to his death with his horse from here. By all accounts he was a nasty piece of work.'

'A shame about the horse,' said Titus, who was still breathing hard from the climb.

A group of merry walkers came towards them. They exchanged greetings and moved on to do the same with Mary and Phoebe, who were drawing near. They didn't join the two men but hung back within earshot, talking to each other. Thus Phoebe was able to hear her father say apropos nothing, as it seemed: 'Excess appalls me, you know, even in nature. I've always felt morally ill at ease with people who have too much of anything . . .'

Titus made no reply but looked in the direction of the walkers who had now reached the edge of the wood and were queuing to pass through the stile. There was a wistful look on his face such as Phoebe had never seen before.

Following Titus's gaze, Rupert Whelan observed, 'Local folks and friends. You meet them out walking on Boxing Day as you do in church and in the village throughout the year. Some of them you've known way back from your childhood. You know them and their habits as intuitively as you know the land round about. Spots where you've played with schoolmates. Nooks in rocks by the river where your parents hid things for you to find.'

Titus turned to give Rupert a momentarily penetrating look. Phoebe saw it, and a vague but intense anxiety gripped her.

'Yes,' Rupert went on, smiling at Titus, 'my roots run deep in this region; So do Mary's. Her people are from Ripon, about thirty miles to the south. My parents were hill farmers not far from here. We were a large family. At times we only just made do. The only things we always had in ample supply were love, fun, and faith.

'I was lucky to have got into a grammar school. Luckier still, and delighted to have won a scholarship to Oxford. But I've never been very ambitious. Not in the service of the Church, anyway. I never wanted to be anything other than a rector in this part of England.'

'Is that so?' said Titus.

'Yes, absolutely. Mind you, many years ago, I did consider joining a mission in Africa, but after a week I decided – probably arrogantly – that spreading the Gospel the missionary way was contrary to God's design,' said Rupert with a self-deprecatory twinkle in his eye.

'What is God's design, in your view?'

Rupert laughed. 'God knows. Maybe just being nice. Helping others to be the same. Helping others in general. I can't think of a better purpose for religion, can you?'

'I haven't given much thought to religion, I must say.'

'Ah,' said Rupert, adding after a long pause, 'I'll tell you one thing without, I hope, sounding self-congratulatory which I'm not. If I've ever succeeded being what I set out to be, it's chiefly because I've never lost sense of where I belong and where my priorities lie . . . And, of course, because I have been lucky to be partnered by someone who is very different to me yet at the same time fundamentally similar. You see, I do believe

149

that diversity enriches only up to a point. Not limitlessly. And beyond that point, it creates disharmony.'

'Dad,' Phoebe called out, 'shouldn't we be turning back?'

When they reached the village Titus excused himself and went into the inn saying he would join them shortly for lunch.

'I hope the walk hasn't tired him,' Rupert Whelan said over a glass of mulled wine by the hearth.

'Of course it hasn't. Don't make a geriatric of him, Dad.'

'I honestly don't know what to make of him, love. I don't think I ever met anyone like him.'

'Because there isn't anyone like him,' said Phoebe crossly. 'I mean, it's hard if not impossible to apply normal categories to someone like Titus. That's why you don't understand him. I'm not sure I do.'

'Oh, I see . . .'

'Sorry, Dad, I didn't mean to snap . . .'

'I think he's a very lonely man,' Mary said, in a way which sounded like a dismissal, albeit compassionate.

Phoebe had sensed Titus's loneliness before, yet for all the love she felt for him, for all the will to assuage his loneliness, she could never convince herself that it was a disadvantage he suffered from, let alone an affliction. And anyway, how could she assuage something she didn't understand? But this morning she did at last, or so she thought when she saw that look on his face as he stood listening to her father by Percy Myre Rock. She actually believed his secret vulnerability was, for a flicker, exposed to the raw air, not so much by what her father had been saying as by the ordinary encounter with the jolly walkers.

Looking at her parents, she remembered Titus telling her once – she couldn't remember in what context – that goodness, like deafness, wasn't uniform but came in peaks and troughs.

'I think he's here, Rupert,' said Mary. And Rupert got up to open the door.

After lunch Titus suddenly announced that he had decided and arranged to fly back to London from Newcastle Airport later in the afternoon.

'Why?' Phoebe asked as she walked with him back to the Rose and Crown.

He shrugged his shoulders and said, 'Because,' adding, 'You needn't drive me to the airport, I'll order a taxi.'

'I want to drive you to the airport.'

'The weather is turning.'

'Doesn't matter. Was it awful?'

'Of course not. Your parents are very nice. I like them. Thank them again for me for a wonderful . . .'

'Oh, stop it, for Christ's sake,' she said.

He put his hand on her cheek and smiled.

'I was right. You shouldn't have come. We should have gone to Switzerland, like you wanted.'

'Let's pretend we did,' he said.

Past Durham and on the A1 to Newcastle, it began to snow.

'Well, I'll be damned,' Titus said.

'You owe me a hundred pounds,' said Phoebe.

He told her when she returned to London that on another sudden caprice he had flown direct from Newcastle to the Christmas-card setting of St. Moritz for an impromptu reunion with Wanda and Theo.

12

T I T U S

'Titus, just think what marvellous stories you could tell your grandchildren!'

A very English lady, with whom I once had a brief, relaxed affair, said that to me. Placidly intelligent in the manner of her class, her passion was only implicit in her love-making. But she became warmly explicit whenever she talked about children – grandchildren in particular. We were both in the grandparents' age group at the time. She had several grandchildren; I had none that I knew of.

I remember her with much affection. And her urging me to tell my story. Well, why not? If Theo could write and publish letters to imaginary grandchildren, why can't I privately spin my life's tales to descendants who might, plausibly, exist? And I'm lucky to possess a perfect vessel for my story-telling: Charon!

Charon is a machine. A super-futuristic computer, more than state-of-the-art technology; without too much exaggeration, I might say a prophecy on man-made intelligence realised a generation or two ahead of its time. I refer to Charon as he; we've developed a personal relationship, Charon and I.

In addition to storing all of Alston Group International's data, down to the last consignment of coffee for office use, Charon can access into vast information resources worldwide, analyse market trends at the blink of an eye, produce company development models and investment plans of mind-boggling sophistication, translate into and out of seven different languages, minute meetings, take care of salaries and company bills, regulate the heating, fire alarm and security locks in the entire building . . . The list of what he does is staggering. With-

152

out Charon, the Alston Group operations would grind to a halt, globally, within a matter of hours.

It actually happened once, during Charon's teeth-cutting infancy. Don Proud, the American genius who created him, administered first aid by telephone. Then he flew in from L.A. with a team of technologists. A day later Charon was restored to full power. It cost us a clean $1 million but Charon never faltered since.

Don Proud built Charon, and wrote a successful book about him. But I imagined him in the course of seven sleepless nights. Then I commissioned Proud – reigning computer supremo of the world and Californian guru of the future – to put flesh and bones, so to speak, on my conception.

Charon lives in a specially designed habitation on the thirteenth floor of the Alston Group International building in St James's Street, London. I have named his room 'The Sacred Sanctuary' – 'Sanctum' for short.

I hardly attend board meetings any more. Nor do I make many executive decisions. This is done by my chief lieutenant and appointed heir, John Lefebre, who passes me his decisions for approval. I'm the superannuated constitutional monarch of the Alston Group, whom all revere but whose demise they nevertheless impatiently await so that they may get on with turning the company into a presidential business republic under John Lefebre.

So I spend many hours – day and night – here in Sanctum, with Charon as my sole companion. Do you know many people who have by their own volition and design abdicated power? I'm one of them. Without regret and *sans* remorse.

For the pleasure I get from Charon, and for all this superfluity of time I've not been accustomed to, I have to thank Don Proud once more.

'Here's a little computer game I've designed for you, Titus, to amuse you,' he had said in his donnish self-effacing manner.

The game is a kind of intellectual literary valet service: as I talk to Charon, he takes down what I say and edits it with supreme competence. When I command recall, I may choose between monitor display, hard copy, or vocal output of which Charon has a selection of five. My favourite is a synthesised

153

impersonation of John Gielgud. I key in the command and at once the passage in question is read back to me. As I listen I think in wonder: Did I really say this? Hey, maybe I'm not such a crusty old dragon after all!

The most important thing about Don Proud's gift – all the kinder for being unsolicited and unrewarded – is that it is invincibly private. Only I have access into this file. Never will anybody else be able to hack into it, because if ever the first barrier against unauthorised intrusion is overcome, the second is instant and irrevocable erasure of the entire programme's contents. Don Proud had sworn on that.

In truth, I never as much as contemplated recording my life's story until I was seduced by Charon, my discreet, unobtrusive amanuensis and editor. Then one morning I remembered my well-born English lady love and thought, Shouldn't I? For the sake of understanding myself better? So that I may be able to balance the good things I've done against the dreadful misdeeds and see if, at the end of my days, I may close the account in credit rather than in debit?

I'm not a philosopher like Theo. Rather, I'm the kind of man who makes things happen . . . Or did, once upon a time.

'Once upon a time' is a good way to begin my story, for it conceals a reality of terror in the coming, with the gentle assurance of a fairy tale. However, I'd like to preface the beginning with an apologia of a sort.

I've been called ruthless, manipulator. It has been said that luck and cunning rather than moral probity have kept me on the right side of the law, and only just, at that. I'll not waste time refuting all that humbug. Is there a power on earth that is managed by angels, I ask?

A business is a living organism. It has brains and muscle and instincts and appetites, but it has no soul. You create it; you nurture and protect it through its early vulnerable phase of life. Then it moves on, devouring and excreting, creating and destroying, getting larger or diminishing, until it falls prey to other businesses. The bigger the business, the less influence you, its creator, personally have on its progress. This is a fact of life that tycoons conceal even from themselves, because they fear impotence above all else.

If my career has demonstrated anything at all, it's simply that the pure quest – the fun and danger of the game – can be as strong a motive as greed in the creation of wealth.

And my contribution to business evolution? Call it Boardroom Darwinism. From 1960 – when I headed the admittance queue into that exclusive club of top international financiers – and on, I set a live or die rule to all who worked for me: Take risks, but win! No remission for failure and no protection in dull cautiousness. Everybody was on his toes day and night. Only the very best survived. Well? Isn't that good? Is Nature more merciful?

As a player – that's essentially how I've always seen myself – I gasp with incredulity as I look back on my life. Not because of what I've achieved, but because my good luck has been so perversely consistent: the more outrageously I defied the odds, the closer I edged towards a fall, the more munificently I was rewarded. Fate has stood at my side and whispered, 'I'm overriding your self-destructive impulses. Win, until I choose to end your run of luck.'

I haven't been hearing Fate's whispering for sometime. Not since I relinquished power; not since I began – despite myself – to love Phoebe. I know that Fate, a cunning auditor, will be merciless when it calls to settle the account.

'Sanctum' is dominated by Charon's presence. His electronic eye glints; his muted hum pulsates against a silence encapsulated by yards of plate-glass windows through which you see bird's-eye vistas of London. Here is the contraption I sit in, more versatile than a dentist's chair. Control buttons on its arm rests will raise or lower me; sit me upright or in a reclining position; turn me to face St Paul's Cathedral or the opaque shimmer of the hidden Thames by Westminster.

There's also a mock Jacobean cupboard – incongruous but functional – containing a few souvenirs from my past: a time-yellowed copy of *War and Peace* in Russian, a Czech-made Mauser pistol with three empty clips, and a Tartar bow with five steelheaded arrows in a horseskin quiver – a gift from the Soviet governor of Uzbekskaya. A composite of horn and wood glued together, then bound tightly with treated twine, the bow

155

is a lethal weapon of immaculate craftsmanship. In the hands of an expert archer its arrows will penetrate body armour and kill from a distance of a hundred metres.

When I am inside 'Sanctum', a red light glows outside above the door, to warn against intrusion. Phoebe has nicknamed 'Sanctum' Titus's Cryonic Sepulchre. She hates the place.

Adjacent to 'Sanctum' is the Alston Group Conference Room. Once it was starkly functional. I had ordained simplicity, to reflect the Group's image, as I saw it: muscular no-nonsense business, without distractions. I know that behind my back they used to whisper, 'The old ogre is murderously irritable. Avoid waffle like the plague. If you can't put an idea across in five minutes flat, forget it, it won't be listened to, let alone considered.'

Things have changed since John Lefebre became Chief Executive. The room has been redecorated and refurnished. Now it is cluttered with modern art which John describes as investment.

Incidentally, a few years back, I renamed the Conference Room 'Sanhedrin', after the law-giving Jewish council of rabbis in the days of the Talmud. And those who attend it – my eighteen-strong team of top executives – Sanhedrists. When the word got out, the Alston Group's equities dropped on all the world's main stock markets, only to bounce back a week later a few points above their former value. Curiously, the only two Sanhedrists who dared to object were Jewish. I promptly sacked them.

Several Jewish Zionist organisations from various parts of the world approached the Group for donations. I said, 'Not a bagel!' A mooted proposal to plant a forest in Israel bearing my name was dropped.

The Alston Group logo, a minutely slanting elliptical white ring against Oxford blue background, heads our stationery and proudly flutters from a mast on the top of the building, next to a helicopter landing platform that never became operational. Various interpretations have been forced on it, most of them irreverent: anal-retentive fantasy; collapsing zero; the gape of a sodomised Cheshire cat; the disembodied mouth of the Norwegian painter Edvard Munch's celebrated painting *The*
156

Scream, to list a few. In truth, it's no more than a stylised bagel. I designed it myself, as tribute to the humble matrix of the mighty Alston Group International, about which only Theo knows.

Detractors have put it about that funds of disreputable provenance are at the foundation of the Alston Group. I've been implicitly accused of selling defective armament to a number of dubious regimes in Africa and Latin American. But if the regimes in question were dubious and the weaponry I've allegedly provided defective, does it not follow that I had done a good thing? It was rumoured that I made a fortune laundering money for criminal organisations. What organisations? How? When?

Then there were speculations that I had been on the KGB payroll for years. Huh! If you could get rich on that there would be more millionaires in Whitehall and the City than there are beggars in Calcutta.

My lucrative contacts with the Soviet Union have all been above board. Also, they were established only after the Alston Group became a financial force to reckon with, not before. Moreover, they have served a wider range of interests than my own, that's an acknowledged fact.

The truth about the Alston Group is that it was conceived in the metaphorical womb of a ring of baked dough in North London.

I came to London from Paris in the spring of 1953. Wars were raging in Korea and in Indochina. Tension was mounting in Berlin. A craze of murderous persecution in the Soviet Union had come to a halt with the sudden death of Stalin, ushering in an interlude of suspenseful uncertainty And in the UK? The economy was picking up a mere step behind the faster moving national confidence. A popular radio programme called *The Goon Show* regaled the public with a zany cocktail of the absurd in the best tradition of English eccentricity. I laughed like I'd never laughed before.

Standing amidst the cheering crowd in Whitehall, on 2 June, I watched the coronation procession roll past back to Buckingham Palace from Westminster. The young Elizabeth II in the Golden Coach waved to the multitudes, who went wild with

157

joy, on a day of pageant recalling an imperial glory long since departed. I said to myself, 'Here is a country of grand illusions, and pleasant manners, and humour that isn't bitter. Shouldn't I settle down here?'

I had arrived with £100 in my pocket and a pretty Russian icon in my suitcase. I rented a bed-sitter not far from Finchley Road. It had a tiny gas fire which would light only after you had slotted a shilling coin into it. I hate this kind of petty meanness. In less than an hour I devised an undetectable way of cheating the mechanism – my first un-British act.

I took my icon to Christie's. They evaluated it at £120. It realised twice that amount at the auction. I visited the English Tourist Board Office.

'Where are the best, most exclusive casinos in this town?' I inquired.

'Casinos? There are clubs, sir. In Mayfair, mostly. One has to be a member,' the woman official explained, and showed me on the map.

Money is membership, that much I knew. Unlike the continental gambling places, where the reckless anonymities of wealth and desperateness play side by side, these were clubs, like the lady said. I started with the less exclusive and graduated upwards. A fortnight later I was £13,900 richer, and had my first introduction to the English class system. Then a chance encounter made me take my first small but telling step towards tycoonery.

Walking along Finchley Road one afternoon, I stopped absent-mindedly by a pastry shop called Finkelstein's Nosh. It had a rundown look about it but the goods in the window were appetising and I was mildly hungry. The shop assistant was busy moulding into shape a heap of bagels in the window beneath a sign that read 'Can you inveigle a bagel?' She had glossy brown hair, rosy cheeks – not from cosmetics, I could tell – large blue eyes and a massive bust. Since she was otherwise slim, that voluptuous exaggeration of curves made her resemble one of those overblown beauties you see in humorously salacious comics. She looked up, smiled, and gave me a slow wink. I went in. There was no one else in the shop.

'Are they good?' I asked, nodding at the bagels.

'The best there are,' she replied.

'How can you tell?'

'I made them myself. And what I don't know about bagels isn't worth knowing. Take it from me.'

I liked her friendly self-assurance. I bought two. While she was putting my bagels in a paper bag, I said, 'What does "inveigle" mean?'

'To tempt, more or less.'

'Could I, then, inveigle you to have dinner with me?'

'Cheeky, aren't you?' She laughed, brandishing a hand with a very conspicuous wedding ring. 'Can't you see I'm a respectable married woman?'

She came that evening all the same. I took her out to a small Italian place in Swiss Cottage. Her name was Madeline Lesser. Her husband had taken off and disappeared ten months ago, she said. 'Good riddance to him. Best thing that ever happened to me.' Her very words. She said she came from Leeds.

I said, 'I've heard of Kyoto, Isfahan, Pensacola, even Birmingham. Where the hell is Leeds?'

She laughed so loudly people were beginning to stare.

At close quarters, she looked older than she did at first glance, in the shop. But wearing a wine-red dress with a cleavage so deep you could lose a howitzer in it, she was sensational. I told her so.

'Really?' she said, like a stock response to a familiar gambit.

'Absolutely. In the same class as *Swan Lake*, Rolls-Royce, and Niagara Falls.'

'You foreigners say such wild things,' said Madeline with a sidelong glance that didn't conceal an invitation.

The next morning, over breakfast of tea and buttered bagels in her small but neat home in Crouch End, Madeline confided how hopelessly incompetent her boss, Solly Finkelstein, was. If it weren't for the fact that she herself virtually ran the shop single-handed, Finkelstein would have gone bankrupt long ago. He was depressive, lazy, and up to his eyebrows in bad debts. He would sell out tomorrow if he could only find a buyer.

'You're right about the bagels. They're terrific. Maybe I should buy the shop,' I said in half jest.

159

'You could have it for a song and all,' she said with down-turned mouth.

'I'll think about it.'

She ran a finger down my wrist. 'How long?' she purred.

'For as long as I can hold my breath.'

I pulled her round the table, sat her astride my lap, and opening the front of her dressing gown, sank my face between her warm enormous tits. When I came up for air I announced that I would bid for Finkelstein's Nosh.

I bought the shop lock, stock, and barrel for six and a half thousand. I had it redecorated and re-equipped. And I renamed it 'Bewitched, Bothered and Inbageled' – an adaptation from the song. I hired two more pretty girls and promoted Madeline to manageress.

'Don't wear those boring white aprons. Wear the dress you wore the night we went out,' I instructed. 'And if I ever catch you dining out with a customer, I'll cut you off without a shilling!'

Can you believe it? 'Inbageled' became the rage of North London! Jew and gentile were guzzling our bagels like they came piping hot straight from Belshazzar's Feast. Hotels were ordering them by the hundredweight. Never before or since, anywhere in the world as far as I know, had the simple Jewish bagel attained such a status as a fashionable object of culinary desire. Within ten months Inbageled was raking in higher profits than I could dream of.

I had become a dab hand at playing on the London shares market. I rented the property adjacent to the bagel shop, fitted it out as an office and, using Inbageled as a collateral for a loan, created the Hermes round-the-clock motorcycle courier service – the first ever in London, I believe. An auspicious contract with a City merchant bank, leading to more, and eventually to one with Whitehall, ensured that Hermes went from strength to strength.

Then, when I was just about ready, came the first big break. An official in the aforementioned merchant bank, whom I befriended, informed me that a certain small but up-market Surrey-based electronic firm called Mallard Automation would shortly be up for grabs. The firm was starved of investment and had been poorly managed. But the work team was young and creative and automation was in the fast lane to the future. It would be the bargain of a lifetime, opined my contact.

I needed no persuading. First I transferred to London all the money from my locked but not forgotten Swiss bank account. Then, after night-long deliberation, I sold both the bagel shop and Hermes, but not before offering them both as collateral securities for the biggest bank loan I could get, from the same merchant bank, as it happened. Then I bought Mallard Automation the very moment it came on the market, outbidding no less than a dozen competitors.

The coup was achieved in two hectic days, with the help of certain sharp and not strictly kosher practice by a clever lawyer and his accountant partner. Mallard Automation, which eventually disappeared forever, was the direct progenitor of the Alston Group.

Barely three years after arriving in London I was a millionaire, playing audaciously but skilfully with serious money, for ever-rising stakes, on the high finance playing tables of the world.

It's early morning in Sanctum. Outside and below, London stirs in the crepuscular light of dawn. I make myself a cup of strong black Russian tea, which I imbibe through a lump of sugar in my mouth, like Pugachev used to do in the old days when, hearing him suck at his tea, the horses, tethered a stone-throw away, would prick up their ears. I sit in my chair and wake Charon from his watchful slumber by keying in a code to access my secret file. A message flashes on the monitor screen: *Guai a voi, anima prave!*

I key in: *Per me si va nella città dolente;*
            per me si va nell' eterno dolore;
            per me si va tra la perduta gente.

Charon responds with: *Lasciate ogni speranza, voi ch' entrate.*

The verse is from Dante's *Inferno*, Canto III. Don Proud's erudite black humour. For in addition to being the world Numero Uno in computer hardware and software design, Proud was a Classics and Renaissance scholar of renown. Alas, poor Proud is no more. He had married a former student,

161

twenty years his junior, and as the young bride gazed in wonder at the Grand Canyon, announcing innocently that it gave her spiritual orgasm, Proud returned to their honeymoon hotel suite and shot his brains out. They suggested at the inquest that her remark brought home to him a fatal flaw in his character: he could never settle for anything less than perfect.

One more coded pass number, and Charon is ready at my service. Let me, then, begin at the beginning . . .

13

I myself chose Titus for a name. It followed the first independent decision I ever made, which was to run away from the Tree of Life Jewish orphanage where, as a foundling, I had been deposited nearly thirteen years earlier. The decision to flee was a negation without reason: out of a pubescent erotic dream surfaced a big No demanding satisfaction. What else could I do but escape?

Titus in my case wasn't a tribute to the noble Flavius Sabinus Vespasianus Titus, conqueror of Jerusalem, scourge of the Jews, and Caesar. I named myself after a dog. A large grey dun wolf-like creature with slanting amber eyes, it hung around the orphanage and chose me, of all others, for a friend. The last I remember of him was his cocking a leg against a heap of rubbish before vanishing from my life. My Roman connection, if that isn't stretching a point, is slenderly symbolic: the orphans Remus and Romulus were nurtured by a she-wolf and grew up to found the mighty Roman Empire. I, befriended by a dog of obvious wolfish ancestry whose loyalty sustained me through some of my hardest moments, survived to found the Alston Group.

In England, once I became respectably rich, I adopted an English surname. Let's face it, a name isn't what you *are*, it's like the clothes you wear, and it has to suit the rôle you choose. I sat in my rented furnished flat in Lowndes Square, London SW1, and pondered over the problem. The owner of the flat, an eminent English traveller, had a purpose-built chess board mounted on a swivel, so that he could spin it round when playing against himself, which was apparently his main preoccupation when not travelling. I placed an AA map of England on this idiosyncratic piece of furniture, gave it a twirl, then brought a pencil down on the map. It hit Alston, a small town in the Pennines whose sole distinction, it seemed, was to be the highest market town in England, annually cut off from the rest of the world with the first heavy snowfall. Moreover, it almost resembled my own former name – itself borrowed, though not by me. I never visited the market town Alston. Phoebe told me it's a pretty, friendly place, where sheep graze all around, and favoured by tourists.

I was born in Odessa. That is the only certain detail in my coming to the world, and the fact that I was discovered by two pissed down-and-outs, lying in the frozen yard of a deserted house in one of the less salubrious parts of town where poor Jews lived. If they hadn't been stone drunk, Ovrom the janitor said, for it was he who took delivery of me, those two would have as soon as not, eaten me from the look of them.

Why the Etz Hachayim orphanage? Because on unwinding my dirty swaddling clothes my humble redeemers beheld my little willy, swollen blue from recent circumcision, and figured I would be worth a bowl of soup each at the nearby Jewish orphanage. What they got, said Ovrom, was a kick up the backside to send them on their way. I ask you, if there were a just God, would He not have afflicted the pious Ovrom for that humiliating rate of exchange?

My birth certificate, too, is once removed from the real circumstances of my birth. A male infant had died, having lived but for two days. Improvised details of my identity were filled in on the document intended for him: Tevya Abramov Altermann. It was signed by Rabbi Mordechai Semionovich Laskov. Tevya, in Hebrew 'God's bounty', reflects irrational Jewish optimism. Abramov is a derivative of Abraham, ancestor of all Hebrews. Altermann was the name of a destitute teacher at the orphanage who had died quietly on the premises barely a month before I arrived.

Since the estimated date of my birth coincided with that of the Christian Saviour according to the Georgian calendar, they wrote down the Hebrew date that fell on 30 December 1903, a narrow but safe margin.

Of all the fraudulence that occurred in my life, in this the

164

first at least I was an innocent victim, an unconsenting accomplice.

I must have been an exceptionally robust infant to have survived such a beginning. Nevertheless I certainly would have starved to death even in the orphanage, were it not for Lara Ismaelova Kagan, the orphanage's washerwoman who fostered me. Lara's mother was a Don Cossack Christian. Her father was an Uzbek Moslem. Lara herself, converted, lived with a Jewish peddler on the outskirts of town, mothering children at yearly intervals. I drank her milk and lived. From Lara I learnt my first Russian words.

I don't remember her children, my foster brothers and sisters. In years to come I would think of them, wondering whether unknowingly I may have met them . . . fought alongside some? Killed others?

An English friend once asked me why I returned to Russia on the eve of Hitler's invasion, knowing what awaited me there. I replied, because there was nowhere else to go. Because there are times in life – mercifully few – when past illusions return to outweigh remembered and expected suffering. Because if I had a mother, a father, a brother or a sister alive, they were in Russia. Because an intimate language of my subconsciousness summoned me there. What else does one fight for? I searched for Lara, by the way. She was gone. So was the Tree of Life orphanage.

Say I'm Jewish in blood. From Lara I imbibed milk of Christian and Moslem loving-kindness. That makes me ethnically ecumenical, I suppose, no? Since my Jewish pedigree is questionable, put it down to mongrel vigour: I was an attractive child. Quick to learn, adaptable, strong. No bully pushed Tevya Abramov Altermann around. Among my peers, I called the shots.

But a more rigorous authority in Etz Hachayim was superimposed upon the hierarchy of natural merit. My lowly status as a foundling denied me sponsors. I got no presents in the Holy Days from some benevolent warm-hearted Jewish family. During the Feast of Passover I stayed at the orphanage while other children were invited to homes. Books were in short supply, often only one shared among the class. It wasn't in

165

acknowledgement of my precocity that I was always seated facing the book the wrong way up. Thus I acquired the far from useless facility of reading upside-down print.

But against all that, I had Lara. So, in retrospect, I consider myself lucky. I remember her placid tenderness, the laughter bubbling from her depth; the silence of her reproach. How often I dreamed she was my real mother. And when I abandoned her to seek my fortune, I told myself it didn't matter, that she was too weary to grieve over me anyway. Even as a child I could rationalise cruelty.

Don't imagine I ran away because I had a hard time. Things weren't that bad for me in Etz Hachayim. I never went hungry for a start, as I did on many days and nights later in my precarious freedom. Bar mitzvah was at hand. A few possessions had come my way ahead of schedule – a prayer shawl, phylacteries and a *sidur* from Rabbi Mordechai Semionovich Laskov, a warm soldier's coat from Lara restored by her skilful hands, a pair of boots and a winter hat – things to stir the nomad in me?

The passage from the bible I was to recite at my bar mitzvah, which I was learning by rote, was full of Yahweh jealously smiting all enemies in sight hip and thigh, against a background of stony pastoral wilderness. I don't remember much of the passage; I didn't stay to have bar mitzvah. I recall with equal obscurity random reading. Seed spilt. Proliferating. The arbitrary balance thereof of wrongdoings and reward. And one simple message like the sound of a reed pipe out of nothingness: God's first marching orders to the father of all nomads, Abraham.

It's pitch-dark in our dormitory, and freezing cold. On the mattress next to mine sleeps Misha. A half-wit, he wets his bed and often cries at night. And when he doesn't cry he snores, as he's doing now. They've put him next to me because I protect him from the others, although at times I too give him a good wallop with a pillow, when his snoring gets too loud. I won't thump him tonight. I have a more urgent imperative: the great escape, in preparation for which I lie cock in hand, conjuring visions I'd never seen – hips, thighs, tits. Hot sperm hits my face. I'm a man! Ready to go, Lord.

Lying curled up against the wall, Titus raises his head to greet me with a lupine smile. Man and dog set out across the dawn-lit snow.

Odessa isn't really Russia. Call it Alexandria on the Black Sea, if you like. A hybrid city full of cafés, hotels and foreign restaurants, Odessa was proudly cosmopolitan long before the word took on an unpleasant connotation. In Odessa you find French, English, Germans, Italians, Tartars, Uzbeks, Armenians . . . above all, Jews. But the Russian spirit halts some distance away to look longingly towards Moscow.

Icicles stab down from the eaves of houses. There's snow in the streets, rutted by the runners of horse-driven *drozhkas*. A dark luminosity of sky squats over the inky water of the harbour below the city. I register such details for the first time with a kind of excited apprehension. For I'm not merely a runaway orphan. On the way out I stole Ovrom's six-inch clasp knife and a hunk of black bread. I'm an armed thief on the way to Moscow! Where is Moscow? Somewhere far away. How will I get there? I don't know, I'll find a way. I'm not afraid, you see, not really. I'm a tough, smart kid. There's a knife in my coat's pocket and a large dog at my side.

At a Jew's junk shop I trade Rabbi Laskov's bar mitzvah gifts for a tattered knapsack and a few kopeks. I buy myself a steaming mug of sweet black tea from a street vendor, and a chunk of decidedly unkosher sausage from which I slice two pieces, one for me, one for Titus.

A train is standing at the station, steam billowing from under the engine's wheels. Soldiers everywhere. They have lit a fire. A samovar is propped over the red embers. One of the soldiers is playing a balalaika and singing. Some are playing *gorodki*, throwing sticks across a stretch of snow. Their rifles are stacked in pyramids.

We've heard of the war at the orphanage. We've heard how the Imperial Army has been taking a beating all the way across Poland. But you wouldn't think so looking at these lot. They look sloppy, mischievously indolent, but not beaten.

Titus sits down. I can tell he isn't happy here.

'C'mon Titus,' I plead. He won't budge, just sits there, head

167

cocked to one side, looking at me as if to say, 'This is where we part company. Take care.'

As I watch him trot away, leaving me, the full meaning of what I had done sinks in. I'm no longer a smart, tough kid, let alone a man. I am nothing. Nobody. Alone with nowhere to go. If I turned back there would be a mean-looking angel – like Ovrom – with a flaming sword of something, barring my return to the Tree of Life.

'Hey, sonny, what's the matter? Why are you crying?'

It's one of the soldiers sitting with the balalaika player, a big fellow with a red face and little pale eyes close together bracketing a small blob of a nose.

'I'm not crying.' I tighten my mouth so as not to blubber.

'What's the matter? Your mutt's gone and left you?'

'It wasn't my dog. He followed me for a bit, that all. And he's no mutt.'

'Really? What is he then, a fucking dragon? Come here. Don't be afraid. You want some hot *chai*?' He points at the samovar. I nod. I could do with something hot in my belly.

More of the soldiers now show interest. They are bored. In their idleness they have become like boys, no longer grown men.

'So what are you doing here? Run away from home? Your daddy belted you too hard?' the red-faced soldier asks.

'I have no home and I don't have a daddy either.' The tea has restored some of my confidence. 'I'm going to Moscow.'

'That elicits a great roar of laughter.

'How old are you, sonny?'

'Fifteen.'

'Fifteen, eh? Hear that, fellows? The *durak* says he's fifteen. Like I'm eighty. What do you want to go to Moscow for? Haven't you heard they eat rats there?'

'I'll be a soldier. With the Guards.'

'You don't want to go to Moscow *durakchik*. You come with us. We're better than any Guards, aren't we, boys?'

'Yeah . . .'

'What's your name, sonny?'

'Titus,' I reply.

168

'We had a little pig called Titus. He was our mascot, until we ate him. You want to be our mascot?'

War is something that's happening far away. Now to the west, now to the north, War plays hide and seek with us. I see things they tell me War had done. But the *real* thing, where is it? They call War she. Mother Russia is gentle and plump and smelling of onions, like Lara. War is a tall thin crone, grinning like a bear trap.

The train chugs across snow-covered land, past woods and frozen rivers towards Kiev. Eventually we'll reach Kursk where General Anton Ivanovich Denikin has his headquarters. There's no hurry: War has broken Time to bits. Wherever the train stops, peasants swarm to it hawking potatoes, black bread, the ubiquitous gruel – *schi* – which they ladle out of blackened pots. Then there are the beggars, with hands extended, broken smiles, empty eyes. Bloody *schi*! Day in day out, that's what we eat. It runs in Mother Russia's veins.

I clean the rifles. I sew buttons on coats. I run errands the length of the train. I learn bawdy songs and how to cheat at cards. 'Tatya,' says Corporal Lyova Ilyich, 'remember this. Soldiers eat like pigs, fuck like dogs, die like flies. That's a soldier's life for you.'

They tell me, my comrades: 'Eat your *schi*, Tatya, and you'll grow bigger, make good cannon fodder.' They tell me: 'Look at Russia, how pale she is from so much bleeding. Just as well you don't have a mother to weep over you.' They tell me that in Moscow, Voronezh, Kiev, people eat dogs, cats, crows, anything. Some would burn their mother's icon for a moment of warmth. And I'm glad Titus the dog is safe in Odessa, at the orphanage, where they'd sooner starve to death than eat him.

I listen to soldier's talk. Things have gone from bad to worse, they say, since the Tsar kicked out Grand Duke Nicholas and personally took command of the army. Now he sits in Mogilev not knowing what to do, while the Germans pound us to a paste. Only Rasputin could put an end to all this senseless carnage. Oh no. *Bozhemoy*, dear *Gospedyn*! Such talk is blasphemy . . .

'C'mon, lads, remember last summer, how General Brusilov

beat the enemy in Lutsk? In spring, we'll do it again, this time all the way, to the end.'

But there are no guns! No bullets! So what? We have men. Yes, to pick up the rifles from the dead and die in turn. When the Tula munition factories grind to a halt Russian mothers will go on pumping out baby sons to fill the ranks.

'Dear God, I could puke from all that *schi*! I want meat.'

Chug chug chug whoooeeee. . . .

They've heard soldiers were deserting in droves. General Kornilov? He was running out of trees from which to hang deserters! Quiet! What's the matter with you lot? Taken leave of your senses? Don't you know Okhrana secret police have ears everywhere? We'll all end up in Siberia.

'Not you, Tatya. It'll be a monastery for you. *Schi* and bread for the rest of your life. Keep away from Yefim Igorevich at night, or he'll bugger you to hell.'

This calm obliging boy Tatya is a necessary guise. Even the Angel of Death, *Maloch hamoves*, looks like a respectable rural court clerk going about his business. As a mascot, I was a failure. It simply wasn't my destiny to be one. I am an agent of Fate's caprice, if anything; of the spirit which evermore denies. When I think about it, throughout my life all my gifts have been preceded by a denial of some sort.

The train pulls into Kiev on its last gasp of steam. There are troops in the station, and they surround the train the moment it stops. They look tense, unfriendly, holding their rifles at the ready. The commander, a tall major with a beard like a slab of granite, wears a coat down to the tops of his shiny boots, and an untidy black astrakhan hat. His hand rests casually on the butt of his pistol above the holster strapped round his waist. My first encounter with Cossacks?

There is sporadic gunfire in the distance. It draws closer, then recedes, then gets nearer again. When we step onto the platform, as ordered, we can see smoke rising in places above the houses. Has the War lunged into Kiev? No, it can't be, asserts Lyova Ilyich. More likely Cossacks up to something. Who can tell who's mutinying against whom nowadays? Safer not to ask questions.

'Who's in charge here?' bellows the major.

Our commander steps forward. All eyes are on him. I sense he is not being treated with the courtesy due to his rank. That must be bad news for the entire unit. After a short terse conference with the major, the men are ordered to set down their weapons in a pile on the platform and line up some distance away. That done, the major tells us that the regiment we were to augment has deserted rank and file. We are to be redeployed elsewhere. Meanwhile, we shall be quartered on the outskirts of town until it is decided what is to be done with us. I hear whispers about deportation and executions. Nobody moves.

Except Yefim Igorevich the sodomite, who goes crazy. Throwing his arms in the air, he bolts. The men watch in silence as Yefim springs across the snow, pursued by a whole section of soldiers. They don't shoot at him. Nor do they shout at him to stop. When they catch up with him, they knock him down and stand over him beating him all over with their rifles. But Yefim won't die. Even though his blood stains the snow and his face is a mess of raw meat, he struggles to his feet and staggers forward, only to be knocked down again. And he isn't even a big strong man. Who could imagine Yefim had so much blood in him! All the while the major doesn't utter a word, doesn't even look. When it is over, when Yefim lies lifeless in the bloody snow, he says, 'Well now, shall we get on with things, or does somebody else here wish to die?'

My erstwhile comrades stand stony-faced. No one as much as looks in my direction. Unnoticed, I slip between two carriages and away, into the city, to begin a brief phase of scavenging.

When I heard of Rasputin's murder, I thought again of Yefim Igorevich. He wasn't a bad fellow, not really. He had a *babushka* in his home village whom he wanted to see before the war killed him. Such obstinacy to live. Like Rasputin. They said Prince Yusupov and his friends poisoned him, shot him ten times, bludgeoned him, then threw him in the River Neva, and still Rasputin wouldn't die. Perhaps they were relatives, Yefim Igorevich and the *starets* Rasputin: both Russian through and through, with a special gift for bleeding.

171

Kiev is choked with cavalry. The horsemen ride to and fro; they loiter everywhere, lighting fires with smashed furniture in open spaces. Sometimes they shoot just for fun. Everybody else keeps well out of their way. Horseshit and fear fill the streets.

I look at the little sparrows and ask myself, 'If they can survive, why not me?'

I found a piece of felt in a heap of rubbish, and a stained copy of Tolstoy's *War and Peace*. I tore the felt to strips which I wrapped round my feet inside my boots and up my calves. The book I put in my coat's pocket. I found a sheltered space at the back of a house where I could curl up to sleep. Only hunger kept me awake. I tried to steal from a baker's shop but lost my nerve. I tried to beg and got slapped.

On the third day, I cried, pointlessly and profusely. Why? Well, picture a square in the heart of Kiev. A squadron of cavalry sit around a fire. They are roasting potatoes on wooden spits. There's a samovar, too, embers glowing red underneath it. I am standing not far away, looking on. The horses are tethered in a row to a length of rope, each with a feed bag attached to its head. A flock of sparrows dart in and out among the horses, warming themselves at the steaming piles of fresh shit. As a horse tosses its head, pinches of grain fall to the ground, a meal for the sparrows.

That's when I began to cry. Those fucking birds!

And suddenly there's a hand on my shoulder.

'What are you doing here, boy?'

I look up. It's an officer! A bandolier slung across his chest, he has a moustache like buffalo horns. Vodka and garlic linger on his breath. His voice reaches down to the soles of your feet. I don't care; he can kill me if he likes.

'I'm crying. Can't you see?'

He stares at me, mouth open. 'Hey, you're not Ukrainian?'

'No.' I tell him everything, except about the orphanage.

'Spunky little beggar. I'm glad you're not Ukrainian. I hate the mother-fuckers.' He slashes his hand across his throat. 'You know who we are?'

'Cossacks, sir?'

'From the Don, little soldier. So you know how to clean guns and brew *chai*?'

172

'Yes, sir.'

'You afraid of horses and hard work?'

'I'm not afraid of anything.'

He starts tweaking his moustache and smiling. 'Well then, there isn't a cavalry regiment worth its salt that couldn't use an extra shit-shoveller. You want to join us?'

'Oh yes, sir.'

'Good. I'll enlist you officially. You ride with the supplies wagons. Try to run away and I personally will whip the hide off your arse. Get that?'

'Yes, sir.'

'*Davai, galupchik.* Let's go.'

I'm a soldier in Prince Bagritsky's 13th Cavalry Regiment. I get fed. I spend nights in makeshift stables warmed by the horses' nearness. I get paid a few rubles sometimes. Sometimes I get whipped by Zulin the Quartermaster, then dream of shooting him dead. I never promised myself that one day I'd be a billionaire; I prayed that one day I'd make a grand for every shovelful of horseshit I ever moved in my life.

Ice! It groans when the horses cross it, a hollow rumble like a deep hungry belly. I shall hear it in my dreams for the rest of my life.

We rode north to Gomel, then west towards Bobruisk. We advanced then retreated. Somewhere, generals were having fun moving army units like pieces on a chessboard. That's war for you. Tolstoy is right about one thing: war is more about motion than fighting. Only the end result is decided by men in the field in few crucial battles which often occur through sheer accident.

Who are the real losers? Those in the path of the moving juggernaut. Those whose lives are centred on place and possessions. See them trudge across wind-swept tundras, through rubble that was a town, always with their laden carts and bundles and an uncomprehending look of catastrophe on their faces – streams of debris flowing to nowhere.

And the aftermath of a battle? Consider Prince Bolkonski in *War and Peace,* lying wounded – fatally, as he believes – on the

173

battlefield of Austerlitz. All that high-minded reflection on the meaning of life and love. That's Tolstoy talking; that's art. What actually happens is different. The wounded soldier thinks: 'O God, why isn't someone coming to save me? Oh God, am I going to die? Please, God, I don't want to die. Mother, mother, make this unbearable pain go away. Forgive me my sins and take me into your loving bosom, God, since my time has come . . .'

The soldier who walks away unharmed? He says: 'Thanks be to God that I'm alive, not lying dead on the cold earth, a feast for carrion crows.'

The scavenger says: 'Here's a pair of boots, I'll take them. Here's a good warm coat, just what I need. What luck! A gold ring. I'm not stealing, the poor sod won't be needing these any more. May God have mercy on his soul.'

From the day when Cain brained his brother Abel, God and War have been going together hand in glove, both conspiring with the poet to portray killing as an ennobling experience. But the soldiers, those who survive, are the lucky ones in this sorry business; they are the moment's regimented hordes of nomads for whom losing is relatively easy.

I learnt to ride the Cossack way: instinctively, like you and your mount were one, your mind and upper body free to fight. Round and round they lunged me endlessly on the long rein, graduating from bareback to a saddle without stirrups. The Cossacks loved to see me fall off. The better I got, the more difficult became the horses chosen for me. Bets were made on the duration of my staying on. I was turned into a recreational asset. One day they wheeled in a huge mean draught gelding. No sooner was I astride the beast than a practical joker stuffed hot pepper up the horse's arse. It bucked ferociously. I held on for a few seconds before flying off and was knocked out cold. All bets were off on that occasion.

'Tatya,' said Sergeant Ivan Ivanovich, 'today you've earned your spurs. What shall we teach you next?'

'The sword and gun,' I replied to loud cheers and applause.

The generals promised victories, like Brusilov's the last

summer. We knew better. Everywhere Germans were advancing behind barrages of artillery. So confident were they that one bright morning in February a horse patrol trotted right into our midst. There followed a short skirmish. Four prisoners were taken. After they were interrogated, they were led out to be shot.

Our commander stood by and looked on as the four were positioned in a line, hands cuffed behind their backs, facing the firing squad. They showed no fear. The section detailed to do the shooting took aim. The sergeant shouted 'Fire!' The volley shook the air. All but one fell backwards, dead. The one who didn't staggered, then sank to his knees. His breath came out in broken wheezes. He kept trying to look up but each time his chin slumped against his spattered tunic. Our commander pulled out his revolver. Turning his head, his eye caught mine. He motioned me to approach.

'Go finish him off,' he commanded.

I began to tremble all over.

'The man's already more than half dead. Put him out of his misery.' He shoved the pistol at my chest.

I must have taken a step back, for suddenly the commander's heel was grinding hard on my toes.

'Do as I tell you. Now!' He barked.

I went up to the German. When he saw me standing over him, pistol in hand, he smiled, then his head dropped as if he was already dead. I shot him in the small bald patch at the crown of his cropped head. He fell sideways and didn't move again. Don't ask what I felt. I truly don't remember. Memory, you see, works for self-preservation. Any assassin will tell you that.

My reward was the German's pretty sorrel mare and weapons. I was not yet fifteen, but now I had a horse of my own, a Mauser pistol, a cavalry sabre made in Solingen. And blood-stained hands.

The mare, oh, she was nimble, sweet-natured, and sure-footed. I named her Lara. Was it not an irony of fate that this lively docile German mount continued her intended progress into the heart of Russia, under a different rider, and in defeat?

175

The soldiers sing clapping their hands:

> Fill your eyes with Alliluya
> for a glass of vodka she'll screw ya
> Mother Russia bring us luck
> save us for just one more fuck . . .

The said Alliluya doesn't mind. She winks and sticks her buttocks out. But anyone who lays a hand on her gets a sharp slap. Alliluya knows her worth and that is a good deal more than vodka which, in fact, she serves in this inn somewhere west of Slutsk where we are. Not a young girl, she is nevertheless pretty in a buxom earthy way. Fair-haired and rosy-cheeked, Alliluya flaunts her charming abundance provocatively but not lewdly.

It is March 1917. Our regiment has been decimated more by illness and desertion than through action. The men are tired; there's no more fight left in them. The horses are thin, listless and dull-eyed. Russia has lost almost all of Poland. The munitions industry has all but ceased production. There are riots in St Petersburg. There is a talk of revolution.

Then, all of a sudden, it happened: Tsar Nicholas II abdicated.

Heading the government is Aleksander Feodorevich Kerensky, whom none of the men has heard of. There are rumours he is a Jew. Shock and disorientation are tempered by apprehension. There are rumours that the new government is giving out the land to the peasants who work on it. A land rush is under way – *muzhiks* are dropping their rifles and going home; nothing will stop them. At the front, officers shoot anyone who as much as thinks of deserting, all to no avail. The war over?

Kerensky has other ideas. Appointing General Lavr Gregorevich Kornilov Commander-in-Chief of the armed forces, he declares his intention to press on with the war to victory! Through blood and heroic sacrifice!

'Kill the shit! Bring back the Tsar!' the men say.

We don't know where we are heading. We don't much care, either. Except that we've had blood and sacrifice up to our back teeth. There's no past and no future. The present is vodka and Alliluya, whom none can afford.

176

In truth, Alliluya doesn't excite me nearly so much as she does my comrades-at-arms, who are by now pretty topped up on booze. I have a throbbing toothache. That apart, my mind is on my beloved mare Lara. For three days now her left foreleg fetlock has been swollen hot. Nikanor Budin, the regiment's mounts officer, isn't optimistic. If she doesn't get better in a week, that's it. Bang! I cannot bear the thought of losing my Lara, whose doleful image as she stands in her stall, a poultice bandage up to her knee, superimposes itself upon the spectacle of Alliluya's wobbling cleavage.

I'm too engrossed in my misery to take in my comrades' surreptitious fund-raising, aimed at initiating me into manhood, until Alliluya's sunflower smile looms a few inches away from my face.

'Hello, little darling, *daragoy moi*. Your friends have made you a present. Come along, don't be nervous . . .'

'Go on, Tatya. Stick it in her, you lucky devil! Show her what you're made of!'

I rally. Rising to my feet, I acknowledge their support as though I were their champion stepping into the ring.

Behind the scullery is a small box of a room strung with sausages. Here, between a barrel of pickled herring and a suspended side of smoked pork, I stand naked before Alliluya like a peeled banana. She squats over a sack of flour, letting her breasts out, a mass of undisciplined flesh.

'Ah, poor little *chupchik*, he won't rise. What's the matter, shot your load already? Never mind, let him rest a little.'

She puts her hands on my buttocks and rocks me caressingly between her breasts.

'There, nice, cheeky sceptre. What a pretty helmet you wear. A foreign little fellow, aren't you? You want loving, don't you. Yes, yes, everybody needs love.'

Between her thighs, uncovered by the hitched-up skirts, lurks a glistening rancid hedgehog eager to devour . . .

14

I once said to Theo: 'To those who dream of worldly power I say, go on dreaming. What it promises is not what you get in the end.'

'Is there power other than worldly?' he asked.

I replied, 'Now that you've asked, I don't suppose there is, actually.'

He said, 'So what is it that you get in the end, which I presume you already have?'

'Being totally, irredeemably superfluous, Theo.'

He pulled a face. 'Nothing new in that, or exclusive to worldly power. Read Ecclesiastes: Vanity of vanities; all is vanity.'

I've wondered a good deal about Theo. Is he a cold man? Does he bear me a grudge for what I had done to him in Copenhagen and in Paris?

I have a dream that keeps recurring year after year: somewhere I have a twin sister who was separated from me at birth. She's like me yet totally different – a mirror image of opposites. And this twin sister of mine is searching for me as I must search for her, because neither of us can ever be complete without the other.

Often, with Theo, I've seen my sister's eyes looking at me through his. I've never told him. And when he stood there, at the battlements of his citadel, gazing down on me, the barbarian below, with my cohorts of uncouth horsemen, I saw my twin sister standing behind him, peering at me from over his shoulder. I offered gifts, proposed a treaty, moved on. Because Theo, too, has power: ideas can create and destroy more thoroughly than guns and money.

The way I go on you might think I was obsessed with power. I'm not. But I am at times regretful of how I misused it when

I had it. Occasionally, before I begin my outpouring to Charon, I fantasise what I'd do if I were, say, a minor deity, possessed of all my experience in addition to certain divine attributes. I'd be a good little god, for a start. I'd work diligently to improve the world in some specific practical way.

Take this sprawling London darkness I see looking out of Sanctum. The smudged orange sunrise struggling against an oyster grey mass of polluted air. (They tell us daily we are screwing up the planet with our cars.) I say it's all down to poor management. As a godling on duty in the early morning shift, I'd push the button for a radiant multi-coloured dawn! Let sunlight flood warmth onto the night-chilled bones of down-and-outs in cardboard hovels, all the way from Catford to the Embankment! Let Beethoven's Ninth cascade through the city and wake up lovers, young and old, to a joyous morning fuck!

And when, at the end of my time, I'm commended for my diligence, I'd submit to the Chief Deity a report recommending terminal abolition of all revolutions, everywhere – on earth as in heaven!

The real Revolution which brought Vladimir Ilyich Lenin to power came in October 1917. One war had effectively come to an end. Another, deadlier still, had just began.

I had a friend, Arckady Pushkin – no relation to the poet Aleksander. Arckady was four years older than me. A sensitive man, he read a lot. Whenever there was a moment's respite there was Arckady, immersed in a book. He was a good soldier. Loved his horse. Kept his weapons clean. Wept when a comrade died. He wrote poetry and kept a diary, too.

The agent who had testified against Arckady at his peremptory sedition hearing, read from his scrap book.

'That's very good, Arckady Arckadevich. Very good indeed. Clearly, you are a gifted poet.'

'Thank you, sir,' replied Arckady, beaming all over his face.

He was still smiling when they shot his brains out. An example to us all! I remember that agent with his tight gin trap of a mouth. His name cropped up from time to time over the years. After the Okhrana ceased to exist he joined Lenin's

179

Cheka, survived its various name mutations and outlived his boss Lavrenti Beria to retire with the pension of a KGB colonel.

'Titus,' said Arckady shortly before he died, 'do you understand the meaning of a great country? Of course you don't. You're a simple lad. Listen. When a country can rise from defeat after defeat, and tear herself apart and still never lose her soul, that, Titus, is when a country is great. Only Russia is like that. Mark my words. Maybe China, too. But not America. A country's greatness, Titus, is measured not least by her capacity for suffering.'

Another of Arckady's pearls of wisdom: 'What do historians tell us about civil wars, Titus? Think of a group of kids. Teacher has gone and left them to their own devices. Two big boys face each other. They choose sides from among the rest, like in a football game. Then the game begins. Only this game is about killing. All games are about killing, in the mind. Civil war is killing for real, no rules, either.' With his innocence he might have lived to be a great commissar, Arckady Arckadevich Pushkin.

So the game began.

There was a mutiny in our regiment. First, they shot the quartermaster. Then the commander. Then the officers who didn't mutiny. When there was no one else left worthy of shooting, the whole regiment broke up. The Cossacks rode back home, raiding the countryside on the way for any food there was still to be found. It was a cruel winter.

I asked myself 'Where is the heart and soul of this great country?' And Arckady's voice rang in my ears: 'Moscow!'

I lead my mare Lara out into the snow. Dispirited, she looks at me, head hung low, fetlocks shivering on the ice, ribs sticking out of her matted coat. I pull out my pistol and press the muzzle between her eyes. But I can't do it.

'Go away!' I shout. 'I can't feed you! I can't bear the way you look at me! Go find someone who can.'

She won't budge. She's all spent. Nobody wants her now that she's in this condition. Left alone, she wouldn't last a week. Wolves and wild dogs would tear her limb from limb if she didn't die of starvation.

To kill her would be merciful, as with her former owner, the German I shot. Only I love my mare Lara. And love is selfish.

I take her back to the barn where she has been standing, which is now empty. I say to myself as I walk out never to see her again, 'Betrayal is like all other things that hurt; you move on and get over it.' But it hurt more than any other betrayal I ever committed.

Years later, on my frequent business flights into Moscow, there would be a Zil limousine waiting for me on the tarmac. The chauffeur would touch his cap deferentially: '*Pazhalsta, Gospedyn Alston, kak pasheveiti? Khorasho?*'

Of course *khorasho*. Why the fuck not? The Zil won't break down. If it did, there'll be another one around in minutes to take me to my VIP suite in the Sovyetskaya Hotel. Or to an official apartment in the heart of the city, overlooking the Kremlin and the River Moscow, depending on how sensitive was the nature of my visit.

I wouldn't be standing in queues. A team of apparatchiks would be on hand to attend to all my needs. And a chaperon to see I didn't get lost when I took a walk. And an amazonian secretary – 1 meter 80cm, a bust of Himalayan proportions (KGB research on me concluded that I liked 'em big!), fluent in six languages and a martial arts expert. There would be caviar galore, and venison. A selection of my favourite Crimean wines. Tickets to the Bolshoi.

I'm a big shot, you see. And although underneath it all I'm as Russian as any of them, I make a point of wearing Savile Row suits and Jermyn Street shirts in Moscow. Just to remind them where I stand; that I'm *Gospedyn* to them, a big time capitalist with a pull. Not some jumped-up *Tovarish*.

Leonid Brezhnev in his dotage had asked me which was the better car, Cadillac or Rolls-Royce. He was crazy about cars. I answered that it depended who was behind the wheel. He looked bemused. But Yuri Andropov smiled.

Before leaving, I would take a good look at Moscow. Highrise buildings; the ugly ordinariness of intentional urban uniformity – Stalin's idea of progress. And I would say to all this with a touch of nostalgic affection: 'We've come a long way,

181

Moscow, you and I. And although you now shave your armpits and wear make-up and high heels, I remember, I know what you really are.'

River Moskva, a distant tributary of the Volga, is frozen over. A dense sky droops over it. The city which illuminated my child's imagination like a vision of Jerusalem wears a Tartar's face. To the west are the wooded Vorvoroi hills. Secluded behind the crenelated Kremlin walls, the golden domes of the Assumption Cathedral and the pewter-coloured ones of the Twelve Apostles glint like the multiple eyes of a huge petrified insect. Alone at the end of Red Square stands St Basil's Cathedral, Slavic down to the last brick: 'Hallowed be the space between us and the Almighty!' say its fairy-tale onion-shaped domes.

Here is the body of Moscow, from which cobbled streets packed with trodden snow spread outwards like a spider's web among two-storeyed houses with green and red roofs.

The silence is charged with a latency of motion. The people are conserving energy, or else are too cold, hungry and tired to stir. They say the church bells have stopped ringing these last few weeks, since Lenin and Trotsky had moved in from Petrograd to make Moscow Russia's capital and centre of government. Why? What has this city to offer, except memories? Even Tolstoy thought it was a backwoods dump. Because Petrograd is too European, a fountain of rebelliousness. You want ongoing revolution? Stay in Petrograd. In Moscow you'll find the native Russian fatalism which, along with General Winter, defeated Napoleon.

The city's population has swollen with hungry destitutes crowding against each other, feeding on hope, waiting to see what salvation the new regime will bring. Hunger, like bereavement, is assuaged by company.

Consider the genesis of a great capital: an adventurous prince from far away, having progressed along an ancient trade route with no definite destination in mind, reaches a plausible resting spot. Here there's a river. There are forests. There is open space and hills not far off. Weary of the long journey and homesick, his men are fractious.

'How much further to go?' they demand to know.

'No farther, lads. This is it,' says the prince. 'Let's erect a stockade. Sooner or later an enemy is bound to come along. We'll be in business.'

'Splendid!' cry the priests. 'We'll build a church. What use is an enemy if you don't have a church in which to pray for God's help?'

Thus a city is founded.

The prince is Dologorukov. The year, Anno Domini 1156 or thereabouts. Moscow can't boast of antiquity. But when it comes to enemies and churches, she's in the top league.

I come into Moscow a walking alimentary system craving for food. There's not a scrap of official paper on me to say who I am. The Mauser is long since gone, sold for a few rubles on the way to Moscow. (The one I keep in Sanctum, by the way, is a later model with just as sinister a history.) All I have in my pockets is a few kopeks, a mouldy crust of black bread and the yellowing pages of my book – Count Lev Tolstoy's *War and Peace*, the world's greatest work of fiction.

Drifting through the streets, I set up a provisional agenda for this new chapter in my life. Two imperatives: food and shelter. For the first, I scavenge; behind houses, outside eating places, in depleted markets. Luck guides me to the second.

It is bedtime. Standing not far from the Twelve Apostles Cathedral, I stare at an enormous ornate cannon, its muzzle a dark orifice the size of a tub. Aha! A home! I sense some warmth as I slither down the barrel. My foot makes contact with something soft, which moves.

'Oi! Piss off! This is my place!' a woman's voice screams at me.

I tell the woman, who happens to be small and hardly much older than myself, that the Revolution had banished chivalry. So, if anybody's going to piss off, it's going to be her. And to make my point I grab her by the scruff of the neck and haul her out so that she's half spilling out of the gun barrel. She is practical. I'm reasonable. We negotiate a contract. I become Varvara Dimitrovna's lodger. At the end of a day's scavenging we load ourselves into this imperial artillery piece, feet against feet – she at the fuse end, I at the other. But on rent nights

183

we fuck, jammed against each other with the inner wall of the barrel pressing on our backs.

One day I wandered in the vicinity of the Bolshoi Moskovski restaurant where food, good food at that, was still available for the right price to the right kind of people. But the smell of the food which wafts out of the restaurant's door as it opens, is anybody's to enjoy for free. It being rent night at the cannon, I thought I'd linger a while outside the Bolshoi Moskovski so as to regale Varvara with descriptions of an imagined feast.

A couple came out. We stared at each other, I boldly, they with pained embarrassment. Reaching for his pocket, the man gave me a coin, then quickly marched away with his woman. I looked at the coin. One lousy kopek! You wouldn't dare give that to a doorman in a third-rate hotel! It took me a few moments to realise what had happened. I touched my face. I felt rough skin over hollows covered with stubble. My hair had grown long and matted – I couldn't remember when I'd last had a wash. I passed a hand over my body and registered how much more space there was now between flesh and clothes. At the back of my mouth there was a cavity the size of a crater, where two molars had been. I had incipient gonorrhoea, courtesy of my landlady Varvara Dimitrovna.

I saw myself for the first time since my desertion from the army as I really was; as though my alms giver had thrust a mirror at me: a scarecrow beggar! The lowest of the low in human hierarchy.

'Tatya! Tatya Altermann! Can this really be you? I can't believe my eyes!'

Neither can I, for the man who addresses me outside the Metropole Hotel where I make my begging pitch is none other than Yuri Danilevich Tabenkinov, the cheerful Jewish sidekick of my former regiment's itinerant supplier.

'My poor dear fellow, what a sight you are!' Arms stretched out, Yuri advances but stops short of coming too close.

'In heaven's name, what are you doing here?'

I can't resist a laugh. 'Being an ordinary Russian. Looking for justice, can't you see?'

Yuri stiffens. I suddenly realise that he is not alone. Standing

184

a few steps behind him is a tall man with a lantern jaw and fiercely innocent blue eyes, a foreigner. Yuri gives him a nervous smile.

'And you, Yuri Danilevich, what are *you* doing here?'

He looks well-fed, well dressed, in an army greatcoat and decent boots. A length of red scarf is looped around his neck. A revolutionary cap perches rakishly on his balding head.

'Tell me where I can find you. No, better still, meet me here tomorrow at the same time, won't you? I'll be back, I promise,' says Yuri, *sotto voce*.

Of course I don't believe him, but that's okay. I'm about to ask for a handout when the stranger intervenes. An Englishman, he wants to know who I am and why a mere kid like me looks like something washed up by the sea a long time ago.

To his credit, Yuri comes back with an answer which, while not quite accurate, is at least humane. I am his former comrade-in-arms, who he thought had perished, he tells the Englishman. And now that he has found me, he naturally wants to help. And he wants to know what had happened to me and so many of his former comrades.

The Englishman is interested. Why don't we all get back inside where it's warm? he suggests. Misunderstanding Yuri's hesitation, he adds firmly, 'Good heavens! If they make any fuss, I'll jolly well pack up and go to another hotel. And they won't hear the end of it either.' The crazy arrogance of the man. Where does he think he is, London?

'Tatya,' Yuri pleads in a whisper, 'for the love of Mother Russia, don't say anything bad or I'll be in real trouble. I'll explain later.'

The Englishman is a writer, a left-wing intellectual who believes in the Bolshevik cause. His name is Lawrence Deere. He has come to Russia to write a book. He even speaks our language, after a fashion. More importantly, he has a powerful friend in Moscow – one of Lenin's lieutenants, Nikolai Bukharin, no less.

'First, I want this young comrade to have a square meal,' he insists.

The two of them had already eaten. I am not used to eating alone, being watched. The opulence of the place makes me nervous. A waiter brings a generous portion of roast chicken on a gleaming china plate, positions it on the snow-white table-cloth, in between silver knife and fork. I want to stuff chicken, bread, and cutlery in my coat's pocket, and make a run for it.

The wine in the crystal glass throws a red halo on the table-cloth. '*Nazderovye*! To the Revolution!'

After a few bites I feel sick: my shrunken stomach can't cope with this sudden ingestion of richness.

'Take a rest, there's no hurry,' says the Englishman solicitously. 'We can talk another time, when you feel better.'

A gentleman. A lord, who is campaigning back home to renounce his hereditary title so that he may run for parliament as a socialist commoner. I warm to him.

No, I tell him, in a moment I'll be all right. Some tea and a cigarette would help. I look longingly at the food, wondering how I might carry it away, or at least retain a little of all this warm cleanliness when I crawl into the cannon's muzzle later. My memory unlocked, I lean back and let go. He sits there, the Englishman, notepad in hand, scribble scribble scribble. Every now and again he looks up and asks me to repeat something I had said.

At the end of my story I feel faint. Not because of the experiences relived in the telling, but because of the unexpected form my story takes, and the novel joy experienced in its creation. In an instance I've embraced Man's most delectable addictions: the magic of story-telling.

The Englishman gives me a banknote. English money. I've no idea how much it's worth.

'Please accept this. Not as a gift, you understand, but as a well-deserved payment.'

I take the money not with gratitude but as a prize, an acknowledgment which is both elating and supremely satisfying.

Night sneaks along the walls, across Red Square, down towards the river, searching for victims. What are all those churches, now that God is banished from the city? Ghosts in the freezing mist. I close my hand over the crisp banknote in my pocket.

This precious fee tells me I'm a beggar no more but the fountainhead of a story.

'Hey, Tatya, let's have a look at the money the Englishman gave you.' Yuri feels the banknote between his fingers. 'Five pounds! A fortune!' He whistles through his teeth. 'Want me to change it for you?'

'It can wait.'

'Okay, please yourself. I wouldn't charge a commission, even though I introduced you to the Englishman. Hey, only a joke. You don't think I'd seriously think of taking your money, do you?'

'No, Yuri. You're a friend.'

'And don't you forget it! What luck we met. I'm not going to let you spend another night out there in the cold. I have a place where there's food and vodka and a fire. You can stay with me for a while. What are friends for? I look at you, Tatya, and say to myself, "It could all have happened to me." Let's go.'

Poor Varvara Dimitrovna, shivering inside the cannon, waiting in vain for my body to block out the chill draft. I didn't as much as give her a thought. There are friends and there are friends, *mutatis mutandis*.

Yuri's place is in Arbat. A four-bedroomed apartment, formerly the home of a timber merchant who fled with his family to Ekaterinodar, it now houses, apart from Yuri Danilevich, six other young Bolsheviks including a dour woman called Lyuba Savitskaya. Everything that was worth taking has long since been pillaged, but thanks to Yuri, who has lost none of the professional touch, there is an assortment of furniture: beds, a few chairs, a door laid flat on four boxes to make a table; above all, a large German cast-iron wood-burner that was too heavy to be stolen. Only fuel is in short supply, now that most of the doors had been burnt, as well as virtually all other detachable combustible material in the place.

My arrival is greeted with something ranging from resentful suspicion to indifference. A closed meeting is held in the kitchen to determine my status. Yuri prevails, with a qualification.

187

He is to forfeit his privacy, since I'm to share his room. He isn't too happy about that; he had rather hoped I would be shoved in with the woman Lyuba, whom all detest. On one item unanimity has been achieved: I'm to be forthwith disinfected by the supreme luxury of a full hot bath, complete with liberal use of precious soap. Also, a set of clothes is donated to replace my rags, which are to be cremated with the fuel for my ablution. Yuri pays for all that, as for my rent which, he tells me, he will duly reclaim from my story-teller's fee when it is converted to rubles.

He sleeps in a proper bed. An upright coffin where he hangs his clothes stands against the wall, topped by a photograph of *Tovarish* Vladimir Ilyich Lenin. On a bedside cabinet at Yuri's head stand an oil lamp, a battered radio, a half-full bottle of vodka whose level Yuri marks, not too surreptitiously, with a shopkeeper's indelible pencil before he extinguishes the light. At the other side of the room I lie, covered in two horse blankets, on a lumpy mattress. Yuri snores and farts in his sleep. I stay awake, contemplating the inscrutable power of the word.

Yuri Danilevich Tabenkinov is nobody's fool. He got to know a man who knew a man who commended him to one Dimitri Didyuchin who, by virtue of being acquainted with Nikolai Bukharin, himself got a job in the culture department of the Moscow Soviet, in charge of liaising with important foreign visitors. Yuri became his deputy. Hence our fortuitous encounter outside the Metropole Hotel.

His qualifications for the job are total obedience and ever-demonstrative gratitude. That apart, Yuri is conversant in Yiddish which, bent and stretched, will attune to any language known to man.

De-loused, re-dressed, and cured of gonorrhoea, I am launched on a timely apprenticeship in social intercourse at Poet's Café, the meeting-place of Moscow's creative intelligentsia, where Yuri Danilevich Tabenkinov is a regular visitor.

What a place! Set in a former back-alley laundry, Poet's Café is a long narrow room. Its entrance is painted black, with the name scrawled on the door in red letters. Inside there are rough tables covered in fustian tableclothes. A *burzhuika* gurgles in a corner, giving off an intimation of warmth. The walls are painted all colours in savage abandonment. Here, wearing a worker's cap and a red scarf, the poet Mayakovsky holds court to a new world. It is plain to see on whom Yuri has modelled his appearance.

Hunger stalks the streets. Here there's food and booze galore – to wash down resonating poetry and the slogans of the day: Left march. Left left left! Mayakovsky, again.

Face flushed from vodka and verse, Yuri grabs my arm. 'Well, Tatya, haven't I done well for you? Drink up and remember these moments for as long as you live. What you're witnessing is history in the making!'

I take in my fellow witnesses. A stately woman with auburn hair and intelligent eyes, whom everybody adores. Aleksandra Kolontai is her name, the reigning queen of Socialism. Surrounded by men with guns, she preaches free love. Then there are others described by a wag in residence as 'bourgeoisie who haven't yet had their throats cut'. Why are they waiting? Why don't they flee? Because, like a serpent's prey, they are mesmerised by the eye of chaos.

There are guns everywhere, displayed proudly on the tables by full or empty glasses. Yuri too has a gun, stuck in his belt pirate-fashion. A survivor, like me, he fulfilled a destiny of a sort; he fought in Berlin under Pugachev, then crossed over to the Americans. Told them he came within an ace of storming Hitler's bunker. He ended living in New York, a writer of horror fiction.

As I loosen up to absorb the atmosphere in Poet's Café, I begin to recognise the source of Moscow's street graffiti, which I have passed unnoticing in my search for food. Red corpuscles of the Bolshevik struggle moving on . . . left left left!

But the news! It seeps in from the outside. Whites slaughtering Reds on the Don. A train from Rostov, stuffed with mutilated bodies of Bolshevik fighters dispatched north to their starving comrade as 'frozen meat'. They will win who have more Cossacks fighting on their side; and more Cossacks to choose from, now that a treaty to end the war has been signed in Brest-Litovsk. Poland gone, the Ukraine too, and all the

Baltic states. The English and Americans have invaded from the north; the French have occupied Odessa (good for the Jews and Titus the dog! I see him in my mind's eye lolling a hungry tongue at a French rifleman – *tiens, mon pauvre chien, un peu du viand russe*). We need food! Shake the bloody Kulaks who are hoarding up grain for the black market. Crush the buggers! *Tovarish* Lenin's own words.

Specialise, specialise, that's the survivor's order of the day!

'Tatya, you're a cool card, handy with a gun, aren't you?' says Yuri.

You bet your life, comrade. Anything for a regular supply of *schi*, bread, and cigarettes.

'There's a man I want you to meet. He's looking for fellows like you.'

The man is Aleksander Tsiurupa, newly appointed head of the Dictatorship of Food Supply. A tough customer, he understands farmers like the butcher understands the lamb. They say about him that he can smell a hidden bushel of grain a verst away.

The operation is warlike; we form like posses in a cowboy movie. We come into the village, round up the Kulaks.

'Where have you hidden the grain, you bastards?'

'Grain? What grain? We have no grain. Can't you see we're starving? Look at our children, at our women,' wail the Kulaks.

Bang bang! We shoot a few, just to show we mean business. So the grain is brought out. Then we shoot the rest and torch the village. Thus the hungry working masses of Moscow and Petrograd are fed, the women in munition factories go to work on full bellies, singing revolutionary songs . . . Left left left!

I'm sickened by this work. My unreformed soul yearns for the complicity of a horse if I'm to kill. And Lady Luck intervenes once again, lifting me from the cold dictatorship of nutrition to be at the side of *Tovarish* Kliment Efremovich Voroshilov, who is on his way to defend Tsaritsyn against General Wrangel's advance.

15

Of all my so-called Caligulan caprices, there is one act I cherish above all others, because it led indirectly to my meeting Phoebe Whelan.

This is what I did.

On a certain day in the autumn of 1978, I convened a special meeting of the 'Sanhedrin'. On the stroke of midnight I announced to my stupefied executives that I intended to sell a third of my shares in the Alston Group leaving 29 per cent of the total in my control. I invited them to buy on ridiculously favourable terms, way below the shares' projected initial market price. Over the next few days there was a god-almighty scramble to buy. I was pleased. I wanted stronger, lasting commitment; and none is stronger, more durable, than that which flows from self-interest or, to put it bluntly, greed.

Later I unfolded the Group's New Business Philosophy: let there be a total devolution of initiative – all the subsidiaries operating independently, each determining its own scope and pace of development. Let imaginative enterprise, acumen, inventiveness, and drive decide the fortune of each.

I commissioned an international head-hunter to poach for me the best business brains available. The quarry turned out to be a youthful high-flyer called John Lefebre, from a Californian software company. I appointed him Chief, briefed to implement my ideas and accountable only to myself. John Lefebre reshuffled the Sanhedrin. A chronicler of the Group would probably describe the period as The Days of Terror. Then everybody settled down to a still leaner, more muscular regime.

Lefebre, let me say, isn't only the most imaginative, toughest, ablest, most ruthless operator I've ever come across, he is also totally amoral. Which made him a most effective agent for just about anything I wanted to do. If, for example, I said to him 'John, transfer X amount of money to a certain party, but make sure it's untraceable'; or, 'I want this or that rival company pulverised and ground to dust', Lefebre will do it without batting an eyelid. And no questions asked.

Having reorganised my empire, I sold more shares, leaving me with a mere 15 per cent of the Group's equities and a personal wealth in excess of what I could reasonably spend in what was left of my life. I arranged for a limited number of shares to be offered to all Alston Group employees of more than five years standing. At a meeting soon after, a certain Sanhedrist formerly from the Bank of England, saucily quoted *King Lear* at me. I said nothing. A second, taking courage from my silence, made a discourteous reference to the extinction of dinosaurs. I turned to my new Chief.

'John,' I said, 'do I still have the power to fire here?' 'Well,' he drawled, 'I guess so. Depends who.'

'These two,' I said.

In the event they weren't fired. What's more, to their credit, the two took it with a smile, albeit a wry one. That was the closest the Alston Group ever came to a coup d'état.

But the extent of my abdication soon became apparent in the following way:

I happened to listen to a radio feature about a dead Cambridge novelist whose name slips my memory. In one of his novels, set in seventeenth-century India, a prince, weary of court venality, renounces his title and takes to the road with a staff and a begging bowl, leaving all his worldly riches and power behind for his relatives to squabble over.

The next morning I took an early train to Lincoln. I checked into the White Hart Hotel opposite the Cathedral. At a nearby shop I bought a whole new set of country clothes, a farmer's cap and a walking stick. I walked about the city. I admired the cathedral, and had a drink in an out of the way pub, where I fell talking to a farmer.

'You're a tourist?' he asked. Yes, I said. 'You speak good English. Where do you come from, then?' Siberia, I told him. 'Hrr, you must find it very warm here and all,' he commented, raising his eyebrows. 'How do you like our beer?' I said I liked it fine, and bought him a pint. So this fellow invited me home to see his farm in a village on the outskirts of the city: it wasn't every day one met an old man from Siberia in the heart of Lincolnshire.

He farmed some three hundred acres of cereal and livestock. His wife bred champion fell ponies. We talked horses well into the night, then he drove me back to the hotel. I walked on average six miles a day before returning to London, with colour in my face from the wind and sun.

Nearly a whole week had gone by, with no meetings, no consultations, no decisions to face, no telephone calls, no appointments. You'd have thought I would be missed, at the very least. Nothing of the sort: Alston Group, recaptained or on automatic pilot, had sailed on smoothly on course without me.

Tieless, and wearing a sports jacket, I took my place at the head of the table in Sanhedrin. A collective look of bemused anticipation focused on me. Old dragons were unpredictable and prone to erratic behaviour, a known fact which, presumably, I had already proved. So what now? Resignation? I could read it in their faces.

'Gentlemen,' I said. 'Hands up all who know what is, one, a fell pony. Two, a Suffolk tup. Three, a blue-faced Leicester. Four, when the lambing season begins. Five, what sheep farmers mean when they talk about mules. Six, how long it is by train from King's Cross to Lincoln, and the cost of a return ticket, second class.'

Stunned silence. What were they thinking? Old Alston's marbles beginning to shake loose? One apple dropped out of the picnic basket? What planet is he talking about, anyway? Then the most timid of the Sanhedrists raised a hand.

'Excuse me, Titus,' he said with an icy smile, 'I'm sure we're all delighted to see you looking so well. Would you kindly explain what relevance these questions have to our hard-pressed agenda?'

That was when the revelation of the year faced me like a death certificate: they were no longer afraid of me. More than that, if the Sanhedrists ganged up on me under a new leader,

193

who was sitting on my right, and called for a shareholders' general meeting, I could actually be deposed! I had by my own volition made myself disposable.

I decided to summon my American heir apparent for an in-depth sounding of the situation. He preempted me. Overruling one of my early-morning engagements, he presented himself for a private interview. We began with a relaxed discussion about the general state of affairs in the Alston Group. All was well. Defying international market trends, the Group was, in fact, going from strength to strength. A steady growth in most subsidiaries, attended by an impressive consolidation of assets world-wide. All thanks to my entrepreneurial vision, the new flexibility I had introduced . . . My place in Commerce and Industry's Hall of Fame was assured . . . blah blah blah. Like a doctor cheerfully chatting you up before telling you cancer was snuffing out your lights one by one. So unlike Lefebre.

I said, 'John, what's all this about? Cut the bullshit and get to the point.'

He leaned back and blew a perfect smoke ring into the air, the first time he had ever smoked in my presence. Then he smiled.

'There isn't a point, Titus. Only, well, I was worried about you. We all were.'

'Worried?'

'Sure. You disappearing like that without telling anybody where to. Irresponsible, Titus, don't you think?'

I had to agree.

'I mean, you're not just an ordinary pensioner, are you? You're the chief of a great international organisation. You go out all alone . . . Hell, man, anything could happen to you.'

He was diplomatic enough not to add 'at your age'.

'The tabloid press. Can you imagine what a feast they'd make of it, given half the chance? "Head of Alston Group lost in countryside tells farmers he's a tourist from Siberia." How would that look on a front page?'

'I wasn't lost. You contacted the police?'

'Damn right I did. Half the country's police detectives were out looking for you. And I won't tell you how many reporters went on an expensive holiday abroad at the Group's expense.

194

Titus, there are terrorists about, a whole collection of nasty guys with guns out there who'd love to get their paws on you for the ransom. Thought of that, huh?'

'How many people know of this?'

'Nobody, just me and Phoebe Whelan. We managed to keep it all very quiet. It wasn't easy, believe me.'

'Who's Phoebe Whelan?'

'She works here. I'll tell you about her in a minute. I just wanted...'

I laughed. I said, 'Okay, I'll behave myself. Is this telling off official, by the way?'

He laughed too. 'Nothing's official until you say it is, Titus. Next time you feel like having a fling, let me know. I could come up with some suggestions.'

I said: 'John, level with me. Are the Sanhedrists grumbling? I mean seriously grumbling?'

He gave me a look, raw ambition momentarily showing through the Anglo-Harvard polish. Well, wasn't it partly for that that I had hired him?

'I wouldn't put it quite like that, Titus. Let's say things are changing somewhat. Your doing, you know. There are many big fellows in the game now. The shareholders demand more accountability.'

Two icon words in business politics. The first denoting anonymous but powerful opposition; the second, a veiled warning not to be disregarded.

'Now, Phoebe Whelan. You mentioned something about wanting a personal assistant, right?'

'Not a top priority, John.'

'Wait. Let me just tell you about her, okay? She's been with us a year and a bit. She came from a very good place. She's a first class Cost Analyst, with a memory like a bank vault. She knows the ropes and who is who in the world of just about everything. Titus, she is bright. She's gorgeous. She's a honey. And she's nobody's fool. You'll love her. And if you don't, I'll have her myself.'

I said, 'I take it you've talked to her. How does she feel about being a personal assistant?'

John spread his hands out. 'I guess she must like you. Titus, you and she are made for each other. Trust me. I'll have her personal file sent to you. Do me one personal favour, see her, won't you?'

A month later I saw Phoebe for the first time. I had kept putting off the interview for days. I read her file. On paper at least, she was everything John Lefebre said she was, a 20k a year high-flying whiz-kid with a First in Economics from York University. Previous employment, a very respectable City merchant bank I had nearly ruined two years before.

And then, at last she was standing before me in the empty Sanhedrin, the sun in her hair and the dome of St Paul's at her right shoulder.

I thought, how simply she dresses. And yet this very simpleness enhanced her looks as if by a deliberate cunning. I thought, what assured tranquillity she radiates; such calm intelligent eyes. I thought, what is this lovely, silly excitement I feel, damn it!

'May I sit down?' Phoebe asked.

I invited her to sit beside me. 'What have they told you about me?' I demanded.

She started listing achievements. I cut her short. 'I meant, what did they tell you about me? The kind of person I am to work with.'

'They warned me you might be difficult. Impatient. They said you were like nobody I would ever meet again. That you don't suffer fools lightly.'

'Do you suffer fools lightly?' I asked.

'I was brought up to accept imperfection,' she replied with the bare intimation of a smile.

'I see. What else did they tell you?'

'That's about it.'

'Were you impressed?'

'In a vague sort of way.'

I had misjudged her. She had not yet accepted the position. She was assessing me no less than I was assessing her. More purposefully, if anything.

I said, 'Let me put it to you straight, Miss Whelan. With your record you'll probably go a long way, with us or elsewhere. But

196

now, in terms of your near-to-medium term career, you've been Abishaged. That's the plain truth of the matter.'

'Abishaged?'

'That's right. From the bible. Read the bible?'

'Bits of it. My father is a vicar.'

I told her about Abishag the Shunemite, the poor bimbo they brought in to warm King David like a hot-water bottle, when he was old and doddery.

'That's the situation you're in. Metaphorically, of course,' I said.

She looked at me steadily for a long moment. I tried to imagine what she would look like when she was older. Beautiful, I decided. Intensely beautiful.

'Do you consider yourself old and doddery, in need of a living hot-water bottle, metaphorical, of course?' she asked at last, in the measured voice of a psychoanalyst.

'I don't. But they do.'

'They?'

'You know who I mean.'

'Your people. You appointed them to be what they are.'

'That's neither here nor there.'

'You are the boss, aren't you? You decide things in the Group. That much I do know.'

Was she humouring me, instructed by John?

I said, 'I know the score better than anybody. I wrote it. I can tell you that this job is a dead end. When I go, they'll get rid of you. You'll be given a golden handshake and you'll be out, it's as simple as that.'

'Surely that isn't imminent,' she said, smiling. 'I mean, I might leave of my own accord well before you go.'

'Maybe. However, I thought you ought to know that working with me wouldn't be quite the grand promotion you may have been led to believe it was, that's all.'

She drew in a breath, her breasts swelling over the rim of her bra against the prim upwardly mobile executive blouse she was wearing. 'Am I to understand, Mr Alston, that you mean to discourage me from accepting this position?'

'No. What I mean you to understand is precisely what I've just told you.'

'OK. I'll think it over and let you know my decision by this time next week. Will that be all right?' She half rose.

'Miss Whelan,' I said, 'I have always had a high regard for good staff. I wouldn't want you to go away feeling you're losing an opportunity for an advancement you clearly deserve. Therefore, I offer as an alternative option a promotion anywhere in the Group where there is a suitable opening.'

She sat down again. 'That's kind. May I, in turn, offer a compromise?'

'Like what?'

'I'll start working with you. If, after a period, either of us finds the arrangement unsatisfactory, I'll take your offer and move on.'

I accepted her terms with relief, I have to admit, because already I liked her. She had style. And courage. And independence of mind. She was not in awe of me. That, too, I liked. Yes, this charming nanny my minion John was pushing at me, made me want to work. I could surprise him yet, along with the other all too cocky Sanhedrists.

'When would you like me to start?'

'Next week will be fine,' I said.

She reached for her briefcase, pulled out a sheet of paper in a transparent plastic envelope and handed it to me.

'I've outlined some of the areas where John said I might be particularly useful to you.'

As I watched her leave, I wondered if she was sleeping with John.

Before Charon, I often calculated on an old Russian abacus. A wooden frame crossed with wires on which rode large polished beads, it made a noise like a baby's rattle. I would have it in front of me on the table at meetings, playing with it desultorily while others talked. It mesmerised people – particularly outsiders. I could all but hear their minds protesting, 'Is this for real? Titus Alston's making fun of us!'

It was for real all right. Flicking those beads with the adroitness of a shop assistant at the Moscow GUM store, I could shift millions of dollars and percentages as fast as blink. After I no longer needed the abacus I still kept it on my desk, a toy for relaxing, like rosary beads.

Phoebe saw me playing with it one morning, and asked, 'Does this thing really work?'

'Sure. I'll give it to you, for your first-born child. Put it in the cot and the baby is guaranteed to grow up into an Einstein.'

'Can you calculate serious stuff with this?'

'Try me,' I said, even though I'd fallen out of practice since Charon's instalment. 'Make it as tough as you can.'

She puckered her mouth. 'OK. How much is the entire Alston Group worth on today's market?'

'That's easy. In what currency?'

'US dollars.'

'Right. Watch this.' I pushed beads furiously back and forth. '28 billion, 900 million, 730,256, give or take a couple of hundred grand.'

Phoebe laughed, clapping her hands. 'You've made it up.'

'No, I haven't. Want to check with Charon?'

'Ah, you knew all along.'

'Of course I did, more or less. I have to, don't I?'

'I didn't realise just how big we were, in terms of capital,' said Phoebe, as if confessing to a weakness.

'Like a black hole, which swallows and swallows and gets bigger and bigger, involving more and more people who toil to make it grow bigger still because their livelihoods depend on it. That's what big business is about,' I said.

'A monster,' said Phoebe, turning her head away.

She has a pale birthmark at the hollow in the nape of her neck, just touching the hair-line. Whenever I look at it, I want to kiss it.

'How much of all this is yours personally? No, don't tell me. I shouldn't have asked. I don't want to know.'

'No secret. Around 11 per cent. Work it out, if you like. Next, what will happen to all this lucre when I die? It will be given away, all of it. I'd consider a short list you might suggest of worthy charities.'

Poor Phoebe started shuffling papers about.

'Next,' I continued, 'what has it all brought me? Lots of fun and, strange as it may seem, protected oblivion.'

She gave me a look as though I had just announced I had some dreadful illness.

I laughed. 'When we step out onto the street, Phoebe, does anyone recognise me? Would a passer-by say "Look, isn't that old what's-his-name who controls capital the size of half the third world's annual GNP? Without whom our trade deficit would plunge into the red down as far as hell?" Can you imagine a passing newshound squeezing into the nearest phone booth, ringing a tabloid to say, "Guess what? I just saw Titus Alston on a walkabout with a smashing blonde half a century his junior. For half a grand I'll shadow them for you." '

'Is that what you want, Titus?'

'You know I don't. In fact I give myself high marks for remaining anonymous when Alston Group has become a household name.'

'You're not anonymous. You have four inches in *Who's Who*.'

'I mean, people don't recognise me in public places.'

'Maybe they do and you don't notice. Anyway, what's so worthy about that?'

'Well, I've created what I've created, then stood aside, letting it account for itself. Doesn't that show I'm not vain?'

'Doesn't that show your vanity is of a less innocent nature?' said Phoebe, smiling at me from the corner of her eye.

'Why don't you book us a table at the Caprice, and get tickets for tonight's performance of *The Magic Flute* at the Royal Opera? We'll put my public invisibility to the test. More to the point, we'll have a lovely night out,' I said.

The Monster. My voracious, expanding *golem*. What are its components? I needn't consult Charon to remember a random selection: petrochemical industry and research labs in Texas, Mexico, Venezuela and Baku. Software companies in California and Japan. Luxury hotels in most of the world's capitals. Prime real estate in Manhattan, Miami, Rio, Monaco, London, Birmingham, Singapore. Satellite TV networks in Monaco, Sydney Australia, Perth, Scotland and Hong Kong. Half of Abu Tor in united Jerusalem – a birthday present from an ingratiating junior Sanhedrist whom I promptly sacked. Cattle ranches in Brazil and Montana, USA. One loss-making newspaper in Cape

Town. A Geneva-based pharmaceutical firm, world leader in genetic engineering, currently in the last stages of creating a sensational elixir of life. Vineyards in Tuscany and Provence. Shares everywhere. A money-spinner international legal firm, staffed by the brightest, meanest sharks in the business – essential for the aggressive take-over bids which have accounted for much of Alston Group's growth. A commercial rocket satellite-launching programme – a joint venture with the Chinese government. Russia, which has been at the basis of my financial empire-building, I've more or less written off.

Last but not least, my new baby, born of my association with Phoebe: a pure science DNA research institute, based in the heart of Yorkshire, not far from Ilkley. One day the world will bless my memory for that.

In theory, the Group could feed starving Africa for a decade. Or foot the bills for half a dozen or so expensive wars of liberation.

As for me personally, I have a house near Primrose Hill, appointed for utility. No car. Four or five suits which have grown a little too large for me. No works of art. In fact, nothing that an upmarket self-respecting burglar would risk his career for.

Maybe Phoebe was right, about the nature of my vanity.

16

Our commissar, Iliya Savitzky, became depressed. He stopped talking to us. There were no more exhortations, and no lecturing. Savitzky sat apart, muttering darkly to himself, ominously playing with his revolver. We lost touch with the leadership in Moscow; we didn't know how the war was progressing on other fronts because Savitzky, whose job it was, among other things, to keep us informed on such matters, had fallen silent. However, before he could get round to blowing his brains out, Pugachev had sent him packing. Pugachev didn't give a damn about official pronouncements, nor about commissars, whom he anyway despised. But it offended him that anyone in his command should not pull his weight – he had no time for a soldier who had lost his nerve; that's how Pugachev was.

The replacement arrived two days after Savitzky had departed. His name was Oleg Asimovitch Tartayev. He was a burly man with fixed, staring black eyes and a slit of a mouth hidden in the depth of a thick black beard. No sooner had Tartayev settled down than he let it be known that he was a crack shot, and that he had studied to become a priest in the very same theological seminary in Tiflis to which Comrade Josef Vissarianovich Stalin had gone. Then he set about interviewing the men with the cold passion of a grand inquisitor. No one – not even Pugachev – was left in doubt that now the Party's ears and eyes were deep into the heart of our Cossack cavalry, through the untiring agency of Comrade Oleg Asimovitch Tartayev.

By the time we went on the offensive, Tartayev had learnt to ride passably well on his large-footed, dun-coloured gelding. We fought a battle outside Voronezh, and routed an élite White cavalry regiment. When it was over, we rested on the outskirts of a forest some distance away from our wounded, so that we wouldn't hear their groans.

Our quartermaster, a rough Ukrainian, rode in at the head of a party, dragging an enemy soldier who had been hiding under a pile of firewood in a clearing. The captive was young, hardly more than a boy, well-formed and fair-haired. He was so frightened he shat himself. The rope our men tied him with had cut into his wrists; his hands were swollen purple.

'What shall we do with this White piece of meat?' the quartermaster shouted.

Pugachev shrugged his shoulders. 'I don't care what you do with him. Shoot him, if you like. Only not here,' he replied.

When the lad heard that, he fell to his knees and blubbered uncontrollably. Tartayev sauntered across. Standing over him, he said softly, 'Don't cry, laddie, don't cry.'

The boy looked up, wide blue eyes gushing tears. 'Please, sir, for the love of God, don't kill me . . . I haven't harmed anybody, I swear to you.'

His mouth was trembling violently. He couldn't speak coherently for the sobs. I had never seen anyone so terrified.

Tartayev ungloved his hand and laid it on the boy's head. He drew his knife and cut the rope on his wrists. Immediately, the boy threw his arms round Tartayev's legs. His weeping grew even louder as he pressed his face to our commissar's thighs. Tartayev hauled the boy to his feet.

'No one's going to kill you, son,' he said, and stroked the boy's head. 'You're free. Go home.'

We watched the prisoner, still trembling, his face wet with tears and spittle, stagger back a few steps.

'God bless you, sir,' he mumbled. 'My name is . . .'

Tartayev's eyes narrowed. 'Who gives a shit what your name is? Scram!'

So the lad turned and began to run back towards the wood, scampering up the path of trodden snow the horses had made. Tartayev walked calmly to his mount, pulled his rifle out of the saddle holster, took aim, and shot the boy in the back of the head. We heard the bullet smack into him. He fell face down, like an axed tree.

'I changed my mind,' said Tartayev, and sat down amongst us to eat his lunch.

None of us said a word. We feared Tartayev and his ideology of death. Killing was killing. Red, White; it didn't matter much any more, so long as it wasn't you.

Pugachev gave Tartayev a look, spat on the ground but said nothing.

*   *   *

When Sergei Aleksandrevich Pugachev puts on his General's uniform, there is barely room on his considerable chest to squeeze in a pin among the clutter of medals.

Twice Hero of the Soviet Union, Pugachev is what they call a soldiers' soldier, a man who leads from the front; a man civilian officials reflexively detest.

Is Pugachev courageous? Not if courage means simply overcoming fear. Sergei doesn't know what fear is. A total imagination dysfunction in that department. Physical fear, that is, imminent violent danger.

What fear, I wonder, crept into his heart in 1937 when, along with Budenni, he betrayed his erstwhile comrade and commander Mikhail Nikolaevich Tukhatchevsky, and told himself he was acting like a patriot?

In war, Sergei knew only one direction: forward. You need good luck in an open-ended flow to support such heroism. Pugachev had it. Time and time again he had led his men to victory against the odds. Or at least brought most of them back alive, which is the next best thing. Yes, whatever star guided Sergei's fortune through the vicissitudes of war, it served him well. But for one incident, I'd therefore say the Alston Group owes its existence to Pugachev's luck – its godparent.

As a solder Sergei Aleksandrevich surpassed his mentor Budenni. Budenni never developed beyond a Cossack chieftain leading cavalry charges. Yet his legend lived on in songs long after he himself became nothing more than a vodka-sloshing buffoon in a Field Marshal's uniform, pandering to Stalin's vanity. While Sergei made the rank of Lieutenant-General by the skin of the teeth.

My bond with Sergei Aleksandrevich – for a bond it has

been – is full of contradictions. Twice he commended me for decoration. Once, fulsomely – out of guilt – after the incident in Drogichin, when he rode away on my horse leaving me for dead. Then again after the Battle of Stalingrad, deservedly, therefore grudgingly. He saved my life and resented it. I saved his twice, which made him more resentful. Under his command, I submitted to his authority without reverence. He reluctantly acknowledged my worth and later took what I gave him, and hated me for it. Gratitude never came into our relationship.

He loathed Jews, yet married a Jewish woman whom he loved devotedly. Perhaps one of the grudges he bore me in perpetuity was that I lacked those obvious stereotypical Jewish qualities, as he saw them, which made him comfortable being a Jew-hater.

And for all that, of all the people I've ever known Sergei Aleksandrevich Pugachev was the only one whose approval I sought uncritically, even as he was delivered to me in Berlin, a confused pathetic shambles of a man with only his pride left intact.

What would a shrink pronounce on this? 'Now here, Alston, is the sublimation of a complex ambivalence in your feelings towards Russia, which reflect your own sense of rootlessness'?

My feeling for Russia defies categorisation. It haunts me in my dreams; it surfaces in memories of wind-swept land where the Don and the Volga flow with deceptive calm. Where horses gallop amidst exploding shells from Rostov to Tsaritsyn, later Stalingrad; and tanks advancing before grim-faced troops.

With a different hand from fortune, I might have lived out my days here, to an earthy rhythm of rustic love, beneath a bronze moon reflected in the lascivious water of the Volga. Here, Pugachev's life briefly but determiningly intertwined with mine.

International emergencies notwithstanding, the American immigration official was a stickler for routine.

'Welcome to Washington DC, Mr Alston.' A Hollywood smile as she perused my passport.

Chad was at my side, with a bloke from the White House

and the top gun from the airport management. But this nice lady wasn't awed, just went on doing her job. Democracy at its healthiest.

'Your first visit to the USA, Mr Alston?'

'No, Ma'am. I've been here before.'

'Your profession?'

'Tycoon.'

'Is that a fact,' she smiled, leafing through the visaed pages of my passport. 'What is the purpose of your visit?'

I might have said, 'To help save the world from a nuclear disaster.'

Chad smiled. The young man from the White House reached into his jacket's breast pocket like a movie gangster – for a badge or something?

'Fun,' I said.

'I wish you lots of it. Have you ever belonged to a Communist Party?'

'No, Ma'am.'

'Do you, or have you had friends who are or have been Communist?'

I smiled broadly. 'Some of my best friends have been Communists.'

That was where my reception committee intervened. With an official 'Have a nice day' in train, I was whisked through immigration and customs to a waiting limousine outside.

For the record, I was never a communist. Not by persuasion, nor by Party membership. Ideologies give me moral indigestion. Sergei Pugachev, on the other hand, was a Party member. Like his friend Vyacheslav Mikhaelovich Molotov, he unquestioningly defended everything Stalin said and did. But whereas Molotov was a true believer to the end, Pugachev concealed threadbare convictions with artful deceit, all the more convincing because he had learnt to delude himself.

Sergei's memory of our first encounter or, for that matter, of the events that followed, does not altogether accord with mine. So much has happened to us both in and around Tsaritsyn, the Verdun of the civil war. So many died. So many more were still to die twenty-two years on, at the same time of year.

A sprawling, charmless town, surrounded by barbed-wired fortifications and divided by the Volga, it was here that Sergei cut his teeth as a serious commander. It was also here, more or less contemporaneously, that Josef Stalin had his first taste of dictatorship.

Unarmed and horseless I came to Tsaritsyn on a burnished morning in the autumn of 1918. I made my way to Pugachev's camp which lay a few versts north of the town, and, by way of initiation, witnessed an execution.

Budenni's Red Cavalry Brigade, enhanced the following year to a full-size army, the *Konarmiia*, was in its infancy. For a few crucial months in 1918 to 1919, Russia's fate pivoted on Tsaritsyn, just as it did on Stalingrad in 1942. In June 1919, General Petr Wrangel stormed Tsaritsyn at the head of his Cossack cavalry, only to be driven thence soon afterwards. That October, we routed the White Cavalry outside Voronezh. In January the next year, Budenni led us cantering through the streets of Rostov on the Don, where two years before the Whites had their first decisive victory. The war was effectively won on the southern front.

I don't think Sergei realised how close he came to being shot dead when he handed me his loaded pistol on my first day in his regiment, which might have been my last.

How vividly I remember his small cold eyes, fixed in stupid hostility. The bullet head and thick neck, the drooping walrus moustache. The pleasant coolness of the gun as I balanced it in my hand.

I stepped back six or seven paces, until the door was virtually against my back. The empty weariness of the past few days was suddenly transformed into a vast homicidal calm. I raised my pistol arm slowly, button by button up Pugachev's tunic, until the end of the muzzle sight settled in the crease between his eyes. A sepulchral headstone of a torso above the desk, legs booted and bowed and comically irrelevant below, Sergei Aleksandrevich didn't move a hair. He just sat there staring at me, as though the logic of a pointing gun had turned us partners.

I thought, 'If he doesn't die with the first, I'll get him with the second. Three more for whoever comes rushing through the door. The last one for myself, straight up the mouth.'

My finger tightened round the trigger. His face went serious, furrows deepening across his brow. I thought, 'He's going to say something. I won't let him.' He leaned to one side and farted thunderously. Relieved, he smiled. It must have pleased him to trumpet a fart of so distinguished a timbre.

I swung my arm away and pumped a cluster of shots into the orders sheet on the wall. Pugachev was impressed. He had in mind to detail me to kitchen duties, as the cook's assistant. Now he pondered a dilemma: what was better for the battalion, another cook who can shoot like the devil but can't cook, or a new horse soldier, without either a mount or weapons, who isn't even a Cossack.

I saw General Petr Nikolaevich Wrangel only once, during my brief captivity by his troops. An enormously tall man, well over six feet, his face was haughty and forbidding. They said about him that in October the year before he shot 400 Bolshevik prisoners as they were brought before him. No mercy.

Maybe the grey stallion I took from his camp was his, and maybe not. I never much cared one way or the other. Sergei did. The more he coveted the horse, the more it mattered to him to believe it belonged to his arch-enemy. Like some voodoo witch doctor he believed that if he rode Wrangel's horse, Wrangel himself would be diminished. It was a good mount, no doubt about that, but in my opinion not a patch on Lara, my beloved little mare. Pugachev's obsession, not the horse's outstanding quality, entered it into the Regiment's folklore. So it became the accepted superstition that whoever rode that pale stallion was by Providence protected from enemy fire.

When I returned on the back of the stallion, my comrades greeted me like I was a hero. Tatya this, Tatya that . . . But not Pugachev. Legs astride, he smacked the top of his boot with his riding-crop. Not a word. The eyes said, 'Why don't you just get off that horse and die!' I thought, 'This man loves to hate.'

I dismounted and walked the horse to him. Standing before him I held the reins in one hand, away from me though not quite at him. The gesture was clear all the same: all Sergei had to do was to ask. Not even that; 'What a splendid horse' would have sufficed'. I'd have given him the horse there and then.

I'd have accepted in return any old nag that was available. And my rightful place in his esteem.

Pugachev looked the horse over at a glance, turned on his heel and walked away. I swore I would never again try to appease him. If he wanted the horse, he would have to take it from me any way he could. After that, I rode the stallion with pride, mocking the stifled snarl of envy in Pugachev's eyes.

Poor Sergei suffered from stomach disorders. Indigestion and diarrhoea at the base, acute constipation on campaigns. All considering, a more favourable pattern than the other way round would have been, because if there was one thing Sergei dreaded it was that his men might mistake his discomfort for before-the-battle jitters.

When he came to London, he was in a real state. I sent him to a Harley Street specialist, a South African Jew called Joe Greenberg. It so happened Mr Greenberg was absolutely the best in his field. If he weren't, I'd still have sent Pugachev to him, having wickedly decided that a Jewish doctor had to be a part of Sergei's treatment. The treatment lasted six weeks, including dietary instruction. Sergei Pugachev never suffered again thereafter.

But in October 1919, in a bombed-out street in Veronezh, Pugachev's bowels' hitherto dependable pattern of behaviour was suddenly and violently reversed; he was caught short in the heat of battle.

Surrounded by his command group, Budenni saw me from a distance and beckoned me to approach.

'What the hell's holding up Sergei Aleksandrevich?' he snapped.

I said I didn't know but there was bound to be a good reason.

'Tell him to move at once up the street as far north as possible. Go!' said Budenni.

I cantered to where Pugachev was supposed to be. There stood his horse held by one of his lieutenants, himself mounted and fidgeting, but no sign of Pugachev. A moment later he emerged from a nearby deserted house, hitching up his breeches. I was about to deliver Budenni's order when I saw a sniper in a ground-floor window across the street, taking aim at Pugachev's back. I whipped my carbine out and emptied the entire magazine at the enemy sniper.

As Sergei stood directly in the line of fire the hail of my bullets must have come pretty close to him. He glared at me, white with rage, then let fly with a string of curses. I pointed at the window behind him where now only the bloody shoulder of the dead sniper was visible. Pugachev glanced quickly before turning on me, unplacated.

'You mother-fucking *durak*!' he bellowed. 'The last thing I need is to be shot dead by a fool in my own outfit!'

I passed on Budenni's message. He mounted, pulled violently at the horse's mouth. 'I know what I'm to do,' he rumbled, then spurred his horse on.

What do soldiers do on the eve of a battle? They huddle together, singing. They tell smutty jokes, bantering with each other. 'Hey, Tatya, what did Dunia do to you out there in the barn, eh? Measure your cock, did she? "Sorry, *galupchik*, what I need is a dick the size of a ten inches salami." Isn't that what she said to you? Ha ha ha.'

When the jokes run out, when at last the ribaldry is spent, the story-teller begins to weave his shamanistic spell. His stories are simple, mostly familiar. Tales of legends and heroism; of pure selfless love, of sacrifice and treachery; of Good's ultimate triumph over Evil. Always.

Shall I tell you something? I loved this childish pish-posh. Together with my comrades, I sat by the glowing embers waiting for the magic to begin working. Yes, the magic in these stories that transforms distrust to unity, fear to selfless courage, doubt to certainty. Until by dawn you are ready for anything. To die. Be a hero. Accept the absurdity of men butchering each other because someone good with words has labelled the other side the enemy.

So, on one such night, when that stage was reached, a comrade called Vlada, who fell at the first charge the next morning, lit a cigarette from a burning twig of the camp fire and put his arm around my shoulders.

'Tatya,' he said, his eyes brimming with tears, 'something tells me tomorrow we shall part for ever. Tell me where your dearest and nearest are that I may write to them how brave you were.'

I once knew an English civil servant from the War Office. A quiet unassuming man, he rose unspectacularly from junior clerk to heading a unit which dealt with munitions. He lived in Clapham or some similar place, probably in one of those uniform semi-detached houses with a front and a back garden. He had a wife and children, and maybe a cat or a dog or a budgie called Joey. Every morning, regular as clockwork, he would leave home and board the train that took him to work. Every evening at the same time he would return home on a train filled with hundreds of men like himself who all wore suits similar to his own and sat behind the *Daily Express*, just as he did.

He owned no car. Had no debts. Spent evenings at home by the fire, wearing slippers his wife had bought him at Woolworths, listening to the wireless or reading, or watching TV on a set they had acquired on the hire-purchase system. Yearly holidays were always taken at the same boarding-house at some seaside resort. In short, behold the latter-day John Bull of that dour, punctilious species that kept going the largest, happiest empire the world has ever known!

One day, only a few months before retirement, this hitherto utterly dependable brick did a disappearing act; vanished without trace, leaving behind a distraught family. Why? Whatever strange urges secretly ruled his life, could he not have hung on for just a little longer so as to qualify for well-earned pension? Enigma. Where to? Another enigma.

A man from Scotland Yard, or was it MI5, came round to interview me. The vanished civil servant was being investigated in connection with alleged irregular export permits for artillery shells to Nicaragua. Did I, by any chance, know where the fellow had gone? I was certain the man was innocent; moreover, I suspected it was really me they were wanting to investigate.

I said, 'What is this? What am I, some kind of crook? A gun-runner?'

In reply, the officer gave me that 'We have information . . .' line, loaded with veiled threats.

I showed him the door, told him to see my lawyer if there were any charges against me. I never heard from him again. The file was closed – another one of those unresolved cases.

This anecdotal digression isn't quite as pointless as it may seem. You see, like the English civil servant, I might have waited and got honourably discharged, medals and all. Joined the Party. Secured a job somewhere in the endless labyrinth of Soviet bureaucracy. Married a sensible deep-chested Russian girl. Raised a family in a poky one-room apartment in Arbat. Denounced a colleague or two to the KGB. Dutifully slurped up the wife's *schi* day in, day out, until at last, lo, I'm a senior apparatchik with a dacha and a Volga car.

But on the morning of 15 February 1921, still weak from my ordeal at Drogichin, I deserted once again. I arrived in Kronstadt at the beginning of March, a fortress town, battlements and guns overlooking a brooding naval flotilla lodged in the ice-locked sea of the Gulf of Finland. Inside, hunger and anger egged on a crazed population into the savage uprising that was to lower the curtains on the last act of the Civil War.

Barely a year before, I had fought under the command of the Red Army's most brilliant leader, General Mikhail Nikolaevich Tukhatchevsky. Now I was on the receiving end of his assault. When Kronstadt fell, I was taken prisoner with all the others who survived. But in that disorganised lottery of life and death, I drew a lucky number: instead of facing the firing squad, I was sent to Solovki Prison on the bleak Solovetskii Island in the White Sea. Tukhatchevsky, hero of the day, was tried and shot in 1937.

On my time in that once ancient monastery of a prison, memory is blurred, or perversely recalcitrant. Six years, for sure. No trial. No sentence. Days and nights ruled by a prison regime and the tyranny of the stomach. The cold that contracted everything into a bare numb *I am* throbbing with toothaches. I worked building roads no one would use. I read *War and Peace* repeatedly, until I knew it by heart. I taught myself German from a book I got in exchange for a strip of felt and the remains of a candle. I learnt to play poker from a Petrograd card conjuror who hanged himself with his belt. He told me I was a natural.

Having forgotten why I was there in the first place, I greeted my liberation from Solovki more with wary apprehension than with a sense of relief that justice had belatedly reached its hand to me. Perhaps they needed room for the arriving hordes of new prisoners, who knows.

One way or the other, I was taken out one morning and, blinking at the sudden light, sucked into the unfathomed servitude of freedom.

It must have been 1927, or thereabouts.

17

Phoebe is an accomplished musician. A tolerably good pianist, she says. But a first-class flautist – that's an expert's judgment. I come into her world of music-making as an invited guest who is nevertheless excluded from its intimate communion.

A friend of hers, a composer, had written a chamber piece on the theme of the Beatitudes. There was in it a long melodious part for the flute. Phoebe played it for me. I was strangely moved, even though I'm indifferent to modern music.

That evening on the Nine o'clock news there was a more than usually gruesome report from Gaza. Provoked by stone-throwing Palestinian youths, Israeli soldiers opened fire with live ammunition. Eight children were killed instantly. Four more died in hospital. Hysteria spread through the entire occupied territories. There were riots in Hebron, Nablus, Jerusalem. Angry demonstrations were held in Tel Aviv, for peace, against peace. Demagogues of both camps were having a field day. I zapped the television off. Phoebe gets upset by violence, particularly against the Palestinians, with whom she sympathises.

She was holding her friend's composition in her lap, annotating the score with a pencil. She looked up momentarily, then returned to her preoccupation with the music. However, her expression had changed; a tense gravity had set about her mouth. I could tell she was trying to decide whether or not to say something. Phoebe believes I side with the Israelis against the Palestinians. This is not entirely true, I have to say. What Phoebe seems unable to accept is that most losers are losers just so, independent of circumstances; and the Palestinians are a case in point.

At last she spoke. ' "Blessed are the peacemakers . . ." Where in God's name are they?'

'Pensioned off. Gone out of fashion,' I replied.

'Oh. So what's in fashion now?'

'Yuppies. Greed. Thatcher-style small-mindedness. It's a worldwide epidemic. Don't you read the newspapers?'

'Sometimes, Titus, I wonder whether there isn't too much cruelty in your cynicism,' she said softly.

I have seen how tough-minded Phoebe can be, no push-over in any circumstances, so her rare surrenders touch my heart. I wanted to caress the vulnerable curve of her nape. I wanted to hold her.

'What's the point of having power and influence, Titus,' she said without looking at me, 'if you don't put it to some good purpose?'

What could I tell her? That power has its own rules and limitations? That in reality one only has a temporary mandate over its administration, anything more was vain self-delusion? That anyway my term in power has already expired? Then round off with some anodyne banality like, 'My dear, I'm a realist not a cynic'?

I reached over to touch her cheek. She turned her lips onto my hand.

'What would you want me to do?' I asked. She pressed my hand to her face. How young she was.

I need to digress a little at this point. Wagner's *Die Walküre* (Phoebe and I saw it in Bayreuth the year before), last act. Alone with Brünnhilde on a remote rock, Wotan is about to withdraw immortality from the one he most loves. The terror coursing through Brünnhilde's mind at the thought of becoming an ordinary mortal, I can only imagine. But Wotan's sadness, the guilt he feels, and the love, all expressed in his farewell aria, I recognise. Because, in a way, this is what I've done to Phoebe. By taking her to my bosom and into my bed, haven't I robbed her of the brief immortality of youth, unreal though it is? And won't she be left surrounded by a ring of fire, awake not asleep, when I pass away?

She said, 'I don't know. It was just a thought. Forget it.'

The next morning I decided to try my hand at peace-making.

I rented Ditchley for a weekend. A stately home near Oxford turned into a research-cum-conference centre, Ditchley offers an ego-pleasing combination of state-of-the-art communication facilities and aristocratic serenity. I invited two delegations of prominent Arabs and Jews, twenty a side, covering a wide range of political opinion, including representatives of the most intransigent streams in Israel and among the Arabs.

I commissioned the most unerring team of trans-faith caterers that ever came together: super-kosher to the last crumb, Halal to the very comma of every possible injunction in the Koran. No booze, of course. Orange juice strictly from neutral Spain and Italy.

With the help of expert diplomats, I had an agenda drawn that was a masterpiece of inoffensive, non-controversial vagueness. Former US President Jimmy Carter cabled to say he was down with the flu and couldn't come, so in his stead an old Middle East hand from *The Economist* stepped in at the last moment to act as moderator. I accepted a quaint touch of humour in the form of two notices outside the conference room pointing at opposite directions, one saying Check-in point for Uzis, the other, Check-in point for Kalashnikovs.

Jews and Arabs took their seats for the opening session in a reasonably relaxed mood – some actually shook hands and smiled at each other.

'Gentlemen,' I began, 'I want to thank each one of you for coming here. I realise it has not been easy. And I would say that in accepting our invitation you have all shown moral courage . . .'

A string of superlative praises for each people. A sympathetic outline of their respective national aspirations. The suffering they had both experienced for too long. Which was why the time had surely come to turn swords into ploughshares. A god-almighty ego-massage: for this, perhaps historic weekend the destiny of the Middle East lay in their hands; History would not be forgiving if they failed. Blah blah blah.

Then the punch line. An unspecified sum of money in excess of £1 million would be immediately allocated to each side, followed by an on-going review for subsidising any project – Jewish or Arab – that ultimately led to peaceful cooperation. Their part of the deal was to come up by the end of the weekend with a public joint declaration of intent to create a framework for peace negotiations between Israel, the Palestinians and the rest of the Arab world.

I proceeded to outline Ditchley's amenities enhanced by me for the occasion: multilingual secretarial services for each committee room; instant telephone link-up to any part of the world. Data access to diverse international sources of information, through Charon . . .

My guests listened, toying with the personalised gold-plated Parker pens each received as a memento, and smiled tersely at each other.

I handed over to the expert from *The Economist* and swanned off to an adjoining room for a stiff shot of vodka with Phoebe.

All appeared to go swimmingly. By lunch, I was ready for some cautious congratulation, when, leaning across the laden table, Rabbi Shlomo Buxbaum from Kiryat Arba in the West Bank, formerly from Brooklyn, addressed the Imam of Regent's Park opposite him.

'Tell me, Reverence, have you read *The Advance of the Crescent?*'

He was referring to a recently published study of Islam by a maverick orientalist with a notorious tendency to shock. The book, allegedly subsidised by an American Zionist source, was so offensive to Moslems that it provoked a new declaration of *Jihad* against the West by extreme Moslem fundamentalist leaders, notably the Ayatollah Khomeini of Iran. The fallout decimated the value of shares on the London Stock Exchange for a week.

The Imam of Regent's Park frowned.

'You haven't?' Rabbi Buxbaum raised his eyebrows, 'Reverence, you really must. It explains crystal-clear who does what to whom. Who's the victim and who's the aggressor. A thought-provoking book, believe me.'

'So is *Mein Kampf,* believe me,' retorted the Imam.

A moment of deathly silence. Then total fiasco. Bagels,

gefilte fish, humus, shishlick and kebab whistled across the room like missiles.

Phoebe and I drove home, drank more vodka and laughed ourselves to sleep.

I gave up being a peacemaker.

Power, vestigial now in my case, is at the heart of Phoebe's attraction to me. In my heart of hearts, I know it. Yet she has introduced an evangelical twist to it: she wants me to be the man who willingly, demonstratively, threw it away for the sake of something greater. Like that Roman prince in *Quo Vadis* who turns his back on his legions; like some powerful pagan who gives up power and position to become a lion's Christian dinner.

What is there in the entire world that's greater than power? Phoebe thinks its the only thing that really matters to me.

I never told her what I've really most desired, particularly since knowing her. Something very ordinary. Something that would have diminished that vague aura of magic and mystery which are part and parcel of how she sees me. Or have I underestimated her character? Anyway, it's too late now.

I mean a family. A large noisy one. And a yearly cycle dotted with birthdays and communal celebrations. The undirected theatre of kids growing up. The ritualised temperance of bereavement. Life, flowing continuously in a polyphony of heartbeats.

I would envisage a house. Spacious; untidy with books and trivial objects. A rocking horse, and an enormous use-worn table made of testimonial oak, where we all sit together on special occasions to a loud discourse of sons, daughters, grand-children, great-grandchildren.

A child, tugging at its little cousin's hand, would whisper: 'Look, Great-grandpa's fallen asleep!'

'No he hasn't. He's only pretending. He always does that.'

The old matriarch would smile with her eyes, recognising patriarchal escapism.

Yet when Phoebe tells me she loves me, I say inwardly to myself: 'Don't be moved too much, don't charge it with too deep a meaning; just take it for what it is, a term of endearment, nothing more.' That enables me to smile at her instead of touching her lips with a prohibiting finger, as I used to do in the beginning, when she first began to say that.

Another thing I tell myself to ease this necessary realignment of emotion: 'Old men – even more so very special old men – should *love*, but not be *in love*. And they should resist the vanity of wanting to have children whose growing up they will not live to see.'

Does all this reflect the benevolent ruthlessness of wisdom, which is one of old age's few blessings? Or is it a cop-out, a mere disguise of the fear of commitment? A question I haven't yet resolved. Meanwhile, I shower her with gifts. I tell her that I love her, selflessly, like she was my own flesh and blood. Always. In my heart, I fight a rearguard battle against this business of being in love, as though it were an unseemly hormonal rebellion. Outwardly, however, I let it show defiantly, because it's Phoebe, not I, who is on the receiving end of malicious gossip. I would not appear to be anything but totally committed to her.

Sometimes she looks at me as if to say, 'I understand your worries and inner conflict. You must come to terms with them on your own. Only don't take too long.' But how can one put a time limit on such dilemmas, even when time isn't plentiful any more?

How, when, or where it all began between us is of little importance. What matters is what followed from the first awkward occasion of our love-making.

I bought a house overlooking Primrose Hill; her choice. An old mottled dark red-brick house secluded in a walled garden, it imparts at a first glance a mood of diffidence that is peculiarly English. Everything in it reflects her touch, her taste, her personality. I have contrived, by stealth almost, not to stamp my mark on it. Phoebe has registered this without saying a word.

I rationalise, saying to myself, 'She should be completely free after I die. No monuments, no relics which either devalue or appreciate ridiculously with time. Only memories, for her to preserve or discard as she pleases.'

I don't think I really wanted to love her. And then I did, all too suddenly, when I saw her one evening play the flute with a small ensemble of friends. The way she held it. Her breath, transformed into beautiful sound, enticed me into helpless loving on the last lap of my life. Curious, isn't it? Considering I'm not in the least musical.

She goes to church, blessed Phoebe.

'On Good Friday,' she once told me, 'we pray for Jews, Turks and infidels. That's when I say a special prayer for you, Titus.'

'As a Jew or an infidel?' I asked.

'Infidel, of course,' she laughed, adding, 'Praying is good for you. Try it sometime. You don't have to believe, you know.'

'I'll think about it. Whom should I pray for, then, you?'

'No. For yourself. You're a beginner in this business. Praying for others comes later,' she said.

I touch her lovely body and feel ashamed to put my own time-ravaged unlovely self against her. She is sensitive to my shyness, she dims the bedroom light before I disrobe.

'What does age matter, for Christ's sake?' she says, 'Look at Picasso, look at Pablo Casals.'

'My egomania is more modest than theirs.'

'You must be joking! Kiss me. Touch me. I love you.'

My old cock, cajoled to stiffness, poor old Lazarus, raised from the dead almost. And when I see that faraway fucky look in her half-closed eyes and half-open mouth, when I taste her breath, I'm further aroused by sweet, lazy jealousy at what she might be imagining in her pleasure.

I wake up early, full two hours before the radio clock is set to come on at 7.30. My bladder is bursting. As I edge back into bed, Phoebe stirs and turns towards me, her breasts against my chest. Warm puffs of her breath on my neck ... Dear God, gods, demons, whoever's in charge out there, here's a prayer I've just thought of: 'Make me love this beautiful gentle girl steadfastly, with a cheerful rainbow of emotion. And with quiet resignation. Amen.'

Over a breakfast croissant, apropos of nothing, I said: 'When I'm dead, Phoebe, I want you to marry soon and forget me. Find a kind-hearted, sensible, handsome young fellow, one who likes to pray, preferably. Have a good time. Have lots of children. No need to worry about money, ever. I'll take care of that.'

She cried, and said it was nothing, just a bad dream that upset her. Then she left the table to have a bath.

How many women have I slept with? At a rough guess between two hundred and two hundred and fifty. That's not prodigiously promiscuous when you spread it over nearly three quarters of a century. How many of them have I loved? In one way or another, most of them. I certainly don't remember those I didn't. Love doesn't necessarily have to be a great experience. A brief encounter charged with intense pleasure and affection, which leaves you with sweet memories, will qualify.

The heart's Big Bang? That's another matter altogether. That's like a reckless investment with magnified prospects of loss and gain looming against each other. A suspension of normality, I say. Who are the big loves of my live? Minou, whom I loved in Paris, most violently. Phoebe, most radiantly. Wanda? Well, yes, her too; most artfully.

I value Wanda for her courage, for her honesty, for her generosity of spirit, and after this string of obituary clichés, I might as well add that more than anything I'm grateful that we've remained friends.

In mid-August 1982, I think it was, she rang me, insisted that I take her out to lunch. I was busy, I told her. She said, 'You're always busy, Titus. This Friday, or I swear I'll never talk to you again.'

We met at the Connaught. She wanted grouse. I said that in my opinion grouse was overrated, a well-roasted chicken was far tastier, not to mention cheaper.

Wanda said, 'You have chicken. I want grouse.'

She was heavily made up, with bright red lipstick. She was wearing a champagne-coloured Christian Dior number which emphasised the liver spots on the backs of her hands. I teased her, saying wasn't it funny that a Communist intellectual who loathed blood sports for ideological reasons now sat here of all places, relishing the queen of upper-class game birds.

'That was a long time ago,' she said, leaving half the bird

221

uneaten on her plate. 'You were right, by the way, about the grouse. How was your chicken?'

'Chickeny. I'll bet you vote Tory, don't you?'

'Of course. What else?' She still had that throaty bubbly laughter. 'Actually, no. I voted Liberal last time, if you must know. Small, nice, harmless.'

For dessert, Wanda devoured an enormous chunk of rich cake topped with cream. Then she wiped her lips and looked at me.

'You don't remember, do you?' she said.

'Remember what?'

'This day.'

'Remind me.'

She shook her head and smiled. I shrugged my shoulders.

'I can never remember dates and anniversaries,' I said.

She laid her arthritic hand on my arm. 'Darling Titus, for so many years I've been wondering what you really are. Now at last I understand. You're a catalyst. You change other people's lives without yourself changing. You set off chain reactions without giving away anything of yourself. How lonely it must be for you, poor Titus.'

If there were a fuckers' guild to confer prizes, Wanda would have got the top award for copulatory choreography, legs down. The trouble with Wanda's fuckery, however, was that like her emotion it was too intense, like her thinking it was too didactic, and like her love, consuming. No amount of inventive artistry and subtle variation of nuance could conceal the underlying, insatiable voracity of her emotion.

On reaching a climax, she would arch her neck and shout, '*O mein Gott!*', loud enough for the neighbour in the next room to start banging on the wall.

I said, 'How can you, an intellectual Communist, invoke a god in whom you don't believe? Wouldn't it be more honest to shout '*O mein Karl Marx!*' Or at least '*O mein Lenin!*'

She sulked. The next time she roared at the top of her lungs '*O mein Willi Münzenberg!*', he being her Communist boss. 'Satisfied now?' she asked. We both laughed.

222

Berlin is like . . . Berlin is . . . I stop for breath, try again. Berlin is a cacophonous mass of multi-everything that's human. A symmetry run amok. The ideal and ultimate caricature of urban habitation. Berlin is a sublime oxymoron – an elevated debasement, and vice versa. Berlin is the whizzing, buzzing, screeching, laughing and sighing agitation that whirls around, and up and down the Great Tower of Babel. Berlin is the last prophetic delirium of a dying animus. Phew!

I stand on the pavement of the flowing Friedrichstrasse. Rain is sheeting down in a dazzling shimmer, like a liquid glass bead curtain. Then it stops, discharging light into the street, onto the trundling tram-cars. I feel I want to zoom like a crazy aeroplane into the heart of the city and loop in her space. I am the barbarian, come from a whispering wilderness to this seething metropolis. Where shall I turn? Right? Left? Forward? Anywhere but back.

A man comes towards me, opaque preoccupation shielding his face. '*Entschuldigung* . . .' I can't understand what he says.

'*Entschuldigung, Ich bin hier fremd,*' I reply.

He looks through me. He walks on without another word.

My possessions, such as they are, are all contained in one canvas bag, effortlessly portable. I have money in my pocket, Swiss Francs, English pounds, ten US dollars. Not a great sum. How long will it last? A week? Maybe two? I can't tell. I understand that money, like air, like water, is essential for life in a place like this. Yet these crumpled notes, which are to fuel my survival for an unknown period of time, are also a burden I want to shed. They are certificates of my new, conditional freedom, issued by one *Tovarish* Captain Osip Goldstein of the Soviet Security Police.

A thief, like me discharged from prison, had advised, 'Go to Leningrad, the pickings are rich there.' And there, a tired whore mused, 'Ah, if I were younger and prettier, I'd pop over to Finland. What's here but misery?'

I made my way to Vyborg, close to the Finnish border. I'd get a job cutting down trees or something, until I sorted myself out and decided what to do next.

At the border checkpoint he was waiting for me, a short sturdy man with one dark eyebrow stretched across his face

223

like a ledge. A gold tooth twinkled at the corner of his broken sickle of a mouth. There were two troopers with him, sub-machine-guns slung across their chests. All three were wearing army uniforms, complete with fur hats and high boots.

He looked at my papers, flicked ash from his cigarette, his pinky extended. He hummed a tune, trying to fool me he didn't know who I was, that this was just a regular border check. Then he read my papers out aloud with a curious deliberate intonation.

'Well, well, well . . . Titus no patronym Altermann. Parasite with a criminal record. Happy New Year, all the same.'

New Year? What was so happy about it? I was being nicked! I've just been officially described as a parasite. Grotesquely unfair!

'So where do you think you are going, if I may ask?'

Cat and mouse.

'My papers are in order, comrade, aren't they?'

He stuffed them in his coat's pocket. 'Forged. You could get another ten years for that, or shot.'

Correct, alas. But how was he to know, since the forgery was done on official paper by the official in charge himself, whom I had bribed?

I spread my arms out, sighed, grinned. 'I'll come quietly,' I said. 'Or maybe you'd rather shoot me here and have done with. It's all the same to me, comrade.'

The gold tooth flashed. 'Now now, don't be like that. You didn't really imagine you could kiss Mother Russia goodbye and walk away without us knowing about it, did you? Eh, Titus Altermann?'

I looked away.

He grabbed me by the chin and twisted my head. 'Look at me when I talk to you. What do you think we are, eh? A bunch of monkeys? You're dog-shit, that's what you are. *Gavno*! Don't think I wouldn't take you behind a tree and blow your face away for giving me lip. Only it so happens there are some important people who want you alive, so let's be cooperative, okay?'

'Who's important enough to want me alive, comrade?'

'Let's say, a certain hero of the war. A certain General, whom

224

you must thank for breathing free air normally denied to the likes of you.' He let go of my chin and wiped his hand on my chest.

Around us was the silence of forests under snow. If it weren't for the two troopers I'd have kicked his guts out and made a run for it across the border.

'Now then, your papers state mission as the purpose of your travel. Neat, I like that. Why don't we talk about it, eh? Maybe we could reach an understanding . . .'

I saw it all: a set-up. I've paid a bribe with all I had for something which had been already authorised beforehand! I thought I was smart, teaching a canny old grandma how to suck eggs!

The fellow took me by the arm. Away from his comrades, his manner changed. He introduced himself. He too came from Odessa. An implicit tribal familiarity suddenly entered his speech. There was no need for me to break with my country, he explained. Indeed, in exile I would be in a position to serve, which would not be a thankless task. Why not in Berlin? An exciting city, from what he had heard . . . Here was a new travel document, not quite a passport. Wasn't I a refugee of a sort? And the money with which I had foolishly tried to bribe the official, plus a bonus. So it's a mission after all, ha ha ha.

One more thing: a name in Berlin; a telephone number. Laszlo Schultz. Contact him on arrival, then leave the rest to him. 'Only for your own good, Comrade Altermann, be sure to do what he tells you.' A fat finger pointed at me in warning.

I thought, 'What the hell, once I'm away, finding a needle in an acre of haystacks would be easier than finding me.' Goldstein's grip tightened on my arm.

'Tatya,' he said with a sly grin, 'we aren't stupid, you know. There's always a good reason why a certain person is selected for a certain mission. Mistakes you make have a way of catching up with you eventually. And then you pay the price, with interest . . . Also, this General to whom you owe your life would be very sorry if you let your country down. Very sorry indeed, believe me. So be smart. Don't even think of double-crossing us, eh?'

I smiled weakly.

225

'I'm not going to preach ideology to you, that's not my job,' he purred. 'But I will say this to you. We've got you on a leash, a long one to be sure, but a leash all the same. You can't escape it. Think about it.'

I did, all the way to Berlin. Many thoughts passed through my mind: America? Maybe as a later option. England? An island. I've already spent years on one. The mere thought of an island is enough to make me ill. Paris? If they were so clever as to find me in Berlin, they would find me in Paris too. Anywhere in Europe, for that matter.

One thing was certain, find me they might. Take me back, they couldn't. Kill me, then? I wasn't afraid.

As for my saviour, General Sergei Aleksandrevich Pugachev . . . Here my resolve wobbled a little. Could it have been my need to belong? Misplaced loyalty? The tougher survival instincts prevailed: we were even, Pugachev and I; I owed him nothing. Besides, why was I presuming I would be called upon to do something wrong? Who's to judge what was right and what was wrong, anyway?

Stepping out from under a shelter, a street organ-grinder cranks up his contraption. There's a cheap-looking restaurant on the other side of Friedrichstrasse, and I'm hungry. The devil take Laszlo Schultz, whoever he is. I'm free. I want to eat, drink, fuck. Taste everything; have a good time. I'll think again of Schultz another time, maybe.

18

There is a touching parable in nature, for those who survive against the odds: the Little Auk. A young ornithologist once wrote to me, asking for money to help finance a research project he was undertaking. He sent an outline, with an eloquent plea in which he made reference to another, renowned, ornithologist from the Middle Ages, the Holy Roman Emperor Frederick II. I was impressed. The fellow had done his homework: he found out that I was an admirer of the dreadful *Stupor Mundi*.

The Little Auk (*Plautus alle*) is a small pelagic bird barely eight inches in length. It breeds on arctic cliffs in great, noisy colonies. It makes high-pitched squawking noises (the ornithologist enclosed a tape cassette). Its flight, as is its aspect, is endearingly comical. The little creature might had scrambled half-finished off the drawing-board before Nature had quite decided what it should be.

Possessed of marvellous underwater mobility, the Little Auk preys on fish, and is in turn preyed upon by skuas in the sky and arctic foxes on the ground.

At the end of the short arctic summer, the parent birds prepare to fly out to sea, ahead of winter. The fledgling chick has not yet had a trial flight. The cliffs stands a distance of a mile or so from the shore. Between the two safe havens lurks death, whose stalking field the chick must cross on its first solo flight.

Comes the day, and the cliffs echo with frenetic squawks. Above, skuas and gulls patrol the sky. Below, arctic foxes wait, maws salivating.

'Squawk,' say the parents to the young one. 'Pay attention now. Get the wind under your little wings. Flap like crazy. Keep

227

your eyes on the horizon. Fly as fast as you can, straight to sea. We'll be alongside, watching you. Good luck.'

The chick blinks. The sea is so far away. It's such a long drop from the cliff. How can the little chick be sure it can make it, having never flown before?

But there's no alternative. The parents take off. The chick takes a jump and flies unsteadily, escorted by its parents, while squadrons of skuas and gulls dive all around for an easy lunch.

Many chicks are taken in mid-air. Some crash-land on the beach to be snapped up by the foxes; it's a great day for killers. Of those who crash to the ground, only a handful miraculously reach the waves on foot, having successfully run the gauntlet of predators. What then? Their parents are gone. Bobbing in the water, the plucky little orphan chick now faces another survival test all on its own.

I tremble for survivors. Who is their patron saint, I'd like to know? What god of a sporting chance would set such fearful odds against them? Never pass a beggar in the street without giving something! That's another thing I'd tell my grand-children, if I had any.

I found a cheap boarding-house near Alexanderplatz. Just a bed, a tiny closet and a tough-looking room-mate called Rudi Schwann. He had just come out of prison, having done two years for complicity in an armed robbery. When Schwann noticed how I tucked my wallet under my pillow, he said with miffed dignity, 'You don't have to do that, you know. I'm a robber, not a thief.'

I didn't want him to get ideas about me, so I told him in the friendliest way possible that it made no difference to me what he was, I'd take him apart all the same if he tried anything. He looked me over with some respect, then laughed.

'Tough guy, eh?'

'I can take care of myself.'

'You been to prison?'

'Some.'

'I thought so. You want to buy a gun? I got a handy little piece, 7.65mm Beholla.'

I said I had no use for a gun. He looked disappointed. What, a tough guy without a gun?

After a moment he said, 'I know where you could make some good money. No guns. Strictly legal. If you're a tough kid like you say you are.'

He took me to a fairground near Potsdamerplatz, where a man he knew was promoting boxing. There was a middleweight there named Kansas Kid. Rudi's pal was offering fifty marks to anyone who could last three rounds with the Kid, a hundred for a win. I watched the Kid knock out three victims in succession, then climbed into the ring.

'Stand on his foot and slug him in the groin,' Rudi advised.

The Kid gave me a pasting; I pissed blood for three days. But I didn't go down. Rudi pocketed half my purse.

'With a little more experience you'd have beaten him,' he said. 'You're tough all right. You have potential.'

We drank *Molle mit Korn*, beer shot with schnapps. Just the thing to pick me up, said Rudi.

He was in his forties, a large ruddy man, growing fat. He had thick, tattooed arms and square fingernails. 'You can't trust people these days,' he kept saying. That was why he had decided to give up robbery and become respectable. He had considered joining the Nazi Party as a paid-up thug, only he had had enough of taking orders. He preferred to be his own boss. Wanted to find a promising young fighter to manage; there was money in it.

I trained for a fortnight under the tuition of an expert pugilist in a gym near Tauentzienstrasse. My training was prematurely cut short with a big fight opportunity at the Zirkus Busch against Samir the Turk, an aging but still dangerous boxer. 'It'll be a walkover,' Rudi promised.

Samir belted me around the ring for five rounds. My left eye was closing. He had a soft belly for a fighter, and he held his hands high. As he slowed down, I saw my chance. Moving, using the ring, I set to work on his body, banging him in the slats. The referee stopped the fight in the seventh, declaring me the winner.

Rudi wasn't as happy as I expected him to be. It turned out he had bet on Samir the Turk to knock me out in the third round, and lost all the money he had. I told Rudi I'd had enough of boxing, and we parted company. I moved to a boarding-house in another part of town.

Balmy spring was at last edging out a relentless winter. Side-walk cafés were opening all along Kurfürstendamm. The street trams glistened as if freshly painted. A shy intimation of foliage was sneaking into the trees in Tiergarten, lagging demurely behind the impatient display of the women in their new vernal outfits. So pretty they were, the girls, with their bobbed hair style and cocky hats. Even the whores looked enticingly fresh.

Passing by the great ugly Kaiser Wilhelm Gedächtniskirche, I caught the sound of distant bells relayed across the city sky. I went in and sat on a pew. There were a few people here beside myself, most of them tourists. I prayed: 'All-knowing God! I'm so lonely I could die. You too aren't having such a great time, if you'll pardon a bit of straight talking. Face reality, Lord, nobody's taking much notice of you nowadays here in Berlin. But I'm listening. Show me what to do.'

A nun smiled as she passed my pew. I got up and left, reaching the Grunewald-Rennbahn in time for the afternoon's main race. Listed in the field was a horse called 'Day of Judg-ment', a rank outsider, touted at 50 to 1. I backed him with thirty Marks. He romped home by three lengths. I collected, and suddenly remembered Laszlo Schultz.

The next morning I decamped to a small hotel in Alt Moabit. Then again, on and on from one end of Berlin to the other, never staying in one place for more than a night. I told myself, 'I'm learning fast in this lush jungle of a city. What with all I already know, the likes of Samir the Turk would be out cold in the third round. Laszlo Schultz can't be that good. He'll never catch up with me.'

On a bright May Bank Holiday, when heaven inhaled without protest the noxious car fumes of a bustling world, we drove north, Phoebe and I. She said it would do me good to see, for a change, how real people spent their leisure weekend. We came to Reeth, a village in North Yorkshire. The sun was shining. The green was at its greenest, as were the hills all around. Sheep grazed in slanting fields. Day-trippers licked ice-

230

cream on the village green. I had sprained an ankle the day before, getting out of the car. Phoebe bought me a carved rustic walking-stick in a tourist shop and dumped the old one in a dustbin by the bus station. Arm in arm we strolled through the village, past glowing stone cottages set in picture postcard gardens. Phoebe bought – too expensively, I thought – a colourful bowl created by a local potter. A gift for friends in Yugoslavia, she said.

Then, for no apparent reason, my mood changed. Thoughts, dreams, take advantage of old age: they steal marches on it to usurp its idleness. Or was it that all of a sudden I felt more than usually out of context?

Phoebe said with unwonted banality, 'Oh, what a lovely village, quite simply out of this world. Can you imagine living in a place like this, Titus?'

I replied testily, 'A Navaho reservation is also out of this world. You visit, you buy souvenirs. You don't think of living there.'

She ignored the barb. I could tell she was stung, all the more since I had refused to pass through another similar village not far off where her parents lived. I should have said I was sorry, put my arm around her, kissed her cheek. Instead I began to exaggerate my lip, hoping to solicit sympathy. The truth is I longed to be back in London, sitting quietly in the zoo. At least, alone with Charon. Phoebe was sympathetic, all right; she tightened her grip on my arm; she wasn't fooled for a moment, though.

Zoo . . . Two discoveries brought my peripatetic Berlin low-life existence to an end. One was the Zoo. I came upon it as I was walking aimlessly down Kurfürsten Allee past the Sportspalast.

I paid the four Marks entrance fee and went in. The paths were swept clean, the flower beds newly manicured. A strange calm, like a sanatorium amnesty, kept out the buzz of the streets beyond the Zoo's surrounding wall, and cast reflective lethargy on both animals and visitors.

I bought ice-cream, also peanuts and a couple of buns to feed the animals. I wandered about until I found myself exchanging glances with an orang-utan across the barrier in the Affenhaus.

231

The plaque said his name was Moses; a gift to Berlin from the Sultan of Borneo.

A friendly-looking beast, he sat reclining against a tree stump, one hand containing a cascade of chin, and gazed at me.

I said, 'Hey Moses, as one Jew to another, what do you think of life in general?'

I swear he smiled. 'As one Jew to another,' I heard this voice inside my head, 'I reckon in general mine beats yours. See for yourself. No hassle, no shmassle . . .'

I tossed him a bun. He pitched it loopingly back at me. 'Do me a favour, *Vetter*, I get more of these than you get trouble. Come back tomorrow. Bring me a banana, or something . . .'

I did. Without a banana or anything. I never talked to Moses again, either, but from that day on I was hooked on zoos for life. A city needs a zoo like she needs a river.

My other discovery was the Staatsbibliothek in Unter den Linden.

A lofty archway beckoned from the pavement. Through it, you could see a sun-drenched cobblestoned courtyard with a spouting fountain in the middle. A pretty girl was sitting at the fountain's edge, trailing her hand in the water. 'Over a million and a half books,' I heard someone explain. The very notion of such numerical vastness enshrined in one building invited exploration. I went in.

I passed from one reading-room to the next, awed by all that learning. I ended my tour with a beer in the cafeteria on the ground floor, and reached the conclusion that the library, like the Zoo, was a haven.

In bed that night, I mapped out a campaign for an assault on Human Knowledge. The Newspapers Room, I decided, would be best suited as a forward base for my quest. From there, out in all directions the imagination suggested.

I read the *Vossiche Zeitung*, the *Berliner Tageblatt*, *Die Rote Fahne*, *Arbeiter Illustrierte Zeitung*, *Völkischer Beobachter*, *The New York Herald Tribune*, the London *Times*, *The New York Times*, and *Pravda* – cross-section of German political opinion, augmented by foreign press. I perused ancient maps, dipped into Ranke's historical writings. My horizons were creaking from the pace of expansion.

I noticed two men taking a guarded interest in my doings at the Staatsbibliothek. One, an irregular visitor, was always in the Newspapers Room, sitting owl-still in the same place, a newspaper held in front of him. He would peer at me from over the page, then quickly duck when our eyes met.

The other was a full-time inmate. He was there always, in the Newspapers Room, surrounded by bound volumes of old newspapers, or in other parts of the library weaving in and out from behind bookshelves like a nervous hamster. At lunch-time he would come down to the cafeteria and sit alone at a corner table, munching a sandwich with intense preoccupation. He always wore the same clothes: grey baggy trousers, scuffed brown shoes, a shirt which probably had been white at one time, a tightly-knotted tie, a V-necked jumper threadbare at the elbows. I never saw him without a cardboard box which he clutched to his side as if it were an appendage to his body.

At first he gave me furtive glances, followed by a quick movement of his mouth, supposedly a smile. Eventually we got to greet each other with a nod.

One day, as he descended to the cafeteria, cardboard box under his arm as usual, he found his habitual table occupied by the Newspapers Room owl, as it happened. He stood at the entrance distraught, unable to decide whether or not to leave, since none of the other tables was free. Then he saw me. He approached and asked if he might share my table. I said he was most welcome. He pulled out of the box a packet wrapped in a newspaper and a thermos flask, smiled nervously, then began to unravel the packet until a single modest cheese sandwich was revealed.

Just as I had imagined, he was a scholar, an autodidact. He disclosed how he had set out to become the most learned man in Berlin, many years ago: a determined assimilation of knowledge right through the library's catalogue in alphabetical order! Consonants one month, vowels the next. Until, taking a fortuitous leap to 'N' on a consonant month, he discovered Nietzsche, who totally altered his mode of enquiry.

The main precious content of that cardboard box was a one million, 200,000 words manuscript on the theme of the fatal exhaustion of civilisations in history. It had taken him sixteen years of study and writing! The mighty opus was far from finished yet because new thoughts kept intruding, forcing him to scrap and rewrite chapters. In fact he was regressing at the rate of two chapters for every newly written one. The poor man, you see, had fallen victim to perfectionism, the dread affliction of all great scholars. He himself named the disorder the 'Penelope Syndrome'.

Leaving him to his lunacy, I escaped to the Zoo. When I returned two days later, the autodidact was not there. I inquired about him of the librarian. He had collapsed, I was told, with a heart attack, and died pen in hand in front of an open book. I wondered if the Penelope Syndrome he suffered from was a recognised medical condition.

And then I confronted the other man.

He was staring at me more boldly than ever. Whenever I looked in his direction, I saw his owl-eyes boring in on me from the top of his newspaper. I could stand it no longer. I got up abruptly and marched over to him.

He looked up, a small man of indeterminable age, thinning hair and a narrow bony face dominated by pale penetrating eyes behind wire-frame spectacles. A bundle of irritation packed tightly into a grey suit.

'Yes? What is it?' He snapped in a brittle Hungarian-accented voice.

'*Entschuldigung, Mein Herr.* I resent your staring at me. I must, with all respect, ask you to stop,' I said.

'If you yourself, *Mein Herr,* stopped staring at people, you would not be bothered by the absurd notion that you are being stared at,' he replied.

While I cast about for a response to this bizarre logic, he added: 'I was beginning to wonder what I must do to remind you of your duty.'

'I beg your pardon?'

'You are Herr Titus Altermann, are you not?'

'What if I am?'

234

'This is not a matter for haggling. Either you are or you are not. Which is it?' he said with mounting irritation.

The librarian was looking at us.

'Well? Of course you are. We need to talk,' said the little man, getting up.

On the way downstairs various thoughts coursed through my mind. The man was a police detective, something to do with Rudi Schwann. No, I could tell a cop when I saw one and this fellow didn't look the part. A private investigator? To what purpose?

As we entered the cafeteria, the penny dropped, momentarily making me feel sick.

'You should've contacted me as you were instructed,' said Laszlo Schultz, putting down his glass of lemon tea.

'When I settled down, that's what I was told. I haven't settled down.'

'Is that right?' His mouth stretched a little, emitting a short, dry laugh. 'Well, never mind. We'll forget that.'

I bought a Bockwürst to eat with my beer. Schultz scrutinised it disapprovingly.

'Why do you eat this shit? It'll massacre your brain cells,' he said.

I said, 'Satisfy my curiosity and tell me how you found me.'

He shrugged. 'I didn't, you found me. You came here. I recognised your face, and remembered. Frankly, I had all but forgotten about you.'

'Is there anything I could do to make you forget me, this time for good?'

Unexpectedly, he smiled. Unexpectedly, too, it was a friendly smile. He shook his head.

'Okay. What now?'

'Now? Enjoy yourself. Go on reading and improving your mind. Give up eating those shit sausages, if you can.'

'And then?'

He sucked on his teeth, which were irregular, widely spaced. 'You'll keep in touch.'

'For how long?'

'For as long as I tell you. Don't look so worried. In the end it'll work out to your benefit, believe me. Do you play chess?'

'No.'

'I thought so,' he said with a sigh. 'You like cats?'

'Not particularly. I play poker. I like horses.'

Laszlo pulled a face. 'Poker and horses are for dumb Polish officers. You have a woman?'

'No woman, either. Or a gun. Or a false beard and moustache.'

'Now now, take it easy,' said Schultz.

'But I do have a few questions for you, like what is it you want of me. Like when and where it all ends. When you tell me that, I'll tell you whether or not I'll go along.'

He brought his teeth over his lower lip. 'First, I don't want anything of you, yet. Second, when or if I do, you'd have no reason to complain, I can tell you that. Third . . . in your reading here have you come across an English poet called John Donne?'

'Never heard of him.'

'He wrote "No man is an Island, entire of itself; every man is a piece of the Continent, a part of the main." Good, isn't it?'

'I can think of better things. What was he, a geographer or something? What's it got to do with me?'

'Only that you have no choice. You've been set free as part of a deal, right? Let me put it differently. There's us, and there's a bunch of nasty *shmucks* who are against us. Nothing in between. And you had better make up your mind pretty quickly whose side you are on. If you want a piece of friendly advice, stick with us. The alternative would be a costly mistake, believe me.'

We fell silent. Schultz finished his lemon tea, pulled a watch out of his jacket's breast pocket and looked at it irritably.

'Is there a fourth?' I asked.

He smiled. 'Sure. Go get yourself some nice clothes. Meet me here same time on Friday. And don't worry.'

I got up. He remained seated. Reaching into his pocket, he brought out a shiny new pipe.

'A little present for you.'

'I don't smoke pipes.'

'No? Keep it anyway. I make them myself, a hobby, very

236

relaxing. A man should have a hobby. Too bad you don't play chess. It's a good way to make new friends. Poker only makes you enemies. *Bis Freitag. Auf Wiedersehen.*'

'Why didn't you get decent clothes, like I told you?' Laszlo greeted me. 'You look like a perfect *shmendrik.*'

'I forgot. What's a *shmendrik?*'

'A *shmendrik*'s a *shmendrik.* Just what it sounds like. Now, about the clothes . . .'

I promised I'd do it when I had money. He took a wad of banknotes out of his pocket and laid it in front of me. It was a handy sum. I let it rest there.

'Take it, don't be a jerk.'

I had stumbled into a trap, but maybe there was still a way out, I told myself. If I didn't take the money. It was feeble reasoning. I could see from Schultz's smile that he guessed what was going on in my mind.

'They told me you were a smart, tough fellow,' Laszlo sighed, shaking his head. 'How naïve you still are. How much you still have to learn.'

I took the money.

'Good,' said Laszlo, brightening up. 'Now we can get down to business.'

We went to a nearby café off Französische Strasse – Laszlo was too sedentary to walk far. It was a little place overlooked by the Huguenot Französische Dom which dominated the quiet square.

'You like it here?' he asked.

'It's OK. Is this to be our place of rendezvous?'

'We don't have a place of rendezvous. Try the onion soup.'

He began to tell me about Berlin, the museums, the best restaurants, who went where, what galleries I ought to visit, what music to listen to, the names of the editors of newspapers, who was who in politics . . . He was very knowledgeable, quite the man about town, in theory at least. At one point I interrupted.

'Laszlo,' I said, 'what is the point of all this?'

'You must learn,' he said with exaggerated patience, 'to listen more and not to ask so many irrelevant questions. All this is a part of your education. To familiarise you with the territory of your assigned operations, instead of wasting time reading Ranke in the library.'

'What assigned operations, for Christ's sake?'

He pointed a finger at me. 'Later. For now, listen and pay attention.'

The shadow of the Dom all but covered the square when we stepped out of the café. 'Keep alert, get to know the places I told you about. Above all, stay out of trouble, you hear?'

We shook hands. 'It's too bad you don't play chess,' he said.

I worked it all out sitting in the Zoo in front of Moses, my orang-utan companion. Schultz was no ordinary NKVD agent. He was the coordinator of a whole network of spies and hit men into which I had been recruited.

When I was ready, spruced up and trained, and with the rewritten identity and background Laszlo had meticulously cooked up, I'd be sent out to befriend journalists, foreign mainly, but also local, and feed them stories selected and prepared by Laszlo Schultz. I was being tutored and groomed to become a credible source of information on the Soviet Union and its secret connections with various factors in the German government. In short, an undercover disseminator of Soviet propaganda and disinformation. Later, there would be other things.

A hovering premonition of those other things marred the undeniable fun my better specified tasks promised to be. But I wasn't quite as naïve as Laszlo Schultz wanted to believe. I knew as well as anybody that nothing was forever; opportunities came and went. Therefore, I would bide my time and seize the right one as it came. Until then, what more was there for me to do but take Schultz at his word and enjoy myself to the full?

I repaired to Julius Zunker's men's clothes shop in Zimmerstrasse, where I kitted myself out for a new career in the service of Comrade Iosif Vissarianovich Stalin: a suit, shoes, two shirts, silk ties, a hat – all emphatically capitalist. For different contingencies, I bought from a vendor by Brandenburger Tor a second-hand knee-length overcoat with wide inside pockets, and boots.

238

It was in that outfit that I met Wanda in Tiergarten.

Yes, I liked my new employment. Soon I was going beyond my brief, improvising confidently. The key to all successful improvisation in this line of work is informed manipulation of probability and plausibility. I was proving what a natural talent I was at that. Truth, after all, like good and evil, is in the believer's expectation. Always, at all times, the Hotel Adlon was a great place for believing. And Chad Johnson was a great believer.

When I try to list the commendable qualities of supreme mediocrity, I think of him. Diligent, steadfast and loyal, Chad packed in an unremitting sense of duty with an uninquiring imagination. He understood instinctively what was expected and required of him, not least by his editor's insatiable appetite for a good story. And he fiercely protected his sources against all, at no matter what cost.

Starting from a strictly professional association of mutual give and take, in which the taking as the giving inflated progressively, we became true friends.

I was enjoying Wanda. There was an intoxicating sense of transience about our love affair, which echoed life in Berlin. Neither of us ever talked about the future.

And when it all became too rich, a sudden hankering for a taste of low life and danger would come over me. I'd put on my rougher clothes and make for the underworld provinces of Alex and Potsdamerstrasse, where once again I ran into Rudi Schwann.

He looked dejected, thinner, scruffier, puffy round the eyes, as if he had been hocking bits of himself and failing to recover them. The former bulging curves of the lady tattooed on his arm now looked morosely attenuated. I couldn't help feeling sorry for him.

'Titus, buddy! You look like a million bucks!' Poor Rudi, the movie Americanism somehow amplified how low he had sunk. I took him out to lunch.

'Tell me how you've been doing. Still in the fight game?' I asked.

His eyes turned spaniel-doleful. He had had a run of bum fighters, and now he was broke. Maybe boxing wasn't his thing,

239

after all. What could he do, since he owed money to some rough customers and dared not show his face in certain parts of town? There were few options under consideration, none too attractive: 'Cocaine, *vielleicht*.' An assured steady income, nice customers, playboys, artists. No heroin, though. The trouble with drugs was the dealers. 'You can find yourself floating face down in the Lundwehr Kanal, Titus . . .'

I suggested pimping as a softer option. Rudi sighed. '*Ach, ja*, but where to get the girls? It's a closed business, Titus, very protected, believe me.'

'Another beer, Rudi?'

He turned sentimental. We could have had a great partnership, he lamented. With my talent and his contacts there would have been a shot at the title, for sure. I had to laugh.

'You look fit, Titus,' he said, feeling my arm. 'Things have been good for you?'

'On and off. Can't complain.'

'You wouldn't be interested in a fight or two, would you?'

'No, Rudi, I'm through with that.'

'I know of a good one, easy money. It would be a push-over for you. I need it real bad, Titus. Just one, for old time's sake?'

The fighter in question was called Gypsy Joe. In his day he was good. Had good legs, fast hands, could take an opponent out with either hand. Now there was nothing left in him, except his reputation from long ago. His left eye was virtually blind. His handlers were looking for a suitable opponent to give him one last win.

'You'd be a six-to-one underdog, Titus, at least, guaranteed. Just think what we could make! And I'll tell you another thing. Gypsy Joe is still in pain from a fractured rib, on the left. You hit him there a couple of times and he'll go down like a dynamited house. What do you say?'

I agreed, out of pity. Maybe I liked him, too, in spite of him being a swine. Rudi was almost on his knees with gratitude, and swore he'd never forget this, he was my friend for life.

It was more or less like Rudi Schwann said it would be, except that the whole event turned out to be the most down-market prize fight I'd ever seen in my life.

Gypsy Joe climbed into the ring with a confident smile on

240

his face. He gasped as I caught him with the first shot, not even in his bad side. I knew I'd have him going in no time at all. He fought like a tiger, drawing on all his experience, and with a full bag of dirty tricks. It was all over in the sixth. And I had a nasty cut above the left eye from a head-butt.

Rudi couldn't thank me enough. He had bet the hundred Marks I had lent him plus another hundred he scrounged elsewhere on me to win at six to one against. I had been promised a purse of 1,500 Marks. However, it soon became clear that the promoter, who also happened to be Gypsy Joe's manager, had a serious cash flow problem. I had to settle for Gypsy Joe's aged BMW motorcycle, which he had hocked to his manager as security for a loan. Rudi Schwann was shattered.

'I didn't know, Titus, I swear,' he pleaded. 'Can you believe I'd let you into the ring with that bum if I'd known?' He offered to share his winnings with me, part of it. I wouldn't accept his offer.

'I'll make it up to you, that's a promise. Look, if there's anything I can do for you, now, any time, I will, if it kills me. You know where to find me,' he said, grabbing my arm.

I roared away on the motorbike, swearing I'll never allow myself to be made a sucker again, nor have any further dealings with Rudi. Actually, I rather liked the machine. And I quite enjoyed the fight.

Laszlo said, 'Let's go for a walk, it's such a lovely day. A shame to sit indoors.'

The contrast between the commonplace invitation and the sudden gravity of his mood alerted my senses.

He collected a bulging brown leather briefcase from the cloakroom. We stepped out into the sunshine. I offered to carry the briefcase. Laszlo said, 'No, thank you.' It looked natural with him but totally out of place with me, he said. Laszlo was fastidious in matters of symmetry and aesthetics, so I let him lug the damn thing awkwardly along Unter den Linden.

At the University building he paused. I think he had had enough of walking. But there were too many students about, making noise. We walked on, crossed the canal and turned into Lustgarten. Laszlo made for the nearest bench. He took his hat off to fan his face. The sweat-band inside it was greasy and damp with perspiration. He rummaged inside the briefcase and brought out a chisel-like knife and half-finished pipe.

'This one is going to be a beauty. What do you think?' he asked, holding the block of briar at arm's length.

'I'm no good at judging pipes, Laszlo, you know that.'

'It wouldn't hurt you to say something appreciative, all the same.'

'OK. You've got a grand pipe in the making there, Laszlo. Keep working.'

He put it back in the briefcase. 'I hate Berlin when it's hot, you know. It makes me crabby.'

It wasn't really all that hot; Laszlo was simply out of condition.

I said, 'We should've stayed in the Library. It's cool there.'

He looked vacuously across the street where a bus had just disgorged a load of tourists in front of the Schlossmuseum.

'What's the matter, Laszlo?'

He turned his head to me. 'Should anything be the matter? You're doing well, Titus. You look smart. You talk smart. I'm pleased with you.'

'Thank you.'

He poked a finger at my chest. 'See? And you were so tight-arsed about it at the beginning. I told you you'd enjoy the work, didn't I? Look what a good time you're having. Spending money like you had a millionaire daddy, going here, going there, cabaret, opera . . .'

'I do as you instruct me, Laszlo.'

'Sure. Do you hear me complaining?'

He fell silent. When he spoke again his manner had changed: out went the world-weary Jewish humour; in came the interrogator's chilling stealth. Even his Hungarian lilt took on a more Germanic precision.

'You didn't tell me you were living with a girlfriend in Kloedenstrasse,' he said, not looking at me but again across the street, where the tourists were photographing each other at the entrance of the Schlossmuseum.

It was like being caught with a sucker punch flush on the

chin. I needed a few seconds to unscramble my senses. I said, 'I figured you'd find out. Is that terrible?'

He smiled without looking at me. 'You ought to know better than to play smart with me, Titus. Wanda Popper. A nice girl, heart and mind in the right places.' He wasn't going to give away anything more.

'How long have you known?'

'Long enough.' He took his glasses off, wiped them clean with his tie but didn't put them back on as he turned towards me. Without his specs his eyes looked smaller, harder.

'Do you care for her?' he asked.

'Want me to tell you also how many times a night we fuck?'

My defensive petulance seemed to amuse him. 'No,' he said quietly. 'Just what I asked.'

'I care for her.'

'That's good. I'm glad to hear you say that.'

'May I ask what all this has to do with anything?'

'Of course, I'll tell you. The party is over, Titus. For the time being, anyway. Now there's something else for you to do. How you do it will make a lot of difference, maybe to your girlfriend Wanda, too.'

He put his glasses back on, brought out the familiar brown envelope. Only it was thicker than usual this time.

'I see. I get a rise in pay?'

'Expenses,' Laszlo corrected.

'So what am I to do? Recruit a bunch of gunmen and wipe out the whole Nazi party?'

He smiled, not so pleasantly this time. 'What you are to do, Titus, is, shall we say, a minor bit of surgery. Someone has to be removed. You don't recruit anybody. You do this on your own.'

I wanted to walk out on him there and then. Take the money, leave Berlin, disappear and start all over again somewhere else. But there was Wanda. I wasn't lying; I really did care for her. Laszlo's implicit threat wasn't lost on me.

'Think of it as a war,' I heard him say. 'There is a war going on, Titus. A war we have to win, which forces us to do things we don't like doing.'

I had heard Schubert's *Der Erlkönig* – the king of darkness

243

who seductively persuades a frightened child, riding with his father through the forest at night, that death was really a wonderful thing. But I was no child; I had seen Death. I had been in a war. I had listened to commissars extol the virtues of sacrifice, exhorting weary soldiers to destroy the enemy who, when you met him face to face, was frightened and confused, no different from yourself.

'Who is this man you want me to kill?' I asked, and noticed how he winced.

He produced a photograph of a fat-faced man wearing a hat and grinning at the camera. He was like hundreds you might run into in the street any day of the week. Like the picture of me Laszlo had been given?

'But who is he? What has he done?'

'That needn't concern you.'

'Oh yes, it does. You're asking me to kill this man, Laszlo. I have to know who he is and why you want him killed.'

'What if his name is Weiss, or Schwartz, or Braun or Grün? Given half the chance, he'd bump you off as easy as fart. That much I can tell you. The world would be a little less awful without him, believe me. Like I said, Titus, this is war. Not the kind you know, but just as deadly. Deadlier, in fact. And we are soldiers in it, like it or not. You don't ask the enemy soldier what's his name and what he's done. You blow his head off before he gets to do it to you. Understand?'

I made no reply. I was thinking desperately how to get out of Laszlo's snare, cursing my bad luck for having slipped into it in the first place.

'Ever been to the city morgue?' he went on with serpentine patience. 'Every day there are about a hundred bodies found all around Berlin. Some are crooks killed by crooks. Many are assassinated for political reasons. The difference is, we do not kill to settle personal scores. We kill, when we have to, in order to win for ideas that would make the world a better place. Weeding, Titus. That's what I'm talking about. Unpleasant but essential. You have no choice, you know.'

I felt something hard pressing against my arm. Laszlo was holding an oval biscuit-tin. It had a blonde smiling girl on a bicycle painted on it. He opened it, casually, as though it

244

contained a cake to sweeten the bad news he was giving me. Inside, wrapped in oiled cloth, lay a brand new Russian-made Tokarev TT-33 semi automatic pistol. I had never seen one before. The model had only recently come into use in the Soviet Union. One thing I could tell about it right away: it was a very distinct and therefore traceable gun.

'The weapon,' Laszlo announced. 'You return it to me after the mission is accomplished, understand? I'll tell you where and when.'

I feigned professional disappointment. The weapon, I said, was unsuitable.

'What are you talking about? This is the best pistol in the world.' Laszlo knew nothing about guns himself. This one had been selected by an expert from the NKVD in Moscow.

I said, yes, maybe, but not for this job. It made it necessary to get close to the target. That was not what I had in mind; too risky. Besides, I wasn't familiar with the Tokarev. Would he mind if I got my own gun, a gun I was used to?

'Absolutely out of the question!' said Laszlo, slamming his fist on the briefcase. 'This is the gun you use. And I don't care if you get so close to the target you catch a cold from him.'

I was to go home and wait. In a day or two Laszlo would contact me and brief me on where and when I could find my quarry.

'Needless to say, not a word of this to your girlfriend.'

'Needless to say,' I agreed.

'You do this right, Titus, and you'll go a long away, I promise you.' He slapped me on the shoulder. In my mind I had a gruesome glimpse of what awaited me at the end of the long way, if not a good deal before that.

'And if I don't, you'll pass my file back to the NKVD for special treatment, right?'

He laughed. 'File? What file? Listen, *shmendrik*, I keep no files and no papers. Nothing written. Everything is up here.' He tapped his temple with his finger.

I kept a straight face. I thought, 'Poor son-of-a-bitch Laszlo, you may be a chess player at grandmaster level, but in poker you're a loser. And poker, not chess, is the game of life and death.'

I went to the Zoo. Sitting on a bench, I memorised the photograph, then tore it to shreds and dropped them in a waste-paper bin. I passed a building site in Zossner Strasse on the way home. They had dug shafts in the foundation for the cornerstones. These were half-filled with muddy water from a recent rain. I wrapped the biscuit tin in a piece of sackcloth I found, and dropped it down one of the shafts. I was clean; there was no incriminating evidence for a set-up, since it seemed possible that was what Laszlo had in mind.

That night I took Wanda out, for a celebration.

'What's the occasion?' she wanted to know.

'You,' I said. 'I want to see you dress up and looking lovely. I want us to have a terrific evening, then come back here and make love at least three times.'

She wanted to go to the Kabarett der Komiker, where Paul Nikolaus was regaling Berliners with his satirical anti-Nazi monologues. I wanted lighter entertainment, something like the Tiller Girls at the Scala. I'd had enough of intellectual *Schall und Rauch*. We went to Rosa Valetti's Grössenwahn, a compromise heavily loaded in Wanda's favour. When eventually we got into bed, I couldn't even get an erection. Wanda fell asleep. I stayed awake for what remained of the night.

The next day I sent looking for Rudi Schwann. I found him in some sleazy dive in Münzstrasse. I told him I needed a gun.

'No problem, Titus. Anything special?'

'A Mauser C/96 with a shoulder-stock, and ten rounds.'

'Wow!' he said, 'you on to something interesting?'

'Not yet, Rudi. Can you do it?'

'Sure. You'll cut me in if you pull a job, won't you, Titus?'

'I'll think about it.'

He had the gun within two hours, complete with two clips. The Mauser C/96 is a heavier, steadier weapon. With the shoulder-stock it has an effective range of up to a hundred metres. Although it was large, I could comfortably conceal it in one of my leather coat's inside pockets. I bought a pumpkin and had a short target practice in secluded part of Grunewald. I was ready.

Laszlo contacted me two days later. We met, at my suggestion, in the Zoo.

'How do you feel?' he asked.

'I feel fine. And you?'

He looked at me suspiciously. 'What's that supposed to mean?'

'Nothing, just something to say.'

'Okay. Now listen carefully.'

In two days there would be a 1st of May march in Hermannplatz. The police had already announced a ban on the event. But Laszlo knew from reliable sources that not only would the march proceed in defiance of the police, but there would be violence – Nazis fighting communists and both fighting the police. My target was sure to be there.

'What if he isn't?'

'Of course he will! Don't be such a defeatist!'

I was to gun him down – in the head, if possible – and get away. The next day, at eleven sharp, I was to meet Laszlo at an appointed place in Tiergarten, by the river Spree. He brought a map to show me the exact spot. There I would hand back the gun and the picture. Simple.

'You want me to go over it again?'

'No need. I've got it.'

'Sure?'

'More sure than I've ever been about anything.'

'Good man. When this is all over, you'll go on a grand holiday, all expenses paid. Take your Wanda, too. Good luck,' said Laszlo, getting up.

Of course I had no intention of keeping my appointment. More likely it would have been the police waiting for me, tipped by him; or another assassin. My plan was to set out on the mission as instructed, but decide on the spot whether or not to carry it out. In any event, I would contact Laszlo a week or so later and meet him in a public place, probably the Staatsbibliothek. I would make up a plausible story about his pistol and the photograph, depending on how things worked out.

I didn't calculate on Wanda being out there among the banner-carrying demonstrators. To tell the truth, I very nearly aborted the whole thing when she told me she was going. Then it occurred to me that her presence could be an advantage –

how could I go through with it in full view of Wanda? I would reason with Laszlo.

The man I was contracted to kill never turned up, anyway. At least, I didn't see him. I was about to pack it in when I saw Laszlo Schultz less than thirty metres away, surveying the mayhem from a safe corner. He was alone. Had he come to see me at work? Ha ha ha! I remembered his careless utterance about keeping everything in his head. I took careful aim and shot a hole clean through that repository.

Think about it; maybe I've made the world a little less awful by sending Laszlo Schultz on his way out of it.

19

When I sit in Sanctum reminiscing, I sometimes miss the freedom of my Berlin days, but Wanda does not seem to accept changes readily. I had avoided giving her my direct line number, and she had been furious. All reassurances that this didn't remotely indicate disregard had been of no avail. In the autumnal phase of her life, Wanda had become jealously status-conscious.

'If you're going to be bloody inaccessible, Titus, to hell with it. I swear I'll never ring you,' she had fulminated, the Hungarian temperament prevailing against her assimilated Englishness. Nevertheless, she broke her vow and rang me.

'Titus,' she began – not a word of complaint about her circuitous route to me via our busy switchboard – 'have you ever seen bluebells?'

'There are some in the garden, I believe.'

'I mean a whole carpet of them, not just a few miserable prisoners in your garden, stretching on and on. A gorgeous wash of blue among trees.'

It was Friday. Wanda was ringing to invite me for a walk.

'Oldies like us need regular exercise. I'll bet you don't get any, tycooning your last years away in that ghastly office building of yours. You must come, or I'll be very cross with you. I've discovered an absolutely marvellous walk. Only four miles, reducible to three, even two. You can manage that, can't you?'

I laughed. With her typical gutsiness, Wanda was fighting a losing battle against crippling arthritis.

'When you laugh like that, I know the answer is yes.'

'Where is this marvellous walk?'

'No more than half an hour out of London. The Chess Valley.'

'Chess as in chess?'

'Quite so. Sorry, there's no Poker Valley that I know of.'

She instructed me how to get there, and where we should meet, on Sunday at ten, weather permitting.

'And Titus . . .'

'Yes?'

'Be a darling and don't bring along your youthful English rose.'

I didn't mind Wanda's occasional bitchery. I had gratuitously denied her too many times in the past. If she wanted a leisurely oldies' perambulation through acres of blooming bluebells, I wasn't going to spoil it for her. Besides, as it happened, Phoebe had gone north to her parents for the weekend. I asked our car pool manager if he could arrange for someone to drive me to the Chorleywood pub Wanda had fixed as our meeting-point. He said he would be delighted to do so himself, since he lived not far away.

Wanda was there when I arrived, a quarter of an hour late. She was not alone, either. Theo was with her.

'Darling,' she said, 'an impromptu reunion. Don't you think it's a brilliant idea on such a beautiful day? There's no need for this good man to wait for you. I've arranged for us to be met at the end of the walk. We'll drive you back home.'

Dressed for the outing in corduroy breeches, rambler's boots, knee-length red woollen socks, matching anoraks and walking sticks, she and Theo resembled a pair of anthropomorphosed love birds.

We started towards the river, Wanda arm-in-arm with Theo. He limped in a rhythmic gliding motion, as though his body had devised a trick to counteract the force of gravity. He was heading for a hip replacement operation, Wanda confided solicitously, which made Theo laugh and quote something from Goethe.

The River Chess flowed among the reeds, capturing the slow movement of the clouds. Wanda remarked that the scene was like a Constable painting – the fragile incipience of an English summer. Four trusting ponies were grazing in the meadow where the footpath ran, allowing city Sunday walkers like ourselves to pet them as they passed. Wanda delighted in the profusion of wild flowers: these were campions, she pointed out. And those, field forget-me-nots.

From the edge of the wood, the bluebells flooded into the shade of the trees on either side of the footpath. Wanda stopped and gasped.

'Oh, look! Aren't they simply heavenly? I want to go down on my knees and thank the good Lord that I'm here, in England!' she said tremulously.

Theo squeezed her arm. 'Come along, dear, you don't get down on your knees at our age,' he said lovingly. It touched him that after all these years she could still gush with such spontaneity.

Wanda wouldn't budge. 'I wonder if there's some significance in the fact that all three of us have ended here, in this country. What do you think, Theo?'

'I think there's still some way to go before the end, dearest.'

She cocked her head at me. 'But you, Titus, you've always made your own options. Why here? I should've thought America was more your kind of hunting-ground.'

'No,' I said.

'Oh? Why not?'

'No one ever makes his own options, Wanda. The best you can do is select from what's available and hope for the best.'

'Untypically modest, Titus. How you've changed.' She laughed. 'Still, why not the USA?'

'Too many people like me over there.'

Chad, with his penchant for open-ended interviews, once asked me the same question. I pondered it as I walked along Pennsylvania Avenue, Washington DC, on a particularly memorable autumn day. I thought, 'Here is mighty Rome resurrected; all her past impatient vulgarity magnificently amplified. Well, could I?'

A taxi driver insolently ignored my hailing. A man bumped into me, nearly knocking me over, and walked on cursing. I had just been to the White House. I had sat in the Oval Office with President JFK, weighing options to save civilisation from a nuclear apocalypse. And here in the street of triumphal

251

processions, I was just another piece of organic matter taking up pavement space.

Chad was engaged that evening. I went alone to a Thai restaurant in Georgetown. An old couple passed by, stopped to read the menu on the window. The woman, eighty if she was a day, wore a red beret and a smiling mask of cosmetics, wrinkles plastered over and a mouth like a freshly-painted letter box. They hugged and kissed, she and her man, then moved on. I thought, 'They have evolved a new strand of survivors in this country, who can take anything in their stride right down to the last gasp of air!'

Back in my hotel I paid the hall porter $500 to procure me a tall slim hooker with an outsize bosom.

'You'll love this one, sir.' He winked. 'She has a college degree in Political Science.'

At the half-bottle level of airport tax-free vodka, I longed for England . . .

'Take him with a pinch of salt,' chuckled Theo. 'Underneath that battle-worn carapace, Titus is really rather sentimental. He's moved by the sight of bluebells and ancient spires. He loves the gentle triviality of the English. England for him is still an enchanted realm, where pretty story-book children enact charades in William Morris gardens, instead of playing video games. Where a cream tea is enjoyed to the late summer evening song of the blackbird. Where clever adults talk in civilised understatement which they don't mean. He accepts all this grand illusion as the reward of success, don't you, Titus?'

'Theo! Don't tell me Cambridge has made you a cynic. I'd feel cheated,' I said.

'Good heavens, no. Cambridge has made me very happy, and therefore understanding. And forgiving.' He laughed.

'I like to think, Titus, that you're softened by such illusions. The old empire-building killer instinct laid to rest,' said Wanda with a mere hint of reforming intent in her voice.

Handing me her walking-stick, she linked her free arm through mine, drawing the three of us closer together.

'Talking of killer's instinct, I've often wondered about that time in Berlin. Not that it matters now, but *did* you kill someone?'

'No,' I answered. 'Like I said at the time, I killed nobody. It was your imagination getting over-heated.'

'You know, I almost hated you when you disappeared without a word, leaving me to believe I'd never see you or hear from you again. How could you do such a thing?'

'The old killer's instinct, darling.'

I resolved to direct all my energy towards making money, fast. As much as I could, any way I could, while my luck held. Before my time in Berlin ran out.

I had served my apprenticeship in creating fiction. Laszlo had been a worthy master. I knew how to beef up a grain of truth with layers of probability. More importantly, I knew where to garner those precious grains, even in times of scarcity. I sold stories in the Adlon like I was doing an end-of-season sale. To Chad, above all. If newspapers of the West ran speculation parading as informed analysis during that uncertain period, blame me for it. Or give me credit, for a lot of what I had purveyed had come to pass.

I played poker for higher stakes than I could afford. I mostly won. There is a simple philosophy to poker: if you set out to gain, you lose; if you aim at enjoying your opponent's defeat, you win. That was how it worked for me.

My only bow to morality, half-hearted and partly disingenuous at that, was distancing myself from Wanda – resigning her to Tristan Rutland's care. Why? A touch of paranoia, perhaps? Spectres of retribution for Laszlo's killing were beginning to haunt me.

We were drifting apart, Wanda and I. A slow corrosive alienation was eating away at the trust between us. When I said, 'Come live with me in the flat I've just rented in Schillerstrasse,' I knew with certainty she would decline.

There had been some regret, for sure: I am a person who will obey necessities, but not without remorse. The necessity of the day was belonging. Wanda belonged to a losing side, but a side which was nevertheless not yet in disarray. Poor Wanda. Little did she understand how her hero in the Kremlin, with the dedicated fatalism of a mad genius, had set about to undermine socialism in Germany and pave the way for the Nazis to seize power.

I belonged nowhere. Laszlo Schultz, the bailiff of my debt to Russia, was gone. But the debt remained unremitted, waiting to be claimed by a successor.

To compensate myself for losing Wanda, I womanised with as much reckless ferocity as I played poker.

One morning, as I walked into the Adlon, the barman motioned me to a corner. A stranger had been asking about me. 'A foreign gentleman, quite out of place here, if you ask me, Herr Altermann,' he told me. Needless to say, the barman had kept mum. I tipped him handsomely to keep his mouth sealed should the stranger return. I stopped frequenting the Adlon.

When you're exiled from the Adlon, half the fun of being in Berlin is at once removed. I thought it prudent to keep out of the Staatsbibliothek as well. There, after all, I had met Laszlo. More of Berlin's charm eroded.

The Zoo was now my last familiar place of refuge. And sitting in its pleasant open-air restaurant on a sunny morning, a sudden, not altogether unwelcome valedictory mood descended on me. It was folly to expect permanence of any sort, but I had done well. I had learnt good many things. I had had fun, and love. Now I'd come a full circle; time to go, travelling lightly just as when I arrived. Except that now I had a lot more money in my pocket, and a good deal more experience. I would drift on, without regret, and find another country. Try my hand at different things. Maybe eventually settle down?

A strain of vaguely familiar music came from within the restaurant. It was French and evocative in a way that made me think of travel.

'*Entschuldigung, Mein Herr . . .* ' The man's voice, intruding from so close behind, made me jump. He was foreign, I could tell from his clothes. The accent, vaguely Germanic, I couldn't recognise.

'I do apologise for startling you,' he said, grinning bashfully.

254

'My friend and I were wondering if you would kindly take a picture of us.' He held out a Leica camera.

I said I would, with pleasure. He showed me how to aim the thing, and where to press for the take. With the zebras in the background? They were most photogenic, I suggested. No, no, just the two of them sitting at the table, he said.

I sighted the two in the bright rectangle framed by the thin black lines of the camera's viewfinder. Strange, how you use the word shoot both for killing and for taking pictures. Two elderly men, they leaned close to each other, an arm across the other's shoulder, hands joined over a single glass of beer in tender intimacy. I took two snapshots.

'Thank you so much,' said the man who had approached me. We exchanged views about the Zoo, how well the animals looked, and the whole place, so peaceful and agreeable. They invited me to join them for a beer. Was I a Berliner? What a fascinating city! They had come here from their native Copenhagen for a bit of culture, 'before culture was snuffed out'. The latter prophecy was uttered with caution in case I was a Nazi sympathiser. One couldn't be too careful these days, ha ha ha.

The more outgoing of the two was called Henrik Pedersen, owner and director of Pedersen Baltic Line AB – a freight shipping company of more than a century's standing. The other was Professor Erland Friis, Head of Pathology at the Copenhagen Rigshospital. They had been close friends since their university days, and lived together in Henrik Pedersen's ancestral home in Klampenborg, a leafy suburb of Copenhagen, facing Sweden across the sound. Henrik played the piano, Erland the cello. In the evenings they made music, read to each other and played chess. Along with many other interests, they shared in common an aging Labrador dog called Smoky.

I reciprocated with select excerpts from my own life story.

'I have faith in my judgment of character,' said Henrik at the third beer, and immediately suggested we addressed each other in the informal 'du'. We toasted the new acquaintanceship. The reason for the impatience of his faith was soon revealed. Erland had been diagnosed as terminally ill with

255

cancer of the bowel. They were planning a last trip together before the pain became unbearable, when Erland would choose the moment to die in peace and dignity.

We held a moment of silence.

'How sad,' I said at last.

'Not at all. We only think of happiness,' replied Erland.

I reflected on this for a moment. 'Perhaps I've not yet learnt to understand what happiness is.'

'You are young,' he said gently. 'If I may offer you a very down-to-earth definition, happiness is being successful at what you like doing and being wanted. It really is as simple as that. We've both been very happy.'

In a sudden burst of candour I announced that I, too, in a entirely different way, had reached a point of departure in my life. There was nothing left for me here in Berlin; once again I was adrift, a grain of dust carried on the wind. I said this without intended self-pity. Henrik lowered his head and gazed like a sad amiable horse into his empty beer flagon.

'Are you fond of dogs?' asked Erland.

'I knew a dog once, the noblest, most trusted companion I've ever had,' I replied.

Thus, in a lilac flush of mutual sympathy, a solution emerged to resolve our respective predicaments.

'I think you'll like Smoky,' said Henrik with effusive certainty.

'I hope he'll like me.'

'Smoky is a polite, affectionate dog. He has a marvellous gift for friendship. He'll be very welcoming,' Erland promised, smiling wisely.

They were departing for Berlin tomorrow. A week later, they would be back home, awaiting my arrival. Henrik offered to pay my fare to Copenhagen. I thanked him and said that letting me have the use of their house for an unspecified period of time was more than generous. I would arrive under my own steam, no later than ten days hence. We parted in high spirits, Henrik swearing he had a pleasant morning premonition that something out of the ordinary would happen that day. Now that it had happened, he couldn't wait to start charting their travels; they would leave a day or so after I arrived to take charge of Smoky and the house.

I decided not to see Wanda before I left. I didn't want the gloom of a farewell, nor questions to which I knew I'd have to lie. As I bought my train passage to Copenhagen I thought, 'There is neither pattern nor continuity to my life. All is random; all is caprice. So be it.'

I crossed Friedrichstrasse and entered an undistinguished eating-place, just as I had done when I first arrived in Berlin some four years before. A man at a nearby table was reading *Die Rote Fahne* and groping on the stained tablecloth for his cigarette, which smouldered to extinction in an already full ashtray.

An idea suddenly came to me, quickening my pulse. I had two days left in Berlin. Once again I went looking for Rudi Schwann. I knew his haunts. He wasn't difficult to find.

'Rudi,' I said, 'do you know a good safe-cracker?'

'Of course, yours truly. I can do most safes with my eyes closed. What sort of safe are we talking about? Key? Combination? Both? Time lock?'

'I couldn't tell you. For all I know, there mightn't be a safe at all. I want a safe-cracker along in case there is.'

I announced that I intended to burgle the offices of the Kommunistische Partei Deutschlands (KPD) in Kleine Alexanderstrasse 28. The KPD had been the agent of Soviet foreign policy in Germany since 1926. The address was also shared by the KPD's newspaper, *Die Rote Fahne.* This was to be my personal counter-offensive against the NKVD!

'Have you gone soft in the head?' cried Rudi, aghast. 'What's there but a bundle of Jewish protocols? No use to anybody.' He knew nothing about the KPD, except that it was communist and therefore run by Jews.

'Listen, I have a better idea. Why not Lunser the jeweller in Friedrichstrasse? I've already cased the joint. It's loaded; cash, stones, gold, watches. Easy. We'll be in and out in no time. I know a reliable fence . . .'

'Rudi, I'm not interested in Lunser. This is what I want to do.'

'Nah, nah. That's not my line of business, pal. I'm a professional. Banks, yes. Jewellers, factories, restaurants, gambling places, all that kind of stuff. But politics, no. I stay out of politics.'

I reminded him that he owed me one. I cajoled, saying how easy it would be, since unlike a jeweller the KPD offices probably had no alarm system. There might also be money . . .

We hit the place at three on a Sunday morning. Gaining entrance to the premises was no problem. We searched room by room – there were five – until Rudi discovered the safe, concealed behind Lenin's picture. It was an old one, made in Prague, with a key lock, no combination. Rudi set to work on it, with me holding the torch for him. After all his boasting, I had hoped he would pick the lock so that we could leave things more or less tidy. He made a mess of it, drilling noisily for more than half an hour before the old box yielded.

Inside there was a large sealed manilla envelope, and 70,000 Marks in bundles of crisp new banknotes stacked at the bottom of the safe.

'*Gott in Himmel!* Those bloody Commies must have robbed someone!' Rudi whistled.

We split the loot halfway. I broke the envelope's wax seal and riffled through the contents, holding the torch in my mouth. There were five pages, typed with names of Party operators in Germany, Austria, France and Spain.

'Hurry up, for Christ's sake!' Rudi hissed.

My name wasn't listed anywhere. Laszlo Schultz's was, crossed out in red ink, with a factual epitaph scribbled over it – 'Shot by Nazi provocateurs, Hermannplatz Tuesday May 1st 1929.'

I stuffed the envelope into my shirt. I left in the safe 10,000 Marks out of my share; they had salaries to pay, possibly Wanda's too. I never found out whether or not *Die Rote Fahne* was published the next week.

I drove to Wörther Platz, where a well-known pub with atmosphere – frequented by artists and homosexuals – stayed open right through the night. We drank *Molle mit Korn* to celebrate our coup.

'Well, Rudi, this is where we part company. I hope you get your sports shop somewhere, or whatever it is you want, and have a happy life.'

'You too, Titus. You could've been a champion, you know. You had it all, truly.'

'Like pigs have wings.' We laughed and clinked glasses. 'You want my car, Rudi?'

'Sure, why not?'

'Five thousand.'

'Two and a half.'

'It's a deal.'

He counted out two and a half grand and handed them over. 'You want me to drive you home?'

'No, I'll hang around here for a little longer. Goodbye, Rudi. Take care.'

I used to think of Laszlo as I sat in the evenings by the fire in the house in Klampenborg, smoking the pipe he gave me. Perhaps a bad choice of career had made him what he was. Anyway, he carved good pipes, in my uninformed judgment. And he had a point about hobbies. In fact, with ample time on my hands, I too was acquiring one. The bookshelves in Henrik's study contained yards of maritime books and magazines. With Smoky resting his kindly head on Erland's slipper which I wore, I was reading through them one by one, turning myself into an expert on international shipping.

Let Laszlo Schultz, whoever he was, rest in peace. Things forever change; *Those are pearls that were his eyes . . .*

We crossed the river at the weir down from Latimer House, and Wanda, who in her enthusiasm had over-estimated her stamina, said with forced cheer, 'I do believe the miles are getting longer from year to year. I've always favoured kilometres!'

'Look,' said Theo, shading his eyes against the sun, 'isn't that your car over there?'

Wanda's old silver-grey Bentley was parked at the roadside. Mr Gough stood beside it, looking in our direction. She waved her stick in the air. Gough acknowledged the greeting, then disappeared behind the car.

'Perfect timing. Wanda's logistic strategy excels, as always,' I remarked.

'*Posa, posa, Scarmiglione,*' retorted Wanda.

'Dante's way of saying "Down boy!". She's into *The Inferno,*' Theo explained.

'Well, we've earned our lunch box, haven't we? I can hear Theo's guts rumbling. I'm famished, too,' said Wanda.

Away from the road, on a patch of green among the trees, Gough had set a table, complete with a red and white chequered tablecloth which Wanda has adored ever since falling in love in Paris with Bonnard's paintings. There were quails' eggs, Italian white bread, Parma ham, a bottle of Chablis thoughtfully chilled half an hour before, and strawberries with cream for dessert. Wanda had embraced the joys of capitalism with all the passion of a convert.

A group of walkers passed by, looked and smiled. Wanda graciously smiled back. She raised her glass. 'Here's to us, and to all the wonderful years we have shared. Wasn't it a grand idea to go on this walk today?'

'Absolutely,' Theo agreed.

'Do you remember our picnic in Wannsee, Titus?'

'How can I ever forget?'

'Oh, but you can. I know the cunning ways of your memory.' She laughed.

'The food was indifferent. It rained and thundered. We got soaked to the bone. The motorbike terrified you. You hated it.'

Puffs of cloud, scudding peacefully across a stillness of blue, reflected in Wanda's dark eyes.

'No,' she said, touching my arm. 'In retrospect, I loved every second of it. It was the most glorious picnic I've ever had in my life. Only two things make here and now a more perfect occasion. Our being richer in everything, and ...' Turning to Theo, she took his hand. 'You, darling Theo.'

He mumbled something and patted her hand.

'I've often wondered how I'd want my life to be if I had to live it all over again. What about you, Titus?'

I thought of the two gentle Danes whose friendship I had lost, and of Phoebe.

'Just as it has been,' I said.

Except that if I were to be different, I thought, I might ask to be someone whose experience lagged somewhat behind his imagination. Someone with more comfortable appetites, for sure.

20

Year in, year out, the sturgeon swims into the Volga estuary from the Caspian Sea. Lumbering upstream to its spawning ground, it journeys through Astrakhan, past lush meadows defaced by Stalin's ugly farming *kolkhoses*, and on towards Volgograd, formerly Stalingrad, Tsaritsyn earlier still.

Ponderously large, primevally snouted, its flanks dappled silver-grey, the sturgeon lives to a great age. Its flesh is too coarse for the discerning palate, but this pale tasteless flesh encases the precious, delicious caviar.

Along a stretch of the wide, quietly flowing Volga in the blue depth of which suspires the soul of Russia, Pavel Arkadevich Yesenin – distant offspring of that naïve populist poet – and his sons cast their nets. As sub-quartermaster in Budenni's Red Cavalry *Konarmiia*, Yesenin surpassed his peers in siphoning off Red Army provisions to the black market for the entire duration of the Civil War, and lived to dream about it.

He hauls the catch aboard his boat to harvest the treasure from the sturgeon's butchered guts. Part of it goes to the official caviar factory in Stalingrad. The larger part is illegally processed in Yesenin's own backyard, whence, packed in counterfeit official packing, it migrates via Odessa to my humble depot in Dieppe.

My caviar is served on the Orient Express, in Paris's Le Voisin, at Maxim's in Rue Royale, La Tour d'Argent in Quai Tournelle, as in a lengthening list of other prestigious restaurants. An intricate concatenation of bribes notwithstanding, I still compete favourably with the top-grade caviar the USSR officially exports, thus vindicating the superiority of capitalist free enterprise which the Communists interdict.

We sit, Theo and I, in the kitchen of our flat in 15 rue

Lacépède. The window is open. Afternoon sunlight floods in along with the sound of laughter from the street below.

'Eat this caviar, in memory of my past,' I coax him.

Theo pulls a face. 'To be honest, Titus, I don't much care for the stuff. It looks like blobs of moist snot and tastes like nothing at all.'

'That's because you wash it down with wine like it was medicine.' I move his glass out of reach. 'Here. Take a small piece of toast, smear a thin layer of butter on it. With this sacramental silver spoon put on a spoonful, no more. Let it melt on your tongue. Then tell me it tastes like nothing at all.'

Connoisseurs know that caviar with champagne is an overstatement bordering on vulgarity: the one obliterates the distinctiveness of the other. Caviar is best appreciated on an alert palate, quickened beforehand by a small shot of vodka.

Theo is unimpressed.

'No?'

'Not even with a silver spoon and all your evocations. It's a decandent con, ridiculously expensive. Perhaps it's simply that I feel morally uncomfortable with sensual teasers. Forgive me.' He pushes the plate away with the back of his hand.

Poor Theo, what a wretched exile his moral discomfiture makes him! A chronic sufferer from ethical indigestion.

'Really, Titus, what's all this about the past? If you must have an umbilical metaphor, can't you find something more meaningful than a jar of over-priced fishy slime?'

'All right, Theo. Eat salami, it's all yours.'

Theo has no time for self-indulgent umbilical connections. For me it has always existed – a simple fact of life. It tightened suddenly into a tow-line with the coming of the war.

Throughout the winter and spring my 8,000-tonne steamer, *L'Aurore*, had dry-docked in Marseille, undergoing repairs. A week before the Wehrmacht rode past the Arc de Triumphe on Friday June 14th 1940, *L'Aurore* freshly painted in black and white, the French ensign flying from her stern-mast, moored in the dirty water of Marseilles harbour ready to sail. Her hold carried a disparate cargo of tinned meat, tinned fruit, sacks of flour and barley, 1,000 bottles of cheap Burgundy and two factory-greased Czech-made Besa vz/37 machine-guns with 3000 rounds of ammunition that came too late to be shipped to Spain. I had replaced her regular company with a minimal crew comprising two sailors, twin brothers from Novorossysk, both dying to return home, a Chinese cook who didn't give a damn where he sailed so long as the pay was good, and a quick-tempered Estonian skipper whom I salvaged from jail, straightened out behind an empty harbour warehouse and dragged semi-conscious aboard.

Destination? Mother Russia! Odessa, more precisely.

Minou said, 'Take me with you?'

'Not a chance.'

'You said you loved me.'

'I do. That's why I'm not taking you.'

'Why do Jews always run away?'

'Because they're smart. You stay here where you belong. You can count on *les boches* being nice to pretty French girls. There's no cabaret where I'm going.'

She slapped my cheek. Then, taking my face in her hands, she kissed my eyes and mouth, biting my lip and sticking her tongue deep into me. We discarded our clothes item by item on the way to bed and made love right through the night, every way imaginable. In the morning, I left.

I had sold everything except *L'Aurore.* I gave Minou 50,000 francs. With the rest I opened a bank account in Zurich.

I can still relive imaginatively that voyage to the east, and taste the salty air upon that summer-dazzled sea of seas. And marvel at the sudden fall of night, alive with lights from distant shores, when valediction followed us like a shoal of dolphins into the first glorious sunrise on the Aegean.

With a Crimean horizon ahead, I changed direction; call it a fortuitous sea change.

'We sail to Rostov-na-Donu,' I instructed my refractory skipper.

Far smaller than Odessa, Rostov is Russian, not cosmopolitan. My arrival there would have some impact when I announced my homecoming from capitalist exile and presented ship and cargo to the city. I would leave for Moscow at once, seek an interview with Voroshilov, maybe get a job working for him. Something was sure to turn up, it always did.

A naval patrol boat closed in on *L'Aurore* with Rostov in sight a mere few minutes away. We were signalled to prepare to be boarded. The vessel's commander, a swarthy, stocky fellow with pock-marked face, came aboard himself, full of imperious swagger. What were we doing here, when the documents said we were bound for Odessa? he wanted to know. Who the hell was I, anyway? Russian, indeed! More likely a fucking spy!

I was a prodigal son returning home, I began to explain. There was good French wine in the hold. Let the Comrade commander go help himself. My gift. '*Yop tvoyu mat!* You mother-fucker. I'll show you "gift". I'll show you "home!" '

My ship and cargo were impounded. I was taken ashore and promptly detained. As the judges deliberated under what breach of the law to prosecute me, I pronounced with all the self-importance I could muster, 'Comrades, kindly contact Comrade Commissar of Defence Kliment Efremovich Voroshilov in Moscow. Tell him Titus Altermann has come back home to serve his country, and that you have arrested him.'

I probably would have languished in jail for eternity were it not for the two Besa machine-guns in *L'Aurore*'s hold. For I'm convinced it were these which convinced the authorities to contact Voroshilov.

He was not in Stalingrad when I arrived there, under escort, to meet him. His visit had been cancelled at short notice. A not too senior deputy had come instead. A lot of questions followed, asked with patient repetitiveness.

Chad believed I had early intelligence of Hitler's plan to invade the Soviet Union. Not true, of course. When he asked, I smiled enigmatically and said nothing. Poor Chad nodded, pleased with his assumption, and went on believing. I did, however, opine to Voroshilov's methodical sidekick that Hitler would soon turn against Stalin, disregarding the non-aggression pact signed by Molotov and Ribbentrop the year before. I don't think my opinion was passed on to Voroshilov, who declined to see me anyway.

Stalingrad – population nearly half a million – was the busy furnace of Soviet industry, a worm-shaped town stretching some

265

thirty miles along the western bank of the Volga on which steamers came and went bringing in and taking out goods to and from far-flung regions. There were no bridge on the river, only a rail-carrying ferry with a landing-point not far from the railway station at the town's centre. Such ancient pedigree as Stalingrad could boast of had long since been subsumed in modern development. What you saw was miles of white wooden houses with gardens, avenues with trees, three hundred factories belching smoke into the sky. Stalingrad was her namesake's demonstration to the world of the limitless energy of Socialist manufacturing.

To the north were the Krasny Oktober Factory, the Barikady Gun Factory and the Dzerzhinsky Tractor Works, named after the idealistic author of the country's secret police. Beyond, across the Metchetka river which flowed into the Volga from the steppes, lay the suburbs of Rynok, Spartakovka, and Orlovka. Dominating the town with a broad promontory, was Mamayev Hill, providing a sweeping view of the river for miles to either side. Another river, the Tsaritsa, cut a gorge through the high ground as it tumbled into the Volga, dividing the town into more or less equal halves. Not far from its debouchment was Red Square – cultural and administrative centre of Stalingrad – with the Commissariat offices, the Post office, *Stalingrad Pravda*, and the Univermag department store.

Like the town's pretensions, her climate was extreme: scorching hot in summer; freezing cold in winter.

Founded to block the advance of Tartar horsemen from the east, Stalingrad, by sheer accident and conceit, was destined to check and then reverse the progress of no less a menace from the west in what was to be the battle of all battles in modern times.

I metamorphosed from expatriate *flâneur* ship-owner to foreman in charge of a ten-strong track assembly team at the Dzerzhinsky Tractor Works, which was by now rolling off the assembly lines at a hectic pace T-34 tanks, not tractors. I was trebly rewarded: by my superiors' esteem; my workmates' loyalty; and the affection of three women workers, who slept with me on an agreed schedule of rotation.

In June the next year, the Nazi military juggernaut crashed

266

into Russia. The summer after that Armageddon arrived, with smoke and fire, at the gates of Stalingrad. Operation Blau, aimed at the annihilation of Stalin's city, had begun.

At the end of August the Germans attacked from the north, from the south and at the centre, focusing on Mamayev Hill. Waves upon waves of warplanes came flying in V formations and bombed the guts out of Stalingrad. When the planes were gone the cannons started up, and then the tanks, flattening whatever stood in their path. There were fires everywhere. You tasted smoke day and night. The heat of the flames, enhancing the already scorching summer, made you lie awake sweating at night.

General Andrei Yeremenko had arrived to head Stalingrad's defence. He set up his headquarters in the Tsaritsa Gorge. General Vasili Chuikov took command of the battered 62nd Army. Comrade Nikita Khrushchev also came. They were a redoubtable trinity with one message to the populace: here we stand to win or die; not a step back! No one seemed to reflect on the obvious, that dying was fast becoming easier, more welcome than living.

Then, as Stalingrad sank towards defeat, the exhausted invaders ground to a halt before us, the equally spent defenders. From here on this was not to be just another episode in the war but the turning-point; the ultimate contest with no life spared, between two gigantic, malevolent wills: Stalin's and Hitler's.

A bridge hastily thrown across the Volga was destroyed on General Yeremenko's orders. Nothing was allowed that would even admit the thought of retreat. The factories were kept working at full pace, lest their abandonment should indicate weakening resolve. Unpainted, and without gun-sights, T34 tanks went to battle straight from the factory's shop floor until it, too, was reduced to heaps of masonry and twisted iron. By mid September over eighty per cent of the town was in German hands. But we fought, street by street, house by house. Men, women, children – anyone able to hold a rifle. We hung on.

Once again I was a soldier. Armed with my trusty Mauser pistol and a brand new M1940 7.62mm sniper's rifle, I led a section of six men detailed to the southern part of town. The

267

German infantry feared face-to-face combat, preferring to advance behind close formation of tanks, preceded by a barrage of artillery. We waited for them among the ruins, ambushed them, sniped at them from every shelter of a broken wall. We cut their throats with knives at night and when they strayed. We crept up behind their tanks and set them alight with hand incendiary bombs.

They had *matériel* in abundance. We had lives to spare, and women to love us: *O Dunya Dunichka, krassavitsa maya . . . O Dunya Dunichka, Komsomolichka maya . . .*

An unusually warm October gave way to a freak November. The Volga froze over. Wind from the steppes drove in huge tumbling masses of snow. You couldn't see more than ten metres ahead of you for the blizzard. The rats grew bold with hunger: you could hear the Germans screaming as they woke in their foxholes to discover that their frost-bitten extremities had been made a meal of while they were asleep. Isolated and cut off, they stewed their remaining dogs and horses for food, waiting for orders to retreat, which never came.

Hadn't their leaders read about the Russian winter?

On the southern outskirts of Stalingrad I was reunited with Sergei Aleksandrevich Pugachev, General second-in-command of the 51st Army, as he came out from behind a boulder buttoning up his coat.

His eyes were red from lack of sleep. How thin he had grown! A grizzle of beard, prematurely grey, accentuated the hollowness of his cheeks. He limped from a wound in his thigh that had had no time to heal.

'Seryozha!'

'Tatya?'

We embraced, then drew apart and looked at each other.

I loved him at that moment. I'd like to believe he felt more or less the same about me.

'I always knew we'd meet again, Tatya. But here of all places? *Bozhemoy,* you smell like a corpse!' There was moisture in his eyes. From the cold wind?

'You look well, Seryozha, considering.'

'You too.'

The wind howled. Snow raced across the grey landscape. We could barely hear each other speak, which was just as well.

'Come in for a glass of *chai*, Tatya,' he said.

I followed him into his field bunker. There was a brief lull in the fighting. Pugachev's 51st Army included a sizeable cavalry contingent. It had been badly mauled. Now, reinforced and refitted, it was poised to attack on the southern prong of the forthcoming offensive.

The bunker was crowded, officers talking over maps and shouting into field telephones. The air was thick with cigarette smoke. A samovar hissed on the table by a paraffin burner. Leaning against the wall next to it stood a collapsed accordion. We found a corner where we might sit and talk. Even so, we were constantly interrupted by a flow of information which demanded Pugachev's attention.

'There you are, pour this into you, Tatya,' he said, handing me a tin mug full of tea. '*Chai* and vodka are the only luxuries we can enjoy before we reach Berlin.'

He never doubted for a moment that we would win the war, and soon.

Beneath his greatcoat his tunic was soiled, the General's epaulette insignia caked with months of dirt. But he was a General, every tired bit of him. His staff loved and revered him, you could tell.

He popped a lump of sugar into his mouth and slurped the hot black tea through it so loudly it all but drowned the noise in the bunker.

'I see you still have your old Mauser.'

'Not the same one.'

'No?' Deltas of lines deepened at the corners of his eyes. 'So where have you been all these years?'

Not '*What* are you doing here?' nor '*Why* have you come back?'

He was taking me on trust, never doubting that I'd return as if I'd merely been away for a spell.

How did I requite the generosity implicit in that simple friendly question?

Instead of telling him about Paris; about Minou, the fun, the food – he loved food and drink, and good times he had

had little opportunity to experience – at which he might have laughed and found some release from the tension of the moment, I told him a gruesome story.

August 1937, Santander, northern Spain, *L'Aurore* moored in port, having unloaded her cargo of guns and provisions. The Nationalists captured the city that morning. Under the terms of the surrender, refugees were to be allowed out, some to sail away with me. But the Nationalists reneged on their promise. Systematic executions were taking place. In one prison containing intellectuals, they had drawn a chess board across the courtyard. The prisoners, enacting the chess pieces, were forced to play for life and death while the Nationalists looked on. Bodies of the taken pieces were laid out in a line on either side of the chess battlefield. No quick checkmate to end the farce; from 'White's' Ruy Lopez opening, both sides fought to an end-game, heatedly analysing each move in the carnage. *Homo ludens!*

I tell Pugachev *this* – without even first enquiring after his wife and little daughter – on the eve of a battle that might well be our last, his and mine!

And I can tell right away that the moment when I might have truly belonged in that close company of warriors who surround him had come and gone.

'Tell me, Titus,' he said after a pause, 'this Coca Cola the Americans drink, what's it like?'

'I don't know, Seryozha, I've never tried the stuff.'

'I'd have liked to taste it. Just once.'

'You will. After the war.'

He sighed heavily. 'Would you like to join my outfit?' he asked, getting up.

I should have liked this story turned into something really meaningful. That winter in Stalingrad, and what followed. A tribute to Pugachev's humanity and courage, nothing else. A movie? I know someone who could have done it, with dignified restraint and insight. A French film-maker called Raoul Cabarnier . . . My son.

270

Cher M. Alston,

I am writing to tell you that my mother, Mme Milicent Cabarnier passed away two months ago and was buried, according to her wish, in Cimetière de Montmartre.

You are probably not aware of my existence. Maman never mentioned your name until shortly before she died, when she told me you were my father, and who you were.

As you may imagine, M. Alston, this came to me as a bit of a shock, just as, no doubt, learning about me will be to you.

I want you to know that I had no intention of ever getting in touch with you. In the end, I decided I should. I believe this is what Maman would have wished. I therefore offer to meet you. Let us satisfy our curiosity about each other, if you agree.

I propose to come to London next week. Please let me know if it would be convenient for you to see me. I would respectfully suggest that a lunch meeting would suffice for us both at this stage.

Yours sincerely, Raoul Cabarnier

I read and re-read the letter over and over. It didn't give away much. The guarded tone could denote natural reticence, or resentment; how was I to know what Minou had told him about me? Pride could not be discounted, either: a son approaching an unknown father who happened to be one of the richest men in the world! A traumatic revelation for both of us.

He couldn't have been born later than 1941. He would therefore be thirty-eight. Perhaps married, with children of his own.

I faxed him a message saying I looked forward to meeting him, completely on his own terms, any way he thought would be best. I signed simply, 'Yours, Titus'. Meanwhile, I checked him out.

He was well respected in the film world, though as yet

without much international recognition. He had won a prestigious award for a film he made about Algiers, where he had served in the French army. His supposed father, whom Minou had married soon after he was born – one Lucien Cabarnier, a maths teacher from Issoire – had died of cancer ten years before. Raoul was married to a TV presenter called Irène. They had two daughters, Cecile and Rosalie, aged seven and five respectively. They lived at 57 rue Charles Laffitte, Neuilly-sur-Seine.

I thought of him constantly. The photocopy picture of him I had acquired showed a strong intelligent face, with a shock of dark hair. I didn't recognise any resemblance to Minou or to myself.

I staged imaginary scenes in my mind of our meeting, directed and re-directed it and, in the end, despaired.

What could I say to my son Raoul, when all that I've experienced has not prepared me for such a moment? Could I mumble, '*Ah . . . mon fils!*' stretching out my arms, before telling him how I searched Paris in vain for Minou after the war?

No? Better perhaps a simple handshake, to begin the process of mutual probing over lunch. And afterwards? Father and son united? Or a disappointed farewell?

When I think of Paris, I think of Minou. My thoughts, however, are hampered by words. There should have been a better medium, some brain-bursting multi-media display in the mind to express all the sensations and ideas I experienced in Paris during that time.

If we humans survive the next nemesis I'm sure Yahweh is preparing for us, then at some future evolutionary turn, language as it is now will be no more. My pet speculation. Thoughts will take form, be communicated and recorded through an integrated system of sound, light, and plasticity, like dreams before words reduce them to formulae. That's how I should want to express what I felt and thought in Paris with Minou.

Let me anchor a beginning in the pleasing ambience of Chartier, rue du Faubourg Montmartre.

The huge restaurant is full. Waiters in white aprons swan among the tables, balancing plates like conjurers. Acres of mirrors lodged in dark wood panelling reflect and multiply a Renoir assembly of evening diners. A delicious smell of Gallic cooking fills the space. The wine glows from glass tumblers. Debris of fresh baguettes litters the functional paper table-cloths on which the waiters scribble bills with pencils taken from behind the ear.

If I can let an unfocused gaze wonder at leisure from the ringed hand of the woman sitting across the long table from me to her unadorned cleavage, it is because she, too, is looking straight through me. Privacy isn't easily invaded here.

And then I see among the many mirrored faces the half-smiling visage of an apprentice demon, his features uncannily like mine; a new *flâneur's* moustache above a mouth grown somewhat slack from too much pleasure.

'Congratulations!' he whispers telepathically. 'The lucky number you've drawn wins you a Luxury Class stay in limbo. All out amenities are yours to enjoy. Deny yourself nothing. We offer interest-free unlimited credit, expert free advice on fun-management. Don't count the cost. Our Accounts Department will settle at a later date, on easy terms. We strive to please our customers. Our reward is your pleasure.'

I say to myself, 'Well? Why not?'

Considering the impact Minou had made on me, isn't it strange that I have no recollection of when or where we met for the first time? It may have been in one of the Montmartre night spots where she sang, soon after I had met Gonzag Beuzelin. That omission apart, my memory is full of her.

She didn't have a big voice. You had to really listen to appreciate what a great singer she was. Even at a whisper Minou could hold her audience spellbound. She might have been a legendary chanteuse if it weren't for the destructive side of her nature which, in the end, destroyed her art along with just about everything else that came into her life. How she must have changed to become a mother and housewife, married to the maths teacher Lucien Cabarnier! She, whose only discipline was applied to burning herself out!

Her eyes were very dark. Only when you got close to her could you see their blueness. Her hair, straight and ebony black, came down almost to her waist. Tall and statuesque, Minou had pronounced high cheek-bones that made her face appear triangular in the low light of the Tabarin nightclub in Montmartre where she mostly sang. While performing, Minou wore dark dresses that revealed no more than her neck. She said she wanted her audience to concentrate on her face, not be distracted by her body.

She was terrified of ageing, so she avoided being out in the sun. When she had to, she always wore dark glasses and a black wide-brimmed hat. People stared at her in the street, mistaking her for somebody else more famous.

I remember her voice – gravelly when she spoke, from smoking too many Gitane cigarettes. And her gestures, and the teasing inclination of her head when she smiled. I can recall the slightly stale fragrance of her body when she got out of bed while I lay there, wanting her again even after long hours of love-making.

She lived in rue de Bretagne on the Right Bank. When she wasn't singing in Montmartre, she appeared in the Coupole, Montparnasse, which I frequented with Gonzag Beuzelin. It was there, I think, that I saw her for the first time.

Gonzag once told me that she had been Louis Aragon's lover. He himself had also slept with her, I'm sure. And while neither of them ever admitted it, it wouldn't have surprised me if they had gone on sleeping with each other after Minou and I became lovers. On one occasion, when Gonzag was at his most enchanting and depraved, he suggested we three went to bed together, divide between us Minou's lush geography – I take her hilly north, he, the dark and musky south. He said he wanted to wank while we made love.

The scar on my forehead attracts women; don't ask me why. Minou traced it with the nail of her forefinger. We were at her place, as always – she never came to mine.

'Is this the mark of Cain?' she asked

'No. A medal from a stupid war.'

'Who gave it to you?'

'Tell me how many lovers you've had.'

She began reciting a list that might have been a read-through of the Paris telephone directory. Then she laughed to see me turn sullen.

'*Chéri*, why ask what you don't want to know? Now, your scar . . .'

'A souvenir from a Polish Cossack.'

'Did you kill him?'

'No. He thought he killed me.'

'*J'adore les Cossacks!*'

'You know nothing about the savage bastards.'

She laughed, then pushed her tongue between my teeth.

'Tell me, then.'

She had a French cavalry sabre hanging on the wall. A trophy from an officer she had done a Carmen on? I got up from bed, unsheathed the weapon, and with one swooshing swipe decapitated the melon on the table. She wanted to lick the juice from the blade.

The way she was aroused resembled the way she sang: both intense, spontaneous, and exciting beyond anything I had ever known. And both made me feel jealous.

Gonzag Beuzelin remarked perceptively that Minou's creative genius was in her body, not her mind, like athletic prowess. She understood the ephemeral nature of her gift. That was why she ruthlessly pushed it to the limit while it lasted. And because of that she was such an extraordinary, fascinating lover.

I played a rum duel with one of her admirers, an expatriate Polish Count called Kazimir Wanserzky. A poker addict, he played for high stakes, which fortunately he could afford, being immensely rich. Everything about him, from his dandified appearance to his extravagant gallantry, reflected the absurd romanticism commonly associated with people of his caste and origin. He even put it about that he was terminally ill with consumption.

In Neuilly, where he lived with a woman ten years older than himself, called Sophie d'Ibelin, who boasted of Crusader ancestry, poker games were held for an exclusive set of serious gamblers. Rumour had it that cleaned-out losers were actually encouraged to shoot themselves as a matter of good style. I was invited one evening to take my chances, since the Count had learned of my affair with Minou and that I was a poker player.

There were six other guests who, I quickly sensed, had come not so much to play on this occasion as to be entertained by my destruction, which was taken for granted.

Count Kazimir was a small elegant man with a neatly trimmed greying goatee and liquid dark eyes. He greeted me with pointed courtesy. For what kind of stakes would I be ready to play? he enquired. I replied that I had not considered a limit but would try to match whatever he went for. 'Excellent,' he said icily.

Past midnight, the game developed into a dead run between the two of us. After a few hours of attrition, I began to read his game and got into my stride. I slow-played a pair of queens in the hole, bet them on the turn and lured the Count to commit all on an inside straight.

I took him for a full 300,000 francs. He was finished, I could tell. To his credit, he kept a straight face, congratulating me on my playing.

'What do you say we have one more game? Winner takes all,' he suggested as I was getting into my jacket.

'I own a freight ship, at the moment laden with timber from Finland. Ship and cargo against all you've won tonight?'

I didn't bother to ask what the ship and cargo were worth. His tiredness was all too obvious; he had lost his nerve, there was no bounce left in him. I picked up a new deck of cards and put it in front of him, inviting him to deal. But he shook his head.

'We'll play a different kind of game this time. Pure chance and courage. Will you accept the challenge, Monsieur Altermann?' He smiled, pronouncing my name with an unpleasant emphasis.

'Whatever you say, Monsieur le Comte,' I replied.

He leaned over the table, hand stretched out. We shook on it.

Mme d'Ibelin, who had been following the game throughout the night without as much as saying a word, now became agitated. She followed him to the door. There was an exchange

276

in low voices. She held on to his arm but he pushed her away, hissing '*Laisse-moi, Sophie!*' She turned and walked out of the other door, leaving it open.

Presently he returned, a revolver in his hand. The three remaining guests, on seeing this, left in a hurry. We remained alone in the room.

He invited me to examine the gun. It wasn't a common six-in-a-chamber revolver but a beautiful long-barrelled ivory-handled .44 Colt 5-shooter of the kind they used in the American Wild West. He took out of his pocket a single bullet and held it in front of me.

I thought, 'Of all the situations I've ever been in, this is surely the most idiotic!' I handed him back the pistol. He held it tilted sideways, and spun the chamber to show me how smoothly it ran.

'I can see you think this is foolish,' he said urbanely. 'In the ordinary scheme of things, I would have to agree. You see, when you pledge your life to experience the ultimate, you must be ready to pay the ultimate price. I think you and I are very much alike in this respect, Monsieur, no? We go for broke. All or nothing. Isn't that so? So here we are. Unless you want to change your mind.'

He suddenly looked incredibly handsome.

'And if I do?'

He laughed. 'My dear fellow, in that case there would be nothing more to say. You'd leave as you've come, without a sou from what you've won tonight. I take it you're a man of honour.'

'Let's get on with it,' I said.

The truth was that at that moment I was so mesmerised by the man's implacable stupidity that the very loss of life seemed trivial. I also realised that if I backed off, my rival would lose no time telling Minou about it.

'*Bon.* I should have been disappointed to find you an unworthy opponent,' said Count Kazimir, and immediately offered cognac which he meticulously decanted from a straight-lined decanter.

We clinked glasses. He smiled patronisingly as I emptied mine in one gulp, like it was vodka, while he sipped his discerningly. Then he produced a cream vellum envelope which he let fall theatrically on the table beside the gun. It contained, he explained, the necessary documents for transferring *L'Aurore*'s ownership to me, should I win. Did I care to examine the papers? No, I credited him with being honourable, I replied, placing my night's takings next to his pledge.

Count Wanserzky cut a deck of cards and motioned me to pick one. I drew a red five of hearts. His was a black Jack of spades. He leaned back as I picked up the revolver. I gave the chamber a good spin, put the muzzle to my temple and squeezed the trigger. A resounding click of the hammer. I put the pistol down. Without hesitating, the Count took up the gun and did the same. It went off with a flat report. He rocked to one side before straightening again, absurdly and foolishly alive, a black smear on the side of his head from the gunpowder in the blank cartridge. I scooped up money and envelope and left.

A week later I read in a newspaper how Count Kazimir Wanserzky shot himself, this time fatally, in some dark retreat of the Bois de Boulogne, watched by two terrified prostitutes. I never told Minou what happened that night, leaving her to believe I had won the ship in a straight game of poker.

For all the money and prestige *L'Aurore* earned me, I never felt in the least attached to her. I parted with her in Rostov without so much as a twinge of regret.

Say you're sitting in a Montparnasse café surrounded by the pick of the age's artistic talent, each one of them intoxicated with life. It is late. Much wine has been drunk. A surrealist poet has just read a new outrageous poem he had written that morning. The American beauty sitting next to you – herself a poetess dying for immolation of some sort – puts a gorgeous hand on your arm.

'Isn't he simply magnificent!' she coos. And she's mildly aroused when you don't quite agree. 'What do you do, by the way?' she inquires caressingly. 'Should I know your name? Are you a painter, poet, or novelist?'

'Well, none of these, actually. I sell tinned baby food all over Europe, and I'm rather rich,' you answer.

278

A glazed look replaces the seductive smile. Any prospect of bedding her before the night is out, vanishes in an instant. You can all but hear her mind working on a suitable disengagement utterance.

If instead you reply with a tormented glint in the eye, 'I'm master of a ship I won in a wager', her eyes would take on that certain moist sheen, her lips part as if to savour a bitter-sweet enigma. Her soul would yearn to embrace the Flying Dutchman you might be. You will have charted the first knot towards the conquest of her heart. For there's something about owning a ship that breeds a string of romantic metaphors on the spot and sets you apart from run-of-the-mill pursuers of money. Even better than a poet, you are an agent of destiny! The lovely lady wants to know what, if anything, you fear. She gasps as if you've touched her intimately when you tell her the only thing you fear is fear itself. Together you gorge on extravagance of literary allusions which youth and the occasion invite. Until the point is reached for love or parting.

When Gonzag Beuzelin heard I possessed *L'Aurore*, our roles reversed: he became the courtier, I the prince.

I met him at the Communist Party headquarters at 120 rue La Fayette. His name was on the list in the safe I had raided with Rudi at the KPD offices in Berlin. I introduced myself as a former associate of Laszlo Schultz. The year before, Wanda's former boss, Willi Münzenberg, had moved his operation to Paris, where he was now publishing the Soviet-backed Editions du Carrefour. As far as I know Wanda never made contact with him, nor with any of her Berlin left-wing intellectual friends who now flocked to Paris. When Wanda decided to change direction she did so without as much as a glance back. Belatedly she had learnt of Stalin's directive that split the Left and enabled the Nazis to seize power: the Socialist Revolution in Germany will be achieved through Hitler, was more or less what he had said. When I told her that in Berlin, she called me an insufferable cynic.

As I had hoped, Gonzag had never heard of Laszlo, nor was he impressed with Münzenberg and his Soviet connections. In France, he explained, the Left was more artistic, more intellectual, and therefore independent. To make the point Gonzag, himself an adherent of Leon Trotsky, sported a silk purple *lavalière* necktie. He was a tall slim man, about my age, though he looked older. A brilliant ephemerality glowed through his Latin good looks; he was like a gorgeous water-fly. Women, and men, found him irresistible. You couldn't help loving Gonzag.

I told him I had in effect retired from political activities after Berlin, but if anything in particular came up where I could be of use I would be glad to help. Activities? He laughed. Why, it all amounted to churning out manifestos composed in Left Bank cafés. Was I interested in art? His work centred on a handful of surrealist intellectuals like Aragon and Breton. I could take it or leave it, I replied. So what did I plan on doing in Paris? he wanted to know. Make a lot of money, have fun, I said.

'*Ah, bon*! I'll show you how to spend it. We'll keep in touch,' he promised. And lived up to his word.

I don't think Gonzag Beuzelin was his real name. *Noms de guerre* were fashionable in his circles. Gonzag relished anything that smacked of *guerre* or intrigue. If it weren't for the fact that he couldn't bear to live for long without an audience to admire him, he would surely have gone to fight in the Spanish Civil War, as did many of his friends, and proved his ephemerality on some foreign battlefield.

L'Aurore needed refitting to serve the dual purpose for which she was now destined: carrying diverse cargo, including my lucrative caviar on some trips, clandestine munitions to Spain on others. The latter came about through my connection with Gonzag. As the money rolled in, I laid down some of the basic principles which later guided the Alston Group: aggressive investment; honour commitments at all cost; never spend more than you earn; extend yourself financially to the limit, but not an inch beyond.

I bought a small news agency which was on the point of bankruptcy. Advisers warned me I was throwing good money away. I didn't mind, I had other plans, specifically to balance the agency's money-losing against undeclared gains from some of my other enterprises. Renamed Star International News, the agency grew and prospered beyond all expectations. People in business circles were saying I had the Midas touch. In truth, all credit where Star International News is concerned must go to its new editor, Bernard Cohen, an American living in Paris, and a friend of Chad's. Cohen was a brilliant pugnacious journalist who worked unrecognised as a freelance until, on Chad's recommendation, I appointed him Editor. A hard-hitting welterweight, his sole distinction at the time was that he had fought Ernest Hemingway and floored him three times in as many rounds, despite Hemingway's considerable advantage in weight.

The agency, thoroughly overhauled by Cohen, who, in the process, introduced me to cocaine, scored an historic scoop, being the first to break the news of the 1939 Ribbentrop–Molotov pact to a stunned world on Tuesday 22 August, a day before it was signed.

The harder I worked, the more energy I found I needed just to keep Minou out of my thoughts. I joined a fencing club in Le Marais. The discipline it demanded was not enough: I longed for Theo.

How deeply he resented my bullying him into joining me, I've never been able to fathom. At times, hurt by his aloofness, I would tell him that it wasn't simply that I needed him; I *loved* him! He was family! That if it weren't for me he'd have never met Wanda! He would gaze at me with opaque benevolence, then say something quite irrelevant, like 'I wonder if I shouldn't get a dog to take me out for walks. What do you think?'

Much later I might have added that, thanks to my ego-maniac wilfulness, he became a celebrated Cambridge professor, instead of ending his life in a Nazi concentration camp.

Theo was immune to Minou's charms. He couldn't have met her more than twice, after which he lost interest permanently. I don't think he ever heard her sing. His comment on her was delayed and oblique: 'Titus, here's something for you to consider. Should the wild caprice of a few inches of hydraulically operated addendum, and an orifice, subvert the functioning of a miraculous organ like the brain?'

Shortly before we parted, Minou gave me a present. It was a little leather-bound romance with pretty engraved illustrations. She had bought it in a second-hand bookstall on the bank of the Seine by Ile de la Cité. Since she knew I was lazy when it came to reading French, she told me the story herself: a man of humble background attains power through the ruthless pursuit of wealth, but in the process loses the girl who loved him. He ends his days in loneliness made all the more poignant by belated wisdom and regret.

I said it was a pretty book and a good story and left it at that.

Poor Minou. She had finally declared her love when for me the apotheosis of its fulfilment had trailed away. If ever there was a case of ships passing in the night . . .

I have cancelled all my appointments for the day. I have instructed Reception that when M. Cabarnier from Paris arrives, I am to be immediately informed. I have had a table reserved at the restaurant of the Stafford Hotel across the road. At first I decided in favour of a small conference room, then changed my mind – it would be easier for us both in the company of strangers.

Waiting for my son, I pace up and down the office, unable to concentrate on anything else. A trivial dilemma defeats me: when he comes, should I go down to meet him or have him brought up here? The weight of so many questions and answers, which I know must be patiently deferred to another time, now flattens the things I have so carefully rehearsed to say.

I engage my mind on how he might look. Athletically built? About my own height? Minou's eyes? French sharpness in a smile all his own? I think of the first handshake . . . Dare I hope for an embrace to follow?

I will give him everything he asks for, and more. I will go to Paris, if he permits, bearing gifts for his children and wife.

It is three. I'm still alone, waiting. No one called Raoul Cabarnier has arrived. And then it's evening. Doors are opening and closing as people leave for home. Teddy Jasper sticks his head through the door. 'You staying in late, Titus?'

'Yes.'

'Anything I can do?'

282

'Just tell someone not to send the cleaners in here tonight, Teddy, thank you.'

Sitting at my cleared desk, I watch the lights come on in London.

My son wrote a week later to apologise that he couldn't make it, adding that on second thoughts he didn't think it was a good idea for us to meet. Too much water has passed under the Seine and the Thames. And life was too short to experiment with retrievement.

That was a long time ago. Such impatience of resolve. Was I ever like that, I wonder.

21

I very nearly lost Phoebe. It shook me nine points on the Richter scale down to my socks. Moreover, I got doubly scared: first, because I suddenly realised as never before how much she really mattered to me, and what an unbearable loss it would be if she left; second, at the notion that I could actually get so profoundly frightened, even in the face of unbearable loss. *Me*!

What was happening? Had the Old Titus Automatic Pilot Defence Mechanism been overridden by love? Had the cunning missionary in her sneaked into victory, surreptitiously turning me wiser, sadder, more human without my noticing? Or was it old age handing me a usurer's IOU?

The whole business unsettled me. I wept. Can you believe it? Vodka-flavoured tears.

The irony of it. You see, in a perfectly serene frame of mind I had decided to cash in my chips. Then I changed my mind. Only what followed locked in on the earlier decision, and Phoebe wouldn't listen.

Like Emperor Henry IV before Pope Gregory VII at Canossa, I humbled myself on bended knees. I promised I'd submit to a spiritual regeneration treatment supervised by any guru she cared to name, have a soul transplant – anything she wanted. She wasn't amused. She said that, for all my reading, deep inside I remained what I've always been: an incorrigible godless savage.

I haggled, 'How about kind, loving, godless savage?' She turned her face away.

Phoebe says that my suicide resolution, and its reversal, both flowed from an arrogance of spirit that was worse than vanity. Wrong.

284

Here is my defence: I lifted mine eyes unto the hills, as the Psalmist wrote, and what did I see? Bloody nothing! Empty, terminal. Then I remembered Corellius Rufus.

He is mentioned in one of the letters of the Younger Pliny, nephew and adopted son of the more formidable Elder Pliny, whom Theo included in my curriculum years before as a part of his programme to civilise me. I don't think I was meant to take Pliny Jr (AD 61–113) seriously. He was merely a treat, like a bon-bon, on my intellectual menu.

Urbane, committed to social justice with the passionless enthusiasm that often goes with a well-groomed conscience, the Younger Pliny survived unscathed the terror years of Domitian. That, as far as I'm concerned, was his greatest achievement. Had he lived today, he might well have been a well-heeled, left-of-centre barrister, living in a Georgian house in Islington and driving a Volvo station wagon. One letter, however, addressed to a friend, Calestrius Tiro, stuck in my mind. It was the reason I took the book out of the London Library. The letter concerned another friend, Corellius Rufus.

Rufus had attained everything a man could wish for. He was rich, he had influence; his reputation was unblemished; he was blessed with a loving family and many devoted friends. Thus, in every way, he had reached the zenith of an illustrious career, from where the view was of slow, mellow, descent – like a cool hillside planted with vines. The luckiest of men, you might think. Yet at this peak of eminence Rufus put his affairs in order, bade farewell to his friends and family and then killed himself. An act decided 'by the supremacy of reason which takes the place of inevitability for the philosopher', writes Pliny.

All because Rufus suffered from gout! Philosophers – excluding Theo, but only by a whisker – are seldom survivors.

I pondered lengthily over the letter. I'm a good deal older than Corellius Rufus was when he died. Unlike him, I'm way past the height of my powers – without regret, I hasten to add. The media no longer solicit my opinion on world events. Probably they have forgotten I am still alive! I no longer get invited to late-night informal consultations in the House of Commons Strangers' Bar on the eve of budgets. Ah well, I did enjoy the beer, and the gossip.

But I'm not unwell, far from it. Thanks to ten minutes daily of *Alston's Cossack Spine-stretching Exercises* I'm no sloth. I can move pretty damn fast when I have to, and touch my toes without bending my knees, and do a whole range of other things that would surprise you. The manual, by the way, published in a slim illustrated volume, has earned over £10,000 in royalties – all donated to a charity for ill-treated horses.

I know my own body: tough, stubborn and resilient, it would, given the chance, fight without regard for form and dignity, all the way until its last reflex is snuffed out.

What I dread is not the unimaginable nothingness at the end, but the long wait in the anteroom; the bleak ordinariness of fading away helplessly, like a power cut, in stages. And most of all, seeing my own disintegration in Phoebe's eyes, made impatient for bereavement by fatigue.

So why shouldn't I go out now, when I am in control, at the moment of my own choosing, by my own hand? And let the world await the discovery of legions of skeletons in closets all over the place? Ha! Did I ever pretend I didn't have feet of clay concealed somewhere, among my other remissions?

Of the method I choose for my demise, suffice to say it is mildly quaint – a modification of Mynheer Peeperkorn's cobrahead contraption, from Thomas Mann's *The Magic Mountain*, to which Wanda had introduced me in our Berlin days. I had had it manufactured long ago. Painless death, in one minute thirty seconds flat, guaranteed.

My exit, on the other hand, was calculated to detonate a controversy that would rage unstoppably on and on, in ever-widening circles, implicating people in high places on either side of the Atlantic. I was going to blow the whistle on hypocrisy; I was going to give international politics a god-almighty arse-thump that would shake off decades of dust and set a good few heads rolling. (John Lefebre; how would he wriggle to escape the chop? I have a lingering, undefined sense that a score of a rather personal nature has yet to be settled with him.)

In January 1985, an old friend with connections in the Politburo contacted me. 'Tatya,' he said cryptically, 'isn't it time you had a little taste of Russian winter?'

I flew to Moscow, alone. I didn't check into a hotel but repaired to an apartment in Kuntsevo – a quiet district of the city – which belonged to a well-known political fixer.

My friend had not exaggerated. The situation was serious: Konstantin Chernenko, the Party mummy who succeeded Andropov as President, was on his last trotters. Wags were joking openly that Chernenko had in fact died some time back, and the Party was wheeling about on public occasions a robot in his likeness. Daggers were already drawn for the succession race.

I talked to people. I went to see Viacheslav Mikhailovich Molotov in his Zhukova dacha. There had never been much love lost between us. In fact I had hated him for good reasons. Yet that earthy wiliness that kept him alive dangerously close to Stalin all those years had matured into genuine wisdom. That couldn't be denied. Besides, two years before he died at the ripe old age of some ninety plus, Viacheslav Mikhailovich was so lonely he would talk to anyone, even me. He was absolutely certain that Gorbachev would be a disaster for the Soviet Union and for the rest of the world; he said that in his opinion Mikhail Sergeivich Gorbachev had no sense of history, didn't have a clue what the Soviet Union was about, was too stupid to appreciate how important the East–West balance of power was. I didn't meet Gorbachev that time.

But I was introduced to Yegor Ligachev, the hardline candidate. A true bureaucrat in the old Politburo tradition, Ligachev never smiled at the camera. Always he had that grim Molotov expression on his face. I was impressed, truly. I returned to London determined to do the world a favour, even if it meant sinking the Alston Group International.

That's what my valedictory testament would reveal. How, with the complicity of John Lefebre, who for once did not perceive my intention, I cooked the books to pump no less than $1.7 billion – and as many promises – into a fund aimed at defeating Mikhail Sergeivich Gorbachev's bid for power by all means available, even assassination, should that be necessary. Nothing personal, let me stress; no one would deny that Mikhail Sergeivich is eminently likeable.

Wicked? Read Russian history, then consider the conse-

287

quences of *perestroika*: instead of the hoped-for Western-type, free-market democracy, the inevitable chaos. A valued, dependable enemy is rendered impotent but volatile, therefore feeling threatened, and threatening, and as a result more dangerous than ever. Who benefits? Anarchists, terrorists, lunatics. Had Andropov lived on, the world would've been safer, more prosperous. Ligachev, too, would've been all right. But not Gorby! Definitely not him.

Ask Henry Kissinger, he'll tell you what's good for the world – the assured balance of a well-regulated cold war! Nations, as individuals, need enemies they can trust and friends they can take for granted, if not ignore. Put differently, order and continuity rest on the unsentimental acceptance of life's ruthless diversity (Theo would have liked this).

Alas, my effort failed. All that money – enough to bankroll a revolution, bribe legions of apparatchiks with cars, dachas, gold Rolex watches, trips abroad – gone down the drain! Only the time-proven safety mechanism operating on the principle of terror worked: not a word about the plot leaked out. Quite an achievement, that.

I was going to let it all out, and list my accomplices in that historic venture: three junior ministers in Mrs Thatcher's government, seven prominent Republicans in the Senate and House of Representatives, and a handful of top international businessmen, mostly from the armament industry, as well as a couple of misguided idealistic boobs from the Left.

My motive wasn't spite, nor vanity either. You might call it medicinal.

Nevertheless, how's that for a grand exit? One thing more. The fortune salvaged from the ruins of the Alston Group International, reallocated as follows: £2.5 billion to my pet genetic research project which is, at last, on the threshold of an exciting breakthrough that could improve the future beyond the imagining of science fiction; £0.7 billion in trust for an education fund for destitute orphans; £2 million to help house the homeless in the UK; £1 million to the RSPCA (I've always admired their work); £750,000 for Phoebe; £2,700 for cremation and funereal luncheon at the Green Man, Granchester.

Thus all I own, more or less accounted for. A firm of solicitors

– unconnected with the Group – will shortly commence working on my will.

I smile at the dilemma the media moralists would face: 'Titus Alston – evil manipulator, or saint?' The eternal stock pigeon-holing response frustrated once again; the absurdly optimistic urge to seek answers to the unanswerable thwarted. And, as a bonus, a growth industry for biography hacks.

My last big joke before the Big Nothing.

Then a mellower reflection centred on Phoebe made me change my mind to hang on and face the music.

Going to the loo before dawn, I looked at the mirror and thought, an Indian summer? What the hell, why not? I'll enjoy it to the full. Give it my best. My gift to Phoebe. I owe her that, at the very least.

When the time comes I'll not steal out like a coward, but magnanimously bid farewell to all my friends. After which I'll fly to Nepal, hire a sherpa to take me some way up a Himalayan slope from where I can see the peak of Everest, and leave me there to face alone the splendour of an elemental sunrise – my last! Out-Corellius Corellius by several thousand feet!

I was easing into self-congratulatory lyricism when another idea struck me with great force. That genetic engineering project I mentioned earlier was created by one of my eccentric whims, according to John Lefebre, who wants to slim it out of the Alston Group. Unknown to him, the scientists there are a breath away from creating a new substance that actually *lives*! Something involving a molecular structure of ceramic and yeast germ. I don't have to be a boffin to appreciate the momentous significance of the discovery: a new genesis in the true sense of the word, it will one day help cure the sick and feed the hungry to whom, say my detractors, I had earlier provided means for self-destruction.

Excited, I rushed to my study to jot down notes. From the debris of the Alston Group I shall claim Charon, move him mind and body to the Project – spontaneously nicknamed Ziggy Frankenstein. After I have made my revelation, after I have resigned from the Group, while everything is still in a turmoil, I shall take control of Ziggy with Phoebe at my side as Chief Executive. It will be our love child – born not for profit, but purely for the betterment of mankind.

Impatient to break the news, I came out of the study to see her standing barefooted in her dressing-gown, looking down on *The Letters of the Younger Pliny* which lay face down on the sofa in the living-room.

'How odd, Titus,' she exclaimed, pulling a face. 'Is that what you want me to read to you?' She had been reading to me of late, mostly books of her own choice.

'No. I was reading that myself.'

She picked up the book, read the Corellius Rufus letter and understood at once. The intent, that is, not the underlying idea, because the philosopher's supremacy of reason on life and death is lost on the Christian moralist for whom faith, not reason, is supreme.

She said nothing, just stood there, an empty coldness in her gaze, as though a sudden notice had been served telling her that her life's saving had been embezzled.

What should I have done? Put my arms around her? Told her what's been keeping me busy while she was asleep? The devil in me reared its head.

Phoebe was having her period. She must have had a bad night, for her face was puffy, sullenly ugly. And when she challenged me with that expression of obtuse intransigence, I returned her gaze with what must have been a mocking smile. She closed the book, dropped it on the floor – that really angered me – and left the room. I heard her splashing in the shower. She returned dressed, make-up stupidly applied to excess. I saw, 'It's all over' writ large on her face. I started to say something. Her hand came up like a stop sign.

'Not now, Titus, I'm going out,' she said in her office-decision-making tone of voice.

'Where to?'

'To see a friend.'

'When will you be back?'

'Whenever. I don't know.'

I watched her through the window as she loaded a suitcase into the boot of her car. I listened to the Alfa's throaty roar trailing away . . .

Later, unable to stand the emptiness, I decamped to the office. I stayed in Sanctum all day and night. At dawn I rang home, only to hear her flat voice on the answerphone. At around noon, a for-your-eyes-only message scrolled onto Charon's monitor screen: '*Titus – I'm taking a short holiday. When I return I plan to resign. We'll talk about it in due course, but you might as well know that my mind is made up. I've also decided it would be best for us both if I moved on and left you in peace. I mean, left the Group altogether. See you when I get back. Phoebe.*

I rang John Lefebre to ask whether he knew where Phoebe had gone, when she would be coming back. His personal assistant informed me that he too had left for a few days. She had been on the point of passing his note to me.

John had never before gone away for half a day without letting me know. I scribbled on my yellow pad: 'Item for emergency Sanhedrin agenda – *Sack Lefebre! To hell with the consequences!*'

An hour later, I relented. My own chosen heir, he was brilliant. Besides, I could no longer fire him even if I wanted to.

But once before I very nearly did, decisively, humiliatingly. I recalled the incident not without shame. It hinged on the takeover of a lame company headed by an incompetent upper-class fool – John's coup. I had overruled the generous terms he had offered.

'Why?' he protested. 'We've won, hands down. We got what we wanted. Be generous in victory. Your principle, remember? What you want to do is bad for business, bad for the Group's image. You can't do that, Titus.'

I suspected he and that unsavoury aristo got on just a little too well with each other.

'I can do whatever I like and I don't have to give reasons,' I replied, glaring at him.

'Jesus, Titus, what's bugging you? Is it because the guy's a fucking earl or something? What's the matter, did he snub you? Refuse to kneel and beg for mercy?'

I made no reply.

'Okay. I'll talk to Phoebe. Maybe she can make you see sense,' he said, half rising.

'Leave Phoebe out of this, John.'

He sat down again. 'I see. We're being King Saul today, madly melancholic, are we?'

I looked at him for a long moment. He didn't flinch. Then I said very slowly, 'Be careful of what you say, because when you say things that smack of disloyalty you eat into your credit irrevocably.'

He rose abruptly. 'I never dreamed I'd hear you speak to me like that, Titus. Does it mean you want me to resign?' And he left.

The next morning I had a top-of-the-range Rolex delivered to his office. I've often wondered what he and Phoebe said to each other about this; at times I've regretted I didn't accept his resignation.

I called for a car to drive me to the Zoo in Regent's Park. The driver, a young man called Jimmy Elliot, remarked what a beautiful day it was; he couldn't blame me for wanting to spend it in the Zoo with so many flowers and people about. When he was a school kid he came here on science class outings, he reminisced, what fun it had been. We parted by the gorillas' enclosure. Tactfully leaving me alone, he said he was going to the gents.

The dominant silverback squatted on a rise from where he gazed with thoughtful apathy at his young ones' antics in the sun.

Phoebe, who never shared my enthusiasm for zoos, had nevertheless wanted a home overlooking nearby Primrose Hill, so that she could hear the wolves howling. That's the beauty of wild animals, they take their peculiar solitude into captivity. We squander ours, mistaking separateness for denial.

I ask to learn to miss Phoebe, if I must, without bitterness. And be with her, if I can, without presumption. I ask – if there's no other way – to watch over her with concealed awareness, like this silverback.

'Look, Brenda, isn't he enormous?'

'Why is he sad, Mummy?'

'He's not sad, darling, that's how gorillas are. Come along now, it must be near feeding time for the sea lions.'

One such summer afternoon, long ago, I sat on the sidelines

watching Phoebe trounce John Lefebre in two sets of tennis; and, like him, admired the golden vigour of her thighs as she rose to slam home a volley. Pulling out of his embrace, she had run to kiss me laughing, as though I had partnered her in the victory.

And there was that night in Moscow, in a borrowed dacha by the woods on the outskirts of town. I had started out of a nightmare, covered in sweat.

'What is it, love?' Phoebe had risen on an elbow, hair streaming down her naked shoulder.

'I had a fearful dream . . .'

'Tell me?'

'I can't. Maybe it's a touch of food poisoning . . .'

Out there, the forest was whispering.

'A bad dream, darling, nothing more,' she said, brushing my damp forehead with her open mouth. And I thought, 'Perhaps there's a shoot of me trembling in her womb.'

'Well, Jimmy, shall we drive back now?'

'Sure, Mr Alston,' said Jimmy Elliot, licking ice-cream from his lips.

I rang home from Sanctum that night, and left a message on the answerphone, saying, 'Please come back, I need you.'

A calm North Sea soughs to the twilit coast. The brooding mass of Dunstanburgh Castle stands guard over a vastness of water – *Oed' und leer das Meer.* In the plain below, now blurred in the fading light, sheep huddle sleepily together.

There's music inside this mediaeval church: an old Northumbrian hymn of Nordic sombreness. Phoebe's thoroughbred mezzo is all but drowned in the rough-throated chorus of the congregation. And I'm caught up in the collective hallelujah fervour that throbs against those rugged church walls.

Thus I accept and return love, understanding its fragile limits without remorse. As I believe in giving and receiving without appraisal, so I believe in the healing mercy of illusion, not divine loving kindness.

The pendulum swings forever between extremes; from greed

293

to charity, from cruelty to kindness, from barbarity to enlightenment. The violence interred beneath the castle's ruins shall be resurrected, here as elsewhere, I know all this. Such must be the design of The Great Experimenter, from his first 'Let there be . . .' Therefore, if prayer is valid at all, let us pray for courage, nothing more.

On this premise, dissembling repentance, I kneel beside Phoebe to mumble with her the Lord's Prayer.

22

'Well,' said Chad, looking at each in turn, 'shall we get on with it?'

Phoebe nodded. She took out of her handbag a pair of dark sunglasses, which she put on before getting to her feet.

'Come, Sergei, we're going,' said Wanda in a stentorian voice.

From the path leading to Grantchester Meadows you could see the river bend and, beyond, the distant spires and steeples of Cambridge. Washed by intermittent showers, the trees radiated fresh, glistening green. A vast sky rolled above, driven by a gusty breeze. The lush meadows were full of cows – brown, white, brindled and black.

Having wrapped an exotic kerchief about her head and buttoned up her coat, Wanda linked her arm through Theo's. 'Well, Theo, onward for the last rite.'

'We could get a little closer with the car,' he suggested.

'Car? Nonsense! We walk, Theo, even if it's the last thing we do. I feel stronger today, anyway.' Thrusting her walking stick in front, she commanded, 'Forward march!'

Phoebe led the way, with Chad at her side, followed by Wanda and Theo. Pugachev lumbered behind, muttering to himself.

'What car, Theo?' Wanda suddenly stopped. 'Don't tell me you still drive!'

'Of course I do.'

'The same old Riley?'

'The very same one Titus gave me. The seats' leather is a bit worn, so is the walnut fascia, the springs are getting stiffer and the engine grows tired, like me. But the dear old car goes on. I said to my mechanic the last time he prepared it for the

MOT, "Young man, you must take good care of this old car, because I want to drive it to the very end, wheel in hand to the sunset." '

'Oh, Theo, what a wonderful, faithful old friend you are. Only today we walk arm-in-arm to Titus's sacred ash tree. Right?'

'Absolutely, *Liebchen*. You know, Titus thought this landscape had . . . Wait a moment. Yes, "magical immanence" were the words he used. He was always looking for a hidden meaning in all this pastoral tranquillity. So it doesn't surprise me, this request.'

Wanda stopped walking and squinted contemplatively in the direction of Cambridge, which gave off a pale honeyed light against the darkening shades of the fields and the river.

'I think he had a point. Where is that tree, though?'

'I'm not sure I remember.'

Chad and Phoebe had reached the spot and Chad, shading his eyes against the sun, turned to wave on the others.

Huge, ancient, and split-trunked as if cleft by lightning long ago, the ash tree imparted a mood of brooding, stricken majesty.

Wanda gasped. 'Are you sure this is the right spot?' she appealed to Chad.

'Phoebe says this is it,' said Chad.

'Maybe that tree over there,' said Theo, protectively tightening his grip on Wanda's arm.

'It's right here. He showed me exactly,' insisted Phoebe.

'Okay, how about a compromise? Half here and half there?' Chad suggested.

'No. It must be right here. I can almost sense Titus,' Wanda said in a subdued voice. 'Besides, I'm not taking another step in any direction other than back.'

That settled it. Phoebe took the urn out of her bag. She looked at each in turn. The others nodded. She removed the top and, sinking to her knees, sprinkled the ashes on the bole of the tree. Chad stretched a hand to help her up. They all stood there for a long moment, staring in silence at the damp spot of earth into which Titus's ashes were slowly soaked up.

Chad was the first to look up. All of a sudden he felt old.

They had all become so old and tired, he thought. Titus, who like a pagan deity had influenced their lives for so long, for better, for worse, in war as in peace, had at last reached out to retrieve an illusion of the timelessness he had given them.

That was it, Chad thought, finished. He'd never see any of them again. He wanted to be back home in his Virginia ranch with Martha. He wanted it so much it hurt. He was grateful that she knew of Titus but had never met him. Something in him, something terribly important yet undefinable, died with Titus, and he only felt it fully here and now. The journalist's habit of mind mercifully overrode his emotion like automatic pilot and pronounced, 'End of an Era'.

Phoebe recognised the valedictory look in Chad's eyes. Like him she understood that, except for Wanda and Theo, none of them would ever meet again.

They started back towards the village. Chad came over. Putting his arm round her shoulder he said, 'Well, honey, I guess that's it.'

She kissed him on the cheek, 'I guess so. Thanks for everything, Chad.'

They walked arm in arm behind the others, to the Green Man. In the parking space Chad said, 'Now you take good care of yourself, okay?'

'Sure. You too, Chad. Would you like a lift to London?'

He half-turned and pointed to a rented Hertz Ford that stood not far from her Alfa Romeo. 'I've got transport and I'm taking the General home. Thanks all the same.'

Sitting in her car, Phoebe watched Wanda get into her old Bentley, helped by a young chauffeur who wore a sports jacket, not livery, then Theo, as he coaxed the old Riley to life. Chad had settled Pugachev into the front passenger seat and clicked the safety belt round him. Then he himself got into the car, turned, and waved to Phoebe. 'Keep in touch,' he called.

She waved back.

It started to rain as she joined the stream of motorists speeding towards London on the M11. There was an analytical report on the radio about the latest mini-crash on the London stock exchange; they were discussing it as though it were a national game. Overruling her habit of listening to such information,

297

she switched over to Radio 3, where a romping Mozart piano concerto was in full flow.

The music soothed her spirit and she was able to look at the events of the past few days for the first time without the distracting effect of grief. She was free; not unmoored from her experience, but free to sail away with it and make the best of it just as Titus would have wanted her to do.

If her years with him had shunted her out of the regular progress of life, they had at the same time enriched and strengthened her. She was the custodian of his secret legacy, with authority to negotiate an entry to a new kind of life more or less on her own terms. She could, if it came to it, put in perspective the wild agitation Titus's disclosures were bound to generate.

He had taught her a good deal more than disciplined toughness and, if the price for her education was loneliness, she could cope with that; she had the patience for enduring; she could see affirmation in the way she was going to develop.

An open car full of noisy youths whizzed past her at over a hundred mph. They waved and honked as they drew level with her.

It suddenly occurred to her that she should travel for a year before taking fresh stock of her life. She could do anything.